THE KID'S ESCAPE

I aimed my carbine at the back of the house. The fire crept ahead until there was no more than ten feet between the leading edge and the house. The Regulators had but seconds to escape or fry.

Then it happened.

The silence exploded with a barrage of gunfire. Out they ran—Billy darted out first, pistols in both hands firing in all directions at once, cursing as he ran, one of the few times I ever heard him say a bad word. I sighted my carbine on his chest and could have killed him, had I pulled the trigger.

Somehow Billy made it through the wall of lead and reached the picket fence, turning to shoot a Murphy man who jumped up from behind the adobe wall. Billy shot him in the head. All his target practice had saved Billy's life. . . .

THE DEMISE
OF
BILLY THE KID

Preston Lewis

BCI Producers of **The Holts, The Patriots, The First Americans,** and **The White Indian.**

Book Creations Inc., Canaan, NY • Lyle Kenyon Engel, Founder

BANTAM BOOKS
New York • Toronto • London • Sydney • Auckland

With the exception of historical figures, all characters in this novel are fictitious. Any resemblance to living persons, present or past, is coincidental.

THE DEMISE OF BILLY THE KID

A Bantam Book / published by arrangement with
Book Creations, Inc.

Bantam edition / November 1994

Produced by Book Creations Inc.
Lyle Kenyon Engel, Founder

ISBN 0-553-56541-9

Published simultaneously in the United States and Canada

Bantam Books are published by Bantam Books, a division of Bantam Dou-
bleday Dell Publishing Group, Inc. Its trademark, consisting of the words
"Bantam Books" and the portrayal of a rooster, is Registered in U.S. Patent
and Trademark Office and in other countries. Marca Registrada. Bantam
Books, 1540 Broadway, New York, New York 10036.

PRINTED IN THE UNITED STATES OF AMERICA

RAD   0 9 8 7 6 5 4 3 2

For Harriet,
who makes everything worthwhile.

Introduction

Just as the earth spins on its axis and revolves around the sun, historical research often goes in large unseen circles as well. Though I failed to realize it at the time, I literally fell into such a research orbit one summer evening three years ago. It was near closing time at the Southwest Collection, a historical repository on the beautiful campus of Texas Tech University, when the collection's director, noted ranching historian David J. Murrah, Ph.D., saw me gathering my materials to leave and came over to visit.

At the time, I was working on a two-part article for *True West* on the Battle of Yellow House Canyon, an odd little affair between drunken buffalo hunters and sober Comanches. This fight, which occurred just a few miles from my home in Lubbock, was the only pitched Indian battle ever fought in what became Lubbock County. The battle intrigued me not only as a historical matter but also as comic relief from the overdrawn renderings of most battles fought between men, red and white, in the Old West. I titled the article "Bluster's Last Stand" and was honored when it received a Spur Award from Western Writers of America as best nonfiction article of the year. The significance of the battle was best summed up by the Texana columnist for the Dallas *Morning News*. After

1

reading my *True West* articles, he dropped me a note saying the battle had indeed "changed the face of the West to blushing pink."

When I mentioned my research on this offbeat battle and my abiding interest in the irreverent West, Dr. Murrah cocked his head and eyed me as skeptically as he would have a suspected historical forgery. I was a bit surprised by his hard gaze, because in my job with the university's public information office I had worked well with him over the years. And, too, he and his fine staff had been of invaluable assistance when I was researching my first hardback novel on Doc Holliday's fabled relationship with the beautiful woman gambler Lottie Deno in Fort Griffin, Texas.

Finally Dr. Murrah just nodded and told me to come with him. I pointed to the door where one of the research assistants was waiting for me to leave. He told her to lock up and go on home and that he would let me out later. I followed Dr. Murrah from the public research room into the stacks crowded with books, boxes, file cabinets, maps, and all the assorted papers and records that the archives had acquired over the years. I had been allowed in the stacks before, but never had I been this excited. Though I didn't know what he was about to show me, I had the feeling that this would be one of the moments I would remember the rest of my life.

After climbing three flights of black metallic stairs and marching past a dozen rows of bookshelves, Dr. Murrah stopped and pointed at two large trunks. It was an early summer evening, and I will never forget the sunshine angling in through one of the high windows and spotlighting the two trunks in a pillar of gold light.

"You are looking," he told me, "at the H.H. Lomax collection."

The name meant nothing to me that day, just as I suspect it means little to most people today. It wasn't as if Dr. Murrah had shown me the papers of outstanding Americans such as Teddy Roosevelt, Leland Stanford, or

Buffalo Bill, or even of lesser Americans such as Billy the Kid, Jesse James, or Doc Holliday. But as Dr. Murrah explained and I later got to know firsthand, H. H. Lomax had known or at least claimed to have known all of those and many other men and women whose names are readily recognized by those with even the slightest interest in the Old West.

I opened the first trunk and found it full of papers and tablets, many tied together with twine. Dr. Murrah told me to look at a stack of papers. I lifted one bundle and began to read the delicate pencil of a feeble hand. I was astounded at what I read:

> Of all the fellows I met during my years wan-
> dering about, not one was more likable than
> Billy the Kid. Something about the Kid—maybe his
> squirrel-toothed grin, his big ears, his infectious
> laugh—won you over. That's why I'm glad I didn't
> kill him when I had the chance. Maybe I should
> have, because he had threatened me, but it was
> nothing personal, just that we had both taken a
> fancy to the same señorita.

My eyes surely wide, I glanced up from the bundle at Dr. Murrah and asked if this was true. Dr. Murrah shrugged and answered that nobody knew. Though he had discussed the Lomax collection with a few historians and a couple of English professors, not one expressed more than a courteous interest in the papers. The historians dismissed them, in large part because of their unproven authenticity. Though historical accuracy didn't matter to the English professors, they discounted anything written by an average man on the Old West as too provincial for their broader vision of literature.

As a former newspaper man, sometime writer of west-ern novels, and full-time devotee of Western Americana, I lacked the wisdom of those scholarly academicians. When Dr. Murrah offered me the chance to organize, study, and publish the Lomax papers, I gladly accepted. How could I have turned him down? If the paragraph I had just read were authentic, I held in my hand a paper written by a hand that had shaken the hand of Billy the Kid. This paper was a direct link from me to Billy the Kid, a sort of historical genealogy that put me just one person removed from some of the great names of the Old West.

How accurate that perception was. By the time I had managed to read most of the papers, I had made a link through Lomax's hand to a virtual Who's Who of the Old West, including Jesse James, Geronimo, Leland Stanford, U. S. Grant, Hanging Judge Isaac Parker, Wyatt Earp, Wild Bill Hickok, George Armstrong Custer, Bat Masterson, and more.

But who was H. H. Lomax, other than a peripatetic soul with the good or in some cases bad luck to have been where Western history was being made? From his writings and from examinations of the census records for northwest Arkansas, Henry Harrison Lomax was born in Washington County, Arkansas, on January 9, 1850, the son of George Washington Lomax and his wife, Abigail. Born while his father was in the California goldfields, Lomax was the next-to-youngest of nine children, followed in birth only by a sister. He matured during the turbulent Civil War years and appears to have been involved in the Battle of Prairie Grove. After the war, when the battles had ended but the sniping hadn't, he ran away from home, apparently at his mother's urging. That began his adventuresome life throughout the West.

By his recollection, he rode with Jesse James on his first bank robbery, then was hired by Joseph McCoy to spread word in Texas about the railhead he was establishing in Abilene. Lomax helped drive one of the first herds of Texas cattle back to Abilene. He witnessed one of the greatest Indian gatherings ever at the signing of the Medicine Lodge Treaty. After that he joined the transcontinental railroad and shot buffalo with the man who would become known as Buffalo Bill. He was present at Promontory Point for the wedding of the rails.

He tried mine speculation in Virginia City, Nevada, but was cheated out of a wealthy mining claim, or so he wrote. In San Francisco he came near marrying the daughter of a merchant who was grooming him to take over the business, but was blamed for missing funds. He ran a saloon for a while in Dodge City until a run-in with Wild Bill Hickok sent him onto the Texas Plains to hunt buffalo and fight Comanches and Kiowas. He tried mining again in Leadville and, though he is vague on the circumstances, may well have bushwhacked a lawyer.

And all of this was before he met Billy the Kid, the subject of the first bundle of papers I picked up that day in the stacks of the Southwest Collection. Later he witnessed the gunfight at O K Corral, toured with Buffalo Bill's Wild West Show, ran in the Oklahoma Land Rush, and prospected in the Klondike, among other things.

By my estimate, there were more than 22,000 pages of handwritten material in those two trunks. Additionally, there were dozens of copies of *Ranch Romances*, *Frontier Times*, and other pulp magazines that ran pioneer reminiscences. I thought perhaps those magazines had given Lomax the impetus to start writing down his recollections, but subsequent interviews with his grandniece, Mildred Ruth, in California provided a more complete picture of his final years and why he began writing.

Mildred Ruth was the granddaughter of Lomax's youngest sister, Harriet Lomax Scott. When Lomax ran in the Oklahoma Land Rush, he claimed a fine site with good water but realized he didn't have it in him to settle down and farm. So he turned the land over to his sister and her husband with the understanding that when he was old and needed a place to live out his years he could stay with them. In 1912 he returned to Oklahoma for payment. By then Harriet Lomax Scott had lost her husband and had turned the land over to her daughter and son-in-law, Mildred Ruth's parents, to run. Of the twenty-one years

until his death on May 22, 1933, he lived all but the final
two on the Scott place.

Mildred Ruth, who was twelve when he came to stay,
remembered him as a crotchety old man who occasionally
took to drink. She recalled locking up the guns and getting
out of the house whenever he found a bottle. Though he
was a grand imposition on the family, they owed the land
they farmed to him and figured they should swallow their
feelings and let him stay. Even so, he became quite a pest,
always interfering with the proper running of things and
always talking about the good old days and all the famous
men and women he had known. Finally, after five years of
his incessant stories, his sister Harriet got tired of his runs
of the mouth, as she called his braggadocio, and flopped
a tablet and pencil in front of him on the table with
instructions to write it all down so everyone wouldn't
have to listen to him. Though angered, he took to writing
and realized he had called his sister's bluff. For a period
he wrote just to annoy her, including in his recollections
scatological and sexual humor that angered her whenever
she found his "papers," as he took to calling them, lying
around the house. Over time those papers became an
obsession.

In 1931, when Mildred Ruth's parents lost the Lomax
farm to the Depression, they moved to California, where
years later I was able to locate the unmarried Mildred
Ruth in a Bakersfield nursing home. Lomax did not ask
and was not invited to go to California with the Ruths.
Instead, he and his two trunks were dropped off at the
railroad station. Somehow he wound up in Hodges, Texas,
staying with the Camp family in an old stone house by the
community gin. He lived there two years until his death
at age eighty-three.

In 1975, before the house was demolished, local farmer
John Bracken found the two trunks of papers among the
junk in a small attic that may have been Lomax's room
the last two years of his life. Bracken, who had earned
an agricultural degree from Texas Tech, examined the

papers, thought they might have some historical interest, and contacted the university's history department, which referred him to Dr. Murrah at the Southwest Collection.

I was so enthusiastic and Dr. Murrah so excited the first night I read the Lomax papers that it was almost midnight before we left. I would spend countless hours in the coming months with Lomax's papers. I came to enjoy his incisive writings, his Ozark idioms, and his unusual perspectives on life and death in the Old West. However, I am uncertain I would have liked him as a person.

Now, as to the authenticity of these papers, I am confident they were all written by H. H. Lomax. As to the veracity of his claims, I cannot be certain. Had he really met all these people or had he made it all up to impress his sister with his adventures? While much of his writings cannot be proved, they cannot so easily be disproved, either. Granted, the vagaries of memory can often turn truth into fiction; nonetheless I suspect that his memory, even in his later years, was better and more accurate than his imagination could possibly have been. Where possible, I tried to check his recollections against the historical record, and generally they hold, though I admit I am not patient enough to be an academic historian.

Today we may scoff at the notion that one man, especially an obscure man, should have seen so much history firsthand, but we forget that we live in a different society now than he did then. We are chained to a small plot of this country, generally within the triangle made by home, work, and grocery store. And when we travel great distances, we fly over the land on commercial jets or drive past on a generic interstate highway. Lomax, by contrast, was bound by no chain and was easily pulled where excitement or money or even the possibility of money beckoned.

His life was no more improbable than that of hundreds of men who roamed the Old West. We might think it unlikely that one man could hunt buffalo in Kansas, fight Comanche at Adobe Walls in Texas, serve as sheriff of

Dodge City and marshal of Trinidad, work as a bodyguard to the heir of Jay Gould's railroad empire, and end up as a sportswriter in New York City, but Bat Masterson did. We might think it unlikely that one man could survive the most famous gunfight in the west, referee a disputed championship prizefight, and become a consultant to the burgeoning film industry in southern California, but Wyatt Earp did. It would be even more unlikely that a lowly trapper, freighter, and buffalo hunter might win a Congressional Medal of Honor as a civilian, then establish a cowboy circus that would take him all over the world and make him the confidant of presidents and royalty, yet Buffalo Bill Cody did just that.

This, then, is not H. H. Lomax's story, but rather just one of his stories edited in a way to preserve the intent and tone of his writings, if not the punctuation and spelling. I started with his recollections of Billy the Kid because they were the first I came to when I learned of H. H. Lomax. To try to put all his papers in chronological order and then truncate his life into the typical historian's colorless prose would have been a great disservice to his perspectives on many of the famous personalities of the Old West.

As I said at the beginning, historical research often travels in circles. For me, the Lomax odyssey started while I was doing research on the battle of Yellow House Canyon. Near the bottom of Lomax's second trunk I found three tablets bundled with twine and labeled "The Pocket Canyon Fight," an early name for the Battle of Yellow House Canyon. The memoirs of H. H. Lomax had taken me full circle.

—PRESTON LEWIS
Lubbock, Texas
January 1994

Chapter One

Of all the fellows I met during my years wandering about, not one was more likable than Billy the Kid. Something about the Kid—maybe his squirrel-toothed grin, his big ears, his infectious laugh—won you over. That's why I'm glad I didn't kill him when I had the chance. Maybe I should have, because he had threatened me, but it was nothing personal, just that we had both taken a fancy to the same señorita.

I never intended to ride into New Mexico Territory, but I didn't intend to get hanged, either, and that's what would've happened had I stayed around Leadville, Colorado, after the killing. It seems a lawyer up there, who was no more than a polecat in a fancy suit, took a shotgun blast to the back. He didn't take it well, because he just up and died. But like all skunks his killing raised a stink, and folks figured I was the man who had performed this valuable public service. These folks, a lot of good and decent people when they were sober, decided to throw a necktie party in my honor, but I declined the invitation, thanks to a little help from a friend and a mule I called Flash.

As fast as Flash could carry me, which was a little quicker than I could walk and a lot slower than I could run, I angled southeast toward Trinidad and the New

9

Mexico line. From my buffalo-hunting days in West Texas I knew the southeast corner of New Mexico Territory was a good place to hide, an outlaw's paradise. Of course I didn't feel like an outlaw, but those fine folks in Trinidad hadn't really considered my thoughts when they decided otherwise. I wasn't an outlaw. An outlaw galloped away from trouble on some fine stallion, but there I was trotting through Colorado on a damned mule. A few years later, when I ran into an acquaintance from Leadville, I learned that Flash, slow as he was, probably saved my life; the law couldn't figure out how I could have gotten out of town since no horses were reported stolen and nobody had seen me get on the stage.

This was back in the fall of 1877—I remember it because just a few weeks earlier we had celebrated the first anniversary of Colorado's becoming a state—and the trains still hadn't reached Leadville, in large part because of a dispute between the Santa Fe and the Denver and Rio Grande railroads. Everybody thought the railroad was progress, and maybe it was for law-abiding citizens, but on this trip I had my doubts. The problem was, the telegraph followed the railroad wherever it went, and the railroad was planning to go everywhere, if you believed every land speculator with a deed and every promoter with a dream. The telegraph sure limited a man's freedom, especially when he couldn't escape one county without the sheriff in the next learning of his departure.

Without any problem I made it past El Moro, a little burg that was the southern terminus of the Denver and Rio Grande Railroad and the end of the infernal telegraph. In Trinidad, though, I wasn't so lucky. I was just riding through town, hunkered low on the mule's bare back, my hat pulled down over my eyes, when a clump of schoolboys started hurrahing me for riding such a superb animal as Flash. I don't know that it hurt the mule's feelings, Flash being no faster of mind than he was of foot, but it kind of riled me that here I was minding my own business and these six yearlings were laughing at my mode of transportation. It didn't help my dignity any when Flash broke wind and those six whistles took to slapping their knees. I didn't have a razor strop to impart some manners on their backsides, but I had a pistol tucked in my britches. The problem was, I only had three bullets and I couldn't get those boys to line up single-file for me. If I was going to get blamed for a positive contribution to society, like shooting a lawyer, I might just as well do something bad so when the law caught up with me I wouldn't be going to jail for nothing. I jerked the halter on my mule, figuring to teach those schoolboys a lesson in manners, but Flash just kept trotting. For a mule, he had good sense for avoiding trouble.

Outside of Trinidad, Flash began the ascent up the rugged trail leading to Raton Pass and New Mexico Territory. That trail was carved out of the mountain almost single-handedly by Uncle Dick Wootton, a grizzled pioneer who was so damned proud of his work he charged a toll of everyone passing his place. It was getting dark, but that was fine because I was broke and figured I would have to slide past the wooden gate and hope Uncle Dick Wootton and his hounds didn't discover my trespass. Getting by Wootton's gate unpaid was akin to slipping daylight past a rooster, but I was lucky. It took to storming and raining, driving the dogs to shelter and Wootton to his stove. I squeezed past the toll gate free and got a cold shower to boot. On the downward slope of Raton Pass I breathed easier, knowing I was in New Mexico Territory and beyond the reach of the telegraph.

By then I'd about worn my neck out looking over my shoulder, but I kept riding south toward Lincoln County. At that time it took up the southeast quarter of the territory and was said to be the largest county in all of the United States. The eastern half was grassland broken down the middle by the Pecos River valley. Without owning a single acre, the cowman John Chisum controlled this grazing land from south of Fort Sumner to near the Texas border. The county's western half was a

series of mountains and valleys where the Mexicans had
lived pretty much peacefully for decades and where white
men were moving in to set up farms. The county was
a paradise for rustlers because of John Chisum's huge
herds to the east and all the mountainous hiding places
to the west.

A man on the dodge grows suspicious of everyone, so
I had gone out of my way to avoid people, trouble, and, the
way it worked out, food. After two weeks on the owlhoot
trail, the back side of my belly button began to rub against
the front side of my backbone, I was that hungry. I stuck
to the foothills in the western half of Lincoln County,
figuring Flash could never outrun a good horse on the
flat land, but he could at least carry me to cover where
I could defend myself with my three bullets.

Hunger can cloud your judgment like a thunderstorm
blots out the sun. One evening just before dusk I caught
a whiff of the best thing I had ever smelled in my life—
roasting beef. By then I didn't care if the devil himself
was cook as long as I could have a few bites.

Riding down a draw, I saw a half-dozen men lounging
around a big campfire, the carcass of a dead yearling nearby. For rustlers they were rather lackadaisical, me getting
within fifty yards of them before a single one noticed me
and then only after Flash broke wind. A couple of them
grabbed at their six-guns, but when they saw the mule
I was riding, they didn't think me much of a threat and
let their guns slide back into their holsters. All but one
of them, a redheaded fellow, returned to cooking. The
redhead, though, angled away from the fire and toward
me. He eyed me pretty closely, never saying a word until
I pulled back the halter on Flash. The mule stopped not
twenty feet from the man, whom I took to be the leader.
For what seemed like forever, he stared at me and I
stared back.

"Fine-looking mule you're riding," he finally said,
then narrowed his eyes at me. "You lost or just get tired
of plowing?"

Well, I'd plowed enough to know what the backside of a mule looked like, and I'd lived long enough to know a thief when I saw one. This fellow would've stolen flies from a blind spider. No doubt he and his cohorts were bad men, but I was downright hungry and not too choosy about who I took as friends as long as they shared their food.

"Is this Wyoming?" I asked him.

"Why, hell yes," he lied.

I just grimaced. "Damnation, then I am lost. I was trying to find New Mexico Territory."

The fellow just grinned. "Jesse Evans is my name, and I'm from Texas. You ever rustle any cattle?"

Well, I'd done some cowboying in past years, even helping drive one of the first herds from Texas to Abilene, Kansas, so I knew a little bit about that line of work. I shook my head. "Can't say I ever did rustle any cattle."

Evans's face clouded for a moment.

"Branding strays is what I always called it," I continued. "In fact, there's no better steak than one from another man's beef."

"Then, hell, you ought to love supper, compliments of John Chisum himself."

Taking that as an invitation, I started to slide off my mule until Evans's voice turned cold as ice. I froze atop Flash.

"No man eats beef I've butchered without telling me his name." He stood there staring with his cold gray eyes. He was a modest-sized man, maybe five feet six and a hundred and fifty pounds at most, but like most men that claimed to be Texans he looked bigger and meaner. The problem with Texans was they were easily insulted. Call one a bastard and he might not think a thing of it, likely because it was true or he didn't know the meaning of such a big word. But forget to introduce yourself and it was like spitting on the Alamo.

To make amends for my lack of social graces, I announced myself. "Henry Lomax." Instantly the five men hunkered around the campfire shot to their feet and lined up in a semicircle behind Evans, their hands sliding toward the guns in their holsters.

Evans's gray eyes became narrow slits as his hand fell to the butt of his pistol. Apparently I had now insulted his fragile Texas disposition as well as that of all his thieving partners.

"You any kin to a fellow named Gadrich Lomax?"

I could honestly say I wasn't, my kin not being stupid enough to name a kid Gadrich. I shook my head. "Never heard of him."

"A damned swindler. If I ever catch him, I'm gonna kill him. Where you from?"

"Arkansas," I said.

Evans's hard gaze softened. "Gadrich Lomax was a damn Yankee, New York or New Jersey." He paused, spitting in disgust at the ground. "I sold him a blind horse for a good wad of greenbacks—counterfeit greenbacks, it turned out. The sheriff threw me in jail for passing the bad money."

I fought the urge to laugh. Here a cattle thief was complaining about being taken by another crook.

Evans lifted his finger and pointed it at my nose. "If I ever find Gadrich Lomax, I'll kill him, or if I find out you're his kin, I'll kill you." Behind him his cohorts dropped their guard and gathered back around the fire, pulling slabs of meat out and chowing down.

I was about to pass out from hunger before the cloud of Gadrich Lomax passed from Evans's strange disposition. Finally he nodded that I could join in the meal. I fairly fell off Flash and darted for the fire, but Evans kept me from taking a steak until he had introduced me all around. I don't remember all their names, but three of them—Tom Hill, Frank Baker, and Buck Morton—would later join Jesse Evans in the killing that lit the Lincoln County War.

I knew these were all bad men, and I didn't much care for them, but I sure liked their food. I rode with them for two weeks because I was hungry and because I figured if I tried to leave them, they just might up and shoot me in honor of Gadrich Lomax, whoever the hell he was. Further, Flash could never outrun their horses in an escape. All the rustlers seemed amused by me riding a mule and carrying a gun with only three cartridges. They went around loaded down with enough ammunition to feed a Gatling gun for a week.

We'd generally have beef two or three times a week, whenever Jesse got the urge to kill someone else's animal. Mostly we'd steal cattle for Lawrence G. Murphy, who ran a big store in Lincoln and held the government contracts to sell beef to the Mescalero Apache Reservation in the mountains and Fort Stanton in the foothills. Murphy made almost pure profit on those contracts, since he used somebody else's cattle to fill them. Though he paid the rustlers good money, they mostly returned it to him through the overpriced goods he sold in his store and the watered-down liquor he dispensed in his saloon. There was a lot of talk, though, about an upstart Englishman who was opening a competing store and jeopardizing Murphy's virtual economic monopoly on the entire county.

In the two weeks I rode with them, we stole maybe three hundred head of cattle, and I had put a little distance between my belly button and my backbone. I was getting itchy to leave, figuring the sheriff would run into us sooner or later and throw us in jail.

Well, I was half right. Sheriff William Brady rode out one day just as we were butchering a stolen calf. I was beginning to think a military brass band could slip up on the Evans gang, with no harder a time than the sheriff and I had had. Well, the sheriff caught us dead to rights, and I figured he might even be looking for me because of the Leadville incident. Like a skunk when the wind changes, I thought my past had blown back to me. But instead of arresting us, the sheriff did an odd thing. He gathered wood and started the fire that cooked us all a good beefsteak. There's nothing tastier than a stolen beefsteak. It rests good on the stomach if not on the conscience.

We were eating around the fire when the sheriff asked me my name. Not accustomed to running from the law, I never thought I ought to use an alias. Of course the whole gang knew my name by then, so I admitted to being Henry Lomax.

"You been up in Colorado within the past month or so?" Brady asked. "I got a flier at the office on a Lomax that killed a lawyer up Leadville way."

All the heads around the campfire jerked toward me, and I saw a look of newfound respect in the rustlers' hard eyes. I shrugged, then stammered a moment before Jesse Evans interrupted.

"Lomax's been riding with us for six weeks," he said. "You sure it wasn't Gadrich Lomax? Now, there's a son of a bitch."

The sheriff shrugged and asked for another slab of steak.

We had just about finished supper when a rifle blast pierced the night air. Everybody dove for cover and their guns. All of a sudden the night was still as death, with us trying to find the location of our assailant amidst the broken and rocky terrain. Suddenly we heard this giggling, then laughing, out there behind a couple rocks. Cursing, several of the men picked themselves up, dusted themselves off, and shoved their pistols back in their holsters. With the barrel of his rifle this fellow raised his hat above the top of the rock. When no one fired, he stood up and walked into camp, slapping his thigh with his hat and carrying on as proudly as a puppy with two peters.

That was the first time I ever saw Billy the Kid. He had a gangly, awkward look about him, and he damn sure wasn't a handsome kid, not with those two buckteeth and big ears, but what he lacked in looks he more than made up for in spirit. I still had my pistol pointed at his heart and could've killed him as he sauntered in, but Jesse Evans strolled by and pushed the barrel of my gun toward the ground. "It's just the Kid," he said, as if no more explanation was needed.

"You boys better hope we stay on the same side of things," the Kid said as he ambled into camp, howdying everyone he knew and eyeing me suspiciously. Approaching me, he pointed his finger at my nose. "You're the man I'm looking for."

My flesh began to crawl. Did he know about Leadville? My gun was still in my hand, but I didn't feel too secure about my chances, not with the cool confidence in the Kid's eyes and the sheriff squatting over his stolen beefsteak not twenty feet away.

"I've been looking for a partner," he informed me, "and you're the one."

Before I said I wanted anything to do with him, the Kid told me to be ready to head out come morning. Engaging and confident, he had a way of dragging folks along for the ride.

Just after sunrise I left with the Kid, him funning me for Flash and promising to trade the animal for a horse, just in case we had some hard riding to do.

"Why'd you want me for a partner?" I finally asked.

"I didn't," he answered. "You just don't have the look of the hard types you were riding with. I figured they would get you in more trouble than you could get out of."

The Kid was right. Jesse Evans and his gang were nothing but trouble.

Chapter Two

Billy was no more than seventeen years old at the time, a full decade younger than me. I mean, Billy wasn't many years removed from clinging to his momma's skirt or eating dirt outside, yet here I was throwing in with him like he was a U.S. senator. He had a winning personality and could've well become a politician except for one flaw—he was basically honest. Unlike Jesse Evans and his men, the Kid had a sense of right and wrong. Most men drifting through Lincoln County had no more conscience than a Democrat had sense.

Billy was a natural lead steer. I'd been on enough trail drives to know that no matter how big the herd, one animal always emerged as the leader. A good lead steer can start a herd moving when some animals are balky, can keep a herd calm when there's reason to panic, and can give a herd direction. The Kid was a good lead steer, and though many older men would eventually follow him, I was the first.

For all his ability, Billy didn't look like a lead steer. He stood no taller than five foot seven and would've barely weighed a hundred and fifty pounds dressed and armed, but what there was of him was hard-muscled and wiry. Whether atop a horse, afoot, or on the dance floor,

he moved with a gracefulness that was almost snakelike.
That grace gave him his deceptive speed both on foot and
on the draw.

His oval face was almost lost between those two flaps
he called ears. His two top front teeth were dispropor-
tionate with the others and protruded slightly, but they
weren't that noticeable in the shade of those ears. His
hair was wavy brown and, to look older, he tried to grow
a beard and mustache, but the result was little more than
peach fuzz that made him seem even more boyish. His
mouth was as wide as his blue eyes because he generally wore a smile, but his quick temper could sour his
grin quicker than vinegar curdles milk, especially when
someone mentioned his tent-flap ears.

He wore a plain vest, dark pants, work shirt, yellow
bandanna, cheap boots, and an unadorned Mexican sombrero that shaded his light skin. High on his right hip rode
a revolver. He favored a Colt Thunderer, a .41 caliber
double-action revolver that could be fired without cocking
the hammer, and he was never far from his Winchester
'73 carbine, which used .44-.40 center-fire cartridges. As
heavily armed as he traveled, he would've frightened
most people had it not been for that constant and dis-
arming smile.

Except for funning me for Flash and telling me I
didn't belong with Jesse Evans's hard types, Billy said
nothing else until we were out of rifle range of the rustlers
and the sheriff. His words surprised me. "Honest work is
hard to come by in Lincoln County."

"Must be, if the sheriff eats stolen beef with rustlers."

"Well, tell me, Henry Lomax, if you were sheriff
and came upon a half-dozen rustlers, just what would
you do?"

"Damn sure wouldn't eat with them."

The Kid laughed. "You've been eating with them a
couple days or weeks, ain't you?"

"I ain't sheriff."

"You're practical and so's the sheriff. You threw in with them until you got some food in your belly."

Billy had a point, but I hadn't taken an oath to uphold the law in Lincoln County, either. "I didn't have a choice."

The Kid shrugged. "Neither did Sheriff Brady. That's why there's little honest work in Lincoln County. The only man who makes choices in these parts is Lawrence G. Murphy."

"Ain't heard of him," I answered.

"You will, if you stay in Lincoln County long," Billy replied. "Lawrence Murphy's a damned Irishman who runs a store everyone in Lincoln calls 'the House.' The good sheriff has to straddle a fence between what's the law of the land and what's the law of the House. He does a fair job of it."

I shook my head. "Not when he doesn't arrest rustlers."

Billy laughed. "Jesse's gang is known in these parts as 'the Boys.' The Boys work for the House. Brady's doing the best he can without doing the House's dirty work. Most folks know he's honest."

"Sounds to me like the sheriff's an empty sack," I offered.

The Kid scratched one of his big ears and shook his head as he studied Flash. "Big talk for a man riding a mule."

"I've ridden worse," I admitted.

"I haven't," Billy shot back, a wide grin on his face. "And I'll not have my partner being seen on such a poor animal."

"I ain't got any money."

"You got me, and that's better than money in the Lincoln bank."

"There's a bank in these parts?"

"Yes, sir, the Englishman and the lawyer are opening one in Lincoln, trying to drive the House out of business."

I couldn't help but laugh. "There's the sheriff, the House, the Boys, the Englishman, and the Lawyer. Is 'the' everybody's first name in these parts?"

"Not everybody," said Billy, "but there's only one 'the' you should worry about, and that's the Kid."

Billy was as cocky as a cage full of roosters, but right. Of all those in what would become the Lincoln County War, Billy was involved in more shoot-outs than any other man.

As we rode out of the foothills and away from the Boys, we climbed a rise and looked to the east across the vast yellow plain that stretched all the way to the Pecos River. Wordlessly we reined up our mounts, the Kid, his black stallion, and me, my dependable mule. We sat silently staring across the gentle rolling terrain, where longhorns by the thousand grazed on the sunburned grass of fall. So many cattle reminded me of the great buffalo herds I had hunted on the Texas plains.

Finally Billy lifted his hand and pointed. "That's part of John Chisum's herd. Eighty thousand head stretching along the Pecos from Fort Sumner to the Texas border."

"It ain't fair that so much belongs to just one man," I said.

Billy replied, "Old John worked for it and earned it, plain and simple."

"It still don't seem fair."

For an instant, Billy's voice lost its confidence. "Life ain't fair, and you're a fool to think it ever will be." He nudged his horse forward. "Come on, we're going to Roswell."

I steered Flash in beside his mount, but no matter how fast I got the mule to trot, the Kid kept his stallion a half length ahead of me because he didn't want to talk. He rode silently for a couple miles, and I quickly learned that when something bothered Billy, he could sull up quicker than a bullfrog in a dry pond. Most of the time he chattered like a widow woman. When he wasn't talking, he was usually humming or singing, "Turkey in the Straw" being his favorite tune. But when he was silent, either he sensed danger or something was gnawing at him.

When he finally let me draw alongside him after a few miles, he was ready to talk again. "My mother was a lung-er. She died three years ago. Life wasn't fair to her."

Tuberculosis being a bad disease, I didn't know what to say, and I don't think Billy expected an answer. He just wanted me to know what had sulled him. It touched me because my mother was alive, though I hadn't seen her since I left Cane Hill, Arkansas, a dozen years earlier and hadn't written her but a half-dozen times since then.

Billy and I talked on into Roswell, and I learned as much as any man about the Kid. After his mother had died of tuberculosis, his stepfather had abandoned him, and Billy had fallen in with bad men who got him into trouble. That seemed to gnaw at him like ugly dogs on a ham bone. I never understood why it was always so easy to take up with the bad crowd and so hard to ride with decent folks. It must be that preachers and their type don't have a sense of humor. And to young sprouts, a sense of humor seems much more important than the sense of honor the bad crowd lacks.

As we rode through John Chisum's vast herd, I learned that Billy enjoyed dancing, didn't smoke, rarely drank, and cussed only out of necessity. He did enjoy gambling and warned me point-blank never to make a bet or play monte or cards with him. Though he was known mostly as the Kid, his given name was Henry McCarty. He admitted he had killed a man in self-defense at Camp Grant, Arizona, and, not wanting to bring dishonor to the family name, he had taken to calling himself William H. Bonney, largely because he liked the tune to "The Bonnie Blue Flag."

It was late afternoon when we approached Roswell, an adobe oasis that had sprouted up beside the Rio Hondo near its junction with the Pecos River. Tall cottonwood trees lined the Hondo, which was bled by irrigation ditches leading to scattered fields of yellowing corn and occasional orchards of ripening apples.

As we rode past the scattered adobe farmhouses, Billy would slow and stare. At one house near the road, a young Mexican woman came running out, waving and crying his name. "Bill-lee, Bill-lee," she called, then exploded into Spanish that shot past me like a runaway freight train. A comely young woman with black hair and matching eyes, she wore a plain skirt and a colorful blouse that highlighted her shapely body as she darted for the Kid.

Billy laughed as she grabbed his leg. *"Me permite acompañarle a su casa?"* he asked.

"No, no. Padre."

"Buenas noches," he answered, rattling the reins of his stallion, which pulled him from her grasp.

She ran her fingers through her hair, then dabbed at her tears.

"What was that about?"

Billy tossed me a sheepish grin. "She likes me. Most of the señoritas do, and I like them, but her father was home, and that would make it difficult for us to be together."

I quickly learned that the Mexicans, and most especially the young Mexican ladies, all liked Billy. He spoke their language and respected their traditions and, in the case of the young ladies, their fiery charms. Curious why he was slowing at each adobe we passed, I ventured a question. "What are you looking for?"

"A horse for you."

I looked back over my shoulder and saw a few horses in the pens of houses we had passed. "What makes you think anybody will sell?"

He flashed me a wide grin. "Who said anything about buying a horse? I'll convince them to give you a horse."

I couldn't help but shake my head. "Someone's gonna give me a horse?"

"For your mule." He was as confident as a Bible drummer at a Baptist convention.

Jerking my thumb over my shoulder at the houses
we had passed, I asked another question. "What's wrong
with some of those horses?"

"Mexicans live there. Their daughters wouldn't like
me if I outtraded their fathers."

As we neared the edge of town, Billy pointed to a
large adobe house some hundred yards off the road. A
half-dozen horses pranced around a substantial wooden
corral beyond the house. "Your horse is in the corral," he
said as he turned his stallion off the road.

Not knowing what to expect, I followed him to the
front of the house, where a mongrel dog emerged from
the shade, all hunkered down like he was ready to lunge
and bark. Billy whistled softly and the cur relaxed, then
trotted out to greet us.

Billy reined up his stallion. "Howdy the house," he
called a couple times. The door swung open and a grizzled
fellow emerged, lifting his suspenders over his shoulders.

"Damn dog," he said. "He's supposed to bark before
someone gets this close to the house."

"Your mongrel needs a dosing," I told him, drawing
Billy's surprised stare.

"A dose of what?"

"Sprinkle a little gunpowder in his food for a couple
days. That'll straighten him up, make him more vicious."

"Hell, fellow, I just want to get him off his ass, not
blow it clear to hell."

I could tell the farmer didn't believe me, but I had
seen it work back in the hills of Arkansas. A dose of
gunpowder once a week or so kept a dog off his haunches
and cleared him of worms.

Billy gave me this odd look like I was ruining his
chances of trading Flash for a horse, then turned to the
farmer. "I'm Billy Bonney. I'm looking to trade my friend's
mule for a horse."

The farmer must have been suspicious, because he
didn't give his name. His eyes narrowed as he looked

from Billy to me and back. "Why doesn't your friend do his own trading?"

"He's eaten too much gunpowder to think straight."

The farmer laughed, but still didn't introduce himself. "I don't have any horses to trade."

Billy shook his head and removed his sombrero. "Sir, I don't want just any horse, I want your best horse."

"You've got gall, I'll hand you that."

"I'm just a kid and don't know better. Now, some kids wouldn't stop to make an offer on a good horse. No, sir," Billy said with a smile as wide as his sombrero, "they'd just poison the dog and come back at night and steal the animal right from under your nose. No, sir, I don't operate that way."

The farmer scratched the fuzz on his chin. "You the one they call Billy the Kid, the one that's ridden with Jesse Evans?"

Billy shrugged. "Some call me that and I did ride with Jesse, though I'm none too proud of it."

The farmer scratched his head, then adjusted his suspenders. "Keep your mule. I've got a horse you can have."

Cocking his head at me, Billy plopped his sombrero atop it and smiled as smugly as a merchant with a government contract.

I thought the farmer had caved to the implied threat in Billy's comments, but the old dirt-scratcher didn't seem the least bit intimidated as he led us and his lazy watchdog past a couple apple trees to the corral. He pointed out a bay gelding. "He don't look too good," the farmer said, "but you can have him."

Billy and I dismounted at the corral, propped our arms over the top rail, and studied the bay as it pranced about. Despite the farmer's assessment, I thought the gelding was a decent-looking horse. He had good lines and a well-proportioned head.

"Why you giving him away?" Billy asked.

The farmer spat through the fence at a fresh pile of horse apples. "Like I said, he don't look too good. He's a riding horse but don't take well to the harness and wagon. So he's just eating up my feed. He's yours, and I'll throw in a halter to boot as long as you promise me no trouble."

By then I was ready to take the horse, but Billy turned suddenly suspicious. "He stolen?"

The farmer coughed into his fist. "Odd question coming from one of the Boys."

"Not anymore, I'm not."

"I got papers on the animal, and I'll give you the same."

"We'd be obliged," Billy replied.

The farmer pointed out a worn halter, its leather stiff and cracked, hanging from a fence post. "There's your halter. Put it on your horse, and I'll go to the house for paper." As the farmer retreated, I took the halter and started toward the gate, but the Kid grabbed my arm.

"That's why you should never bet against the Kid," he reminded me. "I'm too good a horse trader and judge of people."

"You scared him, Kid. That wasn't horse trading, that was intimidation."

Billy opened the gate and bowed at the waist with a mocking gesture as I passed. The other horses danced around the pen and dodged me, but the bay seemed bewildered and was easily cornered. He tossed his head as I approached, but I grabbed his mane and held him long enough to slip the halter on. A horse that won't take to a harness is often balky, so I was surprised when he followed me readily. The Kid opened the gate just as the farmer walked up and handed him a receipt. Holding his nose high in the air, Billy shoved the receipt in his vest pocket.

After closing the gate, Billy tied Flash's reins to his stallion's saddle and mounted. He pointed to the apple trees near the house. "Mind if we have a few apples? My friend and I are powerful hungry."

"Help yourself." The farmer smiled like he had a secret.

"What's wrong with those apples?" Billy inquired.

"Not a thing," he replied.

I grabbed the bay's mane and jerked myself aboard, anxious for the Kid to talk someone out of a saddle to make my mounting and riding a bit more comfortable.

"Obliged," Billy replied. "We came along at the right time."

The farmer nodded. "Just call it blind luck."

Billy nodded and with a tip of his sombrero called out, *"Muchas gracias."* He reined his stallion around and led Flash back to the road, me following. After guiding his horse into the trees, he stood in the stirrups to grab a couple big apples from the upper branches. His stallion and Flash had time to snatch an apple apiece from the lower branches before Billy aimed them for the road.

I pointed the bay for the apple tree, and he plunged into the lower branches without stopping, almost knocking me off his back. "Whoa," I cried, jerking back on the reins and backing him out a bit.

Billy glanced back over his shoulder and laughed. "Maybe you should stick with your mule if you aren't better than that." He jiggled his reins, and the stallion trotted away, dragging Flash.

I had never seen the mule move so quickly. I watched for a moment before reaching for a couple apples. I plucked a pair and waited for the gelding to get one for himself. As I took a bite, I watched his frustrating effort.

The bay kept tossing his head and lunging for an apple but missing terribly each time. He knocked two apples to the ground, but that was as close as he came to the fruit.

"Hurry up," yelled Billy.

Impatiently I jerked the halter and pointed the gelding at Billy, then nudged him with my heel. The gelding started and stumbled a step before catching its balance. He had an uneasy, tentative gait and kept tossing his head as he ran. Then the farmer's words came back to me. *He don't look too good! Blind luck!*

My worst fears were confirmed when I reined the horse down the road toward Roswell and he stepped in a shallow hole he should easily have missed.

The gelding was blind!

Chapter Three

Riding a blind horse ain't a proper way to enter a town. It's worse than riding a mule. Astride a mule, folks think you lack money. Atop a blind horse, they think you lack sense. Near dusk only a few folks were about as we rode the dusty street into what there was of Roswell, but everyone seemed to be staring at me and my mount. I felt dumber than stump water.

The cool air prickled the skin and carried the sweet aroma of burning pine. Somewhere supper was cooking. I could smell it like a preacher smells sin. Whatever it was, it smelled better than the stolen beef I had been eating with Jesse Evans and the Boys.

The Kid turned down a trail I'm sure the locals thought was a street, but I had seen better paths to the outhouse back in Arkansas. My disposition didn't get any better when I saw a couple Mexican boys, barely school age, pointing at me. Those two brown beans said something in Spanish, then took to giggling at me and my blind gelding. I didn't know enough Spanish to understand them or to impress them with the more eloquent cuss words of their language, but that didn't mean I didn't know how to express my mood. After all, I had been educated in Arkansas. I stuck my tongue out. They were equally eloquent, not only returning the gesture but

29

also stumbling along the trail like two blind dwarfs beside my sightless gelding.

I was trying to figure out a way to punish that overgrown crib trash and restore my dignity when my blind bay slid off the trail just enough to rub my leg up against the spindly arm of a cholla plant. Those sharp needles poked through my britches faster than a drunk can uncork a full flask. I cursed, impressing those two house rats with my broad vocabulary. After I extracted a couple thorns from my flesh, I thought about shooting the two of them, then turning the gun on the bay. The arithmetic worked out perfectly, as I still had my three bullets, but I discounted that option when I realized it would be too merciful a punishment for boys and animal. Instead, I considered giving them my blind horse and climbing back aboard Flash.

Billy, though, never gave me a chance to rid myself of the blind bay. He reined up in front of a long, squat adobe building and quickly dismounted. My bay would've butted his head against the adobe wall had I not jerked on the halter and saved him a headache.

"Adobe" was a fancy name for dried mud. Living in an adobe is akin to living in a hole, only it's aboveground. It's a fine dwelling if you're a gopher or a bullsnake, but it wouldn't impress many folks in Cane Hill.

I dismounted and tied my horse to the hitching post. As I walked around his other blind end, I saw the two boys across the trail just grinning at me, their white teeth shining like stars. I was still carrying one of the apples I'd plucked from the farmer's tree. I tossed it between my hands as I considered whether to give it to the horse or the two boys. The bay might snap my wrist off if I came anywhere close to his mouth, so I pitched it to the boys. They rushed to catch it, and one of them snatched it from the air. They both grinned and marched away, alternating bites.

Billy ambled toward me, slapping Flash on the behind as he passed. I wished he'd hauled off and cold-cocked the bay instead of hassling my faithful mule, but I didn't say a thing about the gelding's infirmity. I turned around to stretch and studied the building, concluding it was a mercantile. Through the glow of yellow light that seeped like stale urine out the shuttered window, I saw a sign tacked on the door: CLOSED TILL MORN.

"It's closed."

"Not for me. The storekeeper's a friend who rooms inside."

If Billy knew the storekeeper like he knew horses, we'd be lucky to get inside by the end of the year.

"Name's Ash Upson. He's a windy sort, lies so much he has to hire someone to call his dogs, but he's got a grand curiosity. Never once has he seen a bottle that he didn't want to know what was at the bottom of it. Now's the time to trade with him, 'cause he's probably had a nip or two."

If Billy traded for goods like he bargained for horses, we'd probably leave the store with a sack of weevily flour, a slab of spoiled salt pork, and a tin of rock-hard crackers.

Billy sidled up to the plank door and banged on it.

He was answered by a crash of tinware. "Damned illiterates," cried Upson. "Can't you read we're closed?"

"Open up," answered the Kid. "It's me, Billy."

"Billy who? Billy goat?" Upson chuckled at his own joke.

With a shrug the Kid glanced at me, his skin sallow in the yellow light. "I can't remember the name I told him," he whispered to me, then called to the door. "It's me, Billy Bonney."

"Don't know a Billy Bonney."

"Henry McCarty, then."   •

"Don't know him either," shouted Upson, his voice muffled.

"Kid Antrim?"

"Hell," called Upson, "how many of you are there?"

"Them's all me," Billy called back.

"Damn, feller, I'd hate to go to one of your family reunions."

For such a good friend, Billy had a heck of a time convincing Upson to open up.

"We need a few supplies," Billy continued.

"Thought there was just one of you."

"I need some ammunition, a few groceries, and a blanket for my partn—for myself. I'll take them tonight, pay you tomorrow."

There was a long pause, like Upson had never dealt out such easy credit. "How do I know you'll be back to pay me?"

"How do you know I won't come back tonight to burn you out, slit your throat, and steal all your liquor?"

I didn't know how adobe would burn, but there was a long pause before I heard the bar being lifted on the door. Like I say, Billy had a way with people.

Slowly the door cracked open, and Upson peeked through the slit. I could just make out a big eye staring at us. Then the door swung wide, and Ash Upson stood before us in the rancid light. "Why, Kid," he said, "why didn't you tell me it was you?"

Billy walked in, and Upson started to close the door in my face before Billy stopped him. "This is my partner," he said.

Upson startled when he realized I was right in his face. A short, frail man with a broken nose and a face pitted from smallpox, he studied me. "You Bonney, Antrim, or McCarty?"

"I'm Lomax," I replied.

Upson pursed his lips and studied me all the more closely. "You the Lomax that's been passing bad money in these parts?"

I shook my head. "Nope, that's Gadrich Lomax. I'm Henry Harrison Lomax."

"Another one named after a president," he said with disgust. "Here we're living in a county named after the martyred Lincoln and every other white man you meet's named after a president. William Henry Harrison, the ninth president of these United States and the first to die in office. Tippecanoe and Tyler, too. A good Whig politician, but a politician nonetheless. We need more real heroes so mothers can name their children after them instead of politicians. Every other male born in this country is named George Washington this or Thomas Jefferson that. Congratulate your mother, though, Henry Harrison Lomax. At least she had the decency to name you after a president who only lasted a month in office, not enough time to damage the principles upon which this great republic was founded." Upson stepped aside and allowed me to pass.

Billy already had an armload of supplies by the time Upson closed the door behind me. I stepped toward him, but Upson grabbed my hand and began to pump it vigorously.

"Allow me to introduce myself," he started. "I'm Marshall Ashmun Upson, storekeeper, postmaster, teacher, journalist, and, the grandest honor of all, notary public. That means I'm trustworthy."

From the thickness of the liquor on his breath, I was tempted to add bartender to the list. Extracting my fingers from his lingering handshake, I stepped over a pile of tin plates and cups on the floor.

"Get what you need," Billy called to me. "I've got credit."

"Credit," boomed Upson, banging the tin plates together, "is the downfall of mankind." He was on his hands and knees picking up the spilled tinware from the floor. He went on to explain his views, but I gathered supplies instead of listening. Upson could gobble with the best of gabbers. He could gab the ears off a corn patch and still have enough words left to feed the hogs.

But even if he *was* a talker, I didn't feel right about taking things from his store. Still, I didn't feel right riding around Lincoln County on a blind horse with only three bullets to my name. I picked up a cheap holster, a carton of bullets, a wool blanket, and a coat to help keep me warm as the days and nights turned cooler. Billy pointed at a Winchester carbine, but I declined, figuring I'd taken enough for a man who was dead broke and riding a blind horse.

Billy took a pan, a can of tomatoes, a couple potatoes, a bag of coffee, and three cartons of .41-caliber ammunition for his pistol. He picked up a canteen and tossed it to me. "You'll need that."

Behind me Upson finished stacking the tin plates on the table, then stood with his fists on his hips admiring his work. He turned to Billy. "You wouldn't be stealing from me, Kid, would you?"

"I'll be back in the morning when you're thinking straight to settle up one way or another."

I didn't really believe Billy.

"You'll remember what you got?"

"Sure thing," Billy replied. "The only thing we're taking is the whiskey, Ash."

Upson stood stunned, glancing back and forth between me and the Kid. That was when I learned how to tell when Billy was funning. He had this odd habit of poking his tongue against his cheek when he was teasing. It looked like he was shifting a tobacco chaw in his cheek.

His shoulders slumping, Upson shook his head, as dazed as if he had misplaced his private parts. "You wouldn't do that, would you?"

I felt sorry for him and saw Billy did too. The Kid walked over and patted Upson on the shoulder. "No, Ash, I was just funning you."

Upson smiled and opened the door for us as we left. "You'll be back in the morning to settle up?"

"We will," I said firmly.

"Yeah," Billy acknowledged.

As we rode away, I glanced over my shoulder and saw Upson still standing in the light of the door, staring at us until we had surely disappeared in the dark.

Billy led us away from Roswell's scattered houses to a copse of cottonwood trees along the Rio Hondo. There in the darkness we tied our mounts and began to gather wood. It was cool enough that we didn't have to worry about rattlesnakes, but it was still spooky gathering wood in the dark.

The Kid built a fire, then marched down to the stream and filled with water the pan he had taken from the store. He fished some jerky from his saddlebags and tore the dried meat into pieces, which he dropped into the pan. Taking a knife from his belt, he cut the potatoes and added them to the mix, then opened the can of tomatoes with his knife and dumped them into the stew. He gave me the knife. "Keep it stirred while I do my practicing," he ordered.

"Practicing?"

Ignoring me, he stepped away, and at the edge of the fire's glow he pulled his pistol from his holster, slowly at first, then more rapidly. The first time he fired, I about spilt the stew. He squeezed off five more shots. No wonder he had taken so much ammunition from the store.

Many a night I would eventually spend with Billy, and on nearly every one—except when dances were held—he would spend an hour or more practicing with his pistol or his carbine. He would pull the revolver from his holster or toss it in the air and catch it with the opposite hand, then try to squeeze off a shot as quickly as possible. I was amazed at his speed. He could twirl a revolver in each hand and snap off shots in opposite directions, scorching his target. He practiced with guns like gamblers with cards, like musicians with fiddles, like preachers with offering plates.

That night on the banks of the Rio Hondo, as I stirred our pot of stew, I watched him in amazement. I had never seen anybody better with a gun, whether a pistol or a carbine. There might have been a few better shots against game or targets, but not a one could match up to the Kid when someone was firing back. With

Billy, the tighter the situation, the better he handled a gun.

The stew was bubbling good and smelling tolerably well when Billy reloaded his Colt the final time and shoved it in his holster. He strode to me. "I'll finish up the stew. You need to practice."

I was content to stir the stew and talk. "I'm doing fine."

Billy would have none of that. "You've a new holster that's stiffer than a convict's middle leg and you're telling me you don't need to practice?"

I protested, but he scooted onto the slick log I had dragged near the fire and forced me off the end. Now, I had to admit, the holster was not worn in and my revolver did cling to the stiff leather, but I wasn't planning on getting in any more trouble than I had already gotten into in Leadville, unless, of course, I had another opportunity to shoot a lawyer for the good of mankind. Grumbling, I rose slowly to my feet and stepped away from the fire. I crouched, then jerked my gun from the holster. It flew from my hand and landed a few feet in front of me.

The Kid shook his head. "The object is to hit your enemy with your bullets, not your pistol."

I picked up the gun and dusted it off, then glanced at Billy across the fire. "I ain't cut out to be a fancy shootist."

"You ain't cut out to be *any* kind of shootist, from what I see."

I shoved my pistol back in the stiff holster, dropped my hand away, then grabbed at the weapon. I pulled it free and in one fluid motion cocked the hammer and then squeezed on the trigger. The gun exploded with a flash, and another piece of lead plowed into the dirt somewhere across the Rio Hondo. I was damn proud of myself and turned around to see how much Billy admired my fine handiwork. Billy, though, had his hand to his mouth like he was wrestling with the stub of a cigar between his teeth.

I was watching him when he glanced my way. Seeing me staring, he looked as sheepish as a ten-year-old boy in a whorehouse. He pulled something from his mouth, then screened it with the back of his hand as he spat something to the ground. I figured he was snitching some things from the stew.

"Nice draw," he said. In the firelight I saw his cheek wiggle like he was shifting a chaw of tobacco in his mouth.

"Yeah," I answered, knowing he didn't care as long as he was confident he could outdraw me. The way his cheek poked out, I knew he was up to something, but I couldn't figure out what, unless he was planning to throw a bullet in the fire and watch me panic.

I marched farther away from the blaze, drew again, and fired another shot. Hearing a noise from the tree where we had tied the horses and Flash, I glanced that way and could just make out the Kid pulling something from his saddlebag, then starting back to the fire.

As he entered the ball of light thrown off by the fire, I could see he was carrying two tin plates and a couple spoons. "Let me serve up the stew. It's time to eat."

I was hungrier than a tick on a skeleton, so I ambled that way as Billy unknotted his bandanna and used it to pull the pan from the fire. Seeing me coming, he shook his head. "Just a minute, now. I'll call you when it's ready."

To my way of thinking, Billy hadn't done enough of the cooking and stirring to be ordering me around, but I was so hungry I didn't want to waste time arguing. He dumped stew onto both plates, stirred it around a bit, then returned the pan to the edge of the fire.

"Come and get it," he yelled.

Sauntering over, I saw the result of his mischief. One plate had about twice as much food as the other. I was beginning to think he was lower than a snake's belly for shortchanging me on grub, but then he stood up, a plate in each hand, and extended them both to me.

"Take your pick," he said.

It was a generous gesture. Me being a decent fellow who believed in sharing and sharing alike, unless I was starving, I took the one with the most food on it. Before Billy could reclaim the log I had dragged to the fire for a stool, I sat down on it.

Billy scurried around the fire and settled down on his haunches. He held his spoon up in the air and motioned for me to go ahead. "I don't say no blessing before I start my eating," he said. I guess he thought that was a joke because his cheek took to bulging out.

Not needing further encouragement, I filled a spoon, then filled my mouth. Even bad food tastes good to a starving man, but before I finished that first bite, I realized I wasn't starving. In fact, I wasn't near starving. I had been ready to cram supper in with both hands and stomp it down with both feet, but that stew had a taste as bitter as a dying spinster's tears. Billy, though, must have been accustomed to it, because he sat across the fire, just eating steady and grinning like he knew something I didn't. I studied my stew awhile but couldn't see much from the campfire light. I contemplated the dangers of eating it, but figured I could manage my portion if Billy could manage his. A few bites couldn't do my system any worse harm than that first one had, though I strongly believed this stew was potent enough to revive the dead or at least warm their bodies.

"Eat up," Billy said, lifting his spoon in the air.

I was made a mite uneasy by his left cheek poking out because it told me something was as uneven as a one-legged man's gait. Taking a deep breath, I shoveled the stew nonstop into my mouth. It singed my tongue, curled my nose hairs, and watered my eyes before I was able to clean my plate.

No sooner had I finished than Billy took to giggling like a politician in church. "I figured to make you a little meaner." He laughed and slapped his knee. "Just don't fart toward the campfire tonight or you might blow us to hell."

It took me a moment to catch on, and then I cut loose with a string of words that would do a bullwhacker proud. The son of a bitch had put gunpowder in my stew like I had suggested the farmer slip in his watchdog's bowl. While I was practicing my gun handling, Billy had been working the slug from a bullet casing for the powder to dump into my stew. I looked down around my boots, and sure enough, there was an empty bullet casing on the ground. I bent over, plucked it from the ground, and threw it at Billy.

He laughed as it grazed his shoulder. "I only powdered the stew in your plate. What's left in the pan is yours. It's not doctored."

"You think you're smarter than a perfesser in a nuthouse," I challenged.

"Pretty near it," he said, tossing his plate and spoon aside.

"If you're so damn smart," I shot back, "how come you traded for a blind horse?"

Billy went silent for a minute.

"Like the farmer said, 'The horse don't look so good,'" I reminded him. For a moment I didn't know if he was going to doubt me or shoot me. Then that cheek of his began to bulge out, his lips began to quiver, and finally he started laughing.

That was when I learned Billy could take a joke on himself as well as he could pull one on someone else.

Chapter Four

Come morning the Kid was still laughing about powdering my stew and being taken on the blind bay. Neither was as funny to me since I had eaten one and ridden the other. He examined the gelding and admitted the bay was blind.

"You coming from Arkansas," Billy said, "I wasn't sure you knew how reins worked, the way you kept running into everything."

We had a breakfast of jerky, but the taste reminded me too much of the previous evening's gunpowder stew, so I just ate a few bites. Eating jerky's about like chewing an old boot, though not as tasty.

After finishing our modest breakfast, we rolled up our bedding and started for the mounts. Billy surprised me by throwing his saddle on the blind bay.

"Are you as blind as the bay?"

"He may be a blind horse, but he's one more horse than we had yesterday."

Since Billy didn't offer me his black stallion, I threw my blanket roll over Flash's back and climbed aboard. At least the mule could see.

After cinching his rig on the blind bay and tying the black's reins to the saddle, Billy mounted and surprised

me again by turning toward Roswell. "We're going back
to see Ash Upson."

I must've stared too long at him.

"You didn't think I was going back, did you?"

I admitted I had my doubts.

Billy said, "I stick to my word. Upson's a decent sort
who's always treated me fair. I intend to be fair to him."

"How long you known him?"

"Going on two weeks," Billy replied, not thinking a
thing of it.

That was Billy. He took to most people like a puppy
to a kid. But if folks ever treated him like a dog, he could
turn meaner than a rabid cur.

The morning was cool, and my new coat felt good.
We took our time riding into Roswell and reached the
adobe store before Upson had opened up. Billy ordered
me to dismount and tie my mule and then his black
stallion to the hitching post. As I did, he rode the blind
bay back and forth in front of the store, finally ranging
as much as a quarter of a mile beyond the store on the
dusty trail.

Finally Billy did a foolhardy thing. He took off his
sombrero, swatted it against the bay's flank, and sent him
charging back down the trail at a dead run. Though that
was risky to do on a blind horse, Billy had no more fear
than a sailor in water. He charged down the trail, yelling
and creating a commotion.

I watched him gallop by, then pull up on the reins,
bring the horse to a halt, and start him back to the store.
Billy winked as he rode up and tossed me the reins. I
caught and tied them to the hitching rail. We crossed our
arms and waited for Upson to open for business.

To pass the time, I studied the adobe and decided it
looked twice as good at night when you couldn't see it.
"Damn ugly buildings, these adobes."

"Bet it's nothing like the palace you had in Arkansas."

"We've more whittle shavings on our floors than
there is wood in one of these."

"But can you patch an Arkansas house with mud?"

Billy had a point, I had to admit, but before I could counter, the store door swung open, and Ash Upson stood there looking at us with his bloodshot eyes.

He aimed his forefinger at Billy. "You were here last night, promised to come back and make good on the merchandise you took."

"That's what we're here for," Billy admitted. "I didn't figure you'd remember."

"Naw," answered Upson. "It was you and Lomax and McCarty and Antrim and Bonney, wasn't it, Kid?"

Billy laughed. "Close enough."

The Kid and I marched inside. The adobe, though bigger than the average house, was kept surprisingly warm by a potbellied stove in the corner. Adobes did hold the heat in winter and the cool in summer.

Upson scurried by us, beating us to the back counter and opening a ledger book. "What was it you took last night?"

"A can of tomatoes, a couple potatoes, some coffee, four cartons of ammunition, and a pan. Lomax took a coat, a cheap holster, a canteen, and a wool blanket."

His listing squared with my memory.

Upson did a little ciphering and looked up. "That comes to twenty-three dollars and two bits."

The Kid grimaced. "That's more than I got on me. You don't know where there's honest work, do you? Is Old John Chisum hiring?"

Upson crossed his arms. "Kid, I can't give you credit without the owner's permission. You know that, don't you?"

Billy acknowledged he did. "Well, you've treated me fair, Ash, and I intend to do the same by you. Only thing I know to do is trade my horse to cover my debt."

Upson pointed at me. "What about Lomax's share?"

"I'm covering it, Ash. We're partners, Lomax and me. My horse should take care of both accounts."

Stroking his chin, Upson eyed Billy suspiciously. "Let me see this horse."

"Now, Ash," said Billy, "I want you to know this horse don't look so good."

Sighing and shaking his head, Upson looked at Billy. "That mean he's ugly or blind?"

Acting insulted, Billy marched outside and untied the bay from the hitching post. Quickly he mounted, then slapped the reins against the horse's neck and kicked his heel against the bay's flank. The bay started at a gallop down the trail away from town, Billy shouting and jerking off his sombrero and waving it overhead.

I was impressed by Billy's daring or his stupidity as he galloped away atop a blind horse. I understood now why he had raced the horse a couple times in front of the store. He wanted to give the bay a feel for the trail.

A quarter mile past the store, Billy jerked the bay to a halt, twisted it around in a tight circle, never leaving the trail where a gopher hole or stone might trip the animal, then charged toward us. He barreled past us, the bay's pounding hooves kicking up dirt and pebbles in our faces. When he jerked hard on the reins, the horse rose slightly on his two back legs.

I could tell by the smile on Upson's pockmarked face that he was impressed. He lifted his hands and clapped as Billy let the bay walk back. "Magnificent," he called, "for a blind horse."

Billy slumped in the saddle and plopped his sombrero back on his head. "He's just a little blind, Ash, and I don't know how I'm gonna pay you unless you trade him for the goods." He dismounted and tied the reins back around the hitching rail.

"I didn't say I wouldn't trade for him, Kid."

Billy glanced up, the swagger returning to his step. "You ain't kidding me, are you?"

Upson led us back inside. He marched around the counter and stroked his cheek. "I string for some newspapers back East, and they're always interested in news stories from these parts."

The Kid was perplexed. "String?"

Upson nodded. "It means contribute stories to them."

"Go on," Billy said.

Upson gave a sweep of his arms toward the store's dingy walls. "Not being as robust a spirit as you, Kid, I am imprisoned by these walls."

Billy crossed his arms over his chest. "And these walls hold more whiskey than you can find on the plains or in the mountains."

"Indeed, Kid, you understand well my predicament. But if in your travels you can bring back facts I can fashion into the truth of existence in New Mexico Territory, I will take your blind horse in exchange for what you have taken."

Billy nodded. "I don't have to write stories, do I?"

"Indeed not. I, Marshall Ashmun Upson, am the writer. You just make notes. I am the one who can shape your reports into the prose that will catch the eye of editors at newspapers you've never heard of, prestigious papers like the *New York Herald* or the *Cincinnati Enquirer,* in places you've never been."

"I reckon you're wrong, Ash," answered The Kid. "I was born in New York City and came out west young with my momma."

"You provide me news of what's going on and I'll take this blind animal off your hands and not tell anybody you traded for him."

"It's a deal," Billy replied, "if you throw in a saddle for my partner, Henry Harrison Lomax, here."

Upson turned to me, shrugging in disgust. "Another damn one named after a president."

"What about the saddle?" Billy reminded him.

"You're into me too much already to throw in a new saddle."

"Doesn't have to be new," I answered.

Upson jerked his thumb over his shoulder. "There's the mortal remains of an old one in the back room. It's not much to look at and in need of repairs, but it's leather and does resemble a saddle."

"It shouldn't matter. Lomax is riding a mule, anyway."

The storekeeper motioned me around the counter and pushed open the door, giving me entry into a musty-smelling room that held sacked goods, wooden crates, and a variety of farming tools. He pointed to the corner and a hunk of discarded leather lying on the floor like a slaughterhouse carcass.

From afar it didn't look too bad, but up close it looked old enough for Adam to have ridden on it out of the Garden of Eden when the Creator foreclosed. A saddle of good leather will creak when it's moved. This one just crackled. Good saddle leather has a sweet aroma about it, but this one had no more smell about it than a dead man's nose. Good saddle leather feels slick to the touch; this felt rough as the scabs on a miner's knees. I stroked the rough seat with my hands and it felt grittier than a pot of unwashed beans. After estimating my bottom would last no more than a week before it would be sanded down to the bone, I grabbed the saddle by the horn and lifted it to my shoulder. One of the stirrups fell at my boots. "You sure you shouldn't be paying us for taking this piece of junk?"

Upson shrugged. "Stop your yapping. At least it don't eat and drink like that blind fleabag the Kid's trading me."

Of course Upson had a point, but then his behind wasn't going to be rubbed raw in this saddle. I squatted to retrieve the severed stirrup. Shoving it in my coat pocket, I straightened and marched back out into the store. My face reddened at Billy's laugh.

"That saddle'll go right well with your mule."

"At least Flash can see."

Billy turned to Upson. "Obliged, Ash. I'll swap out my saddle and leave the bay tied to the hitching post for you."

"You just remember to bring me news of Lincoln County."

"Will do, Ash."

I slipped out the door and tried to shield the saddle

from Flash's eyes. Even if he was a mule, he still had his pride. I saddled him, then grabbed the saddle horn and shoved my foot absently for the missing stirrup. My boot missed once, then a second time before I realized I'd be afoot forever if I kept trying to slide into the missing stirrup.

"Lomax," said Billy as he heaved his fine saddle atop his stallion, "if ever a man was born to walk, rather than ride, it has to be you. Mules, blind bays, broken saddles. Maybe you ought to get a job with the railroad when it reaches New Mexico."

"Only thing I can't figure out, Kid, is why someone with your smarts can't find an honest job."

"Luck, I guess," laughed Billy, cinching his own saddle, then climbing aboard his stallion. "My luck's about to change. I'm gonna ride out and get John Chisum to hire me. You want work, too?"

"I want to eat things that aren't poisoned like your stew, so I guess that means I want to work."

We turned our mounts and started toward the edge of town. As small as Roswell was, it was more edge than town. I had a question for Billy and finally blurted it out. "Why didn't we just wait until this morning to see Upson in the first place?"

"Ash is a smart man, but he don't think as well after he's had a few drinks. If I'd waited until this morning, he'd never have let me take what I took last night."

That was Billy, shrewd enough to figure the angles like a billiards player, but he was leading me toward the ranch of one of the shrewdest men I would ever meet—John Simpson Chisum.

His friends called him Uncle John, while the small ranchers and the rustlers that rode for Murphy's store just called him a bastard. His ranch stretched from the Texas border on the south up the Pecos all the way to Fort Sumner, but John Simpson Chisum owned not a single acre of that land. It was all public domain, there for anybody with the gall to claim it. And Chisum had the gall that comes from being the first man to spot a good thing in the abundant black grama that stood knee-high in places. He quickly realized that whoever controlled the Pecos River controlled the land—and the grass—for miles on either side. So he built himself ranch houses that doubled as fortresses along the river and practically dared anyone to try to move him out. No one did. A lot of ranchers and rustlers nipped at his heels, but not one was brave enough to challenge him face-to-face. In fact, Chisum was about the bravest man I ever saw. He and a damned lawyer out of Lincoln were the only two men in the county, as best I could tell, who didn't wear a gun on their hip.

"A sidearm," Chisum once told me, "will get you into more trouble than it can ever get you out of."

I guess he was right, because he died of cancer in spite of being, undeservedly, one of the most hated men in Lincoln County. If he wasn't right, then he was lucky. While Old John Chisum himself didn't carry a gun, he had no qualms about his hired men carrying them—and using them. That's how he ruled the land he didn't own and hung on to cattle that numbered eighty thousand or more.

His cattle were readily identifiable by his unique brand and ear markings. His brand was the "Long Rail," just a straight line along a cow's side from shoulder to hip. Problem was, the brand was easy to alter. One Murphy cohort at the House had the "Arrow" brand that Jesse Evans and the Boys provided Chisum stock for, and some of the small ranchers came up with the "Lazy P," the "Pigpen," and, as a joke to accompany the Arrow brand, the "Bow."

To counter the brand altering, Chisum developed the jinglebob earmark, so that his cattle were easily identified from afar. The cows' ears were cut halfway down so the outer quarter of the ear drooped over like a wilted flower. But men who branded another man's cattle weren't to be put off, so there were a lot of Arrow, Pigpen, Bow, and Lazy P cattle with jinglebobs. In fact, many of them filled the contracts that other ranchers had with the army at Fort Stanton, about eight miles west of Lincoln, and with the Mescalero Reservation higher in the mountains near Blazer's Mill.

Cattle for rations, and hay and corn for fodder, were about the only commodities produced in Lincoln County that could bring much hard cash. While only a few farmers along the rivers grew corn and hay, everybody ran cattle. When the government accepted bids for cattle to supply the army and the Apache reservation, ranchers bid so low, just to stand a chance at winning a government contract, that they didn't profit much if they received it. Lawrence G. Murphy raised his own cattle, but sold everybody else's he could steal. He always profited despite the low prices.

Chisum's place was four miles southeast of Roswell near where the South Spring, a clear artesian stream filled with fish, flowed into the Pecos. The South Spring Ranch, as it was called, was actually his southern headquarters. Farther up north, nearer Fort Sumner, he had a second headquarters called Bosque Grande. The South Spring Ranch was a rambling adobe house with a high-pitched roof and a picket fence surrounding it. He had abundant water, cool and so clear you could count the scales on passing fish. He had fruit trees and a fine garden in season so there were plenty of fresh fruits and vegetables. He had a long dining table that could seat more than a dozen because he enjoyed good company and good conversation. Of course there probably wasn't enough good company in all of Lincoln County to fill his dining table and still be able to talk about politics or philosophy or to tell a joke as well as Chisum could. He had a keen sense of humor and a generous streak for good, honest folk.

A lifelong bachelor, Chisum had one odd habit that I never understood. He had enough money to buy the softest feather mattress in the country, yet he threw his bedroll on the floor of his bedroom and slept on the wood.

He had plenty of everything he wanted except peace of mind. That was because he had a niece that every randy buck in Lincoln County wanted. Sallie Chisum was cuter than a basketful of speckled puppies and the reason Billy and I didn't get hired by Chisum that day.

Chapter Five

When John Chisum emerged from his adobe ranch house, I had to grit my teeth to keep from bursting out laughing. If any man in all of Lincoln County had bigger ears than the Kid, it was John Chisum. I could've whittled on them the rest of the day and not made a noticeable difference in their size. If I'd sliced them in half, he'd've still had a fine set of ears and I'd've had enough leather to make me a pair of chaps. If his hearing was as sharp as his ears were big, he could hear a flea break wind during a thunderstorm. Right then and there, I figured he had settled on the jinglebob earmark as penance for his own flappers.

Except for his abundant ears, John Simpson Chisum was a handsome man with a distinguished, well-trimmed mustache beneath a finely chiseled nose and piercing eyes that could read a man as easily as a book. His high cheekbones accentuated his eyes and gave his face a narrow, angular look. His skin was bronzed and leathery.

The Kid and I drew up our mounts outside the picket fence that surrounded his ranch house. He came out of the gate, studying us intently. "The answer's no," he stated, crossing his arms over his chest.

Billy shook his head. "You don't even know the question."

Chisum grinned wider than the Pecos River valley. "The question doesn't matter if the answer's still no."

"We were looking for honest work," Billy offered.

The rancher shook his head. "I don't need hands that've ridden with Jesse Evans."

Billy looked from Chisum to me and back.

I shrugged. It was hard to counter that type of reasoning or to argue with a man whose mind was already made up.

"A man's known by the company he keeps, and you two haven't been keeping good company. It's that simple."

"How do you know it was us?" I ventured.

"Men I trust say a kid wearing a sombrero and riding a black stallion was riding with Jesse a month or so ago. Another gang member was homely as the flea-bitten mule he was riding. That sounds like you two." Chisum grinned and pointed at my missing stirrup.

I considered pulling my gun right then and plugging Chisum for insulting Flash. I'd have been more tempted to do so had it not been for a half-dozen of his hands approaching us, their hands conveniently resting on the butts of their pistols.

Billy grinned. "It true, Mr. Chisum, that you used to pay Jesse Evans for riding your range?"

"I made a mistake and let him go as soon as I found out."

"We made a mistake, too," I offered.

Chisum studied us closely, stroking his chin. I knew for certain that he was reconsidering his initial rejection, and I figured he was about to change his mind when fate intervened.

Sallie Chisum appeared from around the side of the house. I caught my breath at the sight of her and jerked my hat off my head in humble admiration. She was about the only white woman of marrying age in all of Lincoln County, and that left John Chisum as uncomfortable as a man in tight boots. Every young buck with any sense in his head would have liked to have her making her biscuits and her bed for him. Too, being kin to John Chisum meant she was related to all his money and due to inherit a great deal of it when Chisum rode across the final river.

Her fingers on her uncle's money would've made her appealing to most men, even if she'd been uglier than a wart on a billy goat's behind, but Sallie was one of the prettiest little ladies I had ever seen. She had long, straw-colored hair and a button nose over a mischievous smile that looked like it could bring a man as much misery as pleasure. She had more curves than a mountain road and filled out her riding pants and shirt like the devil had dressed her.

"Uncle John," she said, cooing like a mourning dove, "give 'em work, especially the one on the stallion."

Chisum's face clouded, but we still had a shot at work until Sallie kept talking.

"He looks like there's a lot of things he could do well." She stared at Billy with doe eyes.

Billy lacked my manners and never took off his sombrero, but he answered her with a knowing grin that suggested he would like to do a little plowing at the fork in her road.

I shook my head and replaced my hat. Though Chisum hadn't spoken since she showed up, I knew Billy and I were still unemployed.

"No jobs," said Chisum, more emphatically than before. "Some of the small places may need help in the Hondo Valley."

Sallie Chisum tapped her boot on the ground and plopped her hands on her shapely hips. She stood staring at her uncle, the disappointment dripping from her eyes like honey—or venom. Sallie was spoiled as bad as rotten beef and needed someone to bend her over his knee and swat some sense into her behind. I would've gladly volunteered for the job, but she was pining for Billy. The closest I would get to her bottom was if I shook Billy's hand.

"Now you boys might want to mosey on," Chisum offered.

"Just a minute," Sallie cooed. "You never send anyone away without a meal." She was working her uncle like a dog works sheep.

Chisum glanced from us to her and shrugged in helplessness.

"You tell me I'm the hostess of the South Spring," Sallie persisted, "and I'm inviting them for meals."

"Meals?" Chisum coughed.

She pointed at me—"Him for lunch,"—then at Billy—"and him for supper."

"We're partners," I broke in.

"Not when it comes to food," Billy replied.

That's when I learned Billy was a loyal partner as long as no woman was involved. A woman could beat Billy with her lashes quicker than a man could whip him with his fists. Sallie Chisum was trolling and Billy had twitchy britches. Me, I was just hungering for a meal that wasn't laced with gunpowder.

"They can stay," Chisum finally allowed, "as long as they're gone in the morning."

Sallie lunged for Chisum and flung her arms around him. "Thank you, Uncle John," she laughed, then ran inside the house, shouting orders to their cook and house help.

"Thank you, Uncle John," Billy said, playfully mocking Sallie.

I never saw John Chisum back down to any man, not even the Kid when things between them soured, but he had trouble standing up to Sallie. "Guess you boys might just as well get off your animals and make yourselves at home. If you see anything you like, just take it. Sallie'd probably give it to you anyway."

I doubted that Sallie would give me anything except a hard time, but I was sure curious about just what she might give Billy. The Kid and I dismounted, happier than egg-sucking dogs in the henhouse.

As I stretched, Chisum came over and introduced himself, grabbing my hand in his strong, firm paw.

"Henry Harrison Lomax," I responded.

"Lomax? Any kin to Gadrich Lomax?"

"No kin," I replied. "What did he do to you?"

"Sold a blind horse to Sallie. Pretty little bay gelding, but blind nonetheless."

I looked from Chisum to Billy, who wore a broad grin.

"I traded him to a farmer in Roswell for a wagonload of hay," Chisum said, glancing warily at Billy, not amused by him, then looking at me as he pointed at my saddle. "I've a saddler and harness maker that can replace your stirrup and recondition the saddle a little for you, if you're interested."

"Sure thing, Mr. Chisum." I replied.

"Call me John."

Billy grew antsy, me getting all Chisum's attention, and started to say something. "John."

"Call me Mr. Chisum," the hard-shelled rancher replied.

I snickered. Billy might have a way of getting along with young ladies, but I was better with their uncles.

Billy shrugged. "Mr. Chisum," he said, "mind if those of us that have horses water them, while those with mules get their saddles repaired?"

Chisum's lip quivered like he wanted to laugh. The rancher and the Kid were both as likable as rich grandmothers. I figure they could've taken a shine to each other, but their interests in Sallie were as different as in and out. Chisum nodded. "Go ahead, as long as you quit stealing my cattle."

The Kid licked his lips. "I tell you, Mr. Chisum, you raise tasty beef."

The cowman gave Billy a hard glare. He might not have liked the Kid, but I think he respected him.

They were still measuring each other when Sallie came out the door. It was as if a caterpillar had entered the house and a butterfly had emerged. She had changed out of her riding clothes and put on a gray dress with billowing shoulders and a high neck with a broach pinned in front. Over the dress she wore a starched apron that by its white spotlessness indicated she did more ordering around than working in the kitchen. Besides donning the dress, she had piled her hair up on her head like women do at fancy dress balls. It was so like her, I was to discover—plain and even unladylike one minute and cultivated and polished the next.

"Well, Uncle John," she said as she strode up to Chisum, "aren't you going to introduce me to our guest?"

Chisum slid his arm through hers. "Certainly," he said, as he maneuvered her around to face me. "Henry Harrison Lomax."

"Lomax," she growled. "Any relation to the one who robbed me?"

Chisum grinned. "No kinship that he admits to, though there are similarities. Like Gadrich, Henry Harrison has brought a gelding you seem to be interested in." With a broad grin that made his cheekbones rise, Chisum pointed at the Kid.

Sallie's face flushed red.

The Kid offered a bucktoothed smile. "Billy Bonney's the name. And always remember, a young gelding's better than an old stallion."

The grin on Chisum's face melted like grease in a hot skillet. Then both men snickered like wary opponents.

Sallie fairly thrust her hand for Billy's and shook it warmly. "A pleasure, Billy Bonney. Let me show you the place," she offered. "It'll be an hour until the noon meal is served. We have time to walk around, and I'll show you my favorite place."

Billy tossed me his reins, then floated away with Sallie at the helm. "See that my stallion's watered, Lomax," he called.

Chisum slapped me on the back. "Partners, eh?"

I didn't find it too funny, but he laughed.

"Come along, Lomax," Chisum said, "and I'll introduce you to our harness and saddle maker."

With the reins to the stallion and mule in my hand, I followed Chisum around the fence and behind the house to his corrals and outer buildings. I wondered what it must be like to run a big ranch and have so many people to do all the work. We angled toward a small shed beyond a couple large corrals filled with horses.

As we walked, Chisum kept looking over his shoulder, eyeing Sallie and the Kid. At the shed he greeted a man he called Dink, a small, wiry fellow with thinning hair and wire-rimmed spectacles over his eyes. His shoulders were crooked and he walked with a limp. Chisum introduced us.

"Dink was the best bronc rider I ever saw," Chisum said.

Ruddy though his face was, I saw Dink blush. "I was okay until a chestnut stallion threw me into the fence, then stomped my leg."

Chisum nodded. "A damn killer horse that had to be shot. I should've never let Dink try to tame him."

Dink laughed. "Oh, I came out okay. Uncle John kept me on to repair his harnesses and saddles. Most owners would've kicked a stoved-up bronc buster off the place, but John gave me a job sitting on my tailbone, repairing other people's mistakes."

Pointing to my mule, Chisum spoke. "See what you can do for his saddle. It's a mite worn and needs a stirrup replaced."

I extracted the stirrup from my pocket and tossed it to Dink.

He caught it, then squinted at my saddle. "Damn poor saddle."

Before I could answer, Chisum said, "Dink, see that the mule and stallion are watered. I want to show Lomax the ranch place."

"Sure thing," the hand answered.

Though flattered to receive a tour, I knew Chisum was really more interested in keeping Billy and Sallie in sight.

We stepped back outside and Chisum studied the place, then headed toward the stream where he had caught a glimpse of Sallie and Billy beneath a big cottonwood tree. As we walked, Chisum spoke in an exaggerated voice and made wide gestures as if he was oblivious to Billy and Sallie nearby.

As we stopped at the stream, not twenty yards from them, they looked at us and just shook their heads. They had hit it off real well, and that was worrying Chisum all the more.

"Clearest water you'll find anywhere," he said, pointing to the South Spring but looking toward Billy and Sallie.

He was right. The water ran like molten crystal, streaked with the silver of passing fish. In the shade of the cottonwood trees the breeze was chilly, so I was pleased when Billy and Sallie retreated toward the ranch house. We ambled down the stream, to disguise the fact that we were tracking them like hounds after a prison escapee. They decided to make a game of the situation. They were two-thirds of the way back to the house and us only a third when they stopped dead in their tracks, like they were waiting for a train to pass.

Of course we stopped, too.

"Now," yelled Billy.

Instantly both he and Sallie charged for the house, running and laughing like unruly children. They ran through the picket-fence gate, then angled for the corner of the house.

If Chisum had worn a gun on his hip, he could've winged Billy and ended this problem. Of course, foolishness being what it is, that would've probably just driven the two closer together and had them hitched by nightfall. Chisum did what any man does when confronted with a situation he can't control; he cussed.

We traced their trail to the corner of the house, where they jumped from behind the wall into our path.

"Boo!" they yelled, laughing like fat kids at a circus.

Their prank spooked me, but Chisum never flinched, though I saw his ears redden with anger. Though he loved her dearly, I could tell Sallie exasperated him. Chisum seemed to understand what she, at seventeen or so, did not. She had led a pampered life, thanks to his wealth. Once he died, her status and comforts would change as sure as the next day would bring another sunrise.

Just as he started to say something, the cook rang the dinner bell in back of the house, and Sallie grabbed Billy's hand and jerked him past me and her uncle.

"Let's get washed up. You can sit by me," she giggled.

By the time Chisum and I reached the table, they were already seated and talking to one another. As we started heaping our plates, Sallie turned her big doe eyes on her uncle like a weapon. "Uncle John, don't we have a job for Billy at the ranch?"

Chisum nodded. "We've an opening on the Bosque Grande section."

"But that's more than fifty miles away," she protested.

"I know." Chisum smiled.

Sallie pouted, looking as useless as a Democrat with integrity.

Unruffled, Billy just ate and grinned, speaking as the conversation demanded. Chisum could carry a conversation as easily as a Republican could carry a bribe, so he, Billy, and I covered a lot of territory as we ate. With her feelings hurt, Sallie didn't say much. The conversation finally turned to Jesse Evans, and when Chisum spoke he seemed to be addressing Sallie.

"Jesse Evans's headed for a fall," he said. "He's like a spoiled kid. The more he gets his way, the harder it is to deny him his way the next time, but one day things won't work out for him."

He looked at Sallie, but she wasn't paying attention.

"Lincoln County's about to explode, boys. I don't know how, I don't know over what, but it'll be something. There's the small ranchers against me, the Mexicans against the Americans, the House against everybody, the Boys against the law, the Englishman against the House, and everybody against the Apaches. This county's strung tighter than a fiddle string. When it breaks, a lot of people are gonna get hurt."

Billy shrugged. "I can look out for myself."

I didn't feel as smug as Billy. Chisum's voice and demeanor were as somber as that of an undertaker at his momma's funeral.

He pointed his fork at Billy's nose. "You better pick your friends carefully, Bonney. Six months ago, I might not have worried that you had ridden with Jesse Evans. Nothing against you boys, but I'm picking my friends and my hands carefully. There'll be fireworks before the Fourth of July."

"My friends are who they are," Billy said.

Chisum nodded. "And your friends may determine who you are. Don't get tied in with the wrong group."

Billy shook his head. "You sound awfully high and mighty."

The old rancher nodded. "John Chisum will survive. I tend to what's mine and don't dig too deeply into other people's troubles."

When we finished the meal, Chisum stood up and stretched, yawning slightly. "It's time for my afternoon nap," he announced. He looked at me and shook his head like he knew he could never prevent what might happen between Sallie and Billy, but he just wanted to make them think twice about anything they did.

I ate my fill, as did Billy; then we both got up with Sallie. The two of them walked outside and I went along with them, feeling about as useless as teats on a boar.

"Your uncle worries a lot," Billy offered.

Sallie shook her head. "He thinks I'm too wild. He figures I'm spoiled. It don't matter that I can shoot and ride like a man, cook and clean like a woman."

"What else can you do like a woman?" Billy teased.

She giggled and blushed and I strolled away, wandering around the place, occasionally encountering them as they walked about. They were as circumspect as a Baptist preacher in a nunnery, but after supper they disappeared toward the tall grass by the stream.

Chisum and I went outside until the air turned cool, and we retreated to the stove inside. We were still there when Billy came in with Sallie on his arm. Her hair was mussed and the back of his shirttail was hanging out. When he looked at Chisum he had a solemn look on his face, but the side of his cheek was poking out.

Chapter Six

The next morning we awoke in the bunkhouse to which John Chisum had banished us after deciding Sallie had indeed been more hospitable to Billy than was truly required. We ate with the ranch hands instead of in the big house with the Chisums.

I thought Sallie was a good girl, just a little bit wild, but I have never understood what women saw in some men and not in others—like myself, for instance. Some fellows, like Billy, could walk into a room and have every female between the cradle and grave interested. Most fellows, myself among them, couldn't turn a woman's head with a crowbar. I chalked it up to the basic unfairness of life. I remember from some of my schooling something about the Declaration of Independence saying all men were created equal. Whoever wrote that must never have seen a bunch of cowboys taking a bath in a river.

Life is damn unfair, I concluded early on. Otherwise, why could I go through life for so long and come away with so little other than my memories? Why could one baby be born into a rich family and another, like me, be born into a poor one? My pa farmed our place in Cane Hill for years. We always had food on the table and laughter on our lips, until the War Between the States at least, but we never had much money. Pa went in '49 with three dozen others to the California goldfields to seek out his fortune. About a third of the men died on the trail or in the goldfields, another third stayed in California, and the final third, my pa among them, returned home. Only one of that Arkansas delegation struck it rich and would've been rich to this day had he not taken to drink and cards, gambling away his wealth.

Pa returned to Arkansas with little but the clothes on his back, the thin-soled shoes on his feet, and the tintype of my momma in his pocket, but he had left Arkansas with them, though the clothes weren't as tattered, the soles as thin, or the tintype as faded. The only things he brought back that he hadn't left with were his stories, a touch of rheumatism that bothered him the rest of his life, and a faded American flag that was supposed to have flown over Sutter's Mill, where the original gold nugget was found.

Those tales of California kindled in me a wanderlust that kept me traveling and looking for the wealth that he never found. I met a lot of folks and saw a lot of sights that few people have seen, but you can't spend memories, you can't sell experiences, and you damn sure can't eat either of them. Whoever said all men are created equal just as well as said life is fair. None of it's true. Some people ride stallions and decent saddles; others ride mules and the scab of a saddle. Some people lead parades, and some people clean up the horse apples afterwards. Life wouldn't be fair unless everybody led the parade, but that turns the parade into a mob.

As Billy and I mounted up, he grumbled about John Chisum not having jobs for us, but I knew his sap was rising and he was going to miss Sallie Chisum. As for me, I had had three square meals and was sitting in a saddle that had two stirrups. Chisum had been as hospitable as a man could be to strangers.

Riding away from South Spring Ranch, I looked over my shoulder and saw Chisum standing behind the picket fence, his arms crossed, his shoulders squared. I lifted my hat in thanks and thought I saw him nod. Billy never looked back.

After riding a couple miles, Billy finally spoke. "He could've hired us."

"Probably would have if you hadn't been hot as a billy goat in a pepper patch for Sallie."

He tossed me a big old grin. "Just call me Billy the Kid Goat."

We rode back to Roswell, Billy occasionally bleating like a goat. I figured we'd follow the road to the mountains, but he turned up the trail to the store.

"What are you gonna swindle Ash out of this time?"

Billy removed his sombrero and held it over his heart like he was hurt, but I saw his cheek bulging. "I've got news for him."

We had seen Ash the day before, and I had been with Billy all the time since then—except when he was with Sallie. "News?"

Replacing his sombrero, Billy nodded. "I intend to live up to my deal with Ash."

"What news?"

"John Chisum ain't hiring men."

"It was just us he didn't hire."

"Seems to me rustlers are stealing so much from his herd he can't afford to hire men. Yes, sir, John Chisum is going broke."

Billy was stretching a grain of truth into an outright lie. "You know that ain't right."

He answered with a toothy grin. "But Ash don't."

The Kid had a point. With his fix on the facts, he met the first rule of being a reporter: Never let the truth stand in the way of a story. But he came up woefully short on the second rule: Never pass a bottle of whiskey without emptying it. Over the years I'd seen more reporters pickled than cucumbers.

I don't know whether Ash never had much business or we just always hit him at slow times, but the store was empty when Billy and I sauntered up like two mongrels stalking a lame cat. Upson looked up from the counter.

"How's the blind bay?" Billy called out.

"Keep your voice down," he chided, then laughed. "A couple army buyers came through yesterday, buying cavalry horses. I ran it in with other horses and they never knew the difference. I made a good profit on it." His frail frame convulsed with laughter.

A grin crept across Billy's face like a stain. Upson fell quiet, knowing he had said too much.

"Then I figure Lomax and I can pick up a few more goods to square things," Billy said.

Upson grimaced, knowing he was caught in the trap of his own jaws. He tried to squirm free. "I took the bay in an even trade."

Billy spread his legs and planted his balled fists squarely on his hips. "Nope. I was to make up the difference bringing you news. That meant we'd settle up once you got rid of the horse. Since the gelding brought more than you expected, you still owe us."

"Hell, Kid, I should've never traded with you and wouldn't have if you hadn't as much as stolen what you wanted the night before." Upson wilted beneath Billy's gaze. "Go ahead, pick out what you need and we'll square matters. Then our business is done."

Billy motioned for me to start gathering what I needed. "I'm keeping my end of the bargain by bringing you news from John Chisum himself."

Upson didn't seem noticeably cheered, particularly when Billy began to pick up cartons of ammunition for his Thunderer. While Billy took nothing but ammunition, I grabbed a saddle blanket, some saddlebags, a trail coffeepot, tin plate and cup plus spoon, fork, and knife, a small skillet, an extra blanket, an extra pair of socks, a slicker, a pair of gloves, and a carbine.

"You need more ammunition," Billy said, putting a carton atop my growing purchase.

I couldn't eat bullets, so I set a sack of coffee and

some jerked meat and crackers on the pile. When Upson added it up, it came to almost nine dollars more than our credit.

"You're gonna have to put something back," Upson said.

"Wait a minute," Billy protested. "I've got news for you that's worth ten dollars."

Upson looked bewildered. "That's more than I earn for getting stories published in some of this country's biggest papers."

Billy gazed around the room. "Ash, is there anything in this store you'll let me set the price on and then pay you?"

Upson stared at Billy like he was nuttier than a pecan pie. "You know I won't."

"Exactly," Billy said. "Now why should I let you determine what I charge for my news?"

"Because your news might not be worth the price you charge."

"Does anything in the store cost less than what you think is a reasonable price?"

Upson's face began to cloud like a norther was blowing in off his forehead. "That's different. You can decide if it's worth the price before you buy."

"Exactly," Billy cried. "The difference is that if I give you the news before you buy, you still have the news without buying it. Ten dollars?"

Upson shrugged and stepped away from the counter, running his fingers through his hair. He sighed, then nodded. "Okay, a deal."

"It's a deal as long as it squares us," Billy said.

Upson rolled his bloodshot eyes. "Let's just say you got even."

Billy laughed. "I always aim to get even, Ash."

"Now, what's the news?"

Billy's cheek poked out as he solemnly shook his head. "Things aren't going well for John Chisum, no, sir, they're sure not."

Upson's eyes widened. "Go on."

Billy had hooked Upson and began to pull him in. "Chisum's quit hiring men, can't take any more on."

"You don't say."

Billy pursed his lips. "The rustlers have been bleeding his herds so that he's strapped for cash, may not be able to pay his hands when their pay's due. He says he knows where the trouble is—in the mountains—and he plans to stomp it out."

By then Billy had woven a thread of the truth into a lariat and had wrapped and hog-tied the storekeeper with it.

Grabbing a pencil, Upson began to take notes. "Boys, Lincoln County could explode if Old John goes after the House." Upson seemed shaken by the news.

"Was the news worth the cost?" Billy asked as he winked at me.

Upson's lip quivered. "Indeed."

I gathered my purchases as Billy picked up his ammunition.

"I'll bring you news from the mountains, Ash, on my next trip."

"Obliged," Upson answered.

With loaded arms I walked out the door with Billy. He was humming a tune and as happy as a bull in a pasture full of heifers. I was amazed at how I had prospered in the few days since I had been with Billy. When I met him I had a mule, bridle, revolver, and three bullets and was so broke I couldn't afford hay for a nightmare. Now I had a saddle and saddlebags, blankets, slicker, ammunition, holster, carbine, canteen, and a few groceries, not to mention a fresh pair of socks. I'd had three full meals and a straw mattress for a night at the Chisum place.

After packing my booty, I rode with Billy and followed the Hondo River from Roswell back toward the mountains, where low clouds hovered like a death shroud, blotting out the sun and throwing a chill over the land and up my spine. We passed clumps of Chisum's cattle,

their jinglebobbed ears dangling like maimed pendants,
their long-rail brands fuzzied by the growth of a winter
coat. Along the river the soil was darker and fertile, but
beyond the gentle slopes of the Hondo the ground grew
rocky, with sparser grass. And while you would find more
hair on a frog's behind than grass on an acre of this land,
there was just so much land that the grass mounted up
quicker than debt. As we neared the rising slopes of the
foothills into the mountains, the land was dotted with
clumps of cholla and ocotillo. A breeze blew down from
the mountains, sending us to shivering.

"Winter's coming," Billy said, "and John Chisum's
a liar."

That struck me as funny, coming from a man who had
pretty near trampled the truth to a powder in his report
to Upson. "How's that?"

"Nobody's gonna have work in the valley, not this
time of year. Maybe como planting and calving time in
the spring we can find work."

"I can't winter without a roof over my head," I said.

The Kid didn't seem too concerned. "There'll be plenty of *bailes* in the valley to keep us warm!" He grinned.

"*Bailes?*"

"Dances. It's what the Mexicans call dances."

"I can't dance all winter."

"I can," Billy replied.

The gray clouds took to spitting water—not enough
to baptize a Methodist, much less interest a Baptist, but it
added to our discomfort. I tugged my hat down and urged
Flash on into the cool, moist breeze. The first freeze of the
season hadn't set in yet, though with all the dampness in
the air, it felt like it wasn't far off.

We made camp at a bend in the Hondo where a steep
bank gave us some cover from the breeze. We gathered
wood and built a fire, the damp wood smoking terribly.
After tending our mounts, we draped our blankets over
our backs and our slickers over them, me staring into the
fire and at the Kid. As the fire burned down, I added a few

more sticks of wood, then slipped in between the folds of my blankets and awaited sleep.

Morning slipped up on us like the fog that settled along the river. We got up and stretched, then built enough of a fire to boil a pot of coffee and warm our innards. We saddled our mounts, broke camp, and headed farther upriver, finally sliding into a narrow valley with tall balding mountains on either side. We spent two days making our way up the valley, stopping at every place we found. Among the white settlers we asked for work and were given a few chores in return for a meal, but no jobs. Billy knew the Mexican way of life and knew they didn't generally have work to give, so he flattered them with his Spanish and managed to get us meals and shelter.

The young Mexican women took to Billy like kittens to a saucer of milk. I was beginning to wish I had ears and buckteeth as big as his. At night I thought I might catch him slipping away to meet one of them, but he never did. He did learn, though, when every dance was scheduled.

On our third day after entering the valley, we came to a modest place just below the junction of the Rio Bonito and the Rio Ruidoso, which united to form the Rio Hondo. By the size of the field and the corral I knew this was a white man's place. As we rode up, we howdied the place a couple times before a broad-shouldered man emerged, holding a Winchester at his side. He was well muscled from hard work and had wide eyes as serious as a barn fire. He squinted a little trying to make out the Kid's face under the sombrero, then gave me the once-over.

Billy doffed his sombrero so the fellow could get a full view of his face. The man stood there, scratching at his pants and shifting on his feet. He seemed a mite uncomfortable, but I didn't know if it was us or something else.

"We're looking for work," Billy started. "I'm Billy Bonney and this is Henry Lomax."

"Frank Coe's my name. Does your buddy Lomax go by any other names?"

"Whatever I call him." Billy laughed.

I did my best to smile, seeing as how Coe had a roof to cover his head for winter and I still didn't.

Coe waved his Winchester in my general direction. "You wouldn't be Gadrich Lomax, would you?"

Billy laughed. "No, but it seems like everywhere we go Gadrich Lomax has been."

"I hear he's a swindler."

"What about work?" Billy asked.

Coe shrugged. "Crop's in, the cattle are grazing in the valley, and my cousin up the river's available to help."

I could tell Coe was suspicious, thinking we were up to no good.

"I can haul and chop firewood for the cold ahead," I said.

Billy nodded. "I can keep you supplied with meat all winter, and I don't mean stolen beef. I can shoot deer, turkey, even bear and mountain lion."

Coe scratched at his pants, then under his arm, like he had the itch something terrible.

Billy pleaded our case. "We'll follow orders, work for meals and the roof over our heads. See what kind of workers we are, and in the spring maybe you can take us on for wages or recommend us to someone else."

Next Coe scratched his head as he thought about our offer. He grimaced like he trusted us about as far as he could throw my mule. "Well," he said, "I guess it wouldn't do any harm, as long as you promise me you aren't running from the law."

"We're not, neither of us," said Billy.

"That's right," I confirmed.

"Fine, then," he said. "You can stay at the house with me. Then at least all the fleas won't try to homestead on me."

Chapter Seven

Frank Coe was right about those damn fleas. They started pestering me almost the moment I walked in the door. By the end of the second night under his roof, I had more itches than a rich girl has suitors. I was scratching here and scratching there until nothing separated the two.

"You get used to it," Coe said, as we got up and pulled on our clothes. He built a small fire in the adobe's corner fireplace to cut the morning chill.

The Kid and I just grumbled. Coe had given us a roof over our heads, but we had become room and board for his fleas. Two thirds of the fleas had fled him and taken up residence on me and Billy.

"I was out working cattle for the Englishman," Coe explained. "Gone four days. When I returned, the door had been knocked open and a couple hogs had made themselves at home. By the time I shooed them out of here, they had shed fleas like a tree sheds leaves."

Coe had grown up in Missouri before moving west to make his fortune. As it was, he was struggling to hold on to his place and put food on his plank table. A rich man had servants; a poor man, fleas. He and his cousin, George Coe, who lived a couple miles up the river, worked their places and did a little ranch work for the

Englishman who had bought a ranch on the Rio Feliz to the south. The Englishman had come to America to invest his father's money and increase the family wealth. Next to the government, the House, and John Chisum, the Englishman was the only other source of hard cash in the county.

"I've tried everything to get rid of those damn fleas," Coe said as he skillet-fried some salt pork in the fireplace.

Billy boiled some coffee, and I just scratched myself. I gritted my teeth when the itch got too bad. Coe forked us each a tin plate of bacon while Billy poured scalding coffee in tin cups.

I took to calling the fleas the "Great Southern Herd," which annoyed Coe, though I was certain more fleas migrated across my flesh than buffalo had crossed the Plains.

After breakfast Billy and I left our plates on the table and rushed outside, breathing in the cool, crisp air. When Coe joined us, we stood quietly watching the sun climb over the mountains lining the valley. Of course we had too much on our minds—as well as on our hair, our armpits, our chest hair, our legs, our crotches—to enjoy the beauty of a new day. I looked toward the Hondo, whose cold waters rippled on their way to the Pecos to water John Chisum's herds.

The gentle breeze whispered through the trees along the river, and we stood so silent that we could almost hear each other's thoughts. Simultaneously we came to a decision. We would drown those damned fleas.

"I'll get the soap," Coe yelled, retreating inside.

"Hope the fleas haven't taken it captive," I answered as I unbuttoned my shirt.

None of us had put on our weapons, and it was probably dumb to have left them inside in dangerous country, but the fleas had destroyed our ability to think like sane and cautious men.

Billy hopped clumsily as he wrestled one boot off, then the other.

Coe popped outside again. "I stole the soap from the fleas."

All together we charged toward the river, our legs churning and our arms windmilling as we flung shirts and pants and socks and long johns. We were as naked as an Apache at birth when we plowed into the water and fell into its icy embrace. The frigid water knocked our breath away. Then we gasped and screamed at the cold shock, thrashing about like fish swimming through shallows. No matter how much of a shock this was to our bodies, it had to be worse for the fleas. The Great Southern Herd was drowning, and I couldn't have been happier.

Coe ducked his head underwater, then came up gasping and spitting. He quickly lathered up his hair and tossed the lye soap to me. I used it for a moment, then pitched it to Billy, who stood up to lather himself.

"Throw me the soap, Billy," Coe yelled, and the Kid obliged. Coe snagged the soap from the air and attacked his batch of fleas.

The water was cold, but the breeze slipping through the valley felt colder. All three of us sat down in water up to our necks and waited, letting the water wash away our problems, save one.

"We didn't bring nothing to dry off with," I pointed out.

"That's a fact," Coe admitted. "Only thing I had was our blankets, and that puts us back to itching and scratching for those damned fleas."

"Same thing with our clothes," Billy said, pointing to the trail of garments stretching from the adobe to our bathing hole. "Once we put them on, we'll have as many fleas as a crippled hound."

We discussed the advantages and disadvantages of going naked for the winter. The disadvantages seemed to win out, though not by much. Even so, none of us had the courage to put his clothes back on, not after what we'd been through the last couple days.

Coe said, "I've got a washpot behind the adobe."

"I wish you had a Chinaman instead," Billy said. "A Chinaman sent me to jail my first time. I wasn't much but a kid—"

"You still ain't," Coe interrupted.

"—when a neighbor stole some clothes from a Chinese laundry and asked me to keep them. Not knowing they was stolen, I did, but the sheriff came a-calling after the neighbor pointed his guilty finger at me. The sheriff found the clothes and put me in jail for a day. I escaped out the chimney. Chinamen aren't good for nothing—except laundry."

Coe stood up and looked around. "It won't get much warmer before spring. We might just as well start washing."

Standing up too, Billy shook his head. "That's woman's work, and I can got a woman to do it for me."

"Not dressed like that, you can't," I pointed out.

Billy tossed me a sheepish grin and wrapped his arms around himself. I could see goose bumps pimpling his pale skin. Billy and Coe made for the bank while I stayed a moment longer, dreading the inevitability of my bare skin, every square inch of it, meeting the naked breeze.

I pushed myself up from the water and started shivering as I ran for the bank, splashing myself with more cold water. On the bank I shook myself off and used my hands to wipe away what water I could from my hair, chest, and arms.

Coe jogged past me for a downed cottonwood tree that had weathered white from years under the sun. He picked up a club of a limb and beat on the side of the tree, splintering the outer layer and breaking into the dry rot. He grabbed a handful of dry rot and crumbled it in his hands, then placed it on a flat rock and with a fist-size stone beat it into as fine a powder as he could manage. Then he scraped up the powder and dashed it over his body like talcum. He glanced up at Billy and me. "There's powder enough for you both. It doesn't smell as good as store-bought, but feels about the same."

Billy and I raced to get our portions. We dashed the powder over our chests, then rubbed it up our arms and down our legs.

As we finished, Coe broke off dry branches from the cottonwood and pitched us each one. "Pick up your clothes with these."

Billy shook his head. "As soon as we go to sleep tonight, they'll crawl in bed with us."

Coe shrugged. "We'll wash the blankets, too. Maybe sleep outside tonight."

"We can't sleep outside all winter," Billy said.

"It's that or fleas," said Coe, starting back for his adobe.

On the way to the cabin we picked up our clothes with the sticks, then piled them near the washpot. From the adobe we gathered the blankets in the same manner, never touching them. I took my new pair of socks from my saddlebag and pulled them over my feet, then found my boots and put them on. I didn't feel so naked then, even though I had on fewer clothes than a whore at quitting time. Billy and Coe admired my outfit and put on their own boots, but nothing else. Billy came to his senses and realized it wasn't smart walking around without his pistol, so he belted his holster over his waist. But he'd never have needed it if something had come to a gunfight. The way he looked, his enemy would've died laughing without Billy having to lift a finger or his gun. Coe and I put on our holsters, too. I don't know about him, but I felt sillier than a lawyer in church.

We stayed busy all morning and into the afternoon, boiling the clothes, soaping them, pounding them on rocks in the stream, rinsing them, then draping them over bushes and limbs so they would dry in the sun. It was damn foolish work, and I began to question whether the fleas had really been that bad.

All the time I worked, I worried our effort would

be wasted if we slept inside again. I was determined to solve that predicament. Come midafternoon my clothes were dry enough to wear. They were cool and a bit damp in places, but they beat the nothing I had been wearing. When I was fully clothed, I turned to Billy and Coe, each in varying stages of dress. "You both stay clear of the adobe until I return."

"Where you going?" Billy said. "We've still got work to do."

"I don't know," I replied, because I didn't, "but do you want to be plagued by fleas all winter?"

"No, I don't," Billy shot back, "but I also don't want you leaving. That's less meat for the survivors."

Coe laughed.

"Where's the nearest Mexicans?" I asked him as I grabbed my pair of washed socks and stuck them in my pocket.

"Several families at San Patricio, five miles up the Ruidoso."

"Hell, Lomax," cried the Kid, "you don't know enough Spanish to say 'duh.' And just because you're clean don't mean no señorita will bed you."

The two of them stood laughing, but I was convinced I was going to show them. "You just wait and be prepared to sleep outside tonight," I responded. "And, Kid, if you're as good a shot as you think you are, why don't you shoot us some game for supper."

They grumbled as I jogged over to the corral and the lean-to that Coe used for a barn. I saddled Flash, then led him out of the corral and mounted. I set him to a trot, hitting the trail quickly and turning west.

I passed a couple places that didn't have what I was looking for. A few miles from the Coe place, I met a solitary rider with a Winchester cradled in the crook of his elbow. He had a vaguely familiar look about him, but I couldn't recall ever seeing the dappled gray he rode. I nodded and he answered with a cautious grin; then we passed each other. He couldn't have been too bad a fellow, because he had a fiddle and bow strapped to the back of his horse.

A couple miles farther up the river, I saw a tiny Mexican village that had what I was looking for—sheep. San Patricio was a small place, with maybe fifteen dusty adobes lining a single street. A dozen or so Mexican families called San Patricio home and farmed the surrounding fields. Besides the homes, there was a store and a cantina.

As I rode down the street I decided I liked this place. Several people looked, including a half-dozen kids, but not a single one made fun of Flash. I figured the folks in San Patricio taught their kids better manners than did the parents in Trinidad or Roswell. I was feeling pretty confident, so I greeted them. "Howdy," I said and tipped my hat.

Their expressions never changed.

"A sheep," I said. "I'd like to borrow a sheep."

Not a person moved or even shrugged. Billy was right; I didn't know enough Spanish to get what I wanted.

I *baaa*ed like a sheep, and the people just stared, their stony expressions never giving away their thoughts, which surely must have been that I was crazy. I rode from one end of the narrow town to the other, and not a single person acknowledged my presence, though I felt the gaze of their dark eyes following every step that Flash took.

When I turned my mule around and started back, I spied a young lady, no more than sixteen or seventeen, standing in the middle of the dusty street watching me. I reined Flash up in front of her.

She had dark Mexican eyes and hair as black as night. Her legs were spread beneath her colorful skirt, and her hands were planted firmly upon her shapely hips. Without so much as a smile from her pouty lips, she spoke. "I speak English."

"Your name?"

"Rosalita," she replied and nothing more.

"I came to borrow a sheep."

She turned her head and looked at her elders sitting outside their adobes. She said something in Spanish, and they all laughed.

"A sheep? To borrow?"

I nodded. "Rid my cabin of fleas." Then I realized how foolish wanting to borrow a sheep must've sounded.

Rosalita translated again. An old man shook his head. "Buy a sheep, no?" she asked me.

"Borrow a sheep. No money to buy. Will return in one week."

"What to trade for borrow?"

I had nothing in my pockets but my clean socks. I pulled them out and dangled them before all of San Patricio. "These."

Rosalita translated. An old man stood up and hobbled on a cane to Rosalita's side. "Sí," he said, then continued in Spanish, which Rosalita translated.

"You borrow a ewe for one week, return. My uncle keep socks." She smiled. "You not return, he come and kill you."

I figured the fleas had a better chance of killing me than this feeble man. I nodded. "Deal." I pitched the socks to him, almost knocking him off balance when he caught them.

Rosalita spoke in Spanish to a boy, no more than ten, in baggy pants and shirt, who raced off and returned quickly, leading a sheep by a rope. I dismounted and took the sheep, tying it to the mule's saddle, then got back on Flash. Rosalita still stood in my way, even when I nudged Flash forward a step. She was young, but she had a wild spirit in her eye. I eased Flash around her, then rode out of San Patricio to the laughter of the whole town.

I got the same reception the moment I rode onto Frank Coe's place leading the sheep. Frank, Billy, and the fiddle player I had met on the way to San Patricio were sitting on benches outside the adobe, enjoying what was left of the day.

"I didn't know you were that lonely," Billy yelled, then took to slapping his knee.

"Does she dance?" Coe asked.

The fiddle player picked up his fiddle and bow, slicing out a little jig from his instrument.

Frank stood up and pointed to his fiddle player. "This is my cousin, George Coe."

Without missing a beat of his tune, George nodded.

"Introduce us to your friend," Billy shouted.

I didn't say a thing, just rode Flash up to the door, untied the ewe, and led her into the adobe.

"Oh," cried Billy, "they want to be alone."

Everybody laughed but Frank when I came back out and closed the door and the sheep took to bleating.

"What the hell are you doing?"

"Keep the sheep in there a few days, and she'll soak up all the fleas like a sponge soaks up water."

"Hell," shouted Frank, "by then it'll smell like an outhouse and nobody'll want to live there."

"We'll sleep under the stars tonight," I said.

"As long as that sheep's inside," Billy said, "I'll sleep outside. I don't want no stories starting about me."

Though still skeptical, Frank settled down.

"A week from now, you'll be congratulating me on ridding the house of fleas," I announced.

George Coe had ridden over to visit and to let Frank know there was a dance the next Saturday in San Patricio. The Kid planned on attending, and I figured I would just as well so I could return the sheep.

We didn't do much that night except talk and sing, George sawing some fine tunes off his fiddle. They were good men, all of them, all working to better their station in life. That was probably the best night I ever spent in Lincoln County.

I kept remembering John Chisum's words that a man had to choose his friends carefully. I felt as good about these men as any I had ever been around. John

Chisum was wrong, though. Maybe a big man like him was known by his friends, but little men like us got caught up in events that we could not control. Just days after the San Patricio dance, the noose began to tighten on Lincoln County.

Chapter Eight

That damn ewe turned out to be a problem for me. Just as I knew she would, she acted like a magnet and the fleas like metal filings. In a couple days, what was left of the Great Southern Herd migrated from the bedding and walls to the ewe. Only problem was, the adobe smelled worse than a gut wagon in July. Instead of using their hands to scratch, Billy and Frank used them to hold their noses. They cussed me like a thieving stepchild, never once thanking me for my contribution to the housekeeping.

Now, I admit a sheep is not the cleanest animal, but life is a series of compromises. I figured getting rid of the fleas was worth the odor, but I began to wonder when those two harassed me about "Lomax's girl," as they took to calling her. I should've returned the ewe before the dance, but they had tripped over my stubborn streak, and I intended to let them suffer a while longer.

The day of the dance, I staked the ewe outside while Frank and Billy aired out the place. I got the shovel and removed droppings from a couple places, but the floor was packed dirt so it did not seem that bad a problem. Of course this was Frank's abode, not mine.

That Saturday, after a noon meal of corn mush and fried bacon, the three of us strolled down to the creek to take baths. We undressed, putting our clothes and guns within quick reach by the stream, then threw ourselves into the Hondo. The water was colder than a well-driller's butt in February, but we didn't care. There were fine señoritas in San Patricio, and we intended to dance the night away with them until we got lucky enough to slip out with one. In spite of the cold water and stiff breeze, our unfulfilled lusts were keeping us warm.

All of a sudden the Kid bolted from the water, scampering for his revolver. I glanced in the direction he was looking. What I saw pretty near made me spoil the clear waters of the Hondo! Riding toward us were a dozen men spread out like geese in formation. Every one of them was armed, and judging by the hard gazes on their faces, they weren't reluctant to use their weapons.

Billy picked up his holster and jerked his revolver free as he hid behind the trunk of a cottonwood tree. "Who is it?"

I scampered out of the water and hopped over to my pistol, figuring I would at least die clean. Frank Coe stood up slowly, holding his flattened hand over his eyes as he studied the riders.

"Take it easy, boys," he said. "It's only Dick Brewer and the Englishman."

The Kid didn't seem so certain everything was okay. Maybe Frank didn't have as much to hide about his past as Billy and I did. Billy had a good nose for danger, or at least had had a good one before the ewe moved into the cabin. His gaze traversed the line of riders. "I've never seen the Englishman before—is he the one on the mousy white horse?"

"That's him, Kid," said Frank Coe. "How'd you know?"

"He rides like a girl, and only some fool foreigner would ride a white horse in this country. Stands out too much."

I studied the Englishman and had to agree he had a

girlish sway. He seemed like he would be more at home in a buggy than in a saddle.

"Take it easy, Kid," said Frank. "They're friends."

"Your friends may not be my friends."

The man in the lead lifted his arm like a cavalry officer and tugged back on the reins.

Frank Coe stood up, shivering and waving his hand over his head. The Englishman seemed oblivious to me and Billy, but the leader had us picked out and seemed to be gauging which one of us to shoot first if it came to a fight.

Coe scampered over to his clothes and started pulling on his pants, then his shirt, as the men stopped not twenty yards from the water. "Howdy, Dick," he called as he jerked on his boots and started up the rise toward the riders.

The man Frank had addressed as Dick nodded. "I'd feel more at ease if your partners holstered their guns."

Frank looked at me, then at Billy, both of us naked. "Without their holsters, I don't know where they would put their guns."

"I have an idea," Dick said, "but I don't think they'll like it."

The Englishman laughed. "By Jove, capital suggestion, but where might that be, Dick—their arses?"

Dick nodded.

The Englishman laughed harder. "Slowly, I am understanding American humor, indeed."

I studied the Englishman and found him not at all what I had expected. He was young, thin, and abundantly haired. His skin was pale but splotched with the remnants of a recent bout of smallpox. With his long, girlish fingers he kept twisting a lock of hair that fell down over his forehead. Though he was dressed in a fine-cut English suit, I sure couldn't picture him as one of the richest men in Lincoln County. As I stepped out from behind the downed log, he seemed to flush at the sight of my nakedness. I thought him a dandy and not much more. I figured if I had a cannon I could blow his arse out of the saddle and show him some real American humor, as he called it.

Billy emerged from his hiding spot and lowered his pistol. Frank introduced us to Dick Brewer, then John Henry Tunstall, the Englishman. Brewer nodded with a face as square as his dealings. Curly, unruly hair tunneled from under his hat and dangled over his ears. His eyes were as sharp and clear as his voice.

"Didn't mean to alarm you," he said to me and Billy, "but the cabin looked abandoned. We feared trouble."

"Dick is the Englishman's foreman," Coe explained to us. "Me and George help him out some when he needs it."

"Been plenty of trouble lately," Brewer said, "but I finally called Sheriff Brady's bluff."

"Indeed he has, by Jove," interjected the Englishman, gazing from me to Billy, who retreated to his clothes, never turning his back or his arse to the riders. "Where the sheriff failed, my good man Dick succeeded."

Brewer nodded, a trace of embarrassment in his eyes. "Jesse Evans and three of the Boys are in jail in Lincoln."

Billy laughed. "Not a better place for Evans."

"Stole my horses, he did, he and the Boys," said the Englishman.

Now, I'd never been impressed by money or titles. The Englishman had neither done nor said anything to change my mind. He had a haughty demeanor that said he was better than us, yet at the same time he wanted to be one of us. I dismissed him as a limey buffoon who should've stayed in London fawning over Queen Victoria and attending socials where they drank their tea holding the teacup handles between their thumbs and forefingers.

As Billy dressed, I felt a bit odd standing there by my lonesome, naked as a jaybird and blue as the sky from the chill. I turned red when the ewe back at the cabin took to bleating.

His cheek poking out, Billy said, "Lomax's girl."

Brewer did not smile, but the Englishman tittered, though not seeming to understand why, and one Mexican grinned before translating Billy's comments to the others, who all laughed.

That damn sheep had caused me more misery than any living creature other than the Great Southern Herd. I began to cover my flesh, if not my wounded pride.

Brewer explained how, with the help of Alexander A. McSween, Lincoln's only lawyer, he had gotten an arrest warrant for the Boys from Squire Wilson, a justice of the peace who was too dumb to be a friend of the House. When Brewer had presented the warrant to Sheriff William Brady, the sheriff opted to lead the posse.

"We got the horses back and the Boys in jail," Brewer announced.

"They won't be in jail long," Billy said as he buckled his gun belt, "not with Brady guarding them."

"That's right," I said, proceeding to stick my foot in my mouth all the way up to my hip. "When I rode with Jesse, the sheriff helped us eat stolen beef."

Brewer's eyes narrowed as he tapped his fingers on his carbine.

"I'll vouch for these two," Frank Coe told Brewer, then pointed at all the men backing him. "If Jesse Evans is in jail, why all the artillery?"

Brewer leaned forward in the saddle, shaking his head in disgust. "While we were after the Boys, more rustlers made off with the Englishman's cattle. They're headed Texas way, and we intend to catch them."

"You need more men, Dick?" asked Coe. "We can ride with you."

I didn't care for Frank's volunteering me to chase down some rich Englishman's lost cattle, not when I had a sheep to return and a dance to attend.

"I need your help here," Brewer said, "to look after my place and check on the Englishman's ranch while I'm gone. The Englishman has business with John Chisum to

discuss a partnership in a bank for Lincoln. He'll ride with
us as far as Roswell. We're riding on as long as it takes to
catch up with the rustlers."

"Between me, Bonney, and Lomax," said Frank, "we
can handle it."

"Obliged," Brewer said, touching the brim of his hat.
"We'll be riding."

"You boys take care," offered Frank.

Brewer nodded. "This'll be easy next to rounding up
the Boys."

"Pleasure meeting you chaps," said Tunstall, as out
of tune with the conversation as a warped fiddle.

"I thought you wore chaps," Billy mumbled, and the
Englishman took to laughing.

"American humor," he chuckled.

English stupidity, I thought.

Brewer reined his gelding downstream, and the
Mexicans followed after him. Tunstall delayed a moment,
his finger still twisting the curl of hair on his forehead.
"Good work will be duly rewarded, men." He turned his
mousy white horse toward Roswell and took out after the
others.

"An odd duck," I said.

"How rich you think he is?" asked Billy. "A thousand
dollars?"

Frank answered without hesitation. "He paid more
than two thousand dollars for the cattle Brewer's chasing
He bought them from a widder woman forced to sell to
cover her husband's debts."

Billy nodded. "I bet every woman in Lincoln County's got her eye on him."

Frank crossed his arms and shook his head. "He's tak-
en to no females. Says he has a sister back in London he
plans to devote his life to when he builds his fortune."

"We have a name for that back in Arkansas," I said,
but neither Billy nor Frank found it funny. They were
acting like the Englishman was as decent as God. I figured
otherwise, but I didn't care to debate the issue. Not when

time was a-wasting and a dance was gonna start a few miles up the road in San Patricio.

I put on my boots, strapped on my gun belt, and started back for the cabin at a rapid clip.

"Must be pining for his girl," called the Kid.

"Baaaa, baaaa," mocked Frank.

They laughed until they realized I might get a head start on them and secure dances from all the señoritas before they arrived. They broke into a jog and I into a dash for the adobe. It startled the ewe, which took to bleating again.

Billy laughed. "She's lonely."

At the adobe I borrowed some of Frank's tonic water to sweeten my natural charm and used his comb to tame my unruly hair. Rushing inside, Frank grumbled at the liberties I had taken, then sniffed the air and griped that I had used a nickel's worth of his smelly water.

Though Frank fussed about everything, the Kid just grinned like he would still get the most dances with the señoritas. Frank offered the Kid his comb, but Billy spurned it with a wave of his hand, running his fingers instead through his brown hair as if to say he could charm the ladies with it all mussed. He was right, though I didn't care to admit it.

When I had finished, I grabbed my coat and started for the open door to saddle Flash.

"You just go on and we'll catch up with you later," Billy said. "Flash shouldn't be too hard to catch up with."

"Sure thing," I said, knowing Billy didn't care to be seen riding with my borrowed sheep. At the corral I caught and saddled Flash, then led him over to the ewe, untied the stake rope, and tied the line to the saddle. I hauled myself aboard Flash and turned him toward San Patricio.

"Adios," I called and received no answer as I rode away.

Before I reached George Coe's place, I could hear the strains of a fiddle drifting back to me. When I came in sight of his adobe, he was dancing out front with his fiddle, just sawing away on the strings to while away the time. The afternoon chill was setting in as the clouds and the mountains to the west began to screen the sun from the Ruidoso River valley.

When my sheep bleated, the fiddle playing screeched to a halt. George turned around from his solitary dance. "Frank and the Kid didn't want to be seen with the sheep?"

"They're not fond of the ewe. Are *you* afraid to be seen with me and her?"

"I'll ride with you. I get edgy standing around waiting," George replied. He disappeared around the side of the cabin and came back in a minute astride his gelding. He held the reins with one hand and the fiddle and bow in the other.

As we rode I told George about the Englishman and the Boys being in jail in Lincoln. Like his cousin, George had a high opinion of the Englishman. I listened and kept my opinions to myself. We were within sight of San Patricio when Frank and Billy rode up.

"Why didn't you wait on us, George?" Frank asked.

"You didn't wait on Lomax."

"He's riding a mule and escorting a sheep," Billy broke in.

"You boys've been hurrahing him too much."

"You haven't been living with his sheep smelling up the place, soiling the floor," Frank replied.

"And you aren't living with fleas anymore, either, Frank."

George shook his head. "We either all ride together into San Patricio or I take my fiddle back home." He was becoming more and more likable by the minute. Frank and Billy mumbled as we rode on into town.

As we passed the first house, the people on the street pointed at me and George. Then the sheep bleated. I could've shot that damn ewe. At that moment I realized George and his fiddle were being welcomed while I was being mocked for borrowing the woolly animal. I fell behind my riding companions and thought about the affront to my dignity. The more I thought about it, the greater the temptation to shoot every San Patricio citizen who was laughing at me. Of course that would probably have cast a cloud over the dance, and I didn't need that, especially since I had my ambitions set on dancing with Rosalita. She had given me a heart-burning.

At least San Patricio's fine citizens didn't mock Flash. I tipped my hat to them, drawing a few narrow smiles. Then I saw a man standing in the middle of the street. Frank, George, and Billy rode around him, but he was looking at me. He was an old man in a narrow sombrero, his leather face etched with wrinkles and his ankles as wobbly as the cane he had planted in the street to steady himself. Not only had I seen this man before, I had borrowed a ewe from him.

He lifted his finger and pointed in my general direction, his hands so wobbly that had he been holding a pistol the whole population of San Patricio would have jumped for cover. He said something in Spanish that I didn't understand, but Billy translated that he was glad to see his sheep back. With great effort he bent awkwardly at the waist, snatched at his baggy pants, and lifted them. I could see my socks on his moccasined feet.

Twisting around in my saddle, I started to unknot the rope, but a brown bean of a lad was already there, untying it and then leading the animal away. When I turned around the old man was struggling to get out of the street. I hoped Rosalita didn't take the first dance with him, or no one else would get a dance all night.

The old man finally made it to the edge of the street and took the rope from the lad. If the ewe stampeded she would drag the feeble fellow to his death, so I waited until he was past the corner of the nearest adobe. Being the cautious animal that he was, Flash didn't seem to mind the delay.

By the time I gave Flash a nudge, my companions were dismounting down the street in front of the cantina. Here I was, finally rid of that damn ewe, and not a one of them, not even George, had waited on me. I was beginning to feel lower than a snake's belly when I caught a glimpse of Rosalita, in a full red skirt and a loosely fitted blouse that dipped enough below her neck to see a sliver of her bronze torso. My mouth went drier than a Baptist convention, and when I tried to call out a greeting, it sounded more like a bray. It sure confused Flash, who flicked his ears and tossed his head. Rosalita saw me and waved gaily. With such a reception, I figured I might be planting a little corn in her furrow by night's end.

Rosalita disappeared behind the door of a tiny adobe, so I rode on down to the cantina, where a couple men were hanging festive lanterns from ropes strung from the front corners to two adjacent trees. Darkness was settling over the valley.

"Hurry, Lomax," called George. "I can't stay out too long or my fingers'll get cold and I'll stumble across my fiddle strings like a drunk crossing railroad tracks."

Billy walked around his stallion and crossed his arms as I dismounted and tied Flash. "Who's the señorita?"

"Rosalita. Why?"

"I'm just staking out my claim," he said rather confidently.

"I spotted her first."

The Kid nodded. "I'm a claim jumper. I just don't want any hard feelings if she chooses me over you, Lomax. We're partners until it comes to the ladies."

"I can hold my own," I answered, as sure of myself as a candidate on election day.

We dropped the subject and started for the cantina door just as a couple matrons came out. Inside, we saw that the tables had been stacked behind the bar, which was nothing more than some thick planks supported at the ends by two barrels. Women were arranging platters and bowls of food on the bar while a couple men covered the bottles on the backbar with a wool blanket.

A man moving a bench to the side wall saw George and called to him in Spanish. The women stopped their work and greeted George with wide smiles. George nodded, and Billy stepped to his side and spoke. The old women giggled like schoolgirls.

"What did you say?" I asked.

"I told them if their daughters were anything as pretty as them, then San Patricio had the prettiest women in all the territory, if not the country." Billy seemed proud of himself. "A little flattery with the mommas makes it easier to get dances with their daughters."

That was when I realized I would have some stiff competition for Rosalita's favors. I figured I needed a little help from Billy to win the trust of the señoritas. "How do you ask a girl to dance?"

Billy grinned as if I had just willed him a fortune. He put his arm on my shoulder. *"Me gustan las ovejas mas que las mujeres."*

I repeated it a couple times, and Billy worked real hard to help me get the pronunciation down just right. I probably should have checked it with George, too, but he was warming up his fingers on the fiddle and that seemed more important than my needs at the time.

One of the entering Mexican men pointed to all three of us and said something that caused Billy to nod his head. Billy pointed to the revolver at my side. "No one allowed inside with a gun. We'll give them to the man at the door. He will keep them."

I was surprised at how easily Billy stripped his gun belt off his waist and handed it to the Mexican. I never figured I would catch Billy without a gun. I found out later he was still armed; he always tucked a pistol in his boot before going to a dance.

Outside it darkened quickly, and the men and women lit more lamps about the room. The cantina was small, with maybe enough room for twenty couples to dance in the middle of the floor while observers sat in chairs against the wall. The room began to fill. A couple Mexicans with guitars joined George on the bench at the end of the bar, and they sat tuning their instruments and accompanying each other for practice.

When it was time to start, George stood up on the bench, his head almost touching the ceiling, and began to saw out a simple, quick melody. As he got the song rolling, the two guitarists stood up and accompanied him. They ended to the polite applause of everyone around.

I checked the room and started to make a move across the dance floor for Rosalita, but Billy caught me by the arm.

"The first dance is for the older men and women. It would insult her to be asked on this dance."

I nodded my thanks because that was a damn generous thing for him to do when we were competing for the same girl. Sure enough, the first dance was reserved for the married men and women and the town elders. The moment it ended the younger men shot across the room to ask the prettiest girls to dance. I outmaneuvered Billy and reached Rosalita before him, but not before a half dozen of the young Mexican men. She smiled at me, and I barged through her ring of admirers.

"Me gustan las ovejas mas que las mujeres!" I said.

Her face drooped like an old lady's bosom, and the men laughed.

"What did I say?"

Before Rosalita could answer, Billy reached through and grabbed her, pulling her onto the dance floor just as the music started. There was still plenty of time to find a partner, but everyone I asked seemed to withdraw from me like I was a leper. I asked every young lady and most of their mothers. I was downright discouraged and took a seat along the wall for several dances, then eased through the crowd to the food, which couldn't refuse me like the women had. What galled me most was Frank and Billy were kicking up dust from the floor and no one would dance with me.

The dance went on for hours. I screwed up my courage and returned to each woman who had refused me. The result was the same. It was well after midnight, just when I was about to give up and seek a good bottle of whiskey, when Rosalita found me. She grabbed my idle hands.

"The next dance is special," she said. "It tells the old ladies who your favorite young man is."

I was damn proud to be chosen by her for this dance, even though she hadn't danced with me earlier. "Why didn't you dance with me before?"

"You never asked me."

"Yes, I did. Billy taught me Spanish."

She laughed as the music began. "You said 'I like sheep more than women.' Many think you borrowed the sheep for evil purposes."

I cursed to myself.

"Then why are you dancing with me?" I boldly asked.

"To scandalize the old ladies," she said.

I could see a mean streak in her eye, and when I glanced down at the floor, shaking my head, I saw something that really scared me. Rosalita's toes were poking through the ends of her dancing sandals. Her second toe was longer than her big toe.

That was a bad sign. I don't believe in superstitions unless there's something to them, but it was a proven fact back in the Ozarks of Arkansas that a woman with such a toe would bully her boyfriend, humiliate her lover, and henpeck her husband. I considered the ramifications of dancing with her, knowing that it was dangerous to let a girl with a big second toe get too close to you.

The music started and several couples rushed to the dance floor. I was so anxious to dance, I couldn't hold back, even though I knew I was taking a chance. The old women's mouths gaped when Rosalita started dancing with me. Rosalita was a dangerous woman even at sixteen, but I figured she was worth the risk.

Chapter Nine

The dance taught me one thing. I'd sooner have Sitting Bull give me a haircut than let Billy Bonney teach me Spanish. What I didn't know was whether Rosalita really liked me or was just interested in creating gossip in San Patricio. I cleared my confusion by taking to drink.

The next day the Kid and my head told me I had consumed too much liquor. Though I didn't remember it, the Kid said I was singing along to the fiddle music and dancing by myself. Had he not put me to telling señoritas that I liked sheep better than women, I'd've danced with them instead of drinking. I have to admit that my periodic weakness for liquor had gotten me in trouble over the years, but singing off-key and dancing alone in the crowd didn't break any of the first Ten Commandments, as I recall. Billy, though, kept reminding me of my shameful behavior for a week after the dance. I put up with it because as long as he rode me about my drinking, he wasn't pestering me about the sheep.

I spent the next week working around Frank Coe's place, then riding with him and the Kid over to the Englishman's ranch on the Rio Feliz. Now, for all the talk about how rich the Englishman was, I was damned surprised when I rode over the hill and gazed upon

his ranch headquarters. I couldn't help but break out
laughing.

"What's so funny?" asked Billy, twisting around on
his stallion.

I'd seen better-looking outhouses and bigger ones,
too. It was a rough cabin made of slick cottonwood logs
with so much space between them that, were it not for the
roof and the stovepipe poking through, you would have
thought it a pen rather than a cabin. It was a religious roof,
no doubt, because it was holier than the Bible. My side
was hurting from laughing so hard. "That's it? That's what
he wanted us to check on?"

Frank nodded. "Yeah!"

Billy began to giggle a tad.

"It's a damn palace." I gasped for breath. "No wonder
the Englishman left England." I exploded with laughter.

Then Billy began to laugh, slapping his knee.

At first Frank held back, like he didn't see any humor
in it. Then he laughed, too, as we nudged our mounts
down the slope toward the cabin and the river. I could've
broken out in a sweat that carried more water than the Rio
Feliz. Back in Arkansas a man could drown in a river, but
out here you could take your boots and socks off and wade
without getting your ankles wet. I was tempted to take a
leak in the Rio Feliz but feared it would cause flooding all
the way to the Pecos. Flash, though, had no such worries.
As we crossed the stream he cut loose and sent the river
to roiling. I figured in a few hours this unexpected flow
would reach the Pecos and back water all the way up to
John Chisum's place. If Chisum was asleep on his floor
when the floodwaters hit, he might even drown. Flash
finally finished his business.

Shaking his head, Billy glared at Flash, then spat in
the water, raising the stream another foot. "Damn mule.
I'm ashamed to be seen with you on that mule."

"He may be a mule, but he ain't blind."

"Nope," Billy admitted, "but he damn sure makes me
wish I was."

Frank swatted his thigh, then laughed at us. "You two can jawbone more over less than any two fellows I ever saw."

As we approached the *choza*, as the Mexicans called a shack, I noticed a wagon behind the place and a horse staked in a patch of grass upstream. Firewood was piled beside the door, and at the corner of the cabin was a stack of fence posts and a set of posthole diggers. The ground around the cabin was bare except for occasional clumps of yellowing grass. A few cottonwoods and a handful of willows grew along the stream. Several magpies in one tree chatted among themselves at our passing.

We drew up our mounts outside the so-called cabin, dismounted, and tied them to the hitching post. I stretched the kinks out of my legs and shoved my hands into my pockets.

Frank pointed to the staked horse, then the wagon. "Gottfried," he called. "Gottfried Gauss. Where are you?"

"Damn," I said. "If the Englishman's got someone to work his place, what are we doing here?" Through the gaps in the cabin wall I could see the profile of a small cast-iron cookstove and a table.

The Kid sauntered around to the back of the cabin, then cut loose a yip of joy. I figured he'd found a naked and willing woman, so I eased around in his direction to share in the excitement. I found him looking at the trash piled against the back of the cabin. Discarded bottles and tins stood knee high. I realized the one advantage of this choza: With the wide gaps between logs, a man could discard his empties without going outside. It didn't matter that residing in that cabin was about like living outside anyway.

Despite that, I didn't see much to get excited about, certainly not the trash. The Kid, though, was happier than a calf in clover.

I said, "I've never seen anyone happier over a junk pile."

As Frank Coe yelled for Gauss, Billy bent over, picked up an empty bottle, and tossed it in the air. "Target practice," he shouted.

Twirling end over end, the bottle peaked, then began its descent. Instantly Billy jerked his Colt free and pulled the trigger. The bottle shattered into a hundred pieces.

The gunshot set off a commotion inside the cabin, a clatter of pots and tinware followed by a few mumbled curses in a language I learned was German.

"Don'ten kill me," cried a frightened voice. "I vas jus' sleepin'. No vork for me to do."

Through the gaps in the logs I saw a grizzled man scrambling to his feet from beside the small cast-iron stove. In his excitement he bumped his head on the stove and yelped.

The Kid reached down beside me, picked up a bent tin can, and tossed it in the air, hitting it with successive shots and drawing an even louder plea from Gauss.

"Don'ten shooten me," he cried out, then barged out the door.

Frank Coe must have been standing there.

"Thanken Gott, it is you," Gauss called, just as Billy fired one more time. Gauss gasped. "Vat's the shootin'?"

"Friends of mine," Frank replied.

"Noise, they maken plenty."

Billy laughed, then replaced the empty hulls in his revolver and holstered it. Together we walked around to the front of the choza, where Frank introduced us to Gottfried Gauss. He stood five and a half feet tall, and his dark blue but bloodshot eyes seemed tired under the weight of the heavy bags beneath them. His sandy hair was mussed and his matching beard, flecked with gray, failed to hide the wrinkles etched in his face. By his look I figured he was born tired and never got rested.

Gauss squinted at us because he could barely see. He couldn't recognize a friend at ten yards, much less an enemy at fifteen. As we howdied one another, he stepped up to us both, almost trampling on our feet as he tried to get close enough to make out our features.

Billy gave him a big-eared, bucktoothed grin, and Gauss took to him like an axle takes to grease. Gauss approached me, stared at my handsome features a moment, then slid back to Billy.

"Vould you liken me to maken you some coffee?"

"I'd like some," I said.

Gauss brushed my request aside with a wave of his wrinkled hand and focused—as best his weak eyes could—upon Billy like he was a long-lost brother. He treated me like I was a damn tax collector.

"Coffee?" Gauss asked the Kid.

"Coffee'd be good," Billy answered.

Gauss nodded, then shuffled past me to Frank. "Coffee?"

"Yep," Frank replied. Gauss stepped back inside and clanged and clattered pots and pans against the stove. He sounded like a better blacksmith than cook. "Gottfried can brew more than coffee," Frank said. "He brewed up four hundred gallons of beer at the old brewery just off the government land at Fort Stanton."

Billy didn't seem near as interested as me, and he edged toward the trash pile behind the cabin. I licked my lips.

"That was before I reached Lincoln County," Frank said, "but I'm told it was some of the best beer folks in these parts ever tasted."

"If it was so damn good, then why ain't he still brewing beer instead of fixing coffee out here in the middle of nowhere in a cabin that ain't much more than a woodpile?" I asked.

"Lawrence G. Murphy. That's the reason."

Billy slowly turned around. "Does Murphy have a hand in everything around here?"

Frank nodded. "Just about. Murphy heard Gauss knew how to make beer. Promised him forty cents a gallon if he'd brew some. Gauss did, four hundred gallons.

Then when it was time for Murphy to buy, he offered ten cents a gallon. Gauss balked and Murphy told him to find another buyer, but who else in Lincoln County could buy that much beer? Gauss crawled back to Murphy the next day to accept his offer, but by then Murphy had dropped the price to seven cents a gallon. A man that was owed a hundred and sixty dollars got twenty-eight dollars instead."

I could only shake my head. Gauss didn't strike me as the kind of man who'd grow bowlegged toting his brains around, but neither did he hit me as a mean or dishonest man. Fact was, I sort of felt akin to him. I'd been cheated, swindled, and lied to before and might have been rich to this day had I not let myself get taken by that lying sort of man. Damn if life isn't frustrating when you bust your tail to earn a decent living, maybe get a little bit ahead, and then some big money man or the damn tax collector comes along and takes away what's yours. Those that got are always walking on those that don't. The big man's always walking on the back of the little man, trying to keep him down, when all the poor working man's trying to do is survive and provide for his family, if he can afford one.

Even though I'd never laid eyes on Lawrence G. Murphy, I could tell I liked him about as much as a circuit rider likes sin. By the time he sold the beer a mug at a time to thirsty patrons of his store, he probably made a profit a hundred times or more his cost. By reputation alone I knew Murphy to be the type of man who was loose with other people's money but close with his own. I figured he was so tight that every time he smiled his peter would skin back.

As for myself, all I wanted was a little more than I ever got—like coffee when Gauss returned. The German came out carrying three cups. He handed the first to Billy, the second to Frank, and took the third for himself.

"What about mine?" I complained.

"You vanted coffee? I had but three cups, no more. One for me, one for Frank, and one for Kid."

I shook my head. No wonder Murphy only paid him seven cents a gallon. I charged around the cabin and jumped into the trash pile, flinging cans and bottles until I found a tin that would do.

"Don't break any of my targets," Billy yelled.

I marched to the river, making sure I was upstream from where Flash had started the flood, and proceeded to wash out the tin. I returned to the cabin just as Gauss came out with refills.

Gauss distributed the cups to Frank and the Kid, then began to sip from his own.

I held my tin up to his face. "Now there's four cups," I announced, taking pride that my empty can was bigger than his cup. "I'm ready for coffee."

"Helpen yourself vith vat's left, vich is noten very much."

Grumbling, I marched inside, taking in the table, two benches, stove, and Gauss's bedding nearby. Reaching the warm stove, I grabbed Gauss's rag and picked up the coffeepot. There wasn't much left, but I poured what there was into my tin, grimacing when I saw the clump of grounds that came out with the liquid. I dropped the pot back on the stove and ambled outside. I've seen courageous men in my time, but until I took a sip of the coffee I never knew how brave Frank and the Kid were. That coffee tasted worse than outhouse runoff and didn't smell nearly as good. No wonder Gauss kept only three tin cups in the cabin. He'd never have need for any more. I figured some coal oil would get the rancid taste out of my mouth, provided there was enough in Lincoln County.

"You can tell by Gottfried's coffee that he's a good cook," Frank said, a grin as wide as Flash's behind across his face.

I wondered how Frank could've consumed two cups of that vile liquid and still manage to stay on his feet. Then I saw two wet splotches on the ground behind him. When Gauss had turned around, Frank had dumped his two cups. As blind as Gauss was, Frank might've been able to do it right under the old man's nose. I pointed to the wet spots. "It runs through your system right fast, Frank."

The Kid laughed, and I saw the spots on the ground where he had done the same thing. It angered me to have gone to the trouble of finding a tin cup so I could poison myself with Gauss's coffee. It angered me more that neither Frank nor Billy had warned me before it destroyed my innards.

I threw the coffee out of my tin can, figuring I'd have no more trouble over it than Frank or Billy had.

"Vhy you throwen avay good coffee?" Gauss demanded.

"Too many grounds."

"I saven the grounds, maken more coffee."

I looked at the wet spot and the string of grounds where I had emptied my tin. "If you want me to scoop up the grounds, I'll do it, but you'll have plenty of ground in it."

Gauss didn't see the humor in that and just kept looking at me like I had slapped his momma and called her ugly. "It's the svindlers liken Lomax I don't liken vhen they cheaten at cards."

"Huh?" I said.

Billy defended me. "Lomax isn't good enough to cheat at cards."

Gauss lifted his finger and pointed at my nose. "Vat you diden to me in Lincoln, I'll not forgetten, takenin' my five dollars—three-card monte, vasn't it?"

"What?" I shrugged. "I've never even been to Lincoln and I don't play monte."

"You're Lomax, yah?"

"Yes."

"Svindler, then!"

Frank grabbed my arm just as I was about to plant my fist firmly in the old man's nose. "Gottfried," Frank said, "it was Gadrich Lomax that cheated you. This is Henry Harrison Lomax."

"Vhat, two of them?" he exclaimed.

Frank dragged me toward Gauss until I was no more than eight inches from the old man's nose. His breath smelled like the fumes of his coffee, and I about gagged. "Look at him, Gottfried. Is this the man that cheated you at cards?"

Gauss squinted, then eyed me as closely as a miser would study a counterfeit dollar. Reading his narrow eyes was about as hard as drinking his coffee.

"Name's the same."

"But is it the same man?" Frank demanded.

Gauss stared even harder. He was as confused as a virgin on her wedding night, but didn't smell nearly as good. Finally he shook his head. "Vhat that I maken a mistake. It's noten the man. Let me given you my sorry."

I took that as an apology and unwadded my fist, but I vowed right then and there if I ever ran into one Gadrich Lomax I would punch him in the nose for ruining my name.

Gauss stepped backward. "Vhy I didn't given you a tin cup vas because I thoughten you vere Gadrich Lomax. No Gadrich Lomax is drinkingen from my cup." He extended his hand, offering me his tin cup with its remaining poison.

"Go ahead," I said. "I've had plenty of coffee."

Frank released my arm. "Has Dick Brewer made it back with the Englishman's cattle?"

Gauss shrugged. "He not bringen them here."

Frank nodded. "When he returns, think he'll need help? The Kid and Lomax are looking for jobs. I don't have the money to pay wages. You think the Englishman does for two more hands?"

"Vell, he payen me eight dollars a month, but I can't do much, my eyes being bad as they are."

Frank looked from Gauss to Billy and me. "Way I figure it, the two of you could stay a few days, do some chores and convince Brewer and the Englishman that you're worth hiring. And I don't see much point in me staying. After all, Gottfried's only got three cups."

Billy scratched his chin. "John Chisum won't hire me. Lawrence Murphy's crookeder than a barrel full of snakes, and I won't work for him. The Englishman's my last chance for honest work."

"Lomax?"

I didn't take to the idea of working for the Englishman, but I didn't like the idea of starving, either. I had tried that line of work after my escape from Leadville, and it was about as low you can fall—unless, of course, you're a politician, which opens up whole new opportunities for lowness. Now, if Gauss's cooking was as bad as his coffee, working for the Englishman and starving might work out to be the same thing.

Before I answered Frank, I turned to Gauss. "How many cattle does the Englishman have on the place now?"

"A dozen, no more. Four hundred he haden until the rustlers comen. Vhy you asken?"

"And horses?" I asked.

"Eight or nine. Vhy you asken?"

"If Dick Brewer doesn't return with the Englishman's herd, there won't be enough work for any of us," I said.

There were nods all around.

"What choice do we have?" Billy asked.

I shrugged. "I figure I can get on with John Chisum, maybe even spark Sallie Chisum."

The Kid gave me a spiteful look, then a narrow grin. "She's a step up from sheep." He laughed and retreated around the corner of the cabin, and shortly I heard him digging in the trash heap, pulling out bottles and cans.

Frank looked at me and shrugged.

"Target practice," I explained.

In a minute we saw Billy setting up a line of cans fifty yards upstream of the house. Then he drew his pistol and started shooting. His every shot made a can dance. I told myself right then and there that if it ever came to a showdown between the two of us, I'd have to shoot him from behind for it to be a fair fight, and even then I wasn't sure I would have much of an advantage.

"Well, Lomax," asked Frank, "you gonna stay or ride on?"

"If you don't have anything for me to do at your place, I'd just as well stay."

Frank turned and pointed to the posthole diggers and the pile of fence posts. "Brewer wants a pen where he can keep an eye on the horses instead of having to hobble them or let them run loose."

"Show me where he wants it," I replied.

"Right up against the cabin," Frank explained, "so Apaches or Jesse Evans and his gang can't get close without someone hearing."

"Hell, if Gauss is the only one around, we better pen them up in the choza where he can hear and see them."

Frank laughed, but Gauss didn't think it was too funny. He stared at me through squinted eyes. "Vouldn't be any kin to Gadrich Lomax, vould you?"

Frank shook his head as he walked to the end of the cabin and stepped off the perimeter of the pen. "Think you and Billy can set the fence posts in this rocky ground?"

I nodded. "We can."

Frank moved for his horse. "I'd best be getting back to my place. If you don't get work here, both of you are welcome to stay with me. Cousin George can even take one of you on, if you can stand his fiddle playing in the evening."

"Obliged," I said as Frank mounted.

He rode out to Billy, who was setting up another string of tin cans. "I'm leaving," Frank said. "Lomax knows what to do. If you work hard, maybe Brewer and the Englishman will hire you."

"Nobody's ever given me a paying job before."

"I would if I could, Kid, you know that. Maybe the Englishman with all his money can do you better."

"Obliged for what you did, Frank, all except the fleas."

Frank nodded, then rode on. Both the Kid and I watched him until he topped the hill. Then Billy went back to practicing his shooting and I picked up the posthole digger and began to bite out chunks of earth to start the corral.

After a couple hours I had but two done; the rocky ground was slowing me down like lameness slows down a horse. The Kid kept wasting ammunition at targets that didn't shoot back. About midafternoon I heard him summon Gauss. Then he fetched his Winchester from his horse and disappeared afoot. He returned an hour before sundown with a wild turkey that Gauss took to dressing and cooking. We had a meal of fried turkey breast and boiled beans. After supper the Kid fetched a dog-eared deck of cards, planning to while away a little time before turning in. He asked Gauss for a candle or lamp, but Gauss explained that the Englishman provided him with neither.

A man who wouldn't provide his hands with candles was not a man I wanted to call boss!

Chapter Ten

My joints were stiff with the cold when I awoke about dawn. Gottfried Gauss was snoring in German, and Billy was curled up on the other side of the stove. The fire that had kept us warm the first half of the night had died long ago—the stove was as cold as a cast-iron corpse—but I didn't complain. As long as the stove stayed cold Gauss couldn't brew any coffee.

I arose and stretched my arms and shook my legs. I rubbed my hands together, trying to thaw my fingers and get them moving again before I pulled on my boots. Then I rolled up my bedding and tossed it in the corner where Gauss was less likely to spill coffee on it. Slipping on my coat, I moved to the door, grabbed the rope handle, and pulled on it, but Gauss had barred the damn thing and it didn't give. Seemed funny to me he had secured the door when any ruffian wanting to harm us could walk up, stick a gun between logs in the wall, and put more holes in us than you could find in a Republican's logic.

With my cold, stiff fingers I lifted the bar and propped it against the wall, then pulled open the door and ambled outside. The morning sky glowed orange to the east. I glanced toward the Rio Feliz where I had hobbled Flash and saw him grazing peacefully beside a half-dozen antelope that had come to the stream to water.

If I had had a Winchester, I might have downed one for more fresh meat, but I was glad I didn't. A gunshot might have awakened Gauss and started him to making another batch of coffee.

I eased to the end of the cabin and looked at the posthole digger leaning where I had left it. I remembered the approximate dimensions Frank Coe had stepped off. There weren't enough posts there to make it work. Fencing was a problem in places like the Rio Feliz where there wasn't adequate or convenient timber to build it. A New Mexico fence would hold a stupid or old animal, but not a smart one. I called them stick fences, and that was being generous because they consisted of a post embedded in the ground every six or eight feet. Between those posts were stuck other posts, branches, and sticks, sometimes all straight but usually not; a few strands of wire were threaded around those sticks and anchored to the fence posts. These fences looked like the work of the devil.

Well, I had never known a real devil's fence until I started poking around at the far end of the post pile. I made out three large rolls of wire. It still being dark and me being ignorant, I reached down and grabbed hold of the wire. Instantly my hand felt like it had been stung by a thousand bees. I dropped that roll of wire quicker than a new convert drops sin and startled the antelopes by the creek. They trotted off as I grabbed my fingers and howled. I had just shaken hands with the devil's wire. Everyone else called it barbed wire.

"Damn!" I said. I held up my hand and saw several pricks and scratches leaking blood.

From inside, I heard Billy call. "What's a matter? You lose your pecker?" He laughed, and Gauss kept on snoring.

I dug in my coat pocket and jerked out my work gloves. I pulled them on my hands but opted not to attack that roll of wire again until I had good light and could see what I was getting into. Instead I sat on the post pile and watched the sky turn pale, then bright, as the sun topped the horizon. The sunlight cut the chill. I stood up and bravely stepped over to the three rolls of barbed wire and studied them. I was right; the devil had had a hand in making this damned stuff. Two-pronged barbs were hooked between strands of wire that were wound around each other. I shook my head, wishing I had been the devil's partner in coming up with something like this. Then I might have become rich enough to trample on the back of someone like the Englishman or Lawrence Murphy.

I left the wire lying and grabbed the posthole digger, ready to start work where I had left off the day before. Posthole digging is damn hard work, particularly in New Mexico's hard, rocky ground, and I went about it figuring the Kid would relieve me after a spell. Before I had finished the morning's first hole, I was hot and sweating. I removed my coat and tossed it on the post pile, then went back to attacking the hard earth. It took about an hour per hole, and I was on my second before Billy sauntered out.

No sooner had he emerged from the cabin than he jerked his pistol from his holster and lifted it over his head. I dropped my posthole digger as he fired the pistol in the air. The gunshot was followed by a commotion in the cabin as Gottfried Gauss bounced off his bedroll and bumped against the cast-iron stove.

"Time to get up, Gauss," Billy called as he shoved his pistol back in his holster. "Lomax wants a pot of your coffee." He laughed and ambled toward the creek and his grazing horse.

"Hold on," I said. "Where are you going?"

"To the stream, maybe look for a little game."

"Hell, I ain't doing all the work, Kid."

"Hunting's work."

"Then I'll do the hunting and you dig the postholes."

Billy grinned. "You're better digging postholes, and you'd waste too much ammunition hunting."

"Waste ammunition?" I yelled. "Hell, Kid, you've burned more powder on target practice since I've known you than was spent during the War Between the States."

"That's not wasting."

I shrugged. "Then I'm not working."

Billy looked at me like I had kicked his first puppy. He stroked his chin, then nodded. "Maybe you're right."

My face must have mirrored my shock, especially when Billy moved toward the pile of posts. He took one, then marched to the nearest hole and dropped the post inside.

"Wait a minute," I called. "You put it in upside down."

Billy shot me a wide-eyed look, then scratched his chin. "It's a damn post. One end's as good as the other."

Now, I knew better than that. I had grown up in Arkansas, where trees meant you had all the lumber you needed to build a good, solid rail fence. I had probably fallen out of more trees than Billy had ever seen, and I knew it was bad luck to put a post in upside down. I shook my head. "No, it's not. The end that grew closest to the ground needs to be planted in the ground."

"This some of your Arkansas folderol?"

"It's bad luck if you don't do it."

"Hell, Lomax, is that all your kin do back in Arkansas, think up nonsense like that? What the hell difference does it make if a post is planted the same way that it grew?"

"It's the difference between good luck and bad," I countered.

The Kid picked up another post and shoved it into the ground without regard to my instructions. "Damn foolishness."

I jerked the posthole digger up and thrust it into the ground, then brought out a jawful of dirt and dumped it beside the hole.

"I suppose the dirt has to go back in the same way it came out."

Shaking my head, I raised the posthole digger as high as I could, then impaled it in the hole at my feet. As if that wasn't enough trouble, I caught a whiff of woodsmoke. "See, I told you it'd bring bad luck."

"What are you talking about?" the Kid asked.

I pointed to the cabin stovepipe. "Gauss's making coffee."

Billy's anger melted like grease in a hot skillet. His cheek took to poking out. "Then there must be something to those damn superstitions." He laughed.

He was still cackling as he picked up fence posts and placed them in every completed hole. Then he sidled over to the cabin door and leaned inside, emerging with his Winchester carbine. "I reckon I'll head on." His jaw was still quivering with laughter as he tucked the carbine under his arm and sauntered toward the stream. "Keep up the good work," he called over his shoulder.

"Sure thing," I replied, feeling pretty good about Billy until it hit me that he was going hunting just as he had planned to do and I was still stuck there digging postholes.

To make matters worse, Gauss emerged from the cabin carrying a cup of coffee for me.

"Vorking already this early, are you?" He squinted like he couldn't tell who I was.

I looked up at the sky. Early? Noon was but two hours away.

"Lomax, right?" he asked as he came close enough for me to smell his breath. He extended his right hand and offered me the cup. "The Kid said you vanted plenty of coffee. I maken you plenty, noten drinken any myself."

"Go ahead," I begged. "Drink all you want."

Gauss mumbled something that I didn't understand, it taking all my attention and courage just to stare at the vile liquid steaming in the tin cup he handed me. The way I figured it, coffee left too long in the cup was sure to eat away the tin. That thought gave me an idea. When Gauss turned around and ambled toward the cabin door,

I dumped the coffee into the hole I was digging. I gave the earth a moment to swallow that godawful concoction, then set the tin cup aside, lifted my posthole digger high, and thrust it into the hole. To my amazement, the digger seemed to slide in deeper than before. I came near pulling out three inches of moist, rocky dirt from the bottom of the hole instead of the usual one to one-and-a-half inches. With enough of the acid that Gauss called coffee, I figured I could finish the postholes by noon. The rest of the morning Gauss kept bringing me refills, and I kept pouring them down the holes, making my work and my life easier.

Near noon I heard a gunshot from upstream and figured the Kid had found game. Two postholes later I saw him approaching, an antelope carcass draped around his neck, right proud of his accomplishment.

I figured I'd get even with him by letting him plant all the posts. If he wanted to scoff at my Ozarks beliefs, I would let him test this one himself. Since the Kid had made such a mess of his own luck already, I decided not to correct any of the posts he had planted. If I just set the posts as they were, the bad luck would be his. That suited me fine.

"How was the coffee?" Billy asked as he came up.

"Better than the help I got from you," I replied.

He scowled. "I bagged us lunch, supper, and breakfast."

"When you get him gutted, you need to plant more fence posts."

"The gutting is Gauss's job, and planting the posts is yours if you don't quit giving me trouble about putting them in upside down."

I hated to do this to the Kid, but he had it coming. "You won't hear me squawking again."

He slid the antelope off his shoulders and pitched it on the ground by the door. "Gauss, there's work to be done."

The German slipped his wrinkled, scraggly face out the door and stared at Billy. "Vhat you vant?"

Billy pointed at the antelope. "Clean him."

Gauss squinted at Billy and at the antelope, then rubbed his hands together. "Long time since I had antelope." He retreated inside, returned quickly with a butcher knife, then dragged the antelope to the stream, where he gutted and skinned the carcass.

The Kid made quick work of planting the fence posts, then retreated around the back of the cabin, gathered some tins and bottles, and headed upstream for more target practice. There I was, once again, left with all the work of digging.

By the time Gauss got the antelope cleaned and cooked, it was nearer supper than lunch, so I called it a day. My shoulders and arms ached from the work, and my hand still stung from the bite of the barbed wire. I went around to the west end of the cabin and sat in the sunshine to soak up as much warmth as I could before the night cool set in. I leaned my aching back against the cabin.

Billy ambled up from the stream, surveyed my progress, and shook his head. "You've still got a lot of work to do."

"I'm out of steam, and it goes faster when there's help," I said.

"Help, hell," Billy shot back. "Gauss is cooking your meals and bringing you all the coffee you can drink, and I'm putting game on the table, sticking your posts where they belong, and guarding you."

I had an idea where he could stick those posts— sideways. "Why do I need a guard? Who'd want this damned place? It ain't worth stealing. I've seen more promising alkali flats."

The sun had disappeared behind the distant mountains when Gauss announced supper. We had fried antelope, fried potatoes, and all the coffee we could stomach. I just drank water from my canteen.

"Vhat," said Gauss, "you not drinken mein coffee?"

I pointed my fork at him. "I drank so much this morning, I'm not thirsty for more."

Billy scoffed. "Hell, Gauss, Lomax didn't drink your coffee. He poured it down his postholes."

Gauss glared at me. "Vhat he sayin's noten true, yah?"

"Billy tells more lies than a drunk Democrat." I shrugged, knowing Gauss would be watching me closely from now on to see what I did with his coffee.

I managed for the next three days to dump the coffee into postholes without him knowing. By the end of the third day I had finally finished all the postholes and was leaning against the cabin wall beside the Kid when I heard a commotion that I knew to be cattle scenting water. They came a-trampling over a far hill from the northeast and charged toward the Rio Feliz. They were bellowing and bawling, kicking up dust and tossing their heads in the air. I heard the whoops and whistles of men and counted three on horseback. One I recognized as Dick Brewer, the Englishman's foreman.

As the cattle hit the stream, about a quarter-mile below the cabin, Gauss came out, wanting to know if the noise was Apaches. I pointed downstream and he squinted. "Vhat should I be seein'?"

"A herd of cattle, Gauss, maybe four hundred head." I pushed myself up and dusted off the bottom of my britches.

Billy said, "Maybe I'll have a shot at a paying job after all."

"Why didn't you think about that before all those damn postholes were finished?" I demanded.

The Kid shrugged. "I didn't figure Brewer'd catch up with the cattle. No sense putting myself out unless it's for a sure thing."

"How many men vith the cattle?" Gauss asked.

"Three," I replied.

"And they vill vant to eaten," he said.

"We've enough food," I said.

"Yah, but vhat we lacken is plates, cups, and forks."

"One of them," Billy burst in, "can have my coffee cup."

"Mine, too," I added.

Gauss shook his head and retreated back inside, mumbling in German, which made about as much sense as his English usually did.

Billy and I were walking downstream when Brewer broke away from the other riders. He was on a different horse today.

He reined up in front of us. "Bonney and Lomax, isn't it?"

"Yep," I replied.

"Almost didn't recognize the two of you with clothes on."

"You're riding a different horse," the Kid pointed out, "so we weren't sure it was you, Brewer."

The foreman nodded. "My horse was shot out from under me, but we got the cattle back and sent the rustlers hustling to Texas. We may have lost a dozen head of cattle, but no more. What are you fellows doing here?"

"We heard the Englishman might be hiring for wages," the Kid said. "Figured if we could prove our worth, we might get hired on. We've started the corral, Lomax and me. We've got the postholes dug."

To my way of thinking Billy was giving a lot more of the credit to *we* than to *me*.

"Don't know that the Englishman needs any regular help right now, but we can pay the two of you for the fence work."

"The two of us, hell," I said. "I dug all the postholes."

"We're partners," the Kid reminded me, then pointed to the two cowhands still downstream herding the cattle. "They work for the Englishman?"

"Yes, sir," Brewer answered, twisting in his saddle to

glance at them. "John Middleton and Fred Waite. Good, dependable men."

I was close enough to see that the Kid's cheek was bulging, so I knew he was about to windy Brewer.

"So you've no room to take on a new hand or two?"

Brewer nodded. "That's about the size of it. The Englishman has more money than cattle, so he doesn't need hands here."

The Kid groaned like he was mighty disappointed and hurt, especially after all the work he'd watched me do on the fence. "Now, if something happened to one of your men, you might be able to take on a new hand, mightn't you?" He dropped his hand to his Colt and patted its butt.

Though I knew it was all a joke, I couldn't tell what Brewer thought. He sat silently astride his gelding for a moment. When he spoke, his voice was as steady as before. "The Englishman's opening a store in Lincoln. Sam Corbett's managing it. He may need some help, especially from someone who knows how to handle a gun."

Perhaps he had seen Billy's hand on the Colt; perhaps he hadn't. I don't know that it mattered. Of all the men I came to know in Lincoln County, Dick Brewer was among the best, ranking with Chisum and the Coes. He had a ranch up the Rio Ruidoso from George Coe's place and worked it as well as managed the Englishman's ranch. I never knew him to hurt anyone except in self-defense. Nor did I ever see him smile.

Brewer had bought his ranch from Lawrence Murphy, thinking Murphy had title to the land. Instead, Murphy sold him a quitclaim deed, which only meant that he agreed not to claim land that wasn't his anyway. So Brewer had a lot on his mind, what with investing muscle and sweat in a place that someone else might come along and claim.

If that wasn't enough to keep a man from smiling, Brewer was running from his past. Unlike a lot of men riding through Lincoln County, he had never committed a despicable crime, unless falling for a girl was against the law. Apparently he had fallen hard back in Wisconsin, but the young lady he courted was torn between him and his cousin. When she refused his proposal by arguing for more time to make up her mind, he quarreled with her, then up and left Wisconsin forever. He always wore a sad, forlorn look on his face, as if he could not escape the thought of the girl he'd left behind.

"Come light in the morning," Brewer told us, "I'll look at your work and see what we can do."

"That's all we can ask," Billy answered.

Brewer sniffed at the air. "I can smell Gauss's fire. I hope he's cooked enough for three more."

"Plenty of antelope," the Kid offered. "I killed another buck at the stream this morning."

"Just the thought tastes good," Brewer said. "We haven't had a hot meal in days and a filling meal in longer than that. Let me get my hands, and we'll join you shortly." He turned his gelding around and started toward the cattle.

The Kid and I headed for the cabin, which glowed from the door Gauss had opened on the stove's firebox for light.

"Tomorrow," the Kid announced, "we'll string that devil wire for Brewer. We're gonna get a job out of this, you just watch."

"Kid," I said, "for the last three days you ain't lifted a finger on that corral. Now all of a sudden you've got an urge to do a little work. What's the difference?"

"You couldn't hire me," Billy replied. "Brewer can."

"What makes you think he'd hire a guy that's threatened to kill one of his hands? He's probably out there now telling Middleton and Waite not to turn their backs on you."

"I was pulling his leg, Lomax."

"Brewer doesn't know that for sure."

"You worry too much, Lomax."

"You don't think enough, Kid. Why do you practice shooting all the time, if you don't plan on killing someone?"

The Kid grabbed my arm. I stopped and turned to face him. "I plan on surviving, that's why. That makes more sense to me than worrying whether I put a fence post wrong ways in the hole. I plan on taking care of myself and my friends, if it comes to it. If you were in trouble, I'd kill to help you. Folks that are decent with me, I'm decent with them."

I had to admit I was flattered by Billy's willingness to defend me, but I didn't understand it. "Why? You're always arguing about everything I say or do."

"I just jaw a lot. You argue yourself. Anyway, I figure we've got jobs here with Brewer after he sees all the work we've done for the Englishman."

"Don't you mean all the work *I've* done?"

Billy released my arm and laughed. "You're arguing again."

I just shook my head. "One thing, Kid—I don't figure on working for no Englishman."

"An Englishman's money'll spend just as good as an American's."

"Maybe so, but it's just a feeling I've got. You said you wouldn't work for Murphy because he was a crook. I feel the same way about the Englishman."

"This ain't more of your Arkansas folderol, is it, like those damn fence posts? You and your damn superstitions."

I started for the cabin, grumbling over my shoulder. "You can say that's a superstition all you want, but it's true."

"I always heard it was bad luck to pour coffee in a posthole," Billy called after me, then laughed.

I ignored Gauss's muddled greeting when I entered the cabin and angled for my bedroll and saddle in the corner. I pulled my tin plate and cup from my saddle-bags, then marched to the table and placed them at an empty spot.

"Vhat you diden is good," Gauss announced.

The cabin was warm with the fire in the stove's belly. Gauss had already placed a skillet filled with fried antelope on the table. He followed that with a kettle of beans, a pot of boiled potatoes, and a pan of biscuits. Some cream gravy would've made the meal near perfect, but for a land that had so many cattle, New Mexico Territory had very few milk cows. The Kid barged in and just stared at me for a minute; then I saw his cheek begin to bulge. He threatened me like I had never been threatened before by grabbing a rag, picking up Gauss's coffeepot, and pouring me a cup.

I could've spit, but I held back because Brewer marched in with two men behind him. They carried their saddles, tack, bedrolls, and carbines and tossed them in the corner near my belongings.

Brewer introduced Billy and me to John Middleton and Fred Waite. Middleton was a big, strapping Texan with a strong handshake. Waite was part Chickasaw Indian, with curly black hair and a thick drooping mustache that dominated his face. He looked meaner than a barrel full of rattlesnakes, but he was actually a college graduate. Middleton and Waite took to Billy right off but seemed a bit reserved with me.

"Geten your plates from your saddlebags," Gauss ordered.

The newcomers obliged. We all crowded around the table and tore into the food, the sound of our spoons and forks against the tin plates the only noise for a while. I noticed Waite staring, and finally he pointed his knife at me.

"You any relation to Gadrich Lomax?"

"No," Billy and I answered in unison.

Chapter Eleven

We spent the next two days on the Englishman's ranch working in the daytime, and all six of us cramped into that drafty cabin at night. John Middleton and Fred Waite were decent fellows and hard workers. I figured the Kid could learn some good work habits from them, but he was too busy staying busy whenever Brewer was around. He could've made a good hand if he'd just stayed at it, but whenever Brewer was out of sight, he slacked off.

The first day we set the fence posts, wedging them in place with rocks until they stood straighter than a preacher's pecker in a whorehouse. Though Billy didn't pull as much work as the rest of us, he was always jawing about something. At least that took the monotony out of our work.

When Billy marched to the river to heed nature's call, Brewer commented, "He's a talker, but he don't let it interfere with his work, I'll say that for him."

I couldn't help but agree. "I've never seen a fellow work so hard when the boss was around," I said. Middleton and Waite gave me wide, knowing grins.

After lunch—no coffee for me—all of us except Gauss set out to string that damned devil wire. It was like handling thorns on a string. We couldn't as much as unroll it without cutting our hands or snagging our britches, and once we got it unrolled, we didn't know how to stretch it, not having the wire pullers we needed. My pa always told me that any job was simple as long as you had the right tools. Besides the tools we lacked the fencing smarts necessary to stretch the wire. Brewer yelled to Gauss and instructed him to bring out hammer and nails to tack the wire to the posts.

Gauss obliged, but he wasn't satisfied with his meager contribution to our work, so he shuffled inside and returned momentarily with the coffeepot in one hand and tin cups in the other. "Vhat abouten some coffee?"

"Not me," I said, rubbing my stomach. "I had plenty for lunch."

"You didn't drink any coffee," Billy interrupted. "I think you don't care much for Gauss's coffee."

"Vhat is this? Not liken mein coffee?"

My pa always told me to tell the truth, but he'd never had Gauss's coffee. I'd lie, cheat, or kill—the Kid especially, for bringing it up—not to have to take another sip of his vile brew. I figured I'd get even with Billy later. At the moment, though, I had to fend off Gauss. "Best coffee I ever drank, but a man can only take so much of a good thing. Let Billy have my share."

Billy passed up on the offer, being no more eager to destroy his innards than I was to destroy mine. He waved Gauss away, but the cook made the rounds, stopping in front of Brewer, then Middleton and Waite, making each the same offer. Then he retreated to the cabin, grumbling that nobody liked his coffee and his cooking.

Once we'd escaped Gauss's coffee, the barbed wire didn't seem nearly as threatening. Middleton, Waite, and I grabbed a strand of wire and stretched it out along the fence line while Brewer nailed it to the first post.

"Help them," Brewer ordered.

"I don't have any gloves," Billy answered.

"Neither do I," Brewer replied.

Middleton, Waite, and I stopped unrolling the devil wire and just watched, our arms crossed over our chests.

"I gotta protect my hands," Billy answered.

Brewer gave him a blank look. "A man's gotta use his hands to work. No way around it, Kid."

Billy nodded. "I don't want my gun hand cut up."

"We ain't planning on shooting you, Kid," Brewer replied. "So hammer the wire to the posts."

The Kid grimaced.

"It's that," said Brewer, "or the four of us will pin you flat and pour a pot of Gauss's coffee down your throat."

With a sheepish grin Billy stepped forward and took the hammer from Brewer's hand. Gingerly the rest of us grabbed the devil wire between barbs and gently tugged, then pulled as we became confident we wouldn't cut our hands. We stretched and nailed wire to two posts without drawing blood. On the next post, though, as we pulled the devil wire taut, Billy drew back the hammer. He swung at the post but missed, striking the wire instead, the sudden jolt loosening our grip. As the wire slid through our hands, we screamed and cursed. It cut Brewer's hand, nicked Waite's thumb, and snagged on Middleton's gloves and mine, pricking our palms.

"Damnation!" I shouted at Billy as we grabbed our hands. "All that target practice and you can't hit a post."

"This devil wire's gonna kill us," Brewer growled, licking the bloody cut along his hand.

The Kid wasn't proud of his accident and shrugged. "You sure you need this fence, Brewer?"

I kicked at the strand of wire and it struck back, snagging my britches leg at the calf and biting into me. I stormed away from the wire and into the cabin, cursing all the way. Bending by the cast-iron stove, I shoved my hand into the woodbox and pulled out a dull hatchet and four pieces of wrist-thick wood.

When I emerged outside, the Kid's eyes went wide as they focused on the hatchet. He wasn't afraid—I never saw the Kid fearful of anything or anybody—just surprised. "I didn't mean no harm."

I looked from him to Brewer. "I'm not gonna let this damn devil wire whip us," I said.

Brewer shook his head. "Burning it won't help."

"If the damn Englishman had bought us some pliers or wire stretchers we could've been done by now," I said, "but I'm not letting the devil wire *or* the Englishman whip us."

As I squatted, Brewer, Waite, and Middleton edged toward me, their curiosity afire.

"What you thinking?" Waite asked.

"I'm thinking I'm gonna chop the head off the next person that asks me a question." I waved the hatchet over my head and they retreated a step, looking at me with newfound respect.

I dropped the four sticks of wood, picked one up and stood it on end, then lifted the hatchet and impaled it in one end of the stick. I pounded the piece of wood against another until it split down the middle. As I grabbed another and lifted the hatchet over my head, I said, "I'd let Billy do this, but then we might have to change his name to One Hand Billy." The hatchet bit into the wood, and I quickly split it in half. I repeated the operation with the two remaining lengths of wood. Finished with the hatchet, I tossed it at the cabin door; Billy jumped out of the way, though the hatchet didn't pass any closer than eight inches to his shoulder.

"Watch out," he cried, shaking the hammer at me.

I tossed the matching halves of firewood to Brewer, Middleton, and Waite, but they stood there looking blank and let the pieces fall at their feet.

"What the devil's gotten into you?" cried Brewer. "What's this for?"

Taking the halves of the last piece of firewood, I stood up, a piece in each hand. "Wire pullers," I said.

"Huh?" said Brewer.

Waite looked at me dumber than a lunatic under a full moon. Middleton bent over and picked up his wood as I stepped to the wire lying limp at our feet. I slipped one piece of wood under and its twin over the wire, then wrapped a hand around each end of the reassembled stick and slid the wooden twins along the wire until they snagged on a barb. Tightening my hands on this homemade handle, I pulled on the devil wire. It went taut quicker than a drunk takes to the bottle.

"Wire handles," I announced in triumph.

"Well, I'll be damned," Brewer said.

Middleton and Waite stood dumbstruck at my genius.

"Hit the wire with your hammer," I commanded the Kid.

He hesitated.

"Do it," I said.

Billy lifted his arm and took a swipe at the wire but missed, drawing snickers from the others.

"Hit it this time," I commanded.

Billy drew back and gave it a good lick, but my handle clung to the wire like manure sticks to a boot.

Middleton stepped behind me and clamped his handle over the wire, and then Brewer and Waite did the same. Together we pulled, stretching that wire farther than a miser stretches a nickel.

Billy hammered away, and we quickly had the first of four strands of wire strung around the corral. When Billy saw that nobody's hands were in danger of being cut again, he traded the hammer for Brewer's wire pullers and let the foreman do the nailing. My system worked slicker than goose droppings as we put up a second and third strand.

When we took a breather before starting the top strand, Brewer walked over and congratulated me. "I don't know what we'd've done if you hadn't figured this out."

"Probably bled to death," I replied.

Billy gave me a cockeyed grin. "You wouldn't've thought of it if I hadn't missed the post and hit the wire."

"Wouldn't have had to," I shot back.

"Come on," Brewer said, "let's get this top strand hung, and we'll call it a day."

We pitched together, four of us muscling the wire taut while Brewer tacked it to the post. We made it around the rectangle of fence posts quickly. When we were done, we all dropped our handles and stood there with our hands on our hips, admiring our work. We were damn proud. The wire was tight, the fence sturdy, and the corral a barbed-wire beauty, the first any of us had ever seen.

There was just one problem—we had forgotten to leave a gate. The smiles on Brewer's face and mine disappeared faster than cookies within reach of a schoolboy. I cursed and Brewer began to laugh. The others looked around, shrugging their ignorance and gesturing for us to let them in on the secret.

"The gate," Brewer said.

"Huh?" answered Middleton.

"There ain't one," I explained.

Then Middleton, Waite, and the Kid began to laugh.

We had a fine corral, but it was no more useful than a book to a blind man. This being the first barbed-wire corral any of us had ever seen, we were on our own to figure out how to make a gate.

Brewer turned to me. "You came up with the wire handles—now figure us out a gate."

I scratched my head and took to thinking. "Give me a little time—alone—to think on it."

They ambled away, though I saw them glancing over their shoulders at me. I strode back and forth beside the corral, wishing I had seen a barbed-wire fence somewhere before. I wasn't having much luck until Gauss emerged from the cabin with a pan of potatoes and a knife and ambled to the Rio Feliz.

I stood watching as he skinned those potatoes for supper. The way the skin peeled back stuck with me, though I didn't quite know why. Then I began to think not about making a gate as much as peeling back that fence. Then it struck me. "Yee-haw!" I shouted, clapping my hands.

The other four came trotting over with wide grins on their faces.

"What did you come up with, Lomax?" asked Brewer.

"A gate that just peels away," I said.

It didn't make sense to them, but I didn't know if I could explain it. Instead I issued orders. "Kid, grab one of those extra fence posts and chop off the end so it's no taller than one that's sticking out of the ground."

Billy hesitated.

"Do what he says," Brewer told him.

Billy skulked away.

I pointed at the fence. "I figure we'll put the gate in the corner where we've got extra wire."

Middleton and Waite scratched their heads and stared blankly at me, though Brewer seemed amused.

Billy grumbled as he chopped on the fence post. "Am I whittling on the good luck or bad luck end?"

I ignored the question and took to unnailing the four strands of wire on the corner post. "Brewer, cut me a piece of devil wire about three feet long."

Brewer grabbed a loose end of wire and dragged it over to Billy. Borrowing the hatchet a moment, he laid the wire across the post Billy was shortening. In one powerful swing he hoisted the hatchet and cut the double strand, then handed the hatchet back to Billy.

"Now," I told Brewer, "unravel the two strands of devil wire and remove the barbs so I have two pieces."

While he separated the two strands, I worked on freeing the remaining lengths of barbed wire from the corner post. By the time I had removed the last strand, Billy was standing beside me with the shortened post. I took it and stood it up a couple inches from the corner post.

"Hold it there," I commanded Billy, then turned to Waite. "Hand me the bottom strand of wire."

Waite picked it up carefully and offered it to me. I looped it around the foot of the shortened post, then held out my hand to Brewer. "Give me one length of wire."

Brewer laid a single strand in my palm. I knelt down and wrapped a double loop around the foot of both the corner post and the shortened post Billy held. I twisted the ends of the wire together so the loop would hold, then nailed it to the corner post about three inches off the ground.

"Now I see," said Brewer, handing me the second strand of wire. "Pretty smart."

I made another double loop of wire around the top of the corner post, then nailed it in.

Waite said, "Good damn idea, Lomax."

I was rather proud of myself, though I didn't admit to Gauss's contribution to my innovation.

"I ain't seen a gate yet," said Middleton.

"Me neither," said the Kid.

Waite had already figured out what I was doing, so he picked up the top strand of barbed wire and offered it to me. I looped it around the post Billy was holding, then pulled it tight. Brewer picked up the hammer and quickly nailed the wire in place. To make it extra strong, I looped the barbed wire around the free post a couple times and had Brewer secure it with another nail. We affixed the bottom strand to the freestanding post as well, the twin loops at the top and bottom of the post going taut from the pressure.

Billy released his grip and backed away. Quickly Brewer and I nailed the two middle strands in place, then stood back and admired my invention.

"How's it work?" asked Middleton.

Brewer motioned for me to demonstrate.

"It requires more muscle than brain." I leaned up against the shortened post, shoving it toward the solid corner post. My effort stretched the barbed wire just enough that I could lift the wire loop over the head of the free post. Freed of the top loop, the wire gate went limp, and I simply lifted it out of the bottom loop and peeled the fence away.

"I say you're damn smart," Brewer announced.

I was inclined to agree with him, though I could tell the Kid still had his doubts or was just plain envious.

Brewer took the loose end from me and toted it back to the corner post. He slid the foot of the post back into the bottom loop, then pushed the top toward the anchor post until he could drop the top loop over it. When he released the loose post, it stood as straight as a tin soldier.

Crossing my arms over my chest, I stood there prouder than a kitten with its first mouse.

"Tonight," announced Brewer, "we can pen our horses."

"If we just put a cover over the top of the corral," I said, pointing to the cabin, "the horses would have better quarters than we've got."

Brewer laughed. "Maybe we should put Gauss to chinking the place before it gets any colder."

The rest of us all nodded.

"Well," Brewer announced, "I've got a trip to make to Lincoln day after tomorrow. I'm taking Lomax and Billy with me to attend to a little business and celebrate the new fence."

"Why don't we go tomorrow?" the Kid asked.

Brewer shook his head. "I need the two of you to help me work the cattle, but that's tomorrow. I think we've done enough for today. Let's wash up and wait for Gauss to feed us."

The Kid, Middleton, and Waite ambled toward the Rio Feliz to wash up, but I stayed behind to gather the hatchet, hammer, and nails.

Brewer watched the three others walk to the stream. "You'd be my choice if the Englishman wants to take on another man, Lomax."

"I don't want to work for the Englishman. Take the Kid."

"He's not as hard and smart a worker as you."

"I ain't as charming as he is."

The ranch foreman nodded. "He's as happy as a schoolboy with a sack full of candy."

"And his tongue wags at both ends," I added. "He'd be a damned good hand if he's interested in work as much as target practice."

"I noticed the empty hulls and broken bottles he's drilled."

"He's damned good at it, better than any trick shot I ever saw."

Brewer scratched his chin. "Way things are going in Lincoln County, we may need some hands who are good with guns."

"Billy's your man, not me."

I could tell by his clouded look that he had his doubts.

After we finished putting our tools inside, the two of us went down to the stream and washed up. "Why is it," I asked, "that the Englishman'll put a few men out here to do his work and not provide them a candle or a lamp for a little light?"

Brewer grimaced. "A lot of the Englishman's money is going into his store in Lincoln. He's up against the House, and that's costly."

"And dangerous."

We followed the other three back up to the cabin. The aroma of Gauss's woodsmoke announced that supper wasn't long off.

"If the Englishman's putting so much into his store," I asked, "is he paying wages regularly?"

By Brewer's pause I knew the Englishman was behind in what he owed his men. That convinced me more than ever that I didn't want anything to do with the damn foreigner.

"He's overdue two months," Brewer admitted, "but I trust he'll pay us."

"He don't sound much better than the House."

Brewer considered that remark carefully. "He's not stealing cattle nor hiring bad men like Murphy."

"When he's not paying his men, it's the same as stealing from them."

Stopping in his tracks, Brewer turned and faced me straight on. "He's our only chance at breaking the hold Lawrence Murphy and the House have on Lincoln County. John Chisum is a rich man, but he doesn't see this as his battle because he can stand on his own two feet. The rest of us need the contracts the House controls, if we're ever to make a go of it. If we don't give the Englishman a little slack, we don't stand a chance." His pained grimace was that of a man who was running out of options, a man who believed in right but saw wrong in charge of his destiny.

I could only nod. "I hope you're right, Brewer."

He grabbed my arm. "Don't talk about it in front of the others. I don't want them getting the wrong idea. The Englishman's bound to pay up once his new store starts bringing in money."

"I won't say a word."

We walked the rest of the way to the cabin in silence, entered, and took our seats on the benches on either side of the table. Gauss added a skillet of fried antelope to the fried potatoes and pot of beans already before us. We helped ourselves as he pulled a pan of biscuits from the stove and dropped them on the table. We ate like the tired men we were, not being too critical of the food as long as there was plenty of it. I even managed a cup of Gauss's coffee, drawing an approving nod from the German.

After supper we ambled outside, Gauss and Waite carrying our dishes down to the stream to wash them off while Brewer, Middleton, and I rounded up our hobbled mounts and led them to the corral. Like us, the horses and Flash had never encountered barbed wire before. All the horses challenged the fence, but only once. Flash, though, apparently learned from their experience and never tried to go over or through it.

As dusk changed to night, we all slipped back inside, moved the table to the wall, and stacked the benches atop it to give us room to throw down our bedrolls. We talked for a bit, then went off to sleep, hunkering up to stave off the cold night air that eventually enveloped us.

Come morning, we had a simple breakfast of cold meat between hard biscuits and as much of Gauss's coffee as we could stand. The single cup I had finished the night before had not changed my opinion of it, so I passed up the hot liquid even though it might have warmed me up a little.

After eating, all of us save Gauss gathered our saddles and tack and headed out to the corral. Flash brayed as we approached, and Billy cursed my fine steed. We opened the gate, saddled the animals, and rode out in search of the Englishman's cattle.

We found them grazing, and Brewer ordered us to separate some from the others. It was make-work, I thought, until I realized he was having me and Billy do most of the chores. He was evaluating our cowboying skills. Even astride a mule, I knew cattle and worked them better than the Kid, who had done little more than steal a few while he rode with Jesse Evans. I had done the same thing with Evans, but I had also ridden with one of the first herds leaving Texas for Dodge City back in the sixties.

The Englishman had a mixed herd of longhorns and cattle without horns—muleys, we called them. While Billy did okay around the muleys, he was a bit shy around the horned animals and wouldn't ride his horse as close as he needed to show the steer who was boss.

When Brewer got me away from Billy, he nodded. "You work cattle better, too."

"I work everything better but guns," I replied, "but I'm still not interested in working for the Englishman."

Brewer nodded. "Where'd you work cattle?"

"In Texas," I replied. "Joseph McCoy himself sent me to Texas after the war to promote Dodge City as the best place to ship cattle up north to market. I rode drag for one of the first herds to leave Texas for Dodge."

Brewer pointed to the Englishman's herd, four hundred or so head. "What do you think of his cattle?"

"Too many muleys," I said. "They don't travel well."

Brewer looked at me like I was dumber than stump water. "How can that be?"

"They don't have horns, so they crowd together more than horned cattle. When they bunch up, the heat causes them to lose more weight than the horned animals do. It may not matter on a short drive less than a hundred miles, but on a long drive when the grazing's poor, those lost pounds cost you money on the hoof."

"Can't afford to lose any more money," Brewer answered. He knew farming better than cattle, but he listened and he learned. By midafternoon we were riding back toward the cabin, ready for a hot meal, even if we had to wash it down with Gauss's coffee. We arrived an hour before sunset, unsaddled our mounts, and watered and penned them. We washed up ourselves, then retreated to the cabin for a pot of antelope stew that Gauss had cooked in our absence.

"Get up and fix us a good breakfast in the morning, Gauss," commanded Brewer. "After that I want you, Middleton, and Waite to start chinking the cabin."

The three men groaned.

"Me, Lomax, and the Kid are starting for Lincoln tomorrow."

Chapter Twelve

Lincoln was a town so sleepy that a rooster the size of the moon couldn't have roused it from slumber. When I first laid eyes on it, I couldn't believe a town so slow and so small could be so important to a quarter of New Mexico Territory.

"That's it?" I said in disbelief.

Dick Brewer nodded.

"It ain't Santa Fe, but it ain't bad," said the Kid. He had the look of a rutting buck about him.

I could only shake my head. "Anywhere there's señoritas ain't bad, ain't that right, Kid?"

Billy nodded as we rode west along the Rio Bonito valley and into Lincoln, which sprang up between the river's south bank and the line of mountains to the south. I'd seen a lot of important towns in my travels, but never one that was so lifeless. I guessed there were maybe five hundred residents, mostly Mexicans, making their homes in the adobes and pole jacales scattered on either side of a single dusty road that ran for a mile from one end of town to the other and then on to Fort Stanton to the west.

Even though it was midafternoon, the air was brisk with the breath of approaching winter and fragrant with the pinyon smoke that hung like a veil over the town. More chickens, dogs, goats, and hogs roamed the streets than men, women, or horses. A few Mexican kids played beside one of the primitive jacales, stopping briefly to watch us pass and then resuming their games. Down the street I heard the sounds of hammering and saw men working on a covered porch for a new adobe building.

Brewer pointed to a small log cabin with small gunports cut in the side. "That's the jail where they're keeping Jesse Evans."

The Kid drew up on his reins. "I figure I should howdy Jesse."

Brewer shook his head. "You don't want folks to think you're in with him, do you?"

Billy grinned. "I want Jesse to think that. There's not a man in Lincoln County I don't think I can beat with a gun, but Jesse'd come closer than any other to being that man."

"Suit yourself," Brewer replied, then looked at me. "I'm gonna visit the Englishman at his store. You want to come along?"

I preferred a down-to-earth crook to an arrogant foreigner. "I'll stick with the Kid."

Brewer nodded and pointed to the new adobe with the laborers around it. "I'll meet you there when you're done."

Billy and I aimed our mounts toward the jail, about thirty feet off the road. At the hitching post, we dismounted and tied our mounts, then stepped up to the building.

"Jesse," Billy called, "how you doing?" He peeked into one porthole, me into another.

I heard Jesse's voice, but it seemed far away.

Billy shoved on the plank door, and to our surprise, it swung open and banged against the wall. The room was empty except for a small desk, a chair, and a coal-oil lamp. One wall was almost covered with wanted posters.

"Hello," Billy called again.

"What the hell is going on?" came Jesse's voice, muffled as if it was seeping from hell.

Billy pointed to a corner of the wooden floor, where I saw an iron grate with a padlock latching it to the thick plank flooring. We eased over and squinted into a dark hole. I made out a flickering candle at the bottom of a ten-foot pit and saw the forms of four men, clinging to the darkness like roaches.

"Is that you, Kid?" called Jesse Evans.

"Yep. I came to see how a gopher lives."

"Well, hell, Kid, if you ain't gonna bust me out, why don't you come down here and take a closer look?" Jesse replied. "It's about time you showed up."

"I brought my gang," the Kid announced. "Lomax is with me."

"Hell, Kid, then we're back to zero if he's your gang. Is Lomax still riding that damn mule?"

"Me and my mule aren't caged up," I called down the hole.

Jesse just laughed. "Jail is just a temporary home for me."

Jesse's companions—Tom Hill, Frank Baker, and Buck Morton—seemed less optimistic about their predicament. They had frowns longer than the Pecos.

"You coming to rescue us, Kid, or you just wanting us to think you are?" Hill called up from the hole.

Billy clucked his tongue and shook his head as he toed at the padlock. "You fellows aren't the most popular men in Lincoln County. Fact is, you've got fewer friends than a gelding has balls."

Jesse laughed. "You our friend or not, Billy? Toss me a gun."

"I thought when you worked for the House, you didn't need friends, that L.G. Murphy himself looked out for you," Billy shot back.

"I've wondered the same thing," Jesse acknowledged.

"Maybe he don't need any stolen cattle to fill his contracts for a while." Billy laughed.

"You gonna help us or not, Kid?" Hill persisted.

The Kid clucked his tongue again. "Here I am trying to go respectable, and you fellows are asking me to break the law. Hell, I might get a good paying job with the Englishman. What do you think of that?"

"I think you'd be working for the man that put us in this damn hole in the ground," Hill grumbled.

Billy squatted over the iron grate. "You got caught stealing his horses. Seems you should've covered your tracks better."

"Just throw us a gun, Billy. That's all you need to do." Hill stood up and reached toward us. "Just drop the gun in my hand."

Billy shook his head. "I was planning to do that, Hill, but dammit if the sheriff ain't coming for us."

I thought it was a bluff but caught my breath when I looked through the open door and saw William Brady approaching with a shotgun leveled at us.

"Get away from there," he yelled, wiggling the barrel of the shotgun at us.

My broad experience had taught me exactly how to handle that type of confrontation. "Yes, sir," I replied and retreated.

Slowly Billy stood up, careful to keep his hands clear of his Colt so the sheriff would not mistake any movement for a threat.

"Dammit, Kid," said Brady, "what're you doing, trying to break the boys out?"

Without hesitation Billy nodded. "Yes, sir, I sure was, but you're such a fine lawman I just never got the chance."

I heard guffaws from the men in the pit.

"Did you give them a gun, Billy?"

The Kid shook his head. "I've only got one and I'm keeping it."

"He's telling the truth," I said.

Brady eyed us suspiciously, then lowered his shotgun toward our knees. "Back into the corner now while I decide whether to put you in the hole with the others."

"Now, Sheriff," Billy began, "you wouldn't want to do that." He eased into the corner, and we stood there with our hands uplifted.

I figured it was all a bluff on the sheriff's part, or he would've disarmed us. I felt pretty good until he lowered his shotgun to the desk and lit the lamp. Instantly I caught my breath. Tacked to the wall was a wanted poster with my name on it: WANTED FOR MURDER: H. H. LOMAX. $500 REWARD. SHERIFF OF LEADVILLE, COLORADO.

It seemed like that poster stood out among all the others. Besides the shock of seeing my name in big letters, I was also surprised by the value they placed on me. Five hundred dollars for killing a two-bit attorney would've been a nice reward had they given it to me for bettering society instead of placing the price upon my head.

Billy saw the poster as well. "Get it when you can," he whispered.

"What are you two whispering about?" Brady said, picking up the shotgun again. "I know you've both ridden with him, so I've gotta think you're here to spring him from jail."

Billy nodded and held his index finger up to his mouth, then pointed to the pit. The sheriff motioned for us to come closer. We slipped around the desk until we stood beside him and within reach of the wanted posters.

"Wasn't planning on it, Sheriff, though I don't want Jesse to know that," Billy whispered so low that the sheriff couldn't hear him. Brady leaned closer to him, and he repeated his answer.

Quickly I lifted my hand and jerked the poster from the wall, coughing to disguise the sound of the rustling paper. I shoved the poster in my britches behind my back.

Turning to me, Brady eyed me suspiciously. "Same go for you, uh, uh . . ."

"Lomax," I answered, "and yes."

The sheriff seemed momentarily distracted. "Lomax . . . Where have I heard that name before?"

"I was with Jesse one day when you had a steak with us."

His face wrinkled as he scratched his head. "Nope, not that. I thought I saw your name before." He turned to look at the wall, now missing my poster. "I don't remember where it was." He shook off his concern, then addressed us sternly. "If I see you boys around here again, I'll figure you're planning to help them escape and I'll arrest you. Understood?"

"Yes, sir," I said.

"Understood," the Kid replied.

"Good," the sheriff said. "Now get out of here."

Billy and I escaped outside, where we untied our mounts and led them down the street. I retrieved the wanted poster, folded it, and slipped it into my pocket. We had barely stepped away from the sheriff's office when the Kid let out a low whistle.

"Five-hundred-dollar reward for murder. I didn't realize you were such a mean one, Lomax."

I shrugged. "It was just a lawyer."

Billy cocked his head and pursed his lips, disbelief as thick on his face as maggots on a carcass. "I never figured a man that rode a mule would be a killer. How'd you do it?"

"I don't know. I'd been drinking. What I heard was I shot him in the back."

"Best way! Saves you from dodging his bullets."

I wasn't keen on telling too much to Billy. My reputation might spread, and Sheriff Brady might come gunning for me. Or worse, every snot-nosed kid who wanted to make a name for himself might come after me. Granted, a lot of men in the West had killed bigger names than I had, but not a one had likely killed a man involved in more crimes than my victim, the lawyer.

I didn't care to talk about it anymore, so I mounted Flash and nudged him to a trot down Lincoln's street. Billy jumped on his stallion and rode after me. We passed the torreón, a twenty-foot-high, circular stone tower with gunports, built more than a decade earlier when Apaches were more of a problem.

Next we passed the Englishman's store, an impressive adobe building with iron shutters and a long porch still going up. It seemed to me the building was designed to serve not only as a store but also as a fortress. A head-high adobe wall abutted the building on both sides and made a huge corral out back. Except for the porch, the store looked finished.

About twenty-five yards down, on the same side of the road, we passed another adobe building, this one with a picket fence around it. The U-shaped building was the biggest house in Lincoln and, as I was to learn, the home of a lawyer. I noticed a comely red-haired woman staring at me as I rode by.

A little farther down the road, we passed the Wortley Hotel. It offered decent rooms and decent meals for a decent price. The Wortley, like the other major structures in Lincoln, stood on the north side of the road. Just beyond it, on the opposite side of the street, stood the store of Lawrence G. Murphy—the House.

It was a huge, double-story adobe structure, over a hundred feet long and designed to withstand an attack by Apaches or unhappy patrons. Besides the horses switching their tails at the hitching rail, the only sign of activity was a man sitting on the front porch whittling. Seeing us approach, he got up and marched inside.

"Care for a drink in the House?" the Kid offered.

"I'm broke, can't afford it."

Billy laughed. "I'm buying."

We added our mounts to the string at the hitching rail, then went inside. The wooden floors creaked beneath our booted feet, and the noise seemed to echo off the tall, thick walls with eleven-foot ceilings. A clerk stared silently at us. For all I had heard about the House, I was shocked by the scanty merchandise. "This is it?"

Billy nodded and turned to an adjacent room, where I could hear the voices of several men. He motioned for me to follow him, and together we entered the saloon. A dozen men stopped what they were doing and stared at us until Billy headed for the bar.

The man behind the bar wore an expensive suit and bow tie. He had a high forehead and a close-trimmed mustache that met at the corner of his lips with a narrow, close-cropped beard. He was narrow between his bloodshot eyes, too, a sure sign that he was not trustworthy.

"Care for a drink, lads?" he said, his Irish brogue as thick as his eyebrows.

"Give my partner a glass of beer," Billy said. "For me, just some coffee."

The man behind the bar drew me a glass of beer from a barrel at the end of the counter, then slid it down the bar to me. He stepped to a corner stove where a coffeepot rested, poured Billy a cup, then returned to us holding his hand outstretched. "That'll be a dollar."

I almost spit out my teeth. "A dollar for a single glass of beer and a cup of coffee? Let me speak to the owner."

The man behind the bar grinned, then thrust out his chest as he hooked his fingers in his suspenders. "I'm the owner. L.G. Murphy's the name. Freight costs make things more expensive in Lincoln." He offered me a big smile, like he owned half the county, which he did. "Take your business elsewhere, lads, because I don't need your dollar, but if you ever come back I'll add the dollar to whatever you buy. Fact is, lads, everybody that does business for long in Lincoln County does it with L.G. Murphy."

Billy counted out coins enough to pay for our drinks and slapped them on the bar. "I'm buying the drinks."

Murphy snatched the money and slid it into his pants pocket. "Well, lad," he said, leaning over the bar toward me, "your back'd really be bowed if you was spending your own money, but I do admire a man that spends another man's money."

I could smell the liquor on his breath, and I had to

admit it did smell better than Gauss's coffee. I took a sip of beer.

"I'm Irish, you know," he said to me. "There was a time when I could outdrink and outfight any four men in New Mexico Territory. I can still outdrink them, but the fighting I leave to my men." He gave a sweep of his arm, and I looked over my shoulder long enough to see a half-dozen men staring at me with gazes hard enough to cut diamonds.

I realized Murphy was trying to bait me so his men would have an excuse to work me over, but Billy came to my rescue.

"You don't want to mess with Lomax," he said.

Behind me I heard several chairs suddenly scrape against the floor as those hardcases rose.

Murphy's narrow-spaced eyes seemed to move even closer together. "You any kin to a son of a bitch named Gadrich Lomax?" There was enough venom in his voice to poison every stray animal in Lincoln.

"This here's Henry Lomax from Arkansas," Billy announced. "He's no kin to Gadrich, who's a damn Yankee."

Murphy glared at Billy. "I fought for the Yankees back during the War of Insurrection. Damn proud of it, too."

Billy lifted his finger and pointed at me. "Even if Henry was kin to Gadrich, you wouldn't want to tangle with him."

"Why the hell not?" Murphy asked.

"Because he's a killer," Billy announced.

I wanted to haul off and knock those buckteeth down his throat.

Murphy eyed me suspiciously, then nodded to one of the men. I looked around and recognized the fellow who had been whittling on the front porch when we arrived.

"He came in riding a mule. A killer don't ride no mule unless he's touched in the head."

Billy didn't let up. "Just shows you how unpredictable he is. He don't look like no killer, but with a gun he can drop men faster than a whore can drop her drawers." He nudged me with his elbow. "Show him the poster."

Damnation, I thought. Here the Kid was promoting me as a killer and increasing the chances that someone, either the sheriff or one of Murphy's hardcases, would try to kill me. I hesitated.

"Show him the poster," Billy insisted.

My hand fell to my pocket, and I removed the flyer and showed it to Murphy.

Much to my surprise, he seemed genuinely impressed that I was a wanted man. He grabbed the paper from my hand and held it up for his men to see. "Five hundred dollars ain't bad for a reward."

I shrugged, then took another swig of beer, figuring I would finish my expensive drink and get out of the House.

Murphy returned my wanted poster and made me an offer. "You like to work for me? I'm gonna need some hard men to drive the Englishman out of business."

"I'll think on it," I said, anxious to leave before one of Murphy's men decided he wanted to try to collect the reward.

The Kid, though, just couldn't shut up. "Lomax killed a lawyer."

"Did he now?" Murphy grew more interested. "Does he specialize in lawyers, or does he just do them on occasion?"

"Whenever the opportunity arises." The Kid laughed.

Murphy didn't bat an eye or crack even the hint of a smile. "We've a lawyer here that needs killing worse than any you murdered. A damned Scotchman named Alexander McSween."

Now I was really getting nervous. The Kid was digging a hole it was going to be tough to get out of. I glared at him as I tucked the wanted poster back in my britches, then glanced over my shoulder to see that most of Murphy's men had sat back down.

"You've got enough men to do the job," I said. "I'd hate for them not to get the credit."

Murphy pounded the bar. "McSween owes me several thousand dollars, and he's thrown in with the bastard Englishman. We Irish hate the damned English, seeing how they starved us and throwed us out of our own land. Besides, there's even talk of John Chisum throwing in with them to create a bank here in Lincoln."

I finished my beer while Murphy insulted the Englishman and cursed all the Englishman's ancestors for poor breeding.

Billy drained his coffee cup, then nodded at Murphy. "Where might Lomax find this lawyer and this Englishman if he decides to put them out to pasture forever?"

Murphy's eyes widened with pleasure. "The Englishman's at the store they're working on down the street, and the lawyer lives in the big adobe house just this side of the Englishman's store."

The Kid nodded. "We'll check them out."

What was this *we* business? I wondered. I was ready to get out of there before I had a bigger reputation than Jesse James. I pushed myself away from the bar and turned around, angling for the door into the store. I heard Billy's creaking step on the floor behind me. We had reached the door when Murphy's voice called out after us.

"One more thing, lads," he said. "You kill the lawyer or the Englishman, and your next drink is on the house."

"Obliged," Billy called over his shoulder before we escaped.

I wanted to run, but the Kid grabbed my arm. "Not so fast."

We paused to look at the tools, then stepped outside, climbed aboard our mounts, and rode back down the street.

"Thanks a lot," I grumbled, "for bringing up my past and building me a reputation that's sure to get me killed by one of Murphy's men, if not arrested by the sheriff."

Billy didn't respond, and we rode silently until we reached the Englishman's store. We tied our mounts outside and went in.

As the door closed behind us, I saw the Englishman talking to Brewer, who stood with his back to us. "The mercantile is not yet ready for business," the Englishman said. "We open in two days."

Brewer glanced over his shoulder, then turned around. "It's okay, John. These are the two that built the corral I was telling you about." He introduced us again.

John Henry Tunstall had eyes as wide as his ambitions. Upon close inspection, I took him for a naive man, ill prepared to survive in New Mexico Territory against the likes of L. G. Murphy, Jesse Evans, and all the other human reptiles that crawled around the countryside. He strode across the room to greet us, shaking our hands vigorously. Despite his enthusiasm, he had a girlish handshake and mannerisms decidedly feminine.

"I should ask you to join us for dinner tonight," he said. "Dick and I are dining with the McSweens, a delightful couple who have been quite helpful to me." He looked around the room, which was crowded with merchandise. "Sam, Sam Corbett," he called.

A man lifted his head above a table covered with tin cans. "Yes, sir."

"Come here," Tunstall said. "See that these chaps have a decent place to spend the night and that their horses are stabled."

"Yes, sir," Corbett repeated as the Englishman turned back to Brewer.

I offered Corbett my hand, and he shook it strongly, then acknowledged the Kid. Corbett wasn't one to stand idly around. He seemed to be at a loss for words and turned back to his chores. "You boys can help."

Billy shook his head. "I ain't a storekeeper."

I didn't care. "What do you need, Sam?"

He pointed to a broom. "Sweep the floor."

Billy took up a position by the window and watched the inactivity on the street. I swept the floor, then helped Corbett move a couple tables. I had to give the Englishman credit—he knew how to stock a store. The tables were laden with merchandise, and ropes hanging from the ceiling suspended saddles as well as other leather goods. After a while I saw that Billy had sauntered over to the Englishman, who was laughing at one of his stories. I had a hard time hearing what he was saying for all the hammering on the walk.

Damnation, I thought. Here I was actually doing work while Billy did nothing except try to charm this damn foreigner. That's the way it always was with life. Some people do all the work while others, like Billy, get by on their charm or their fast tongue.

I was still helping Corbett when the Englishman, Brewer, and the Kid stepped toward the door. "We'll be back," the Englishman said.

As he reached the door, the Kid turned, tipped his sombrero, and winked at me, his cheek poking out. I grumbled to myself about the unfairness of life and work.

Two hours later it was getting dark outside, and I heard the sounds on the plank walk of men approaching and, most disgusting of all, laughing. The Kid was friendlier than a patent medicine barker and had charmed Tunstall as easily as he did all the señoritas.

As the three men walked in the door, Billy and the Englishman wore grins wider than a crescent moon, though Brewer was his usual reserved self. He grimaced at me.

"Good workday, Sam," the Englishman announced. "Suspend your chores for the day's duration."

I glanced out the window and saw there wasn't much day left. Damn generous of the Englishman.

"Obliged, Mr. Tunstall," Corbett said.

Tunstall nodded at Corbett, then looked at me as if he had forgotten I existed. I found out later he was practically blind in one eye, which might have explained his strange look.

Brewer stepped over to me and placed his hand on my shoulder, shaking his head very slowly, his lips tight. "The Englishman decided he could hire another hand, but just one. The Kid."

"I can get work other places. The Kid can't. Besides, the Englishman's a fool," I whispered.

Tunstall grinned and I thought he had heard me, but he turned to Sam Corbett. "Hired us a new chap, I have," he announced. "See that he can bed down in the back of the store outside my room."

Corbett nodded.

"I'm taking Dick and Billy Bonney to dine with the McSweens."

"What about Lomax here?" Corbett asked.

The Englishman stared blankly at Corbett for a moment. "I just told Susan that there would be two extra."

Billy stepped forward as cocky as a man with a new job. "Lomax did help build your corral and came up with a solid idea for a gate. He deserves to go."

"Then he shall, Billy. Capital idea!"

Billy winked at me, but I couldn't decide if he was letting me know he hadn't forgotten about me or if he was trying to impress me with his influence over the Englishman.

"I could use some grub," I answered.

"Grub?" mouthed the Englishman.

"It means food," replied Billy.

"Then excellent," answered Tunstall. "Come along, Lomax, and we shall dine together."

I left the store with them, and we marched next

door to the McSween place. It was the fanciest house in Lincoln and home to the only organ in all of Lincoln County. It was also the abode of the only white woman in town.

Not only was Susan McSween a gracious hostess, she was also the most dangerous woman I ever met.

Chapter Thirteen

Alexander A. McSween, or Alex, as folks called him, could say the longest blessing I ever heard. It must have been the natural windiness of a lawyer because he said more grace over that meal than I figure was said over the Last Supper. Between the time he said "Our Heavenly Father" and "Amen" I lost five pounds.

I have to admit I opened my eyes once during the prayer and saw Susan McSween staring at me. She licked her lips. I figured she was hungry for the mashed potatoes that sat on the table between us until I felt the tip of her button-up shoe against my ankle. I flinched. She smiled.

Not knowing what to do, I bowed my head again, but that didn't please her. She kicked my ankle. I glanced up and she winked at me.

I swallowed hard and hoped no one had noticed, but I saw the Kid grinning. I figured he'd start gossiping quicker than a politician could raise taxes. Of course I wasn't sure it mattered, because I doubted this prayer would ever end. When McSween finally concluded his oration to the Heavenly Host, everyone sighed with relief. The Kid was the first to say something.

"Damn good prayer, Mac."

I knew Billy didn't curse as much as most men in Lincoln County, so I figured he was funning McSween, who looked as if he had been slapped upside the head with a plucked chicken. He hem-hawed around, trying to say something.

"Ahem," started Mrs. McSween, "we don't use those kinds of words in this house, Mr. Bonney."

Right off I saw that Mrs. McSween was the backbone of that marriage. She had more ambition than her husband had courage. I figured Alex couldn't raise his flag without her permission.

"Sorry, ma'am," replied Billy. "Just that the prayer ran past my bedtime."

I tried to keep from laughing, but a grin crossed my face.

Mrs. McSween smiled at me. "My bedtime varies, depending on what I'm doing." I knew she was trying to raise my flag, but I wasn't willing, even if she was.

I tried to ignore her and observe her husband. Alex McSween was the only fellow in all of Lincoln County besides John Chisum who did not carry a sidearm. The difference was, John Chisum wasn't a coward. McSween was. He hid behind lawbooks, thinking disputes could be settled without gunfire or bloodshed. Maybe they could in Kansas City, which he had left because of his asthma, but he was in New Mexico Territory now.

Mrs. McSween set so many tongues to wagging that you couldn't walk down Lincoln's dusty street without tripping over the gossip. The most common was that she had been a prostitute in Kansas City and that Alex had dragged her out west where she could move beyond her reputation. If the foot that kept tagging my ankle was any indication, McSween hadn't taken her far enough west.

She wore an elaborate black gown with a beaded front that accentuated her ample bosom before narrowing into a high collar. She took her clothes more seriously than she apparently did her marriage vows. Her face was colored with a wagonload of rouge and powder. I might have been more taken with her were it not for that red hair piled in wave upon wave of curls atop her head. I'd gone with a carrot-topped girl named Carla once.

She'd called me crazy, but she—not me—wound up in an insane asylum, so I guess she got a chance to see what crazy really was. After Carla I just figured red hair was a sign of lunacy, much to be avoided.

Alex was a pale-skinned fellow with curly black hair and a drooping mustache that looked like it had been caught in the middle of a catfight. He was one of those weak men who didn't have the guts to call you a bastard to your face, but he'd damn sure spread the word behind your back.

McSween twisted his head toward me, then grimaced. "Lomax, you wouldn't be kin to a Gadrich Lomax, would you?"

I pleaded innocent to the charge.

"A shame," McSween said. "Met him in Santa Fe. A good man."

I looked from Brewer to the Kid and shrugged. Anybody that liked Gadrich Lomax wasn't too smart. I decided I didn't like McSween or his wife. But even though I didn't care for them, I must admit they spread a fine table, with an ironed white cloth, bone china, fine crystal, and sparkling silver. And they served up a good meal: a huge roast, the mashed potatoes, boiled cabbage, green beans, corn sliced off the cob, and biscuits so light they almost floated off the table. When I tasted the food, my opinion of Mrs. McSween improved. Maybe I had been wrong about redheads. Then the door from the kitchen swung open and a black servant entered, carrying a pitcher of sweet milk. He had done all the cooking and now would attend to all the serving.

When the servant left, McSween spoke. "I have important news to announce, something Susan and I have waited a long time for."

I figured he was about to announce Mrs. McSween was with child.

"We received a letter today from the Presbyterian Board of Missions. It has approved a missionary for Lincoln. We shall have a real church in Lincoln now."

Tunstall clapped his girlish hands.

"We shall build a church and start a school, bring civilization to Lincoln County finally," McSween went on. "With so many Irish and Catholics around, it's about time we had a civilizing influence, wouldn't you say, John?"

"Indeed, my good Scottish friend, indeed."

"And to celebrate getting the mission we've wanted," McSween announced, "I'm ordering a piano for Susan."

They started talking about religion, but I didn't pay attention. I didn't know too much about religion; I always figured you either believed it or you didn't. If you believed it, you didn't need to talk about it, and if you didn't believe it, you didn't *want* to discuss it. I didn't know much about being a Presbyterian and what was different about it from, say, being a Baptist or a Catholic. Now, were it left to me to decide my religion, I'd pick Baptist or Catholic because they weren't the mouthful that Presbyterian was.

Brewer, the Kid, and I did most of the eating, and Alex and the Englishman did most of the talking. They greatly admired each other, talking as if their breeding made them superior. I guess that's what gave them the idea they could take on a mean bunch like the House and survive. Murphy's men had done so much wrong they had calluses on their consciences. McSween and Tunstall had been so sheltered that they didn't even have calluses on their hands. If I was as smart as McSween and Tunstall made out to be, I'd at least have been worried about being shot by a dumber man.

And Mrs. McSween, well, she seemed to have calluses on her behind as well as her heart. The three of them made as odd a group as I'd ever been around.

"Once we open the store, we'll drive the House out of business and take over," McSween declared.

Mrs. McSween shook her head. "You're fools, both of you."

McSween cocked his head and clenched his jaw.

"Once John opens that store, Alex," she went on, "both of you are as good as dead."

"The law is on our side," McSween answered.

"The lawmen are not. They will not let you beat them."

"I've already beaten them once, Susan, by buying this house." He turned to me. "Mr. Lomax, do you realize you are sitting in what was once Murphy's store? I bought it, enlarged it, and made it into the best home in Lincoln County. Did you know that?"

"I didn't," I answered as I felt Mrs. McSween's shoe toeing at my ankle. "It does have more chinking than the Englishman's ranch house, and your servant is a better cook than Gauss." I don't know why McSween was trying to impress me. Maybe he was trying to impress Mrs. McSween, who kept trying to impress me with her wandering foot and, apparently, her wandering eye.

Brewer had been quiet throughout the meal; I think he knew what Mrs. McSween was attempting. When he finished his gingerbread, he nodded. "This was an excellent meal." He stretched and yawned. "But it's been a long day and I need some rest."

Tunstall nodded. "Rather a long month, don't you mean, Dick? First catching the brigands who stole my horses, then the thieves who took my cows. Take the extra bunk in my room."

"Obliged," Brewer replied.

Mrs. McSween clapped her hands. "Let's retire to the parlor for music."

As we stood Brewer extended his apologies to Mrs. McSween. "I'm exhausted and must get some sleep. I haven't even checked on my ranch since I got back."

"I'll go with you," I interjected. "I'm tuckered out myself."

Mrs. McSween glided around the table and grabbed my arm. "I want you to help with the singing." She leaned closer to me and whispered softly in my ear. "You're

staying, or I'll tell the other gentlemen you were trying
to caress my leg with your foot."

"I ain't scared of your husband," I whispered.

She smiled. "He's a lawyer and can make your life
hell."

I always admired subtlety in a woman, and she had
a certain point that was hard to miss. "Music would be
grand," I said.

Her smiled widened, and she batted her eyelashes.

Brewer left me and the Kid with Tunstall, McSween,
and, worst of all, Mrs. McSween. She escorted us into the
parlor, where she had a pump organ. She positioned me
at her side on the bench.

She motioned for her husband and Tunstall to sit
in specific chairs but ignored Billy. When she sat down
and started playing, I quickly realized there was one less
organ player than organ in Lincoln County. She called it
music, but I think "noise" was a better description. Her
playing had a cadence that reminded me of music you'd
hear in a saloon—or a brothel.

My job beside her on the bench was to turn the
sheets of music. I couldn't read music, but that made
us even because she couldn't play music. Billy took to
snickering and retreated to the dining room to visit with
the servant clearing the table. When Mrs. McSween
began to sing, I couldn't decide whether she was worse
on "The Flying Trapeze" or "Darling Nellie Gray," but
it was clear that the talent she lacked on organ had not
been added to her singing skills.

Finally I could stand no more. "I need to retire," I
said. "The food was delicious and the music was . . . well,
memorable."

"We've an extra bed," she offered, taking my hand,
"a feather bed that'll beat anything John can offer. Can't
he stay, Alex?"

McSween nodded. "Suit yourself."

"I've got to leave," I said, pulling away from
her.

Like a shadow she followed me step for step to the front door. There she grabbed at my arm, but I bolted out the door and down the street, bounding up the plank walk in front of the Tunstall store. I banged on the front door until Sam Corbett brought a lamp to see who it was. He unlatched the door and I slipped inside.

"Brewer wants to see you." Corbett jerked his thumb over his shoulder toward the open door of a lit room at the back.

Steering around the abundantly stocked tables, I managed to reach the back room without knocking anything over. Brewer was propped up in one of two bunks on opposite sides of the room. In addition to the two beds, the Englishman had furnished his quarters with a massive rolltop desk, a rocking chair, a stove for cooking and heating, a rag carpet on the floor, and a small table with chairs.

Brewer spoke with disgust. "I work for the English-man, not Alex McSween or his wife. She's a dangerous woman."

"And she can't sing worth a damn or play the organ," I added.

"She's arrogant, being the richest woman in town. I've come to believe the rumors about her," he said.

I was about to make another comment when I heard the front door open and saw Tunstall with another man. "It's McSween," I whispered.

The two men entered the quarters, nodding around. "Sorry, Dick," Tunstall explained. "A business matter arose. I need to show Alex some materials in private, if you don't mind, chap."

Brewer shook his head. "Not at all." He arose, wearing nothing but his long johns, grabbed my arm, and closed the door behind us. I spotted the Kid's bedroll and mine on the floor.

"Hope you don't mind the floor," Corbett said from behind the counter, where he had a cot.

Brewer walked to one of the windows and stared into the darkness. "You reckon any of them are out there watching?"

"All the time, I suspect," answered Corbett. He eased onto his cot, and the room was silent. At first I didn't pay attention, but gradually the voices of Tunstall and McSween in the next room caught my attention.

"Day after tomorrow," McSween said, "we'll open. Are we ready?"

"I've acquired goods and merchandise from as far away as Denver and St. Louis. The citizens of Lincoln County have never seen a store like this."

"You expect trouble?" McSween asked. "Susan does."

"She's a woman. That's what you should expect from one with a weaker constitution. I'll be ready for trouble. I've already hired an extra man, Bonney. Brewer says he's good with a gun. I may ask Lomax to stay around for a few days, pay him a few dollars. He's not as good with a gun, but he'd make another target if shooting starts."

McSween coughed. "You sure you've got enough money to keep paying all the men you've brought on— Brewer, Middleton, Waite, Corbett, Gauss, and now Bonney and Lomax?"

Tunstall laughed. "Alex, once we open up the store, the money will be piled at our feet. Within the year, at least half of every dollar made in Lincoln County will come to us."

McSween laughed. "I'll need it, the way Susan's been spending."

"With your expertise as a barrister and mine in the mercantile, we'll cut Murphy down. Then Lincoln County will have to come to us for everything."

I could only shake my head as I rolled out my bedding, then took off my boots, gun belt, shirt, and pants and crawled under the covers. Tunstall and McSween were no different from the House. It turned my stomach.

Shortly McSween jerked open the door and stood there looking at me on the floor. "Were you listening?"

"To what?" I bluffed.

"Nothing," he replied before tugging at his moth-eaten mustache. "Susan said you turn the music well, and you're invited anytime to help her play."

The brazen woman, I thought. And the stupid husband.

McSween walked past, aiming for the front door. As he neared Brewer, the ranch foreman said, "Good night," startling him.

"I didn't realize you were here," McSween said.

"You ran me out of bed, Alex."

McSween stepped to the door and unlatched it, then exited the building without another word and without shutting the door. Brewer pushed it to.

"Wait a minute," came a cry from outside.

I recognized Billy's voice and saw him run by one of the windows, then enter the store. "Thanks, Brewer," he said as the ranch foreman closed the door behind him. "I figured you'd already be asleep, as tired as you said you were. Or were you just trying to escape Mrs. McSween's singing?"

"Both," Brewer replied.

"Her singing sounded worse than a catfight," Billy observed. "My ears have threatened to leave me if they're ever in the same house with her again."

I shook my head. If Billy could just persuade half of each ear to leave, he'd have a normal pair.

Brewer marched past him. "Come on, Kid," he said. "Your bed's on the floor by Lomax's."

Billy snickered. "Lomax, Mrs. McSween sure took a shine to you. I can't believe you passed up an opportunity like that."

"Hell, Kid, she's married and redheaded."

"What's that got to do with anything? More Ozark beliefs?"

"I don't like redheads, especially married ones."

"She's just about your age, ain't she, still ripe and juicy?"

The Englishman emerged from his quarters. "Bonney," he called, "what are you talking about?"

"Mrs. McSween," Billy replied.

"Ripe and juicy?" The Englishman scratched his head.

"Her cooking," Billy shot back, and the rest of us laughed.

Tunstall turned to Brewer. "My regrets for evicting you from your bed. Alex and I had business to discuss."

"No harm done," Brewer replied, heading for his bunk.

"The McSweens are quite the couple in Lincoln," Tunstall said. "And she is so elegant."

So unfaithful, I thought.

"You ever gotten into her linen?" Billy asked.

"Goodness, no," replied Tunstall, missing the insinuation. "Her servant always sets her tables."

Billy and I laughed.

Tunstall shook his head. "You Americans and your sense of humor." He closed the door, leaving us in darkness.

The night chill was beginning to take hold. I balled up under the covers, thinking how nice it would be to have a woman, but not a redheaded one, to warm my bed. Shortly Billy took to snoring.

For a while I heard Tunstall and Brewer talking in the Englishman's quarters. I didn't pay much attention to their conversation until I heard my name mentioned.

"I've given it thought, Dick, about your man Lomax."

"What about?"

"Hiring him on."

"He's a good worker, better than Bonney."

"Not permanent, though, just for a few days."

"A few days of ranch work doesn't make sense," Brewer argued.

"No, I mean a few days around the store until it

opens up. We'll have so much business that we may
need an extra hand or two to help out. I assume he
can be trusted."

The Englishman's words angered me. He'd told
McSween he wanted me as an extra gun or target.
I considered marching in there and straightening him
out, but Billy started snoring, and before long it was
hard to hear anything Brewer and Tunstall were saying.
I gradually warmed my nest and fell into a deep sleep.

Light was just creeping into the store windows the
next morning when an awful commotion commenced.
Someone was riding down the street hollering something
I couldn't understand. I sat up and listened. "Sounds like
big trouble," I said, reaching over to rouse the Kid.

He moaned and groaned. "What is it?"

"Sounds like trouble," I repeated.

"It's nothing," he said, wriggling to get out of my
grasp. "Jesse Evans escaped, that's all."

I knew the Boys would eventually break from jail, so
I wasn't surprised until I lay back down on my bedding.

How in the hell did Billy know Jesse was gone?

Chapter Fourteen

Sam Corbett started a fire in the potbellied stove and put on a pot of coffee. In the Englishman's quarters I could hear Brewer and Tunstall stirring. I fidgeted in my bed until Billy rolled on his side and faced me. I propped my head up on my hand and stared at him. "How is it you knew Jesse Evans had escaped?"

Looking around to make sure no one was close, Billy whispered, "Right after I left the McSweens' place, I visited the jail. The guardhouse was empty."

"But why did you help them?"

"Jesse saved me when I was on the dodge for a killing in Arizona Territory. I owed him one. Now we're even again."

I clucked my tongue. "His type needs to stay in jail."

The Kid threw back his covers. "Probably. It looks like we're coming down on opposite sides of things."

"Why don't you get out?"

"And do what? At least the Englishman's given me a job, even if it's the job that belongs to you. A dollar a day is better wages than I ever made."

"He's hiring you for your gun, Kid."

Billy gave me a wide-toothed grin. "That's what I'm best at. It damn sure ain't fence building."

The door to the Englishman's quarters opened, and Brewer emerged, strapping on his gun belt. "What was all the noise?"

"Best I can figure," answered Billy, "Jesse Evans and the others escaped."

"Damn," Brewer managed through clenched teeth.

Billy shrugged. "It was bound to happen. They worked for the House, remember?"

Brewer bit his lip, then doubled his hands into fists. "All that time I spent tracking them, recovering the Englishman's horses, and they just slip away."

"None of them will bother Tunstall's stock or yours again."

I don't know if Brewer realized it, but the Kid had apparently made the Boys promise not to bother their property. With such tangled alliances, Lincoln County was a damned confusing place.

After we got up, Tunstall took Brewer, Corbett, Billy, and me to the Wortley Hotel for breakfast. By the time we returned to the store, the workers were finishing up the porch and overhang.

The Englishman was excited. "Tomorrow's the day we've been awaiting, the beginning of the end of the House of Murphy and the beginning of the rise of the House of Tunstall."

I didn't figure there would be too much difference between the two, except that one was owned by an Irishman and the other by an Englishman. It still cost people like me more than it should to buy goods whether we bought from the Englishman or the Irishman.

"I'll build a fortune," the Englishman said.

"What if you take away all Murphy's business?" I asked. "What will happen then?"

Tunstall laughed at such a pleasant and, to him, realistic thought. "I'll take over his store like McSween did his previous one and make my own mansion."

"Don't you figure Murphy might try to kill you?"

"For all your primitive behavior, you Americans are not barbarians. The law protects the just."

"Murphy's an Irishman, remember? And Murphy controls the law in Lincoln County."

Billy held up his hand. "Enough, Lomax. We'll watch out for the Englishman where the law won't."

As we approached the new store, I saw the law pacing back and forth outside the door. Sheriff William Brady straightened the lapels of his coat.

"Morning, Constable," said Tunstall. "What brings you about this morning? Here to apologize for letting the thieves escape?"

Brady shook his head. "I'm here to talk to the Kid and Lomax, not you."

"A final question, Constable," Tunstall continued. "Why haven't you given chase to the brigands?"

Brady cursed the Englishman. "Now, move on and let me talk to Lomax and the Kid."

Tunstall started to say something else, but Brewer grabbed his arm and jerked him toward the door. Corbett jumped forward and unlocked it so Brewer could get the Englishman inside before he said something that would create more trouble.

Brady stared at me and Billy. "I don't suppose you two had anything to do with Jesse Evans's escape last night."

"Not me," I answered, trying to deflect attention from Billy. "I had dinner with the McSweens, then was in Tunstall's store the rest of the time. Just ask Sam Corbett or Richard Brewer."

Brady turned to Billy. "Kid?"

Billy grinned. "I was out some last night, probably about the time the Boys were sprung, but I was looking for señoritas. Jesse and the Boys didn't have what I was looking for. If you're so upset about losing them, why aren't you chasing them?"

Brady pursed his lips, then stroked his mustache. "The way I figure it, Kid, the Englishman got his horses

back, so he ain't out nothing. Tomorrow's the opening of
the Englishman's store. If I left right now, I'd be gone
several days and wouldn't be around to keep the peace
when Murphy's men decide to make trouble."

The Kid cocked his head at the sheriff. "I thought
Murphy called the shots for you."

"Murphy has sway, I'll be the first to admit, but
he doesn't control me. It ain't easy, Kid, believe
me."

I felt sorry for Brady, figuring he was a decent man
who just got in over his head. He had taken the job to
earn a monthly salary to support his wife and kids on a
small place a couple miles east of town. He had fought
with the army during the War Between the States and
had since become a naturalized citizen. Twice he had
taken an oath of allegiance to the United States and its
constitution. That was two more times than either the
Scotchman or the Englishman.

The sheriff studied Billy. "Kid, I know you were
involved, but I don't understand the timing. If Murphy's
boys had done it, I'd've known about it as soon as it
happened. The timing was right for them, but I don't
understand your timing."

"Coincidence," Billy answered. "I owed Jesse a debt
and I repaid it. I don't forget my debts. Now I've a new
debt to the Englishman for giving me a job that pays
a dollar a day. That's more than I've ever made
before."

Brady shook his head. "I just hope you aren't working
for the wrong boss."

"No boss that pays wages is the wrong boss," Billy
replied.

"Maybe so, maybe not, Kid."

Billy nodded. "We free to go now?"

"Sure thing, Kid, though one bit of advice."

"Shoot," Billy replied.

"You best post a guard on the roof tonight. I hear
there may be an attempt to burn the place down. That's

between you, me, and Lomax, so don't you be spouting off where you heard it."

Billy touched the brim of his sombrero. "Already forgotten."

Both Billy and I stood watching as the sheriff walked away.

"One of these days Murphy's gonna get Brady in a hole so deep he can't get out," Billy said.

We turned and walked into the store together. The Englishman and Brewer were standing at a window watching us, while Sam Corbett tended to the final details of getting the store ready for its first day.

"About what did the constable inquire?" Tunstall asked.

Billy's cheek poked out slightly. "He wanted to know if you had helped Jesse Evans and his men escape."

"Outrageous," Tunstall exploded. "They stole my horses."

"We told him you were at the McSweens' or here in the store all night. He went away believing us."

Tunstall shoved his fists together. "And why isn't he giving chase to the brigands who escaped?"

"Fact is, English," the Kid continued, "he fears the escape might be a distraction to draw him out of town before your store opens. With the law gone it'd be easier for Murphy to attack you."

"He's lazy," Tunstall shot back. "We can protect this store." He patted his coat pocket, where he carried a small five-shot pistol. "I'm armed and prepared to defend myself and my property."

"Besides the bullets in the revolver, English, how many other rounds are you carrying?"

The Englishman crossed his arms over his chest. "None."

The Kid shook his head. "Most men in these parts carry more than a hundred rounds, and they're not afraid to use every one."

Tunstall shook his head in anger.

"He's right," said Brewer.

The Englishman spun around, preferring to ignore the truth rather than face it head on. He thought he was so much smarter than us that we couldn't be right. Maybe he did have more book learning at fancier schools, but you didn't learn about New Mexico Territory from thick gray books on Latin and philosophy. You learned it from experience and from growing up around people who carved their existence out of the land day by day rather than living like leeches on the wealth of their fathers.

While Corbett and Tunstall scurried about seeing to the final touches, the Kid and I took turns walking around the building and making sure no one planned any mischief.

Worried about his ranch, Brewer gave his apologies to the Englishman and rode out of town before noon to check his place and make sure the escapees hadn't burned down his house. He had just ridden out of sight when the Englishman approached me. He had a cocky grin on his face as if he were doing me a favor. "Would you be interested in a temporary job, chap? Fifty cents a day for a week, maybe ten days? Sound fair?"

"You're paying the Kid a dollar a day."

The Englishman blinked at me, shocked that I had questioned his wage offer. "He'll do ranch work. You'll do store work, inside and out of the elements."

"You want me for a gun in case there's trouble and another target to stand between you and Murphy's men. The answer's no."

The Englishman rubbed his soft white hands together, not knowing what to do. He retreated a step.

"I don't want your money. It's bad luck," I said.

The Kid interrupted. "Don't give us that Ozark folderol about something being good luck and something else being bad."

"It's a gut feeling. I'll stay the night and leave tomorrow."

"Fair enough," Billy said.

By nightfall the store was ready, and Tunstall was pacing back and forth enough to wear a hole in the wooden floor. Though the Kid and I didn't tell him what we were doing, we alternated guard duty through the night. I stood the first watch of two hours, the Kid the next, then me, and finally him.

On my second watch I positioned myself atop a storage shed out back. From there I could peer over the ten-foot adobe wall that formed the corral behind the store. It was a good position that gave me an adequate vantage point from which to see all but the front of the building.

The night air chilled me to the bone in spite of the coat I was wearing. My hands were almost frozen to the cold metal of my carbine, my teeth chattered, and my knees shivered so much I almost didn't hear the noise— a slow hiss like steam escaping from a boiler. I realized it was a whisper.

"We need to open the corral and slip inside. Then we can fire the roof," said an unidentifiable voice.

Brady had been right and decent enough to warn us.

I steeled myself as I listened to the soft sounds of men trying to be quiet. I took aim at the noise and waited until the men came closer. In the moonless night it was difficult to make out your hand in front of your face, much less assassins thirty feet away.

I aimed at the darkness and squeezed the trigger. The muzzle of my carbine flashed white. I heard a thud, then a curse. I ducked down, waiting for them to return fire.

"Let's get out of here," yelled one. I heard retreating footsteps and nothing more. Thirty minutes later Billy whistled that it was time to change guards.

When he approached, I told him of the two men I had scared away.

"You sure this wasn't an Ozark superstition?"

"I heard voices, dammit."

Billy was skeptical and wasn't bashful about admitting it in those brief moments before I headed back to my bedding to sleep out the night.

Come morning, I felt a nudge on my shoulder. It was the Kid, holding a tin can of coal oil in front of me. "You were right, Lomax. Somebody was out there, planning to build a coal-oil fire around the place."

I studied the black tin he held before my face.

"Brady was right, and so were you."

Sitting up, I rubbed my eyes, trying to work the sleep out.

I brushed away the tin can. "It's your problem, Kid. I'm leaving come noon."

"Dammit, Lomax, you can't leave. We're partners, remember?"

"The Englishman broke up that partnership by hiring you instead of the two of us."

The Kid grimaced. "You said you didn't want to work for him. I know the job is rightfully yours, Lomax, but I've never had a job that paid me money. Most I ever got was food and keep. The Englishman did me a favor."

I stood up and put my arm around Billy's shoulders. "Folks don't do favors unless there's something in it for them, Billy. The Englishman'll use you to fight his fights."

"What are you gonna do, Lomax?"

"I'll find work."

"But where? The Englishman's strapped, said he could just barely afford to take me on. The Coes can't pay money. Brewer needs help but he's broke. You won't work for Murphy. Who else is there?"

"There's Ash Upson's store. He may need some help."

At the mention of Upson's name, Billy snapped his finger. "I need to write him a letter on the jailbreak of the Boys. There's plenty to—" Billy stopped in midsentence and eyed me like he would a trade horse. "You're going back to Chisum's, aren't you? You're gonna try and get a job with a man that won't hire me."

"The Englishman won't hire me at your wage."

"He can't afford to, Lomax."

"Chisum can't afford to hire you, Kid."

Billy bowed his back like a washerwoman. "Chisum's got more money than any man around. He could hire me."

"He couldn't afford to have you around his niece."

Billy grinned. "Sallie does plow a new row now and then."

"I'll take Sallie and leave you Mrs. McSween."

Billy's grin curdled like old milk. "That ain't funny."

Standing in my long johns, I shivered and edged toward the stove and the warmth of Sam Corbett's fire. Billy, still carrying the tin of coal oil in one hand and his Winchester in the other, followed me. "Sallie likes me. Mrs. McSween likes you."

At the mention of Mrs. McSween, Sam Corbett glanced at Billy and me. He started to speak but froze, his cheeks reddening in anger.

"What's the matter, Sam?" I asked.

He thrust his pointed finger at the Kid's left hand.

"Dammit, Kid, here we are ready to open Tunstall's store and you're going out and buying coal oil from the House."

"What?"

"That's one of Murphy's tins," Corbett answered.

The Kid and I nodded that our suspicions had been correct.

"You got it wrong, Sam," I replied.

Billy jumped in. "Somebody tried to slip up on the store last night, likely to burn it. Lomax drove them away."

Sam nodded. "I remember a shot last night, but just one."

"They didn't fire back. There was two of them," I answered.

"They must've dropped the tin," the Kid explained. "I found it after daylight just outside the fence."

"You told the Englishman?" Sam asked.

Billy pointed to Tunstall's closed door. "He ain't even up yet. No sense alarming him on opening day. We'll just have to be alert."

I held my hands over the stove, warming my fingers, then grabbed a cup from atop the nearby cracker barrel and poured myself some coffee. Compared to Gauss's, Corbett's brew was sweet as nectar. It warmed me all the way down, and I had another cup.

Sam took the coal oil tin from the Kid and hid it behind the counter. "We'll put it in a new tin and sell it as our own."

Looking from the Kid to Sam, I shook my head. "How does a building made of mud burn?"

"The roof," Billy said. "Once it takes to flame, you can't put it out, and the fire falls to the floor and burns up the insides."

"When it's burned out, the walls remain, but everything else is destroyed," Corbett added.

I was still standing in my long johns, drinking my second cup of coffee, when Tunstall's door opened and he emerged, wearing a wide smile and his best suit.

"Good day, chaps," he said, his gaze coming to rest on me.

I nodded a greeting. "Morning."

"Must you stand in your undergarments where you can be seen from the street? It will not help business!"

Billy laughed. "It will if Mrs. McSween gets a glimpse of him."

Sam snickered.

Tunstall never cracked a smile, but crossed his arms over his chest and stood there tapping the floor with his foot. "I shall not have disparaging remarks made about the wife of my business partner."

Billy looked at the Englishman. "What kind of remarks?"

"Disparaging, insulting," he answered.

"It ain't insulting if it's true, is it?" Billy asked.

Sam and I laughed, but Tunstall was drawn tighter than a bowstring that morning and wouldn't have found humor in a joke that made fools of the Irish. He had invested much of his father's money in the store and in the ranch on the Rio Feliz. I took it that his family was well off, but not wealthy. Tunstall was worried.

As he stared blankly at me, I finished my coffee and slipped over to my bedroll to dress. I quickly put on my clothes and rolled up my bedding, then hid it behind the counter.

The Kid rounded up his bedding as well and dropped it with mine. As he did, Tunstall spoke. He had a wistful, almost girlish innocence about what he had undertaken.

"Have you ever been to San Francisco?" he asked no one in particular.

Billy shook his head.

"I have," I answered.

Tunstall said, "There was a time when San Francisco was no bigger than Lincoln, but it grew into the great city that it is because men took risks. One day Lincoln will be to New Mexico Territory what San Francisco is to California."

"San Francisco had the gold strike," I reminded him, but he seemed lost in his own delusions. I guess I wasn't the visionary he was, because I just couldn't see Lincoln rivaling San Francisco. Maybe it would rival Roswell or Mesilla and maybe even Santa Fe or El Paso, but San Francisco? Surely not. After all, San Francisco had an ocean and a bay that opened it to commerce with other countries. I had seen the Rio Bonito and didn't figure many ships would be able to navigate its waters to Lincoln. Maybe Tunstall was planning on digging a canal to the Pacific.

He kept blubbering about the significance of this day. He was getting so sentimental I could've sworn I saw his eyes glaze over with tears. Fact of the matter was, Tunstall was homesick and just couldn't admit it. More than five years earlier, at the age of nineteen, he had left London to make his fortune. Now, at the age of twenty-four, he was taking the biggest risk of his life, gambling with his family's money that he could develop a mercantile empire in the Southwest and turn Lincoln into a second San Francisco.

"Today," he said, "is the start of my future. All my education, all my travels in these United States and Canada, all the knowledge I've acquired over the years have led me to this moment. By the end of next year I'll be in London celebrating my accomplishments with my family."

Or dead, I thought.

Tunstall moved absently past me and stepped to one of the windows. It was still more than an hour until opening time, but already people had gathered across the street.

"Look," he said. "People are waiting to be our first customers."

I eased over to the window and looked. The Englishman was half right. Men were gathering across the street, but they weren't customers. I recognized several from Murphy's saloon. They were Murphy's men, all heavily armed, ready to intimidate anybody who thought about coming into the store.

"Business will be brisk," Tunstall said confidently.

Billy slipped over beside me and shook his head. He knew what I knew about the crowd. "It ain't gonna be as easy as the Englishman thinks," he whispered.

As the Englishman scurried about, helping Sam with last-minute preparations, the Kid took a pencil and paper and scribbled out an account of the jailbreak for Ash Upson. I stood at the window and saw a couple wagons pull up outside, then move on when the men across the way began to taunt them. As opening time neared, I caught a glimpse of one man who was not cowed by

the ruffians across the street. I only caught the back of
his head and could not identify him, but he took up a
position by the door, ready to be the first customer inside. I couldn't help but admire his bravery.

Tunstall, a stickler for opening on time but not a
second early, pulled his watch from his pocket and studied
it. "Now," he announced, turning to Sam, "we shall open
for business."

Sam unlatched the double door and swung it open.

"Tunstall's Store is open for business," the Englishman yelled across the street.

The mob marched for the door, then stopped in a
half-circle around the entrance. The man who had not
been intimidated by the ruffians swung around.

It was Lawrence G. Murphy himself, the high priest
of corruption in Lincoln County, who walked into the
store.

Tunstall froze, finally realizing that the men he had
thought were customers were actually Murphy's hired
hands.

Murphy brushed past Tunstall, nodding to me, the
Kid, and Sam as he strolled among the shelves, picking
up several items and tossing them back down.

"You English bastard," Murphy scowled, "you should
never have opened this store. You English ran me out of
Ireland after killing most of me family. You'll not run me
out of Lincoln."

As he passed me I could smell the whiskey on his
breath, but it was not nearly as strong as the venom in
his eye.

Tunstall's hands quivered, and his eyes widened
with fear. He stood silent. What could a man say,
especially a man whose ambitions and hopes had been
dashed so rudely at the moment of his anticipated
triumph?

Murphy marched to Corbett. "I want to make
the first purchase in Tunstall's Store," he announced.
"Where's your ammunition?"

Sam stood uncertain of what to do until Billy nodded at him. Sam pointed to the ammunition and escorted Murphy in that direction. The Englishman's wide gaze followed his competitor.

"I want forty-five-caliber ammunition," Murphy declared.

Sam pulled a carton from behind a glass counter.

Murphy slid the box open and pulled a single bullet from inside, then reached in his pocket, extracted a penny, and slapped it on the counter.

"That's the last cent you'll get from Lawrence G. Murphy." Holding the single bullet between his thumb and forefinger, he retreated slowly to the door. He stopped opposite Tunstall and held the bullet before the Englishman's eyes. "Not another cent, you English bastard, but you *will* get this back one day."

With that, Murphy walked back outside, and his men trailed him down the street to the House.

Tunstall stood pale and trembling.

"Don't worry about it," Billy said.

The Englishman was scared, no doubt. He bit his lip and ran his fingers through his hair. He wandered wordlessly around the room, straightening everything that Murphy had touched.

Billy took up a post near the door, cradling his Winchester in his arms. It was almost noon before any customers came in, and then it was Alex McSween and his missus.

The lawyer consoled Tunstall. "Business will pick up in a day or two, once people learn of your reasonable prices."

Mrs. McSween winked at me, but I retreated to the counter to collect my things. She joined me.

"Where you going?"

"To find paying work," I replied.

"I've got some things you could do around the place," she teased. "The pay's not cash, but you'll enjoy it."

"Me gustan las ovejas mas que las mujeres!"

"What's that mean?"

"It's Spanish," I replied. "Ask the Kid."

I picked up my belongings and strode past her. The Kid grabbed my arm at the door. He shook his head. "Wish you'd stay."

"These folks ain't my type," I said, pulling my arm free and stepping outside.

The Kid followed me out, looking both ways down the street. He nodded toward one of Murphy's men, sitting on a stump across the street and whittling. "The Englishman's okay," he said.

"He don't have the common sense God gave a cross-eyed mule."

Billy shoved his hand in his pocket and pulled out a letter with an open flap. "Give this to Ash Upson when you see him. Tell him I'll send more when I get the chance."

I took the correspondence and shoved it in my pocket.

"I didn't seal it in case you wanted to read it."

"I might. Say so long to Brewer and the Coes for me. Tell Gauss his coffee's worse than stump water."

Billy laughed. "Yeah, I'm gonna have to ask the Englishman for more money if he expects me to drink that coffee."

I studied Billy for a moment. "You sure you don't want to come with me?"

"Chisum won't hire me."

"You can find work elsewhere."

"Nope, I'm sticking with the Englishman."

I shook my head. "I still got a bad feeling about Tunstall."

"You had a bad feeling about me planting fence posts upside down. No bad luck came of that."

"Then how do you explain Mrs. McSween?"

"Maybe you've got a point." Billy laughed. "Now get along or we'll stand here jawing until dark."

"So long, Kid. You've been a good partner."

"Adios, Lomax. I'll miss you, but not that damn mule."

We shook hands. I went around the store, saddled up Flash, tied down my bedding and belongings, mounted, and rode out into the street.

I gazed a final time at the store. I saw Alex and Mrs. McSween strolling back home. Billy still guarded the porch with his Winchester. Behind him in the doorway stood John Henry Tunstall, his head drooping like his shoulders.

It was the last time I ever saw the Englishman alive.

Chapter Fifteen

On my two-day solitary ride from Lincoln to Roswell, I thought a lot about the Kid, figuring he had bought into a passel of bad luck by throwing in with the Englishman. Tunstall was the same breed of greedy as Lawrence Murphy, though not as vicious.

When I reached Roswell, I headed to a mercantile that wasn't a threat to anybody. It was midafternoon when I rattled the door and marched inside.

Ash Upson looked up from behind the counter and grinned. "Where's Bonney? He was supposed to send me news periodically."

I reached in my britches pocket and pulled out the Kid's missive. "He sent this about the jailbreak in Lincoln." When I handed it to him, I could smell liquor on his breath.

Upson nodded. "Jesse Evans and the Boys escaped?"

"That's right."

"Did the Englishman open his store?"

"Sure did. His only customer the first morning was Lawrence Murphy himself. Murphy bought a single bullet, nothing more."

Upson stroked his chin. "Trouble may be sooner than later. I'd bet on Murphy, if I were you."

"I won't bet against the Kid."

"Then why'd you get out?"

"Nobody'd give me a paying job."

"Hell, you didn't want to get killed, Lomax."

"The Englishman doesn't think Murphy's men are killers."

Upson laughed. "Damn fool limey. The scrawniest of John Chisum's steers has more value than a man's life in Lincoln County." He shook his head and began to read the Kid's letter, nodding periodically. "Bonney doesn't have my flair for writing, but he does okay for a working hand."

"Next time I see the Kid, I'll tell him you're worried he'll take over your seat as Lincoln County's greatest scribe."

With an exaggerated sweep of his arms he shouted, "Blasphemy, you infidel. I am the greatest scribe in all the Southwest. One day I shall write a book that will endure through the ages and prove to all my consummate skills with the English language." Upson had a knack for theatrics when he'd had a few drinks.

"A few newspaper articles don't make you Shakespeare."

Upson was incensed. He jerked the pencil from over his ear and thrust it at me like a dagger. "Of all those arts in which the wise excel, Nature's chief masterpiece is writing well." He scoffed. "You know who said that?"

I admitted my ignorance. "No, and it doesn't matter."

The store clerk looked at me askance, then laughed. "No, I guess it doesn't, because I've forgotten." He cackled. "I write better when I've had a few drinks. Only problem is, I don't remember as well. Want a drink with me?"

I was tempted, but I didn't want liquor on my breath when I approached John Chisum for work. "I best be moving on."

Upson grabbed my arm. "Look around, buy something."

"I'm broke, don't have a cent to my name."

Upson sighed and stared at me with his bloodshot eyes. "Believe me, one day I *will* write a great book."

"Be sure and mention me in it," I said, "so my momma'll know I'm still alive."

"Why not send her a letter? I am the postmaster, remember?"

"Thanks, but I've got to see John Chisum."

I retreated and closed the door on Ash Upson, untied Flash, mounted, and rode to Chisum's place. As I approached the main house, I was intercepted by Chisum's foreman astride a chestnut gelding. A lean, rawboned fellow with a rolled cigarette hanging out of a corner of his mouth and a six-gun on his hip, the foreman treated me as any other saddle tramp who happened to come by looking for work.

"We don't need more hands for the winter," he growled. "You just as well ride on, because I don't hire men that ride a damn mule."

I did what always worked best when confronted by an obstinate pest. I lied. "I ain't looking for work. I'm looking for John Chisum. I've a message from Lincoln."

The foreman extended his hand. "I'll see that he gets it."

"Nope," I replied, tapping the side of my head with my right forefinger. "It's all up here, too important to put on paper in case it fell into the wrong hands."

He leaned toward me. "You can tell me. I'm his foreman."

I leaned forward too, crossing my arms over my saddle horn. "Nope."

After trying to stare me down, the foreman caved. Fact was, he didn't know what he was up against. I had sipped Gottfried Gauss's coffee and lived to tell about it. I was no ordinary man.

The foreman turned his gelding and eased in beside Flash. As we drew up outside the picket fence, the front door swung open and Sallie Chisum herself emerged, carrying a calico cat in her arms. She glanced at me, then turned away. Suddenly she twisted back around, dropped the cat, and called to me. "Lomax, it's good to see you!"

"You know him, Miss Sallie?" the foreman asked, taking off his hat as she ran to me.

"Why, yes, I do. He's a trusted confidant of Uncle John's."

My chest swelled, knowing that she remembered my name and saw fit to lie on my behalf. "Thank you, Sallie," I ventured. "Your foreman treated me rather rudely." Out of the corner of my eye I saw him squirm.

Sallie laughed. "That's what Uncle John pays him to do, so no poor cowboy can get within rutting range of me."

"Now, Miss Sallie," replied the foreman, a tint of embarrassment on his leathery face, "there's no truth in that and no cause to make unladylike remarks."

"You're right," she said, motioning with her hand. "Now go on and I'll see to Mr. Lomax."

The foreman backed his gelding away from the fence, then spun around and galloped off, pulling his hat down as he rode.

Sallie smiled. "Where's Billy Bonney? He coming shortly?"

"Nope."

"Well, damn," she answered. "If I'd known that, I'd've had the foreman rope you, brand you, and send you on your way."

So much for Sallie being glad to see me. Even so, one of her insults was better than all of Mrs. McSween's offers.

"Where's Billy?"

"He's working for the Englishman."

"I wish Uncle John'd hired him. He was a lot of fun."

"That's what all the señoritas say about him, yes, ma'am. They all think he's a lot of fun, whether they're dancing or strolling in the moonlight by the river."

That Billy might have other girlfriends didn't bother Sallie any more than a rainstorm bothers fish. She just smiled. "A fellow needs to stay in practice."

My jaw about dropped to the ground. Sallie wasn't bashful at all about those matters.

"I need to see your uncle."

"About what?"

"Business," I replied.

Sallie laughed. "He's inside the house and not in a very good mood. He just found out Jesse Evans escaped from jail."

"Billy's the one that let them out."

She placed her hands on her hips and glared at me. "You're sure trying to poison me for Billy, now, aren't you, Lomax? But it don't matter what you say about Billy Bonney. I'll not have anything to do with you. You don't have Billy's . . . charm." She giggled.

"Next time I see Billy, I'll tell him you miss his charm."

"Would you?" She strode through the gate. "Uncle John's inside. Just step up to the door and knock. If he doesn't answer, yell for him. Sometimes he's a little hard of hearing."

I watched the sway of her hips as she strolled away. She was damn proud of herself. Nothing gives a woman more confidence than good looks and plenty of money.

After she marched around the house, I dismounted and tied Flash. I pulled up my britches, slapped some of the trail dust off my coat, and lifted my hat while I ran my fingers through my hair. Though the sky was clear, the weather was between fall and winter. I was too warm with my coat on and too cool without it. Snugging my hat on my head, I started for the house and was quickly under the porch shade. I knocked on the door a couple times. Receiving no answer, I called, "Hello." Then, following Sallie's instructions, I yelled, "Hello, Mr. Chisum."

"Come in, darn it, come in," answered Chisum's disgusted voice. "What the hell is it?"

Knowing I'd made a mistake by yelling, I pushed open the door and removed my hat. I heard John Chisum grumbling.

"Can't a man even take an afternoon nap without some peckerwood disturbing his sleep?"

I saw him sprawled out on a sofa in the corner, rubbing his eyes. I wanted to strangle Sallie Chisum. He sat up, resting his elbows on his knees and shaking his head as he stared at me.

I heard footsteps behind me and turned to see Sallie entering from a back room. "Uncle John, did somebody wake you up from your nap? I told him not to bother you."

I considered batting her head up against the wall, but I didn't figure that would help me earn John Chisum's respect and admiration, much less a job. Even so, the temptation was great, especially considering that the old cowman never wore a sidearm.

"I'm sorry, sir."

"The damage's done, Lomax. Now, what brings you here?"

"Business, sir."

"Go on."

"Private business," I said, twisting to look at Sallie.

"Sallie's family," Chisum replied. "You can trust her."

"I'm sure I can," I said, shaking my head, "but I'm a mite uncomfortable discussing some delicate things in front of a lady."

"But, Uncle John," Sallie cooed, "you know I can be trusted and my ears aren't the least bit delicate."

Chisum nodded. "That's true, and, much to my regret, you have been known to use a profane word."

"Sir," I protested, "I'm sure she is a lady, but if she stays I'll be forced to think otherwise, and that would disappoint me."

Chisum laughed. "Move along, Sallie."

"But, Uncle John." He shook his head and flicked his arm at her. Like the lady she was, she stuck her tongue out at me when her uncle wasn't looking, then left the room.

"Have a seat, Lomax." Chisum pointed to a chair.

Sliding into it, I held my hat between my legs and bent toward him. "I'll be honest," I said. "I came looking for a job."

Chisum let out his breath. "You woke me up for that? I can't hire every man that comes along in need of a job."

"I've worked cattle," I said, "and I'll make you one promise."

"What's that? That you won't steal any of my cows?"

"No, that I won't court Sallie."

Chisum stopped laughing instantly. "What's to make me think you're any different from all the others? Every one of them's interested in getting his hands on her linen and my money, if the truth be known."

"She's too independent for me," I replied.

The cowman scratched his chin, then tugged on his mustache. I was glad he didn't start scratching his ears. As big as they were, it would have been nightfall before he finished. "You're not in with Billy Bonney, are you?"

"Bonney's gone to work for the Englishman."

Chisum grinned. "Too bad for both of them. The Englishman's heading for a fall."

I studied him. "I thought you and Tunstall were partners."

"Tunstall and McSween wanted me to go in with them on a bank. I lent my name, but none of my money. I don't trust the pair. If they say we're partners, fine. Maybe Murphy'll believe it and pester them instead of me and my ranch."

Chisum seemed smarter by the minute. I'd have pegged him a pure genius had he up and hired me on the spot. "I thought after our first meeting you might hire me."

He nodded. "I had a need for a hand then. Don't now."

There was no sense in prolonging this funeral, so I nodded, then stood up and shook his hand. "Good luck to you."

"Good luck to you, Lomax."

I pulled my hat on and started for the door. As I opened it and stepped outside, I found Sallie Chisum leaning against the window. She'd been eavesdropping on us.

"Important business to discuss, hah," she said, her eyes flashing in triumph. "You're no better than all the rest, out of work and needing a job." She snickered at me.

Not having anything to lose, I was tempted to punch her in the mouth, but she went suddenly silent and meek before I could lift my fist. Her mouth dropped open and her face went pale as she stared not at me, but beyond me. I glanced over my shoulder and saw John Chisum standing behind me, his arms crossed over his chest, his eyes aflame with anger.

"Sallie Chisum," he said, his voice booming like thunder.

Sallie swallowed hard.

"By sneaking around like a coyote and listening in on a private conversation, you've proven yourself not to be a lady. What do you have to say for yourself?"

"I was funning him, that's all."

John Chisum stepped out of the door. "Young lady, it's no laughing matter when a man's without a job. I guess I've spoiled you rotten and brought this upon myself, but you've never had to work a day in your life, though a lot of women do, just to put a meal on the table and keep a family in clothes. I get you store-boughts, give you servants in the kitchen, and make your life easier than any woman's in New Mexico Territory, and you don't have the decency to treat other people with a bit of dignity. I'm ashamed of you."

Sallie hung her head and cooed, "I'm sorry, Uncle John."

Her coy act didn't work this time. "You owe two apologies. One to Mr. Lomax and the other to me."

Sallie glanced from Chisum to me. Her eyes simmered with the embarrassment of getting caught rather than regret for her treachery. "I apologize, Mr. Lomax. I let my teasing get out of hand." She curtsied to me, then glanced back at her uncle, batting her eyes until they began to water. "I'm sorry, Uncle John."

He nodded gruffly. "How should we make amends to Mr. Lomax?"

Sallie's tears disappeared instantly. "I apologized."

"That's not enough."

"Maybe," she suggested, "you should give him a few dollars."

Chisum shook his head. He seemed genuinely embarrassed. "You think money'll buy anything. Sallie, if you don't grow up, there won't be enough money in all the world to pay for the mistakes you'll make before you're my age."

"Then what should I do?" she cried out, her eyes watering again.

"You've forced me to offer him a job, but I'll be taking his wages out of what I give you each month."

Sallie's tears boiled away in anger. "It was a little mistake. I apologized."

Chisum pointed to the door. "Go on. I don't want to hear another thing about it."

After giving me a hateful stare, Sallie skulked into the house.

"My apologies," Chisum said. "She don't mean bad by it, but she thinks life's one game after another. Maybe it's too late to be teaching her some lessons."

"You don't have to—"

"Yes, sir, I do," Chisum replied before I finished refusing his job offer. "I don't want the Chisum name sullied by her acts." He whistled to the foreman, who came riding up to the fence.

"This is Henry Lomax. I'm hiring him on. See that

he works one of the camps down toward Seven Rivers where we'll likely have trouble with rustlers." He looked at Flash. "You still riding that same mule and saddle?"

I nodded.

"Guess you're an honest man, then. A thief would've stolen another animal and rig by now." He laughed.

I was getting tired of folks making fun of Flash. He might have been a mule and might have been a damned mule, but if he was, he was still a damned good mule.

The foreman escorted me to the bunkhouse, putting some distance between me and Sallie Chisum. I didn't figure the coldest winter would be nearly as bad as the chill of Sallie. I stayed the night and then rode out early the next morning for my winter home.

It was a two-day ride to the line camp, where I joined five other cowboys cramped into a shack in a grove of cottonwood trees near the Pecos. The foreman loaned me a good saddle and a trio of geldings for my string of horses. Two were chestnuts, pretty much indistinguishable in looks and temperament, and the third was a yellow dun. Though his coat was yellow, his spirit was anything but. Maybe he was touched in the head, but he didn't spook. You could fire a pistol right next to him, hit him with a rock, poke him with a stick, yet he wouldn't stampede away like most horses. Of course he was hardheaded and must've thought he was in charge of things, because he was balky sometimes—except around cattle. He could work cattle like a politician works a crowd, but most of Chisum's hands didn't care for a horse with a mind of its own. I took to calling him Sal, which was short for Sallie, which I didn't have the nerve to call him around Chisum's hands.

Those five hands were decent men, but I don't know that I knew their actual names. I told them my name, which didn't present a problem until the wanted poster I had stolen from Sheriff Brady's office slipped out of my pocket one night when I pulled off my pants. One of the cowhands picked it up the next morning and passed it

around to the others before handing it back to me. They
never said a thing, but after that I noticed they didn't
cheat me anymore in our nightly card games, even though
we were just playing for matchsticks.

We spent the next six weeks doing typical cowboying.
We rounded up calves that had been missed in the spring
branding and burned the long rail in their sides and
jinglebobbed their ears. We weaned any calves that were
still suckling to give them and the mother cows a better
chance of making it through the winter, and we jerked
weak and stupid cows from the muddy grasp of the Pecos
when they got bogged down. Periodically we'd round up
small herds that other Chisum hands would then drive
south to El Paso or north to Santa Fe.

All the time we kept our eyes open for rustlers,
always working in pairs so no man was ever alone in
case he happened upon a gang of thieves. The foreman
had given us explicit instructions to save all the cattle
and kill all the thieves we could.

Jesse Evans and his gang had been plaguing herds
up north, and we realized that he would eventually move
our way. We had lost one hand to rustlers up north and
everybody was on edge when the ranch foreman rode up
one night in early December and joined us for supper.
He wasn't pleased to find us playing poker, even for
matchsticks, but he didn't say anything. He didn't have
to. We hid those cards faster than a preacher hides his
mistress.

After a silent supper, the foreman lectured us about
the evils of gambling while in another man's employ. Then
he turned to business. "Signs point to Jesse Evans and the
Boys in these parts. You fellows seen anything one way or
the other?"

To a man we shook our heads.

"You will before long," he said, fetching his saddlebags and extracting a carton of ammunition for each of
us. "We'll be doing gun work instead of cattle work for
a while."

To a man we nodded. When you worked for John Chisum, you were expected to know cattle and how to work them. You were also expected to know guns and not be afraid to use them.

"Any questions?"

"Yeah," replied one of the hands. "How's Sallie?"

"Sallie still ain't engaged," the foreman said. The other hands cheered, as if they had a chance at winning her hand.

"What's the latest from Lincoln?" I asked.

The foreman shrugged. "It's still a standoff. Business has picked up at the Englishman's store, but nobody's doing a land-office business. Lawyers are muddying the waters now. Murphy's lawyer's accused McSween of swindling money from the House, something to do with McSween buying the old store building and not paying for it. I wish they'd all kill each other so we wouldn't have to put up with them or their mischief."

"What about Billy Bonney?"

"Working at the Englishman's ranch on the Rio Feliz and staying out of trouble, from what the stock detectives tell us."

I was glad to hear it, because I was still kind of partial to the Kid. After supper that night we retired earlier than normal and arose earlier the next day. Each day for the next three days, we split up into two groups of three, with the foreman alternating between the two posses.

Around noon the third day, me and the two other hands patrolling the western boundary of Chisum's grazing land spotted a ribbon of smoke and slipped over the rolling prairie until we came to a rise. We hobbled our horses and crawled to the top. As I expected, the fire was heating branding irons for eight or nine rustlers. I recognized Jesse Evans and the three who had escaped jail with him. Since we were outnumbered, we stayed hidden until the rustlers rode off; then we mounted and returned to the line cabin.

The foreman met us as soon as we rode up.

"Any luck?"

I nodded.

"Was it Jesse Evans?"

"Sure as I'm sitting here."

"He's the one we want. Did he spot you?"

"Didn't appear to."

The foreman outlined his plan. "I figure they'll be back tomorrow. We'll split into two groups. I'll lead the first group, and we'll circle wide of where you spotted them today and head into the foothills. The other group will ride out just like you've been doing. I figure you'll run into them. Chase them in our direction, and maybe we can get them caught between us."

I can't speak for the others, but for myself I had a fitful night's sleep, waking up before the foreman roused us plenty before dawn. In the darkness I picked out Sal as my mount. We ate a bite of jerky as we saddled up, me and two others heading out with the foreman for the foothills. The night air was cold and crisp, and the chill cut through our coats as we advanced at a trot. The stars seemed like shards of ice overhead. By sunrise we were well into the foothills and had taken up a position atop one bald hill that gave us a good vantage point for miles around.

We waited and waited, time dripping by like molasses in winter. It reminded me of fishing with a cane pole in Arkansas. If fish didn't bite within five minutes, I wanted to do something else rather than wait all day for what might never come. The foreman, though, was as patient as a rock. I would've given up by midday, but he continued to study the Chisum rangeland with his field glasses. By midafternoon I was ready to mutiny, but just then the foreman loosed a sinister growl. He pointed to the northeast. "There they are."

The other three of us squinted our eyes. I could make out ten or so horses moving east, sticking to the depressions between hills.

"Now," the foreman said, "if the others can just drive them back toward us, we ought to get a sizable number of this gang."

"What if they don't?"

The foreman nodded. "We'll take positions between them and the mountains and get as many as we can." We mounted up and screened ourselves for as long as we could while we made our way toward the rustlers.

It took a half hour before we reached the shallow valley where the rustlers had passed. The foreman ordered two men to dismount, hobble their horses out of sight, and take up positions with their carbines among the rocks on either side of the trail. The foreman took me with him. We were to stay mounted just around a bend in the valley so we could chase escaping thieves.

Even though it was cold, my palms grew tacky, and I was as nervous as a long-tailed cat in a room full of rocking chairs. We waited nearly half an hour before we heard distant gunfire.

"It's working," the foreman called.

My palms grew sweatier, but I forgot about them when I made out the noise of pounding hooves. The foreman and I eased our horses forward just far enough to see down the valley. The thieves charged toward us, shooting over their shoulders, ignorant of the trap before them. I recognized Jesse Evans in the lead.

"It's Evans," I said as the rustlers drew closer. I counted ten of them before the gunfire of our men erupted from the walls of the valley. I saw two men fall.

The foreman yelled, and we reined our horses out of hiding. I drew my pistol and was taking aim on Jesse in the lead. He had a wild-eyed, frightened look on his face when he saw me and the foreman blocking his escape route.

Just as I had Jesse in my gunsight, my yellow dun Sal bolted forward, charging straight into the approaching riders. I was on a horse out of control. I fired at Jesse, but he leaned low in the saddle and

I missed. I shot at another rider and saw him grab his shoulder.

The gap closed quickly between me and the panicked rustlers. I fired at Tom Hill, missing, and Frank Baker, missing again. Jesse Evans and I passed within five feet of each other and exchanged a shot each without drawing blood. Another rider darted by, and I knocked him out of the saddle. I must've pulled the trigger three or four more times before I realized my pistol was empty. I shoved it in the holster, jerked my carbine free, and fired at the three approaching stragglers. One flung up his arms and tumbled out of the saddle. The other two charged by me, one on each side.

I jerked the reins on Sal and spun him around to give chase. Just as I did, one of the stragglers twisted around in the saddle and fired. I felt like I had been kicked in the side by a mule.

I slumped forward in the saddle, then fell to the ground. The whole world seemed to collapse around me.

Chapter Sixteen

Except for the pain, I don't remember much about the trip back to Chisum's South Spring headquarters. The foreman and the hands rigged a travois and dragged me to the ranch house. I felt every rock, hole, rut, and bump on the way. By moving me so roughly, I figured they were finishing off the job that the Boys had started with the bullet to my hip. The slug had lodged against my hipbone, and no matter how I tried to rest, spasms of pain coursed through my body like lightning through the night sky. I could not move without pain. Even breathing hurt. I would've begged them to put me out of my agony, but even talking pained me.

I made the trip somewhere between drowsy and unconscious, never knowing quite where I was or how I got there. I figure we traveled through the night. I do remember getting periodic sips of water but never enough to quench the burning thirst that grated at my throat almost as badly as the pain gnawed at my hip. When the tortuous motion of the travois finally stopped for good, I slit open my eyes and was blinded by a brilliant sun. I squeezed my eyes shut, turned my head away, and groaned at the throbbing pain.

Then I felt arms sliding under me, lifting me off the travois and carrying me somewhere. I groaned so my bearers would know I was alive. I could tell they were carrying me indoors by the sound of their boots on a hardwood floor. Shortly I felt myself being lowered onto the softest bed I had ever touched. Not only was the bed soft, it was also stationary, unlike that damned travois.

Somebody removed my boots, then worked my pants down. I groaned as my britches were peeled off. Next, somebody with mean hands poked and jabbed at my hip. I cursed, wishing I was back on that travois after all. The pain kept shooting up my spine like bullets out of a Gatling gun. Those mean hands squeezed the flesh on my hip, then shoved it against my wound. I screamed, clawing to get up, but the hands wouldn't let me. They belonged either to someone who didn't know what he was doing or to some damned sawbones. I figured I had about a fifty-fifty chance of survival either way.

"How is he, Doc?" I recognized John Chisum's voice.

"Bullet's lodged in his hip. May have shaved some splinters off his hipbone."

"What are his chances?"

"He'll survive as long as we get the bullet out before the body poisons start in on him."

"What are you waiting on?" Chisum asked.

"It's gonna take more men than you got in the room now to hold him down once I start digging."

Maybe it wasn't a sawbones after all, but a miner, the way he was talking.

"Sallie," called Chisum, "fetch some more of the men."

The mean hands pressed my hip, but I tried to roll away.

"He's a damn brave one," the foreman said. "He charged right into Jesse's band, killed two and winged one more before going down."

I heard steps, then more whispered voices. The doctor told them to roll me over on my side. When they did,

I cried out and someone shoved the middle of a folded towel in my mouth.

I felt a liquid being poured into the wound. For a brief instant it felt cool; then it turned mean, burning worse than a branding iron from hell. I bit into the towel as hands clasped my arms and legs and steadied my torso and head. Then before I could think, the doctor attacked me with a damn poker. I tried to scream but someone shoved the towel deeper into my mouth. My hip was afire, like it was being rinsed with molten lead. Finally the pain became so great I passed out.

How long after that I awoke the first time, I don't know, but it was dark and someone was beside me, bathing my head with a damp cloth. I sucked at the moisture, and whoever sat at my bedside gave me a cup of water. The cool liquid cut the cotton in my mouth. I fell back asleep. The next time I awoke the room was softly lit by the light outside. I figured it was near dawn or dusk, my time sense still being confused, but the light didn't change for a while, and I realized it was a cloud-covered day.

At my bedside, asleep in a rocking chair, sat Sallie. "Water," I called. She snapped awake, shaking her head and rubbing her eyes.

Sallie grinned as she handed me a cup of water. "If you'd just accepted my apology instead of Uncle John's job you wouldn't've gotten shot."

Grimacing, I took the cup. The excruciating pain had been replaced by a deep, dull ache that pulsed through my entire hip. I drank the water and gave her back the cup, then carefully touched my waist, hip, and bandage, trying to figure out the extent of my wound.

"Don't worry," Sallie said. "You haven't lost any of your charm."

"How do you know?"

"I already looked!" She giggled. "You picked a good time to get shot." She pointed at the window. "The first storm of the winter rolled out of the mountains. And Uncle John'll want to keep you here until you're recovered." She stood up and stretched. "We've a pot of soup we've been cooking for you."

She strolled out the door, leaving me as confused as a new steer in a pen full of heifers. At least she was cordial, but I figured it was just another of her ploys. I was still contemplating her motives when John Chisum himself walked in.

"Feeling better?" he asked.

I nodded, then winced.

"Doctor said you were lucky. Had the bullet entered a couple inches forward, it'd gone around the front of your hipbone rather than the back. You'd've been gutshot, dead and buried by now. My foreman tells me you rode right into those cattle thieves, shooting like a demon out of hell. Didn't know you had it in you."

I answered softly so as not to awaken the throbbing hip. "My horse didn't know the difference between 'whoa' and 'go.' "

Chisum laughed. "You won't be riding anything for a spell. Doctor says you need to stay off a horse—or a mule—for several weeks. We'll keep you here until you're recovered. And I've told Sallie to care for you. If she doesn't, she won't get any money."

"I heard that," said Sallie, standing in the doorway and holding a tray in her hand. I could smell soup— nothing ever smelled better, unless it was the Ozarks in the spring. She carried the tray in and set it on the table beside my bed.

"You remember what I told you," Chisum admonished her. "We need more men like Lomax. He's to receive your full attention."

"Yes, Uncle John," she replied, gently propping a pillow beneath my head, then spooning me some soup.

That was the first of many meals that Sallie brought me as the days drew closer to Christmas. I gradually regained my strength, but the better I felt the colder Sallie turned toward me.

As I healed, though, I enjoyed newfound respect among Chisum's hands. The foreman took his hat off every time he spoke to me, just like he did when John Chisum himself was around. Chisum had one of his men make me a cane, which I used to hobble around the house. The pain began to subside, though occasionally I would take an awkward step and receive a stabbing jolt up my side.

To pass the time, I played a lot of solitaire with a deck of dog-eared cards. Sallie even offered to play me some poker. Like a fool I accepted and even wagered a few dollars. It was sport to me, but she played for blood. And she cheated. After that, anytime I heard her approaching, I hid the cards.

The attack on Jesse Evans and the Boys was about the biggest excitement in Lincoln County for several weeks. From our sporadic winter visitors I learned that the two sides had taken to squabbling in court with writs, accusations, and all sorts of legal badgering. Murphy accused McSween of embezzling money from the House. McSween accused Murphy of depositing county tax monies collected by Sheriff Brady into the House's account. Tunstall, supported by his father's money, managed to keep the store open and even attract customers, mostly Mexicans with little cash but a great hatred for Murphy and the men who worked for him.

The more I listened, the more I learned that McSween was held in low esteem by many. Some folks were even saying McSween was draining money out of Tunstall faster than the Englishman's father could send it across the ocean. And then there was Mrs. McSween. The rumors reached as far as Chisum's place about her improprieties, and the hands had a few laughs about her. If respect were gunpowder, the McSweens couldn't have put enough together to pop a firecracker.

That's why it came as a great shock to me a week before Christmas when John Chisum entered the kitchen one morning carrying a bulging valise and issuing orders to Sallie and his foreman at the breakfast table. Chisum was heading to St. Louis with the McSweens. When he announced that, I couldn't help but snicker. The foreman nodded that he was thinking the same thing.

Chisum gave us a stern look. "It's not what you think."

"I ain't thinking about it," replied the foreman.

"About what?" asked Sallie.

The foreman and I stuffed our mouths with biscuits.

"Eat your breakfast," Chisum said.

I believed John Chisum and later figured that he realized his run was about over. He was looking to sell his ranch and turn it over to someone else to handle. Had he had a wife and children, he might've willed it to them, but his brothers didn't have the mettle to keep the ranch together, and Sallie was more interested in spending money than in making it.

"Mrs. McSween has a sister in St. Louis," Chisum explained. "Alex McSween and I are, after all, partners in the Lincoln Bank."

"In name only," I said.

"Sometimes a name is enough."

Chisum sat down to breakfast and instructed his foreman to have his buggy hitched up for the trip to Trinidad and the railhead in Colorado. He said he'd meet the McSweens in Anton Chico and accompany them the rest of the way to St. Louis.

Sallie pouted because she wanted to go, but he told her it wasn't safe with the McSweens.

"Then why are you going with them?" she whined.

"Because I can take care of myself," he said. By the tone of his voice I knew the discussion was closed, and so did Sallie. He finished his meal, said his good-byes, grabbed his coat, and slipped outside into the cold December air.

The house just wasn't the same without John Chisum in it; it seemed lifeless, I guess because he was the heart of the ranch. He had invested his lifetime in it, and no one could match that investment.

Christmas came and went. Though Chisum had left presents for Sallie and instructions for there to be a big feast, it was a sad day all about. Without blood family around, Christmas is the saddest day of the year. It'd been twelve years since I had been in Cane Hill and five years since I'd learned of my father's death. I'd written not much more than a letter a year to my mother, always promising I'd return to visit, but I never seemed to get around to it. I was always a vagabond, running away from home several times as a kid, not because I was ever mistreated or anything but because I had a wandering streak in me and the ambition to become wealthy. When I returned home, I wanted to return in style, as a success, a person people knew by reputation.

Though there were a lot of hands around the place for Christmas dinner, I had never felt lonelier. I got so sad eating my meal that I took my cane, hobbled out to the barn, and cried. Only when I saw my teardrops freezing on the ground did I realize how cold it was. I hobbled back inside, just in time for singing. It wasn't the prettiest singing I ever heard, but it was a distraction. I vowed to write a letter to my mother that night, but I just never got around to it. I was glad when Christmas was over.

I figured I'd had about the worst Christmas around until the middle of the next afternoon when a rider brought in a message from John Chisum. He had spent Christmas—and would likely spend several days to come—in the Las Vegas jail. Both he and Alex McSween had been arrested after one of Murphy's lawyers accused them of trying to leave the territory with swindled funds. It was one more reason for me to hate lawyers. News of the arrest upset Sallie, who moped about for a few days as if she had lost her last dollar.

"Your uncle can handle himself," I consoled her. She sighed and whimpered, as lost as a temperance leader in a brewery. Chisum was tough, but he was even more stubborn. Even though he had the money, he refused to post bond and wound up staying in jail until March when the county finally got tired of feeding him at taxpayer expense and released him, all the charges that had been brought against him being overturned in court.

Sallie's spirits rose as she realized her uncle's unfortunate jail term was not going to change her comfortable life. Because it was in the hands of a good foreman and basically honest men, the ranch survived, though not with the same heart as with Chisum about.

I spent January mending, gradually getting around without my cane, though still walking with an obvious limp. My hip didn't bother me much, except when I had to climb steps. On those occasions a sharp pain would burn powder up my side, but I learned that twisting my foot outward would ease the discomfort. By late January I could do just about everything except win a footrace and ride a horse. I made my first venture away from the ranch just after the first of February, when the foreman decided we needed a wagonload of supplies and instructed me to ride to Roswell the next day to pick them up. Sallie volunteered to go with me, but the foreman told her no. She batted her eyes at him, and he told her no in even stronger terms. I liked how he dealt with her.

I left at daybreak the next day. The morning was biting cold; my coat seemed flimsy against the wind. I could've left later in the morning, but I was anxious to pick up any news Ash Upson might have about Lincoln. The best I could tell, most of the battling between Murphy and Tunstall had occurred in a courtroom in Mesilla, southwest of Lincoln near the Texas border.

Since no decent human being except possibly a criminal would ever set foot in a courtroom, nobody could vouch for what was actually happening in Mesilla except that the House, through Murphy, seemed to own the federal district attorney and the federal judge. I'd always heard that justice was blind, but long ago I had concluded that it was the damned lawyers that had blinded her in the first place. And if lawyers were ever able to breed—say like rats—they would cut out her tongue and plug up her ears as well. Lawyers' only redeeming trait—and the thing that kept the country safe—was that they ate their young.

Once I arrived in Roswell, I had to wait almost an hour in the cold before Upson opened up. I drove the wagon around to the side of the building to block out some of the wind, but I felt just as cold as before. Even when I got inside, the store was cold, Upson having let the fire burn out overnight. He moved around sluggishly.

I gave him the list of merchandise the foreman and Sallie thought we needed. Upson read it over, then shook his head. "I've got a third of what you need." He pulled a whiskey flask from behind the counter, uncorked it, and took a long, healthy swig, "Keeps me warm," he explained.

"Tell me what you know about affairs in Lincoln."

Upson studied the flask. "Amazing what fermentation can do to rye." He downed another mouthful, then turned to me. "First, you tell me about John Chisum. Any word from jail?"

"Nothing new. He's the stubbornest man that ever lived."

"Or the tightest." Upson plugged the bottle. "I hear Murphy used connections to jail Chisum along with McSween. McSween bailed himself out, but Chisum was too tight or too stubborn to make bond."

"Maybe too proud."

Upson shook his head. "McSween'd been safer if he'd stayed in jail or gone on to St. Louis like his wife."

"Mrs. McSween still out of Lincoln?"

"Last I heard, she'll be out another four to six weeks."

That was good news. If that woman stayed out forever, it would be even better news. "Where do things stand with the Englishman?"

"The fool wrote a letter to the *Mesilla Valley Independent,* accusing Sheriff Brady of misappropriating fifteen hundred dollars in tax monies. I hear this week McSween and Tunstall are in the Mesilla court defending themselves against Murphy's claim that McSween swindled him."

"Why's the Englishman involved if McSween is accused?"

"Murphy claims they're partners in the swindle."

I shrugged. It was getting too complicated, and there was only one reason I cared about Tunstall or McSween. "What do you hear about Billy Bonney?"

"Nothing since you brought me his letter. Hadn't heard him mentioned beyond the fact he's working cattle for the Englishman."

We visited a bit more, and then I reminded Upson of the supplies I came for. He took a swig of whiskey and started gathering goods and badgering me with questions about my shoot-out with the Boys.

"Hear you rode straight into the gang, blazing away, your reins in your teeth, your carbine in one hand and your pistol in the other. I never picked you as a fool."

"My damned horse didn't know 'whoa' from 'go.'"

Upson scratched his chin. "You're not only brave but humble, perfect traits for a dime-novel hero. You ever thought of becoming a literary legend? All you'd need is someone capable of telling your stories, your adventures and exploits on the dangerous frontier."

"You wouldn't happen to be that capable person, would you?"

He nodded. "I'd make you into Kid Lomax."

"There's only one Kid in these parts, and that's Bonney."

"How about Lone Wolf Lomax? Make that the Legendary Lone Wolf Lomax, a one-man army."

"How about filling my order?"

Upson sighed. "There's money in dime novels. All I need is the right hero, and I can give up this job for honorable work."

"Telling lies is honorable?"

"Absolutely! How else do you explain politicians?"

Upson had a point, but not one I cared to debate. I motioned for him to hurry. "What's the delay?"

"What's your rush, Lone Wolf? Once you leave, I may not have another customer, as cold as it is outside."

"I want to get home before the spring thaw sets in."

Upson clucked his tongue. "I could make you famous, Lone Wolf." He went about finishing my order, even toting a couple hundred-pound sacks of flour out to the wagon. "That's all the flour I got, and I'm out of coffee. You'll have to go to Lincoln for everything else."

I nodded. With Mrs. McSween in St. Louis, Lincoln would be safe for me, and I might get the chance to see the Kid. I settled up the Chisum account with money the foreman had given me, then started for the ranch, getting there too late for lunch. Sallie showed no sympathy for my missing the meal. "It shouldn't take that long to pick up no more than you brought back."

"Upson's out. Lincoln's the closest place to get the rest."

I explained to the foreman that I'd need to make a trip to Lincoln to fill the complete order, but he told me to wait a few days. He was banking on Chisum returning before then. But after ten days he gave up.

"You feel up to making the trip by yourself?" he asked.

"It's been years since I hung on to my momma's skirt."

"I know you can take care of yourself, after what I saw you do against the Evans gang, but I was wondering about your wound. Head out in the morning. I'll have the hands hitch up the wagon. Take plenty of ammunition and blankets to keep warm."

I was pleased to have an excuse to go to Lincoln and find out how things were going with the Kid, the Coes, and Dick Brewer.

When I left the next morning, I rode through Roswell and followed the Rio Hondo into the mountains, camping the first night in the foothills. The weather was cool, but I had plenty of blankets in the wagon and slept warmly in the back. The second day I got up early and followed the Rio Hondo until it split into the Rio Ruidoso and the Rio Bonito, which I followed into Lincoln.

As cold as it was, the street was virtually empty, though I could've sworn I saw faces staring from behind every window I passed. I drew up the rig in front of Tunstall's store. Not another wagon or horse was hitched there, but I didn't think much about it since it was late afternoon and folks that had business had likely attended to it already. I did see two men with rifles standing inside, behind the windows. I didn't think much about that either, figuring Tunstall had just hired a few more men to watch his property.

Entering the store, I was immediately struck by the heat. Sam Corbett was being awfully generous with Tunstall's firewood. I quickly unbuttoned my coat and looked around for Corbett. Who I saw shocked me. Sheriff William Brady stood behind the counter, his shirtsleeves rolled up and his hands on his hips.

I twisted around and looked at the guards by the windows. They wore badges too. "Where's Sam?"

"Sam doesn't work here now."

"Why not?"

"This ain't the Englishman's store anymore."

I felt dumber than a Comanche at a spelling bee. "How's that?"

Brady grinned. "The court's attached the store."

"Attached it to what?"

"The court's taken over the store and is holding on to all merchandise until the charges of fraud against McSween are resolved."

"It's Tunstall's store, not McSween's."

"They're partners."

I shrugged. I had a better chance of changing a fence post's mind than of changing Brady's. I pulled out my list of supplies and offered it to him.

"Damn shame, Lomax, but I can't sell you a thing, you belonging to the Tunstall gang."

"Hell," I shot back. "I work for John Chisum."

"Same difference."

I offered a compromise. "I'll take what I need and pay you cash." I shook the list at his nose.

"Lomax, I can't even let you take a leak in here until the court says otherwise. If you want supplies, I'd suggest you take your list down to Murphy's place. They can fill your order."

I started to argue, but Brady cut me off.

"Lomax, don't give me any trouble or I'll arrest you."

"For what?" I challenged.

"Murder," he shot back.

"What?" I shouted. "Who?" I was haunted by Leadville and the wanted poster.

Brady laughed. "We've got witnesses that say you killed two men back in December. Jesse Evans saw you shoot them."

"They were rustlers and you know it."

Brady shrugged. "Get out or we may let the court decide."

I grumbled, then turned and walked out into the cold. Justice was blind because justice was dead in Lincoln County. Even after the door slammed, I could still hear their mocking laughs. I figured I could stay the night down by the river, then return to Chisum's place the next day. Just then I saw Sam Corbett come out of Alex McSween's house next door. He saw me and motioned for me to join him.

I climbed aboard the wagon, and Corbett pointed me to an adobe corral in back of the McSween house. We unhitched the team and drove the horses into the corral, where a dozen others stood watching.

"Things are going to hell," Corbett said. "The sheriff's got the upper hand, holding Tunstall's store. He's even sent a posse to take the Englishman's cattle and horses from the Rio Feliz ranch."

Corbett led me into McSween's house. The lawyer was there and maybe twenty others, talking and complaining about the situation. I did more listening than talking. The discussion went on until ten o'clock or later, not really settling anything. Throughout it all, McSween kept urging that any action be lawful.

The crowd had about spent itself and was about to break up when we heard the sound of galloping horses outside. Somebody jumped to the window, but before he could announce anything the front door flew open. Every man in the room went for his gun until he recognized the Kid standing there, wide-eyed and lathered.

"The Englishman's dead!" he shouted. "The Englishman's dead!"

Chapter Seventeen

The room exploded in confusion as men shouted questions.

"Oh, my God," cried Alex McSween.

Carbine in hand, Billy pushed his way into the parlor, followed by Dick Brewer, John Middleton, and Fred Waite. They were breathless and had the look of wild stallions in their eyes.

"Brady's posse killed him," Billy shouted.

"Who?" McSween wanted to know.

Billy glared across the room. "Brady's posse, dammit."

Brewer stepped beside Billy and answered McSween. "Jesse Evans, Tom Hill, Buck Morton, and Frank Baker."

"My God," McSween cried, balling his fist and hitting his palm. "There's arrest warrants out for them. They shouldn't have been part of a posse. Are you sure? What were they doing with Brady's posse?"

"Killing the Englishman," Billy growled.

"Where?"

"Up Perry Springs Canyon off the Ruidoso," Middleton said.

Billy stared blankly past me. "The Englishman's the first man that ever gave me a paying job," he said to himself. "I owe him."

I stepped toward him. "No way you can repay him now."

"I'll kill his killers," he said, then seemed to recognize me. "What're you doing here? I thought you worked for Chisum."

"I came for supplies, but Brady's taken over the Englishman's store, and I won't buy from Murphy."

All around us men were shouting and arguing for action until McSween stood in a chair and held his hands up. "Quiet!" He pointed at Brewer. "Dick'll tell us what happened."

The murmuring died. Brewer cleared his throat as he looked about the room. "We were herding the Englishman's horses back to Lincoln. As we neared the Ruidoso, we flushed a flock of turkeys. Me, Waite, and the Kid took off after them, figuring we'd shoot us some supper. Just as we neared a rise, we heard horses riding hard from back down the trail. Middleton yelled at the Englishman, then raced for cover, but the Englishman didn't try to escape."

Brewer paused to catch his breath, and there wasn't another sound in the room. "Evans, Hill, Morton, and Baker topped a rise behind us and rode straight for the Englishman." He fumbled for the right words. "Then they shot him."

"Who?" McSween asked.

Brewer shrugged. "I can't say for certain, just that they all shot at him. One of them killed his horse, too."

Everybody took to grumbling.

Brewer lifted his hand for silence. "By then the rest of the posse came up, Buckshot Roberts, George Hindman, and a dozen more."

"Bastards," muttered the Kid.

"Where's the body?" asked McSween.

"Still in the canyon," Brewer answered. "We asked one of the farmers on the Ruidoso to bring it in tomorrow."

"I'm ready to kill the murderers," Billy cried out. "Who's with me?" Several men volunteered.

McSween waved his hands. "Wait," he pleaded. "There're laws we must follow to see justice done."

"Justice? Laws?" shouted Billy. "The House controls the laws in Lincoln County. The only justice we'll see is the justice we make for ourselves." He patted the Colt Thunderer on his hip.

McSween shook his head. "There's Squire Wilson. He's a justice of the peace."

"He's a babbling old fool," came a voice from behind me.

"Yeah," added another man. "He's all vine and no taters when it comes to brains."

"It doesn't matter," McSween said, "as long as he can issue a warrant." He scoffed at the doubters, then turned to Brewer. "Once the body's here we'll go to Squire Wilson for warrants. Don't anybody do anything until then."

For the next two hours McSween circulated among the men, pleading with them to remain calm. It was well after midnight before the crowd broke up and men returned to their homes. Billy told me to stay with him, and we wound up spending the night on McSween's floor along with Brewer, Waite, and Middleton. Before Brewer blew out the lamp, the Kid stared at me. I'd never seen icier eyes. The glimmer of mischief that I had always seen there was gone.

"I'll kill them," he said, his voice as cold as a barrel of ice water. "Damn shame, Lomax, you didn't kill them when you caught them rustling Chisum's cattle. It true you charged straight into the bunch of them and Jesse butt-shot you?"

"More or less," I said, not admitting the dun's role in my bravery.

"I always pictured you half coward, Lomax." Billy lay down.

"I've killed more of the Boys than you have," I shot back.

"Not for long, you haven't."

Brewer overheard us. "Don't be talking like that, Kid. We'll do it according to the law, the way McSween tells us."

"The law ain't on our side," Billy replied.

"McSween'll change that."

Billy snarled, "The law won't put out this fire, not when it was Sheriff Brady's posse that burned the Englishman. If McSween's smart, he'll start relying on a six-shooter rather than the law."

"That's not his way," Brewer answered.

"His way'll see us all dead, Dick."

Brewer didn't respond, and the room fell quiet for a bit.

"How's Sallie?" Billy whispered to me.

"She's fine, been taking care of me real well," I said.

"She ain't taking care of you that well—and we both know it. You're too tame for her."

I couldn't argue that so I didn't answer, and we lay there in silence. It was a long night; none of us got much sleep. Come morning we had a breakfast prepared by McSween's servant, then went outside to await the arrival of Tunstall's body. The tension in the air was so thick you could cut it with a dull knife. Armed men had posted themselves at the corners of McSween's house because everyone knew the lawyer would be Murphy's next target.

All morning we waited, watching one end of the street for a wagon bringing Tunstall's body in and the other end for activity at the House. Brady's deputies were still holding Tunstall's store, but McSween allies reported that Brady had abandoned it for the House as soon as word arrived of the Englishman's death. Another rumor had Tunstall's murderers hiding in Murphy's store with Brady.

The morning passed slower than a bad sermon, but just after high sun a wagon rattled in from the wrong direction, the west rather than the east. The Kid jerked his pistol and pointed it at the wagon, even though it appeared to carry a family. I'd never seen such wide-eyed terror as on their faces. The man held the reins. A small girl held his arm. The woman clutched an infant to her bosom.

The man braked the wagon opposite me and Billy. "Is this the McSween home?" he asked in as strong a voice as he could muster.

I nodded, but Billy challenged the man. "Who wants to know?"

"The Reverend Taylor Ealy," the man said, then cleared his throat. "The Presbyterian Board of Missions sent me to establish a church and a school."

"We've more need for an undertaker," Billy replied.

The woman beside Ealy gasped and drew her baby closer.

"I'm a doctor and a reverend," Ealy stated.

"You know how to cure the dead?" Billy asked. "They're bringing a dead one in, the only man that ever paid me for an honest day's work."

Ealy pursed his lips and shook his head. He patted his wife's hand. "I'm here to do God's work. Is this the McSween home?"

"Yes," I replied, stepping forward to assist Dr. Ealy with his wife and family. He introduced his wife as Mary and his daughters as Anna, three years old, and Ruth, not quite six months.

Before I could introduce myself, the door to Mc-Sween's adobe swung open, and the lawyer strode out. "I'm Alex McSween."

"Thank God we found you," Ealy replied. "We're from the Mission Board. We've been threatened by men outside of town and told not to ride in if we were friends of yours."

"You're Dr. Ealy?" McSween scurried to their wagon to help Ealy and his family down. "Lincoln has great need of a church of the Christian faith, Dr. Ealy, but the only thing harder than the stony soil of Lincoln is the hearts of its men, a soulless lot of Irish and Mexicans who put their faith in a pope instead of God."

Ealy looked as lost as a suckling calf separated from its mother as McSween hurried his family into the house. "Bring their things inside," he called out. "They will be staying with me."

I didn't work for McSween and didn't like him ordering us around, even if he was a lawyer. Everybody else must've felt the same way, because no one moved and the wagon stayed full until McSween's servant came out later and handled the chore himself.

About midafternoon and long after the Ealy wagon had been unloaded and unhitched behind the house, another wagon approached from the east. This was the wagon that carried the body of John Henry Tunstall, dead just three weeks shy of his twenty-fifth birthday. As the wagon approached, a procession of men afoot and on horseback fell in behind it.

No sooner had the wagon stopped than men circled it, Billy first among them. The silence was eerie as we looked over the sideboards at a lump wrapped in a wool blanket. Billy grabbed the corner of the blanket and lifted it up. I saw him wince; then I saw why. Tunstall's eyes were open wide with surprise at one perfectly round bullet hole in his forehead. A second hole had scorched his coat over his heart. The back of his head was matted with blood, brain, hair, dirt, and dried grass where his skull had been blown away.

"Bastards," Billy whispered. He spun around and glared down the street at the House. "Bastards!" he yelled.

Death is a humbling sight, and I felt my knees shake. I didn't care for the Englishman, but neither did I care to see him dead.

We stared at naked death, our stomachs churning at the brutality. Brewer broke the silence. "We need to get him inside." Brewer, the Kid, and several others grabbed the edges of the blanket and lifted Tunstall's body from the wagon bed. Men took off their hats as it was carried into McSween's house. Before the Reverend Taylor Ealy could say his first public prayer in Lincoln, he was conducting a post mortem.

When Billy emerged from inside, he carried his carbine and dashed down the street toward Squire Wilson's place, returning shortly with the justice of the peace. "McSween wants witnesses for the inquest," he announced. "And somebody go find the constable. He'll be needed to serve warrants." Middleton and Waite followed Billy and the justice into the house, where McSween and Brewer waited.

Several men tried to follow the witnesses inside, but Billy stopped them at the door. "Nobody else comes inside but the constable."

They protested, but Billy stared them down, and they stood solemnly by the door, opening it only for a Mexican identified as the constable.

We waited around a half hour or so, occasionally casting worried glances down the street at the Murphy store. Then the door flew open and Billy strode outside, his carbine in one hand and a fistful of papers in the other. Brewer, Waite, Middleton, and the constable trailed him. Billy shook the papers. "Warrants for Evans, Hill, Baker, and Morton." He received cheers.

"Papers won't arrest the murderers, not with them forted up in the House," I said.

Billy stared at me. "I'll arrest them."

"No, you won't," came a voice from the house.

Everyone turned to see Alex McSween standing in his doorway, his arms crossed over his chest.

"We'll do it according to the law," he announced. "You can accompany the constable, but he must serve the warrants."

Now everyone looked at the constable. He fidgeted, especially when the Kid pointed the carbine at his chest. The constable nodded slightly, and everyone cheered again.

"Let's go," said Billy. He was ready to run through an adobe wall and spit out the straw, but the rest of us were a bit reluctant to commit suicide, not without writing out our last wills and testaments, which would take time.

Fred Waite stepped forward. "I'm with you, Kid."

Middleton and Brewer volunteered as well, but McSween reined them in quick.

"It's best the two of you stay and let Bonney and Waite go with the constable."

Brewer protested. "There's two or three dozen of them in the House. The Kid and Waite won't stand a chance."

"Two more won't make a difference," McSween argued, "not when the four of you are the only ones that saw the Englishman murdered. If they get all four of you together, what's to keep them from killing the only witnesses?"

"He's right," Billy said. "Just me and Waite'll go with the constable."

The Kid and Waite checked the loads in their carbines while the constable adjusted the gun belt on his hip. When they stepped forward, the crowd parted.

"Good luck," called McSween.

Many men followed them partway, ever careful to cling to the sides of the street in case Murphy's men started firing. About halfway to the House, everyone except the trio stopped and watched. I don't remember seeing anything braver than those three striding toward a building full of bad men and uncertainty. Without hesitation they walked to the front of the store and marched in.

When they disappeared, we stood in silence, half expecting to hear gunfire and mayhem. We heard nothing but the silence.

Finally Middleton spoke. "You think they knifed them?"

Having no answer after a half hour, we retreated sheepishly to McSween's place. No one had the courage

to check on the trio, and we stared at the ground rather
than each other as we skulked away. I felt lower than a
gravedigger's foot and half wished for that damned yellow
dun to make the decision for me.

Embarrassed by our cowardice, we stood guard in
shifts, just in case Murphy's men tried something. I began
to worry that they were torturing the Kid to make him
reveal what he knew about McSween's plans, but my
imagination was running as wild as the yellow dun.

I was standing watch a little before dark when I
noticed a man emerge from the House. Holding his hands
in the air, he moved deliberately down the street, then
gradually lowered his hands as he came closer. Suddenly
he bolted forward and ran toward me, shouting something
in Spanish. It was the constable. I couldn't make out a
single word.

A couple fellows ran over and translated that Billy
and Waite had been relieved of their guns and were
being held by Sheriff Brady and the Boys. Brady had
sent a message that, as sheriff, he was still in charge of
Lincoln County—not Justice of the Peace Wilson, not the
constable, not Fred Waite, not the Kid, and especially not
Alex McSween.

Though angered by the sheriff's message, we weren't
mad enough to go charging the House. We grumbled a lot
and tried to put on brave faces, but I figure we were as
scared as a seven-year-old facing the razor strop.

Before dark a wagon pulled up, and a couple men
got out and unloaded a coffin, which they carried inside
McSween's house. A bit later the surgeon from Fort
Stanton arrived with a small military escort and went
inside. Word was passed around that he was assisting
Dr. Ealy with another examination of the body before it
was cleaned and dressed for burial. Two hours after he
arrived, the surgeon and his military escort mounted up
and rode down the street, stopping in front of the House.
In the cool night air we could hear the strong voice of
Murphy greeting them at the door.

"Damned Englishman died, did he? Sure it wasn't suicide?" The drunken Murphy laughed. From our distance we couldn't tell if the soldiers shared his joke, but they did share his hospitality. That was plenty unsettling. All the law and all the might of Lincoln County seemed to be backing Murphy and his operation. All we had was a senile justice of the peace, a nervous but game constable, a lawyer who never carried a gun, and the Kid.

About midnight I went inside McSween's house. Through the door to a candlelit room off the parlor, I saw McSween and Dr. Ealy dressing Tunstall for the last time, then placing him in the coffin and positioning his hands across his waist. Ealy used sticking plaster to plug the hole in Tunstall's forehead. McSween caught me peeking and invited me to inspect the corpse, so I eased in and glanced in the coffin. Tunstall looked about as natural as a dead man could with sticking plaster filling a hole in his head.

"Doesn't he look fine?" McSween asked.

"I reckon."

"Dr. Ealy and I are tired. It's been a trying day," McSween told me. "Would you stay up with him?"

"He ain't going anywhere," I answered, figuring truer words were never said.

McSween, though, looked as if I'd doused him with a chamber pot. "I'm exhausted, and Dr. Ealy and I have many things to discuss about his burial tomorrow. Will you watch him?"

I shrugged. How complicated could a burial be? You dig a hole, drop the coffin in, then fill in the hole. It's pretty damn simple, but like a lawyer, McSween always had a way of complicating things. "I'll stay," I said.

McSween gave me a sickly smile and shook my hand. "I knew I could count on you in these bad times I appreciate all you're doing. So would the Englishman." Then he and the doctor walked out of the room, their heads drooping like their spirits.

The moment they left, the candle flickered weirdly, and I twisted around to study the flame. It must've been an air draft from somewhere, but it unsettled me. I slipped back into the parlor and found my bedroll stacked atop several others along the wall. I extracted it and made my bed on the parlor floor, rather than in with the Englishman, fearing my snoring might rouse him. I slept about as well as a man can sleep in the presence of a dead man with sticking plaster in his forehead. When I awoke momentarily in the night, I realized the candle by the coffin had burned out, but I didn't see any point in lighting another one. The Englishman wouldn't be doing any night reading.

I awoke at the sound of footsteps in the parlor and opened my eyes. McSween stood over me, his arm crossed. "You let me down."

"Did he escape?" I asked.

McSween strode away in disgust. "We'll bury him after lunch."

I arose and rolled up my bedding, shivering at the cold. I followed my nose through the house to the kitchen, where McSween's servant was cooking bacon, eggs, and biscuits. I helped myself and enjoyed both the food and the kitchen's warmth. The black servant didn't care; he seemed glad to have the company and said he admired my bravery for sleeping up front with the body. I told him I admired his bravery for working with a lunatic like McSween. He laughed.

When I heard someone approaching on the wooden floor, I gulped down as much food as I could, then hid my tin plate. It was McSween. I grabbed my coat and went outside in the early morning chill, spotting John Middleton, who was leaning against the corner of the adobe house. He nodded.

"Any word from the Kid?" I asked.

Middleton shook his head, then bit his lip. "Not a word. I should've done something before now."

"They're planting the Englishman after lunch," I said, then moved on. Middleton was in no mood for talking.

Though the morning was still early, the crowd of supporters had thinned considerably, many going to the warmth of their homes or deciding a lawyer as nervous as McSween was not a good man to follow to their deaths. I trailed a couple men with shovels to the back of Tunstall's store and watched them start digging a grave. Although the sheriff's men still held the store, the land belonged to Tunstall.

After wandering past the gravediggers, I ambled over to the stone torreón and climbed the ladder through the trapdoor in the wooden floor that was the upper level. There I found one of McSween's followers sitting on the floor and leaning against the stone wall, asleep. I toed at him with my boot. "I'm here to spell you," I announced.

He awoke with a start, then grinned sheepishly. "I dozed off."

"Nothing happened," I said. "The funeral's after lunch. I'll look after things."

The guard seemed relieved as he stood up and pulled his coat tight against the cold. He slipped down the ladder and disappeared. From the torreón I could easily see Tunstall's store next door and most of McSween's house on the other side of it. At the far west end of the street was the House, silent and sinister in the early morning light.

I stayed the morning in the torreón, mostly watching the gravediggers as they excavated the Englishman's final resting place. Just before noon I saw four men wrestling Mrs. McSween's pump organ out beside the grave. This was going to be the fanciest funeral Lincoln had ever seen. Periodically I glanced toward the House, hoping I might see Billy escaping. I knew he would want to attend Tunstall's funeral, but I wasn't certain he was even alive.

As the time neared one o'clock, people began to gather around the open grave. Then I saw a line of men emerge from the McSween house, a half-dozen of them—Dick Brewer, John Middleton, Frank and George Coe among them—carrying the Englishman's coffin. The Reverend Ealy held an open Bible in his hand and led the procession. Several men carried carbines.

I lowered myself down the ladder and moved to join the mourners. Mrs. Ealy started playing the organ, and folks started singing "Jesu Lover of My Soul." I didn't know the words and didn't sing well enough for it to matter, so I slipped beside Frank and George Coe. They acknowledged me with a nod.

When the song ended I was expecting a prayer, then the burial, but Reverend Ealy stepped forward with that open Bible and began to preach from First Corinthians. I never was much of a religious man because some of that Bible writing was hard for me to follow. I thought we had come to bury Tunstall, but the preacher must have figured this was his last chance to lecture the poor dead fellow, so he cut into a long sermon, made longer by Justice of the Peace Wilson's Spanish translation for the Mexicans.

One verse the reverend read from the Bible said something about the end coming and man being delivered to God and was followed by a verse that I didn't know how to take.

"'For he must reign, till he hath put all enemies under his feet,'" read Ealy.

I wasn't quite sure whether that was a call to battle against the House or if Tunstall was our enemy, religion not being something I took well to. In fact, I kind of wished Murphy and all the Boys had been there to listen. I figure they would've grown so confused by the sermon that we could've gotten the drop on them and ended all of Lincoln County's troubles right then and there.

Ealy would've preached Tunstall to death had he not already died. It seemed forever before he said "Amen." With heads bowed we sang "My Faith Looks Up to

Thee," and as the song ended the pallbearers slipped lariats under the coffin, lifted it over the grave, then lowered it into the ground. I felt sorry for Tunstall, dying so far from home and loved ones. I figured that was the way I would probably die one day, all alone and away from family. At least Tunstall had attracted a crowd of more than two hundred friends. My funeral probably wouldn't attract that many flies.

When the coffin was in place, everyone stood around, not knowing quite what to do. It being winter, there were no flowers to toss in the grave. Brewer fished a silver dollar from his pocket and dropped it on the coffin. I thought that was a foolish waste of spendable money but kept my opinion to myself.

Then Brewer and Middleton grabbed two shovels and began to fill in the grave. As the coffin disappeared beneath the dirt, the crowd thinned out. Though Middleton shared his shovel with the other pallbearers, Dick Brewer worked like a madman. When the grave had been mounded over, he thrust his shovel into the overturned dirt and looked around.

"Any man who had a hand in the Englishman's death," he said, "will pay for it with his own life!" He had become as rabid as the Kid.

Chapter Eighteen

After the funeral the mourners gathered at McSween's house, many squeezing inside and the rest clumping around the door. They groused about the terrible deed but did more crowing than scratching, even when someone noticed Sheriff Brady walking down the middle of the road, cradling a Winchester in his arms. As word spread that the sheriff was approaching, the house emptied of folks, McSween leading the way. He stood at the fence, Dick Brewer and John Middleton on either side of him.

"Sheriff," he called as Brady drew even with the gate, "why haven't you arrested Tunstall's murderers?"

Brady swung the Winchester menacingly toward us. "What did you say, Scotchman?"

"Why haven't you arrested Tunstall's murderers, you Irish bastard?"

Brady's temper flared and he raised his rifle, aiming it at McSween's chest until he realized a dozen or more guns were pointed at his own. His anger, like his Winchester, fell. That was when I noticed he was carrying the Kid's carbine. "The Englishman refused to surrender to my posse. He went for his gun. My deputies had a right to defend themselves."

"Jesse Evans and the Boys, are they your deputies?" McSween challenged.

"It's no concern of yours, Scotchman."

"Where's Bonney and Waite?" Brewer demanded.

Brady laughed. "We're taking good care of them."

"That's the Kid's gun you're carrying," I called out.

Brady smiled. "The Kid let me borrow it."

"You're a disgrace to justice," yelled McSween.

"I am justice in Lincoln County, Scotchman."

McSween shook his head. "Not for much longer, you won't be."

That was big talk coming from a man who didn't carry a gun, but at that moment McSween was backed by a hundred sullen men.

The sheriff reached inside his coat and pulled out a stack of folded papers. "You know what this is, Scotchman? A warrant for your arrest for swindling Mr. Murphy. I'll serve it one day when you're alone." He laughed. "So long, Scotchman. I've got to check your store now, make sure my deputies haven't looted it." He marched on, mocking McSween with his laugh.

When the sheriff disappeared inside Tunstall's store, the crowd began to disperse in twos and threes. We'd done a lot of talking, but not one of us had been nearly as brave as the Kid and Fred Waite. At least we knew we were still alive, though we couldn't be certain about the two of them. McSween, with Brewer and Middleton, retreated into his house, followed by a dozen others.

I mulled over my options, knowing my absence back at the Chisum ranch would cause alarm because they were in need of my supplies. I wasn't going to trade with Murphy, and as long as his men held Tunstall's store, I wasn't going to trade there. I decided I would stay the night and begin the trek back to the ranch the next day.

The rest of the afternoon I spent in the warmth of the house, trying to ignore the big talk of the others. Once McSween approached me. "We can count on John Chisum and his men, can't we?"

I shrugged. "Chisum's still in jail, last I heard. I don't speak for him or his men, just me."

McSween looked as lost as an Apache at a ballroom dance. "He's with us, isn't he?"

"Whatever you think," I replied, then slipped past him, deciding I'd go out back to water and feed my team. It was almost dark when I approached the adobe-walled corral. Several horses were penned inside, but not nearly as many as the day before because fewer men were guarding McSween's place. Like me, most were abandoning the lawyer to return to their homes or their chores.

The horses seemed more nervous than usual at my approach. The moment I closed the wooden gate behind me I understood why. Someone else was in the corral, hidden behind the chest-high adobe wall. I felt a hand clamp over my jaw and the end of a gun in my back. For a moment I figured I'd be sleeping beside the Englishman like I had the previous night. When I heard my captor whisper, I couldn't have been more shocked than if the President himself had gotten the drop on me.

"Don't start a commotion," said the Kid.

I couldn't believe it. How in the hell had he escaped from Brady without setting off a battle?

"Do you understand, Lomax?" he said.

I nodded and he removed his hand from my mouth. I spun around and stared at him. He wore a grin bigger than a slice of watermelon.

"I slipped the wrist manacles, knocked out my guard, then freed myself and Waite."

From the opposite side of the gate I heard Waite grunt and then spotted him squatted low to the ground.

"Have you got your supplies yet?" Billy asked.

Shaking my head, I shrugged. "They won't sell, not with Brady's men in control."

"Good," the Kid growled. "I owe the sheriff a few favors for stealing my carbine and pistol. I plan to take the Englishman's store back. There's ammunition and guns there we need to fight our battles. You're gonna help me and Waite."

The Kid had this way of volunteering you to do things you really weren't set on doing.

"All you've got to do," Billy said, "is hitch up your team and drive it over to the store. Me and Waite'll be hidden in the back. You get them to open the door and we'll rush them."

I grimaced. "What if they start shooting?"

"Duck." The Kid laughed.

Now I wasn't sure I was glad the Kid had escaped, not with me being the bait for taking on the sheriff's men. I found my horses and began to harness them as Billy and Waite plotted.

"There's more men inside McSween's that could assist," I offered, hoping the Kid would want me to rouse them.

He shook his head. "It'd create too much commotion. Our only chance is to take them by surprise, or they might fire the store."

I was as nervous as a frog with a busted jumper on a busy road, but I went along because Billy had a hard look about him. When the horses were harnessed, I eased them out of the corral and hitched them to the Chisum wagon. Darkness had settled by the time I climbed in, took the reins, and started the rig forward. The Kid and Waite rode in the back, their pistols drawn.

I swung wide of McSween's house until I hit the road, then angled toward the store. Its windows were aglow with lamplight. Hiding behind the wagon sideboard, Billy grumbled, "I hope that bastard Brady's still there."

After reining the wagon up in front of the store, I tied the lines and slid out of the seat onto the ground. My knees shivered from the cold—at least that's what I told myself as I stepped up to the door and knocked. Then I retreated a step so the deputies could see me through the window.

"What do you want?" came the gruff voice of Deputy George Hindman, who had ridden with Tunstall's murderers.

"To talk to you about buying supplies," I answered.

"Won't do any good. Our orders are not to sell anything."

"I've got cash," I pleaded. "Is the sheriff inside?"

"Not here," the other deputy replied. "He returned to the House earlier. Buy your goods there."

"I'll pay you for letting me in," I offered.

That got their attention. There was a long pause, and then I could hear them whispering. "How much's in it for us?" asked Hindman.

"Depends on how many of you there are."

"Two," the other responded.

"I'd say twenty-five dollars apiece, and that'd still leave me money for the necessities."

There was another pause, then a rattle at the door as they worked the latch. My knees shook.

The door cracked just enough for Hindman to eyeball me. "Show me the money."

Not having any, I had to bluff. "You think that's wise, me showing you where other people might see?"

The door widened, and I saw both deputies holding pistols.

I stuck my hand in my pocket as if I was going for the money. "I'd feel a little better about this if you'd holster those guns. I get the creeping feeling you might rob me."

Both deputies laughed. "You think we're crooks?" Hindman asked.

"You do work with Murphy," I replied.

They thought that was a good joke and laughed heartily as they slid their pistols back in their holsters.

"I feel better," I announced loudly, "now that you've holstered your revolvers."

I took a tentative step toward the door, then dropped to the walk at the sound of a commotion behind me.

Almost before I hit the planks at my feet, I saw Billy bolt through the door, his borrowed revolver in his hand.

It happened so fast the deputies didn't have time to react before Billy was at their side, relieving them of their revolvers and their pride. The deputies cursed me, but Billy told them to shut up and gave them a message to take to the sheriff.

"Tell Brady I hold him responsible for the Englishman's death and that I intend to get him for it and for stealing my Winchester." The Kid shoved both men past me.

They grumbled until they saw Waite holding his pistol on them. Their manners suddenly improved.

"Unbuckle your gun belts and drop them to the ground," the Kid ordered.

They hesitated.

"Now," he commanded, waving his revolver in their faces.

The two undid their holsters and tossed them aside.

"Now run to Brady. Tell him what I told you or I'll kill the both of you next time we meet." Billy fired his pistol over their heads to speed them along.

Neither deputy needed any more encouragement. Both ran across the street and behind the nearest adobe house to screen their retreat to Murphy's store.

Billy's laugh mocked them as they ran. The shot drew several men from McSween's place. They cheered when they saw Billy and Waite in control of Tunstall's store, then ran over, laughing and shouting questions to Billy. He retreated inside, heading straight for the guns and ammunition. He took a half-dozen cartons of bullets and set them aside for himself, then picked up the single .41-caliber Colt on display to replace his own.

Ignoring the others around him, he turned to me. "Get the supplies you wanted."

McSween appeared. "Don't take anything without paying for it."

The store clerk, Sam Corbett, emerged from the throng of men. "I'll handle the ledger. That's my job, McSween." He gathered my goods, then totaled the amount, which came to more than three hundred dollars.

"Add it to Chisum's account," I said.

With help from Corbett, the Kid, and Waite, I loaded my wagon. Corbett invited me to stay the night in the store along with Billy, Waite, Middleton, and the Coes. We all gathered our gear from McSween's and joined Corbett. He opened some canned peaches, which we ate for supper as we talked about Tunstall's murder. Before we pitched our beds on the floor, I went outside and hobbled my team of horses and covered the supplies with a tarp. I wanted to leave first thing in the morning to avoid trouble and any further delay in returning to the ranch.

Though there were a couple bunks back in what had been Tunstall's quarters, none of us felt comfortable sleeping in them, so we pitched out bedrolls on the floor between tables and piles of goods. Billy wrote another missive for me to give to Ash Upson.

Before dawn I was up, gathering my bedroll and putting my coat on, anxious to leave. The Kid heard me stirring and got up with me, grabbed his sombrero, and helped me carry my gear to the wagon. He removed the hobbles from the horses as I climbed into the seat.

With hobbles in hand the Kid approached me, shaking his head. "You be careful. Sheriff may have a mad on for you for helping me evict Hindman." He tossed the hobbles in back of the wagon.

"I'm riding away from the storm, Kid. Seems to me you're riding into it."

Billy stroked his cheek with his left hand. "The Englishman gave me a paying job, and I owe him for that."

"You paid him back with your hard work, Kid. You don't owe him anything else."

The Kid grinned. "Funny, ain't it, that I'm working for John Chisum now, just like you."

I scratched my head. "What?"

"McSween's offering three dollars a day for any man that will ride Lincoln County and rid it of all its bad men."

"McSween don't have that kind of money."

"He says Chisum's backing him, so I guess you and I are both working for John Chisum."

I shrugged. "I wouldn't put stock in the lawyer unless I heard that from Chisum's mouth myself."

"I got to put stock in someone, now that the Englishman's gone."

"Tell you what, Kid. You pulled me out of Jesse Evans's gang—saddle your horse and ride out with me. Once I return the wagon and supplies to the Chisum place, we'll just keep on riding into Texas and start over again."

The Kid didn't answer for a long time. When he did, his voice was soft but dangerous. "I've got some men to kill first."

"It'll be too late by then, Kid. You know where to find me if you change your mind."

He nodded beneath his sombrero as I rattled the reins and the wagon lurched forward. "Adios, Lomax."

"Take care of yourself, Kid." I aimed the team for Roswell.

The trip back to the ranch took two days. Despite the cold I managed okay, delivering the Kid's letter to Ash Upson and reaching the ranch by the middle of the next afternoon. I received a huge welcome.

"What the hell took you so long?" demanded Sallie Chisum.

"Good to see you again, Sallie."

The foreman shook his head. "I've been a tad concerned about you, Lomax."

"But not worried enough to send men out to find me."

Grinning, the foreman nodded. "That's about the size of it. Our winter crews are short enough as is."

The foreman instructed a couple hands to unload the wagon and ordered me to tell him about the doings in Lincoln. Sallie listened, her interest rising at every mention of the Kid but flagging at the mention of anyone else.

"Those are problems in the mountains," the foreman said. "I can't let them reach the prairie or the ranch'll go to hell."

"Hell," I challenged, "Chisum's already promised to pay three dollars a day to the men who ride against Murphy."

The foreman looked at me like I had been drinking. "I ain't heard about this."

I shrugged. "Neither had I, but that's what the lawyer McSween is telling folks."

The foreman could only shake his head. "They're damn fools if they believe him. Chisum don't think much of McSween."

I was glad to hear that.

Over the next two weeks, we heard occasional bits of information from the mountains. Dick Brewer and the Kid were leading a band of men—Waite, Middleton, and several others who had aligned themselves with McSween or were taken with the Kid—around Lincoln County, trying to serve Wilson's warrants on Tunstall's murderers. They called themselves the Regulators.

We seemed isolated from the problem, though ranch hands occasionally reported seeing the Regulators or their quarry on Chisum land, but that isolation ended not three weeks after Tunstall's burial. The foreman rushed into the house just before dusk one evening and took a Winchester from Chisum's gun rack. "Get you a gun, Lomax. We've trouble approaching."

I jumped up from my rocking chair and grabbed a carbine, then followed the foreman out the front door. He pointed to the south, where I saw a dozen men approaching. At first I didn't recognize any of them in the poor light. I would've taken one for the Kid had he been wearing a Mexican sombrero, but he was wearing a regular felt hat like most white men.

As the group came within fifty yards, I realized it was indeed Billy, following Dick Brewer and two men with their arms tied. "It's the Regulators," I told the foreman.

"I don't like it," he said. "It just means trouble, them coming on Chisum land." As the group drew closer, I recognized the two prisoners as Buck Morton and Frank Baker, two of the men who had killed Tunstall.

About the same time, Dick Brewer saw me and called a greeting. "You running the place with Chisum still in jail?"

The foreman didn't take too kindly to the question, so I introduced him to Brewer. "It's either him or Sallie Chisum in charge—I can't always tell," I said. The foreman didn't take too kindly to that, either.

Brewer took off his hat as he addressed the foreman. "We don't mean to trespass, but we're law, and we caught these men. All we want is to stay the night before heading for Lincoln with them."

Buck Morton sneered. "They ain't the law any more than Lomax is there, and we'll never see Lincoln alive."

Billy laughed. "Wouldn't have been a problem, Buck, if you'd had faster horses."

I sidled toward Billy. "What happened to your sombrero?"

"Had to give it up. I was the only white man in Lincoln County wearing one. Murphy's men could pick me out from miles away."

The posse was a ragged-looking bunch, and that worried the foreman for sure, but he agreed to let them stay the night as long as they left first thing in the morning.

"We'll be gone by sunrise," Brewer told him.

I turned to Billy. "Hate to be the one to tell you, Kid, but Sallie ran off and joined a nunnery."

Billy scoffed as he dismounted. "She just as well have joined a nunnery with you around," he said, "but I didn't come to see Sallie."

Those words told me more than any that Billy had changed. The youth that back in the fall had thought of little but dancing and women now had his mind on other things, revenge foremost among them. He strode over to Morton, grabbed him by the arm, and pulled him off his horse. The prisoner fell to his knees, then heaved himself up awkwardly, shaking his bound hands at the Kid.

Next, the Kid grabbed Baker and jerked him off his mount. Baker, though, was prepared and managed to stay on his feet after a couple steps to catch his balance.

"No call for that, Kid," Brewer scolded.

Billy nodded. "No call for them to be riding with us, Dick. We should've killed them miles back, left them on the trail like they did the Englishman."

"When I was sworn in as constable, I took an oath to defend the law and do what was right, Kid. You took the same oath. I intend to see that we get these men back to Lincoln."

"What then?" challenged Billy. "Turn them over to Brady, who wouldn't arrest them to begin with? They'll never come to trial."

The argument was disrupted by a clatter on the front porch as Sallie barged out the front door and rushed down the path toward us, her eyes fixed on Billy, her hands patting her hair in place.

"Billy," she said, "I'm glad to see you."

The Kid waved her away. "No time for foolishness right now."

Sallie stopped in her tracks, her smile fading like the dying sunlight. She took to pouting like I had seen her do a dozen times around her uncle, but she only drew Billy's scorn.

"Leave me be, Sallie."

She spun around and strode back in the house, slamming the door behind her. Sallie was unaccustomed to rejection.

Brewer issued orders and the other men dismounted, some taking the horses to the stable and others guarding Baker and Morton. The foreman said half the men could stay in the ranch house, but the rest would have to sleep in the bunkhouse out back.

"I'm staying in the ranch house, and the prisoners are staying with me," Billy announced.

Neither Brewer nor anyone else argued.

Billy pointed the prisoners toward the house. "You've eaten John Chisum's beef many a time," he said. "Now you'll get to sleep under his roof." He laughed as he herded them indoors.

The foreman, Brewer, and I followed along with a couple others. They were a solemn bunch, and not much was said. The foreman offered them a share of what food was available, but the cook had not prepared enough to go around, so everyone had a few bites of fried beef, a biscuit, and some coffee.

Sallie helped Buck Morton and Frank Baker with their food since they couldn't eat with their bound hands. Morton spoke with a soft Virginia accent, and Sallie seemed taken with him, not so much because she liked him but because she wanted to make the Kid jealous. She sweet-talked Morton and offered to get him anything he wanted.

"How about a gun?" he answered.

Billy gave Sallie a hard stare. "Don't be fooling with me, Sallie, not tonight."

She patted Morton on the shoulder. "Can't do that. Anything else?"

Morton nodded. "A pencil and paper. I want to write a letter back home."

Sallie left the room, then returned in a few moments with a pencil, paper, and writing board that she propped

on his lap. Even though his hands were bound in front
of him, he was able to write with a little assistance
from her.

While Morton wrote his letter, the Kid kept whispering his desire to shoot the pair on the way to Lincoln
the next day. Morton never flinched. He wrote with a
steady hand, the same hand that had pulled a trigger
against the Englishman. When he finished, Sallie put
the letter in an envelope and stuck it in his vest pocket.
He thanked her.

Sallie sashayed around the parlor, trying to entice
Billy to join her, but Billy's desire had shriveled away
beneath his vow to avenge the Englishman. Finally she
left in exasperation.

With her gone, the men argued about whether to kill
Morton or Baker tomorrow. They debated for more than
an hour, Brewer taking the stance that the law was the
only avenue of true justice, Billy insisting that vigilante
justice was the only kind open to them. I think Billy
was intent less on murdering Morton and Baker than on
worrying them.

"I know this," he said. "If they try to escape tonight
I'll kill them without asking a question."

From their talk I learned that the Regulators had
run into five men on the prairie well south of the
ranch headquarters. The five had split up, and the
Regulators had taken off after Morton and Baker. After
an eight-mile chase Morton's and Baker's horses played
out, and there was nothing they could do but surrender
or fight to the death. They chose to surrender, though
I was beginning to wonder if that truly meant anything
other than a few more hours of life. I grew tired and
repaired to my room, where the foreman was waiting
for me.

"I want you to ride with them tomorrow," he
said.

"Why?"

"I don't want them killed on the ranch. Go as far as Roswell, for sure, farther if you can."

I hadn't ridden much since I was butt-shot, which I reminded the foreman. He didn't seem too concerned. After all, it was my behind, not his. I agreed to his request and retired.

True to their word, the Regulators left the ranch house at sunrise. I went with them. My tail was a bit sore astride Flash, but it was good to be on the mule again. At least he wouldn't be leading me into trouble like Chisum's yellow dun had.

We got to Roswell before Ash Upson unlocked his store, but Billy convinced him to open early. Billy could be a very persuasive talker, especially when he threatened to shoot the place up.

Upon letting us in, Upson saw the prisoners and realized he had a story he could peddle to the newspapers. He grabbed a pencil and paper and began to ask questions and take notes.

"I'm not talking," Morton said, "until you make me a promise."

"What's that?" Upson asked.

With his bound hands he managed to pull his letter from his vest pocket. "See that this gets mailed. It's the last letter I'll ever write."

Upson agreed, taking the letter from him.

"You won't forget?" Morton asked. "I want my family to know what happened to me."

"I promise," Upson replied. Then he questioned Morton and Baker for ten minutes.

The Regulators helped themselves to jerky and crackers for breakfast but didn't offer any to their prisoners. Upson, feeling sorry for Morton and Baker, gave them some anyway.

"It's a waste of food," Billy said.

"It's my last meal," Morton shot back.

When Upson finished with the prisoners' stories, he talked to Brewer and a couple of the other posse members before turning to the Kid. "What have you done since your daring escape from beneath the nose of Sheriff Brady and his men?"

The Kid stared at Morton and Baker. "I've been waiting to get even with the Englishman's murderers. It won't be long now. We need bullets."

Upson put away his writing implements and walked to the counter, pulling out cartons of ammunition from a shelf on the back wall. "That enough?"

"For today," replied the Kid.

Brewer stepped forward and paid for the ammunition, then herded the Regulators out of the store. "We best get going. We've a day-and-a-half ride ahead of us."

I followed them outside and mounted up, riding west out of town. I stayed with them maybe two hours as they followed the trail along the Rio Hondo.

"It's not safe," Billy argued, "us keeping to the main trail. Murphy's men could ambush us. We need to take a back trail."

His argument made sense. Everyone agreed that was the best way to reach Lincoln safely, everyone except Morton and Baker. When the posse turned off the main trail and headed north toward the mountains, I stopped my horse and wished them a safe journey. I knew I would never see Morton and Baker again.

Two days later I learned I was right. The two prisoners had been shot in an escape attempt. At least that was what the Regulators said.

Chapter Nineteen

I learned of Morton's and Baker's deaths from John Chisum himself. The sheriff up in Las Vegas had finally gotten tired of spending public money to feed one of the richest men in New Mexico Territory, so he just up and released him.

The old cowman had a grin as wide as a crescent moon when he arrived in his buggy. Sallie rushed out of the house and threw her arms around him as he crawled out of the rig and tried to stand. He seemed pleased by her welcome.

"How are you, Sallie?"

"Fine," she squealed, "and so is Lomax."

I was touched that she cared.

"Now that he's okay," she continued, "do I have to pay him out of my money any longer?"

Chisum laughed and shook his head. "No, no, just run along and fix me a big supper."

She spun around and marched past me, her arrogant nose in the air. "I don't owe you nothing now," she growled.

"What was that, Sallie?" Chisum asked.

Without missing a beat she looked over her shoulder and smiled. "I told him I was glad he was as good as before."

Chisum just laughed. He enjoyed spoiling her, and she took to spoiling like a kitten takes to a saucer of milk.

I greeted him and shook his hand. "Glad to have you back."

No sooner had I gotten the words out of my mouth than the foreman jogged up. "Welcome home," he called, grasping the cowman's hand and shaking it warmly.

"You heard Tunstall was murdered?" I asked.

Chisum stroked his chin. "He never understood that rough land produces rough men, men with no regard for life." He jerked his thumb over his shoulder toward Roswell. "Ash Upson said a couple of the killers were killed by vigilantes two days ago, out in Black Water Canyon."

"Baker and Morton?" I asked, knowing it was them.

Chisum nodded. "Upson also heard that Tom Hill and Jesse Evans got shot up raiding a sheepherder's camp in the mountains. Hill is dead and Jesse's wounded so bad the doctor at Fort Stanton doesn't think he'll live. All this happened on the same day, the best Upson could figure out."

I caught my breath. Had Billy not pried me away from that band of thieves, I might have been dead like them. With three of the four men who had killed Tunstall dead and the fourth dying, I thought the Kid could leave Lincoln County. He had avenged Tunstall's death. Now we could ride away and look for honest work.

"With so many of the Boys dead, you think the rustling'll die off?" I asked.

Chisum shook his head. "Not as long as Murphy's still alive. He's behind most of the mischief, and he's got connections with the district judge and district attorney, likely even higher. Upson heard that the governor of New Mexico Territory himself had visited Lincoln County. If it's true, he's doing Murphy's business, not anyone else's."

As was his habit, Chisum talked on, but I didn't catch much of what he said. Lincoln County was the

meanest place I'd ever been. A county can't help but
be mean when the law's crooked. Wondering if it was
time for me to leave, I carried Chisum's valise into the
house while the foreman discussed the ranch with him.
I knew I had stayed too long in Leadville and that had
only led to trouble, but I felt I owed it to Billy to take
him with me.

The trouble had changed him for the worse. There
was a mean streak in him that I hadn't known before. It
was a dangerous streak in one so young.

When Sallie announced supper, I joined her,
Chisum, and the foreman. At the table we men couldn't
discuss the news because Sallie was too intent on making
herself the center of attention. That was fine with me
because I had a lot of things to think about.

After sunrise the next morning, I mounted Flash and
rode up the Pecos, trying to clear my head and decide
whether to leave or stay. It was near sunset when I
returned to Chisum's place, arriving just before supper
and just before three horsemen rode up. Two of them I
had seen at Tunstall's funeral, though I didn't know their
names. The other was Alexander A. McSween himself. He
was as wide-eyed and bewildered as I remembered him.
He stopped his horse in front of me without showing a
sign of recognition. "Is John Chisum about?"

I shrugged. "Don't know. I just rode in myself. I'll
see." Inside I found Chisum dozing in a chair. I cleared
my throat, and he awoke with a start. "Alex McSween's
outside," I announced.

Chisum yawned and stretched. "I guess things have
gotten too hot for him in Lincoln. A fool like him ought
to pack a sidearm."

"You don't."

Grinning, Chisum stood up. "I ain't a fool, even if I
did spend a couple months in jail." He marched past me
and out the door, greeting McSween graciously.

"I must ask a favor of you, Mr. Chisum. Might I stay
at your place for a few weeks? Lincoln is not safe for me

right now, and I've written my dear Susan to meet me here when she returns from Missouri. That is all right, is it not?"

"You and Mrs. McSween are always welcome, Alex."

McSween crawled off his horse and marched over to shake Chisum's hand. "Thank you, thank you," he said in a nervous, squeaky voice. "I'm glad I can count on you when so many have turned against us."

Chisum wrapped his arm around the Scotchman. "Is it that bad?"

Nodding, McSween let out a long sigh. "The law's against us."

"You knew that going in," Chisum answered.

"But the governor, too?"

"I hear he came to Lincoln."

McSween spat at the ground. "He did. A fact-finding mission, he called it, but he only talked to Murphy's men, not a one sympathetic to our cause."

"What did you expect?"

"He's the governor, though. Do you know what he did? He invalidated Squire Wilson's commission as justice of the peace—the one man sympathetic to us—and appointed one of Murphy's men."

Chisum whistled.

"Timing was terrible," McSween continued. "That very day Brewer and the Regulators were bringing Morton and Baker to town for trial on warrants issued by Wilson. The two murderers tried to escape, but were killed. The governor's proclamation invalidated those warrants. Brewer, Bonney, Waite, Middleton, and the rest of the Regulators are being sought for murder now."

"Seems you've nothing but bad news, Alex," Chisum said.

"There's worse. Sheriff Brady's carrying a warrant for my arrest. If they ever arrest me, I'll never leave jail alive."

I had always thought a man as religious and pious as McSween wouldn't have feared death, but I was wrong. He was practically cowering on John Chisum's doorstep, even though he was more than fifty miles away from any real threat.

His cowardice turned my stomach and seemed to settle poorly on Chisum, who turned to the lawyer's two companions, still mounted. "You boys are welcome to stay the night and have supper with us."

They declined the invitation. "We need to get back to our places," said one.

"We'd be obliged for some food we could eat in the saddle," answered the other.

Chisum nodded. "I wouldn't abandon my place in troubled times."

I took the cowman's remark as an insult to McSween for leaving Lincoln.

Chisum pointed to the corner of the house. "Ride out back and tell the kitchen help or my niece that I said to give you food."

The men touched the brims of their hats and rode away, leaving the bewildered McSween with us.

"Supper's not long away, Alex," Chisum said, "if you need to wash up."

McSween plodded past us as if he carried the weight of Lincoln County's troubles on his shoulders.

Chisum shook his head. "Some men can live with danger, some can't." He gave me a hard stare. "Murphy's a coward, too. Maybe that's why he hates McSween so. McSween's a naive coward, while Murphy is more cunning. Murphy'll turn tail and run when he loses control."

We went inside and washed up for supper. McSween was waiting for us, and I couldn't help but snicker. Apparently he had washed by splashing water against his face; his cheeks were mottled with alternating streaks of grime and clean where the water had run.

He eyed me, then lifted his hand. "Have we met?"

I nodded. "Lomax. H. H. Lomax is the name."

McSween stared blankly at me. "I don't recall. I do remember a Gadrich Lomax. A fine man, likable man."

Chisum looked at me with a grimace that said the lawyer must be talking about a different Gadrich Lomax from the one he had encountered.

"You related to Gadrich Lomax?"

"Not that I know," I replied.

The lawyer shook his head. "A pity. He's a good man out of fine stock."

"Livestock," I replied, trying to make a funny.

"No," McSween replied, without so much as the glimmer of a smile. "I guess they're mostly dead now."

At that moment I decided McSween was going crazy from fear of death. He'd stepped in a hole and all he could see was a grave.

Chisum shrugged at McSween's comment and pointed us to the dining table, where Sallie waited with arms crossed over her bosom. The thing I remember about supper that night was how distant McSween's mind seemed from reality.

McSween was with us for two weeks before Mrs. McSween arrived from Missouri. I'd asked Chisum and the foreman to send me to a line camp to work cattle, but they'd put me to carrying supplies to the various camps. I told Chisum I'd sleep in the bunkhouse once she got there. "I don't want to be under the same roof with that woman."

"You don't trust her either," he answered. "Shame Alex doesn't have the grit in his craw that that woman has. If he did, he wouldn't be cowering like an abandoned pup under our roof. She'd fight, not run."

"Her fighting's not what scares me."

Chisum slapped me on the shoulder. "That's one way to put it."

A couple days later, Mrs. McSween drove up in a buggy. It was a pleasant late March day that hinted of spring's approach. She was wearing a new dress that

was powdered with trail dust, and she carried a fancy
parasol. In the back of the buggy were two trunks filled,
I suspected, with new clothes. I wondered where she'd
gotten all the money and if there might be any truth to
the rumors that McSween was gradually bleeding the
resources of the Tunstall estate.

Chisum called inside the house, and McSween came
out, squinting against the sunlight. He hadn't been outside much since his arrival because he feared assassins.
He seemed reluctant now to venture beyond the front
door, but he finally eased away from the house, looking
around nervously, and walked quickly to his wife. He
stood staring blankly at her as she sat waiting for him
to help her out of the buggy. After several moments she
climbed out by herself, then put her arms around him
and her head on his shoulder.

It was a touching sight, one that threatened to make
me puke—husband and wife, prey and predator. As she
hugged her spouse, Mrs. McSween saw me standing
beside John Chisum. She winked.

Chisum snickered. "Looks like you won't have to be
reintroduced to her."

"I'm moving my things to the bunkhouse. I'll take my
meals there," I said, spinning around for the door. It didn't
take me near as long to remove my belongings as it did for
Mrs. McSween to see that her trunks were unloaded and
carried inside. From the bunkhouse I watched McSween
struggle with one of the trunks before Chisum came over,
lifted it handily, and carried it in. I wondered if McSween
was good for anything, save maybe target practice.

Over the next two days I was able to avoid the
McSweens, but not Sallie Chisum. She came out to the
bunkhouse the next morning using language that would
make even the roughest cowboy blush.

"I hate that woman," she said, then began to call Mrs.
McSween a few names I found highly amusing though
physically impossible. "She's nothing but a hussy, and

her husband's too blind to see. She's why you moved out, isn't she?"

"I've never been fond of redheads."

"She's been asking about you. Her husband can't remember you, and she can't forget you."

"I don't care for either of them."

She smiled and walked up beside me. "Me neither," she said, grabbing my arm. "Let's go for a walk."

I wasn't fool enough to think she loved me. Hell, up until then she'd ignored me at best and treated me with disgust at worst. She just wanted to strut about with me on her arm and tweak Mrs. McSween's nose. No, I'd learned long ago that the only thing that happened when you got caught in the middle of a catfight was you got your eyes scratched out.

"I've got work to do."

Sallie could be as obstinate as a fence post and a downright pest when she set her mind to something. She squeezed my arms, her fingernails digging through my shirt and into my flesh. I had been taught never to hit a woman, unless, of course, she really needed it. I drew back my fist to pop her on the jaw, but she didn't flinch. She just jutted her chin forward, daring me to go ahead.

Not knowing just how to preserve my manly honor, I was considerably relieved when a man on horseback trotted up. I looked from the badge on his chest to his face and recognized one of the deputies the Kid and Waite had evicted from Tunstall's store.

He studied me. "I'm Deputy George Hindman. You're Lomax, aren't you? H.H. Lomax?"

In Sheriff Brady's absence Hindman had been the deputy in charge of the posse that killed Tunstall. I nodded. "H.H. Lomax. No relation to Gadrich Lomax."

The deputy snarled, "I know Gadrich when I see him, and the next time I see him I plan on shooting him."

"Glad to hear it," I replied.

Hindman pointed his trigger finger at me. "As for you, I've got something for you." He lifted his hand to a vest pocket, pulled out a wad of papers, and leafed through them. "Here you are," he finally said, pulling a sheet from the stack and offering it to me.

I hesitated. "What is it?"

He smiled. "A subpoena." Leaning over in his saddle, he extended his hand.

"For what?" I took the paper from him.

"To testify before the grand jury next week."

"About what?"

"Your part in the murder of Frank Baker and Buck Morton in Black Water Canyon."

"I had nothing to do with that, wasn't even with the Regulators."

"Folks in Roswell saw you leave with them."

"But I came back," I protested.

"Nobody made mention of that." Hindman tipped his hat and smiled. "Now, can you tell me if Alex McSween's staying at the ranch? Some say he is. I've got papers for him."

Sallie Chisum stepped forward, her grin bigger than the back end of a wagon. "He sure is. His wife, too. Follow me and I'll take you right to them."

"Why, thank you, Miss Sallie."

"You're welcome. Another subpoena, is it? What for, pray tell?"

"He's accused of swindling Lawrence Murphy."

I heard Sallie cluck her tongue. "I bet his wife put him up to it. She spends money faster than her lawyer husband can make it. At least that's what I hear."

"You're likely right, Miss Sallie."

Sallie walked to the house, still spewing venom at Mrs. McSween. About ten minutes later I saw Hindman ride off toward Lincoln.

I took supper that night in the bunkhouse, then strolled around a bit, considering whether I should just saddle Flash up and leave the territory. Down by the stream I found Chisum with a cane pole, fishing.

"Having any luck?" I asked.

He lifted his line from the water. Even in the moonlight I could see his hook was naked of bait. "I had to get out. Sallie and Mrs. McSween take to each other like cats and dogs. I tired of listening to their sly insults. Sallie did take a moment from criticizing Mrs. McSween to tell me you've been subpoenaed as well."

"I'm trying to decide whether to stay on or leave the country."

"A man has to make his own decisions, but you can't always run from things."

I had run from Leadville after the most unfortunate death of a two-bit lawyer, and I had survived better than if I'd stayed, so I didn't know if I believed Uncle John or not.

"You've a place here," Chisum offered, "so what are you running from?"

"Mrs. McSween, I reckon."

Chisum laughed. "I don't care for redheads myself, especially married ones, but I guess I'll go with them to Lincoln for the grand jury. He's too weak of heart to face the trip alone. You're welcome to ride along with us."

Shaking my head vigorously, I declined. "I was thinking about drawing my pay and heading up the Ruidoso to see Frank and George Coe. They've been hospitable when I was hungry and needed shelter."

"Long as you're that way, Lomax, you could ride on up to the Indian Agency up at Blazer's Mill. They're taking bids on contracts to supply beef for the summer and fall, and you could deliver my bid. When's the grand jury?"

"The first of April," I replied.

"Good. Bids are due the tenth. After you finish up in Lincoln, head over to Blazer's Mill and drop off the bid. When you get back, we can put you to punching cattle again, if your wound'll allow it."

"It's a deal."

"Give me tomorrow to figure out my bid, then I'll give it to you."

"Thanks," I said, leaving him to his futile fishing.

Late the next afternoon Chisum brought the sealed bid to the bunkhouse and gave me five months' back pay and a twenty-five-dollar bonus for the two rustlers I'd killed. In all, I had almost $175.

"I'll ride in with the McSweens about noon the day the grand jury convenes," Chisum said. "Mrs. McSween said you could stay at her house with the Reverend Ealy and his family."

"Nope, I don't care to get close to that woman or her husband. Why you helping them out, anyway?"

Chisum scratched one of those huge ears and shrugged. "Guess I feel sorry for the fellow. He wasn't meant to live out west. He should be back east, where folks are more civil."

I pondered the wisdom of Chisum's statement, then asked him a question. "If he wasn't meant to live out west, you think he was meant to die out here?"

"Hadn't thought of it that way, but I suspect you're right. For all his faults, the Englishman was a likable fellow. McSween's not. Too pompous, too arrogant. He's a damn lawyer, too."

It did me good to see that Chisum felt the same way I did about redheads and lawyers. He slapped me on the back and wished me luck on my trip.

I was more worried about the grand jury. "What if I'm indicted and arrested?"

Chisum shook his head. "It'll never happen. Murphy has the judge and the district attorney in his pocket, but the grand jury's made up of regular citizens. They're tired of Murphy and all the killing he's spawned."

"Seems to me," I ventured, "that the deaths of Morton, Baker, and Hill and the wounding of Jesse Evans ought to avenge the Englishman."

"Vengeance has a life of its own," Chisum replied as he left.

I awoke early the next morning, took some cold biscuits from the cook for breakfast, then carried my carbine and my bedroll out to the barn, where I saddled up Flash and rode off toward Roswell before the sun popped out of the morning sky. I camped the first night in the foothills, then rode on into the Rio Hondo valley, planning to spend the second night with Frank Coe.

With the weather warming, I expected to see activity along the river, men plowing fields, digging irrigation ditches, cleaning brush along the stream. Instead I saw fields still stubbled from the previous fall's crops, cabins abandoned, corrals knocked down, and stock running free. The valley seemed forlorn, as if it mourned the Englishman six weeks after his death. I realized how sheltered life was on the Chisum ranch. Money could buy security. The folks who lived in the abandoned houses had no money.

A little after noon the second day out, I reached Frank Coe's place. I was disappointed to see that it was no different from the others I'd passed; there was work to be done and no one to be found. I let myself in the cabin. By the furniture remaining and the food still stocked on the shelves, I knew Frank had not abandoned the place, but I could tell he wasn't spending much time there, either. I hid Flash in the small lean-to of a barn and built a fire in his stove, then fried up some potatoes I found in a sack.

About dusk, I heard a scream outside. I grabbed my carbine and jumped for the door. No sooner had I cleared it than I heard a whiz and a thud in the wall behind me, then the retort of the gun that had fired the bullet. Scrambling back inside, I wondered who my friend was. I jerked the door shut and spent a nervous two hours peeking out the window, trying to spot my assailant. I saw nothing, heard nothing.

After a sleepless night I arose and left before light, clinging to the Rio Ruidoso rather than the road to San Patricio. The town was closed up tighter than a preacher's mind. The pockmarked walls told me it was more than just the early hour that kept people inside. Life in Lincoln County had grown hellish; every living person was in danger.

Beyond San Patricio, I came to George Coe's place. I hollered for George, then Frank, but heard only my soft echo shouting back at me. I dismounted and tied Flash to a hitching post, then let myself in. Like Frank's place, George's was full of his belongings and a little food. I knew he would return, because his fiddle hung from a couple pegs in the wall.

I stayed at George's place until the day before the grand jury was to convene, hiding Flash in the barn and never lighting a fire for fear it would draw attention. I depleted George's canned goods and his store of dried apple slices. How I wanted to see the Coes and the Kid. Money in my pocket and no one to share it with—like everyone else in the mountains of Lincoln County, I was afraid to come out into the sunlight.

At noon that day I wrote George a note that I would repay him for his food, saddled Flash, and started for Lincoln, taking the direct route over the mountains that separated the Rio Ruidoso from the Rio Bonito. The route was harder on Flash but safer for me than the regular roads into town.

By late afternoon I was atop the mountains and could see Lincoln below me. It was one of the damnedest sights I ever saw, people coming in from all over and the roads filled with men on horseback, families in wagons, people afoot. Folks were camped out behind the houses on both sides of the street. Even though I felt better about riding into Lincoln, I waited until dusk to start down the mountain. I didn't intend to make my presence known to anyone unless I happened to see the Kid or the Coes.

Once I reached the valley, I skirted the campfires and aimed Flash toward Tunstall's store, planning to toss my bedroll across the street because I figured I'd have a better chance of catching the Kid and the Coes there than anywhere else. I suspected they'd been subpoenaed as well.

Across from the store I found a juniper tree with no one around, so I dismounted and tended Flash. Then I tossed down my bedroll and watched the store for any sign of Billy. The town was quiet, and I was relieved for I had feared trouble. Members of both factions were about, but it seemed as if everyone was tired of all the fighting and trouble.

Come morning the sun shone brightly on Lincoln County, and I could've sworn there was hope in the air, an optimism that the troubles might be put aside. I clung to the shadows of the juniper, not wanting to draw attention to myself, and kept my carbine handy in case I had misread the general mood.

For the most part folks stayed near their camps or homes, awaiting some sign of activity at the temporary courthouse, an adobe building owned by John Wilson, the defrocked justice of the peace.

It was midmorning before I sensed a stirring in the air. I looked up the street toward the House. Five men, carbines cradled in their arms, came marching down the street, glancing nervously from side to side. I recognized Sheriff Brady, Deputy Hindman, and three other deputies. The sheriff was carrying a notice in one hand and a Winchester in the other. The very air seemed to tense as they advanced, no one certain what the lawmen planned. As they drew astride of me I thought I saw a movement across the street at the gate in the tall adobe fence that enclosed the back of the store. I could've sworn I saw the gate crack, then shut.

At the courthouse the sheriff tacked the note on the door, then said something to his deputies. They grinned and started retracing their steps toward the House.

They moved slowly, deliberately, as if they expected trouble. They seemed to note everything except the gate inching open across the street from me.

I saw the tip of a carbine barrel appear in the opening as the lawmen drew even with Tunstall's store. Before I could yell a warning, the gate swung agape and two gunmen jumped into the opening. Two others appeared with carbines over the top of the adobe fence.

Nothing was said; the assassins let their carbines talk for them. It was a pigeon shoot if I ever saw one. Brady took several bullets before he could twist around to see his assailants, then took a few more before he hit the ground. George Hindman was peppered, too, as the other three scattered, dashing for cover and squeezing off shots as they ran. One ran in my direction, and bullets flew all around me. I extended my carbine and rolled under the juniper, levering a cartridge into the chamber.

I squeezed off a shot at the two men firing from behind the wall, showering them with bits of adobe. They ducked for cover. From along the street now, several other guns opened up, splattering the fence.

No one but a fool would've shown his head after that, but one did. He ran out the gate and dashed for the sheriff's body, where he squatted over him, rifled through his pockets, then reached for Brady's carbine.

I drew a bead on the fool and was just squeezing the trigger when I recognized the Kid. I jerked my carbine away as it exploded.

The Kid howled, then limped toward the open gate, a carbine in each hand. He had more luck than a crooked gambler—bullets were flying all around him, splattering him with dirt and grit, and mine was the only one to wound him.

I saw a slash of blood on his leg as he lunged behind the adobe wall and slammed the gate shut. The bullets kept flying for a full minute after they would have done any good.

When the guns went silent, all of Lincoln held its breath. Then there was a commotion of cursing men and frightened horses behind the adobe walls of Tunstall's compound. I heard the bang of a gate against a wall, then the galloping hoofbeats of the escaping assassins.

"Why, dammit, why?" I found myself screaming at Billy. He had gone too far now. Why hadn't he stopped with the murder of Morton and Baker? For his brutal assault on Brady, he was no better than Tunstall's murderers. By their stillness I knew nothing could be done for Brady and Hindman.

And then who should appear at the east end of town, returning for the first time in weeks, but Alexander McSween and his wife. They rode in a buggy with John Chisum himself trailing them on a fine bay gelding. I know it had to be coincidence, their arrival at that time, but it left a bad taste in a lot of people's mouths. Many said Alexander McSween didn't so much as look at the bodies when he passed, but I was close enough to see and I know better. He not only looked, but he spat at Sheriff Brady.

"Brave man," I yelled as McSween passed on the way to his house.

Chisum, though, reined up his gelding and dismounted. He walked over to the sheriff and knelt beside him. He shook his head, then picked up the sheriff's hat and placed it over his head. He marched to the deputy and covered his head as well. When he stood up, Chisum removed his own hat for a moment in a gesture of respect.

Gradually others felt brave enough to emerge into the street. They approached the bodies respectfully. I don't know that I liked Brady, but he didn't deserve to die like a dog.

I dusted myself off, then edged out to the middle of the street, carrying my carbine.

Chisum saw me. "Did you see this?"

I nodded.

"Who did it?"

Though I didn't want to say, I knew I had to. "The Regulators." I looked around at the other men gathered nearby. "What did he post at the court-house?"

A man ran to check the note, then came back, waving it over his head. Chisum grabbed it from him.

"What's it say?" I called.

The cowman shook his head. "Grand jury is postponed until next week."

For Brady and Hindman, court was adjourned forever.

Chapter Twenty

Until Sheriff Brady fell dead on Lincoln's dusty street, the decent folks of Lincoln County were behind the Regulators. But that cowardly deed changed it all. Hope died with Brady in Lincoln County that day. A lot of decent folk had come to town for the grand jury, expecting to see the county take a turn for the better. Instead, they saw two men gunned down like dogs. Many folks packed up and returned home, back to some civilized state—or Texas.

Troops from Fort Stanton rode into town that afternoon. They marched up and down the street, spreading word that the grand jury had been postponed a week. I saddled Flash and rode down the street to the Wortley Hotel, taking a late lunch to avoid Murphy's men, who often gathered there. I paid fifty cents for a meal, then retreated to the McSween place. I humbled myself enough to dismount and approach the house.

I knocked on the door and gritted my teeth when Mrs. McSween answered. She smiled warmly. "Glad you came by."

"I need to see John Chisum."

"Won't you come in?"

"Not today. I just need to speak to him."

Mrs. McSween spun about and marched away, mad.

Shortly Chisum strode to the door. "You weren't hurt in the shooting, were you?" he asked. "Some say you plugged the Kid."

"Maybe I did, maybe I didn't. It all happened so fast. I'll ride up to Blazer's Mill and deliver the bid, maybe stay a few days with friends on the Ruidoso until the grand jury convenes."

Chisum shook his head. "There's likely to be a lot of mischief after Brady's killing. It don't matter if Brady leaned toward Murphy—he was still the law. When the law dies, a lot of men take advantage of it, try to take what they can or settle scores. Be careful."

I nodded, then returned to Flash, taking a moment to check the cinch on the saddle. I mounted and rode past the House, followed the Bonito to Fort Stanton, then angled south for the Ruidoso, where I spent the night. Next morning I got up early and headed upstream several miles west, gradually leaving behind the scrub pinyon and getting into the tall pines. At Carrizo Canyon I turned south and followed the trail to the mill some twenty miles away. The land was well timbered, offering plenty of places for ambush. Somewhere I crossed onto the Apache reservation, and that gave me cause for concern. My dealings with Indians hadn't always been the best, some of them taking an unnatural interest in my hair. And the Apaches still had a fierce reputation, generally because Geronimo was still running wild in Arizona and Mexico. I saw a few Apaches, but they just stared at me with faces so solemn they could curdle whiskey.

I was as edgy as a barrel full of knives and felt much better when the trail topped a low mountain and I looked down on a broad valley that was home to the Indian Agency and Blazer's Mill. The mill was about two miles beyond the agency itself, but everyone called the area Blazer's Mill for Dr. Joe Blazer and his lumber mill. Blazer, a former dentist, supplied lumber to army posts ranging from Fort Stanton, in the north, all the way south to Fort Davis in Texas. Besides the big mill on the stream, he had a huge house and an outbuilding up the bank. His house was so big that he let out rooms to bring in extra money. His wife fixed meals for travelers. After I attended to business at the agency, I figured I'd stay the night with Blazer, then return the next day to the Ruidoso.

Flash carried me to the agency building, a modest structure of sun-bleached wood. A couple Apache men squatting under a nearby tree watched me as I rode up. They chattered in their language and gesticulated wildly. My pride being what it was, I thought they might be making fun of me astride Flash. Holding on to Flash's reins, I dismounted, adjusted my gun belt to make sure the Apaches knew I could take care of myself, and strode to the door. I was feeling as cocky as a rooster at sunrise until I twisted the handle on the door. It was locked. I hammered on the door and waited. No answer. I knocked again.

"Anybody home?" I called.

Glancing over my shoulder, I caught a glimpse of the two Apaches arising from their squat and starting in my direction. They looked pretty much alike to me, except one wore his hair braided and the other loose and straight. Their haircut didn't bother me as much as the knives on their belts did.

"How," I said.

"How's that?" answered the one with braided hair. His English was easier to understand than that of most Yankees I'd ever met.

"The agent? He here?"

"No. Return two sunrises. You bring bid on cattle?"

"Yeah." I nodded. "How do you know?"

"Our stomachs growl for want of meat." He extended his hand. "I take, give to agent."

I hesitated, then shook my head. "My boss says I must give them to agent."

The Apache shook his head. "Two Dogs, my name. I can be trusted. Friend called Big Rock. He can be trusted."

"My name's Lomax," I announced. "I can be trusted."

Both Apaches stepped toward me, their hands on the handles of their knives. "No you can't, not if you brother of Lomax, Gadrich? He crooked as den of snakes, tells more lies than Indian agent."

"Cheats at dice," Big Rock added.

"Don't know this Lomax."

To my relief, the Indians loosened their grips on the knives, though their stares were still skeptical.

"I'll be back in a couple days." Quickly I mounted Flash and rode off toward the mill.

At the Blazer residence, I introduced myself to the doctor's wife, who was sweeping the front porch. I asked her about a bed for a couple nights until the Indian agent returned.

"Pay Dr. Blazer first," she said. "He's in his office in the corner of the barn out back."

I tipped my hat to Mrs. Blazer, then rode Flash around to the back. I guess Blazer had to do something with all the lumber he cut because the barn was as big as the house and likely the biggest in all of Lincoln County. After dismounting I tied Flash to a hitching post, then stretched the kinks out of my legs before approaching the corner office. Through a side window I could see Blazer working at a desk adjacent to another window that looked out over a narrow gully that widened out at the mill on the stream below. I rapped on the door and entered at Blazer's command.

As he finished making an entry in a ledger, I looked about the room, taking in the single bed and mattress in the corner, the desk neatly arranged with papers, and the gun rack holding a .45-.60 Springfield hunting rifle and four cartons of ammunition.

Finishing his business, Blazer glanced up at me. He looked as decent as they come and not the least bit worried by Lincoln County's troubles. "I'm Joe Blazer. What can I do for you?"

"I need a room for two nights until the Indian agent returns. I'm delivering a bid from John Chisum."

When Blazer shook his head, I thought he was refusing me a room. "Damn government doesn't feed those Indians what it promised. The beef bids should've been requested a long time ago."

I shrugged. "Wasn't my fault."

Blazer stood up, extending his hand. "Didn't say it was, and I didn't catch your name."

Grabbing his hand, I shook it warmly. "Lomax, H.H. Lomax."

His hand went limp in mine.

"No relation to Gadrich Lomax," I added, and his clasp returned to normal.

"Rooms are a dollar a day and board's fifty cents a meal. Your mount'll stable free. First rule is this, you leave your guns outside the house." He pointed to his hunting rifle on the wall. "Momma won't even let me keep it inside. Second rule is you pay in advance. Third rule is you don't do any drinking around the place, and the final rule is you don't smoke in the house or around the mill. Can you live with that?" He released my hand and turned his palm up.

"I've lived with worse," I said, sliding my hand into my britches and pulling out a wad of greenbacks.

Noting my money, he smiled. "You can stay as long as you like."

I spent the next two nights under Blazer's roof. I occupied myself sitting on the porch talking to whoever would listen and watching the odd characters that passed by. Oddest of all was a short, grizzled fellow riding a donkey who came by around noon to see if a bank draft had arrived for the sale of his land. From what I overheard, he was getting out of Lincoln County as soon as the money arrived. He figured the county was going to hell faster than a trainload of politicians.

I had an upstairs room that overlooked the barn and mill. The feather mattress was softer than Chisum's bed,

and Mrs. Blazer's food was as close to heaven as you
could get with all your clothes on. I enjoyed the mattress
so much that the day the Indian agent was supposed to
return, I stayed in bed until midmorning. After I got
dressed I went downstairs, and Mrs. Blazer told me I was
too late for breakfast and too early for lunch. I considered
going over to the Indian Agency and dropping off the bid,
but I had time to kill before I had to be back in Lincoln.
After Mrs. Blazer assured me the Indian agent would be
in that afternoon, I decided to walk around the place and
enjoy the fresh mountain air.

I had no more than stepped off the porch and begun
to circle the house than I saw a string of riders coming
out of the woods not a hundred yards away. I knew it
was trouble because they weren't following the road. I
counted thirteen of them, all with carbines resting across
their arms, and I recognized Dick Brewer and the Kid in
the lead. The last time I had seen the Kid, I'd creased
his leg with a bullet from my carbine, so I wasn't sure
what to expect from him.

As I stepped away from the house, one of the men
pointed at me. The Kid nudged his horse and galloped
for me, reining up not ten feet away. He had a hard look
about him, but I couldn't tell if it was the look of the
hunter or the hunted. I noticed a kerchief tied around
his thigh where I had grazed him.

"How are you, Kid?"

"Better if some son of a bitch hadn't scorched my
leg. It's a mite sore, but I'll live. What are you doing up
here?"

"Attending Chisum's business. Why'd you do it,
Kid?"

"Do what?" His eyes narrowed.

"Kill Brady."

Pursing his lips, he studied me but said not a word.

"The trouble could've ended, Kid, if you hadn't killed
him. Folks are tired of the trouble. They just want to go on
with their lives. You settled the score for the Englishman

by killing Morton and Baker. Hill's dead and Jesse Evans isn't in good shape."

The Kid answered with a hollow laugh. "I'd like to know what Evans and Hill were doing at a sheep camp that allowed a damned sheepherder to shoot them up so." He forced another laugh, but it was as humorless as his disposition.

"Why Brady, Kid?"

Billy spat. "His posse killed the Englishman."

"But Brady wasn't with the posse. He was in Lincoln. That's like someone shooting me for your killing Morton and Baker."

"He got what he deserved."

I nodded. "In time, Kid, we all get what we deserve."

Billy just stared at me, his eyes burning with hate or guilt. I didn't say anything else, as others were approaching. I saw the Coes, Dick Brewer, John Middleton, Fred Waite, and several men I didn't recognize.

The Coes greeted me warmly, but none of the others seemed to have a thread of friendliness anywhere about them. Dick Brewer said nothing to me.

"We're gonna buy a meal. You want to eat with us?" George Coe offered.

"Why not?" I answered, looking at the Kid.

He turned his horse away from me and rode around the house. "First hide your horses in the barn," he called over his shoulder.

George Coe jumped out of his saddle and tossed the reins to his cousin. "Take care of my horse, Frank, while I visit with Lomax." He grabbed my hand and pumped it steadily.

As the others disappeared around the house, I stared him straight in the eye. "Were you in on killing Brady?"

The enthusiasm died in his handshake. He shook his head. "It was the Kid and some of the others. Frank and I were behind the place, but we didn't shoot at nobody.

I swear. After the deed, we ran away with the others. I
didn't figure anyone would believe us."

I believed George. "Was Brewer involved?"

George shook his head vigorously. "He was with me
and Frank and didn't know what was happening."

"What are you doing out here?"

"Still looking for the Englishman's murderers,"
George replied.

"Damnation," I said. "Morton, Baker, and Hill are
dead. Evans is dying. They were the ones that pulled
the trigger. Even the Kid and Brewer admit the rest
of the posse didn't catch up with those four until the
Englishman was already dead."

George nodded. "It's true."

"Hell, Brady was in Lincoln when it happened. The
Kid's gonna make murderers out of the bunch of you."

"We're up against a bad lot," George answered.
"Some of them've been seen in these parts—Buckshot
Roberts, for one, and others. If we don't kill them, they'll
kill us."

I felt sorry for him. A lot of good men were getting
sucked into Lincoln County's ills. I wondered if there
would be a decent man left in all the county when this
affair had played itself out.

We made small talk until the others came around
from the barn. Mrs. Blazer stepped outside and took a
head count, saying we'd have to eat in shifts because
her small dining room couldn't handle so many with her
regular boarders.

I ate with George and Frank Coe, Dick Brewer,
Fred Waite, and two men I didn't know and was never
introduced to. Mrs. Blazer fed us beef stew and corn
bread with syrup. When we finished, she ushered us
outside so she could clear the plates and reset the table.
Then she invited the second shift, including the Kid,
John Middleton, and five others inside for their meal.
Claiming a rocking chair on the porch, I sat down, kicked
back, and let a good meal settle in my stomach. The

Regulators, though, were skittish, keeping a close watch in all directions. They feared an ambush, even though it would've been difficult for anyone to come too close to Blazer's Mill without being spotted. Even so, Fred Waite took up a position at the corner of the house. The more I watched the men, their eyes flitting from side to side, the gladder I was that I had parted ways with the Kid. This wasn't any way to live. Except for their eyes, they looked as listless as their conversation.

"You need your fiddle, George, liven things up. Nobody shoots a fiddle player," I joked.

No one thought my comment funny and likely would've told me so had not Fred Waite whistled real soft and long.

"We've got company," he said.

All the Regulators eased to the corner of the house to take a gander at the approaching rider. I got up, stretched a moment as the stew and corn bread settled deeper into my stomach, then strolled to the corner myself for a look.

I saw a solitary rider on a donkey. I soon recognized him as the man who had ridden in before, to check on his bank draft. "Don't worry about him," I said. "He was by here yesterday. He's getting out of Lincoln County soon."

For the first time since the Regulators rode up, Dick Brewer spoke to me. "Your friend," Brewer scowled, "is Buckshot Roberts."

"So?" I shrugged.

"He was with the posse that killed the Englishman. I've got a warrant for his arrest." Brewer shoved his hand in his pants pocket, pulling out a wad of papers.

"If they were issued by Squire Wilson," I recalled, "they aren't worth a continental, not after the governor voided his acts."

Brewer gave me a hard glare. "Whose side are you on, Lomax?"

"My own," I answered.

"If you work for Chisum, then you should be on the same side as us. Chisum's agreed to pay us for our work."

"Chisum don't remember promising you or any of the Regulators such. McSween's wrong to be making promises for Chisum."

Brewer shook his head. "I figure you're a coward, Lomax."

"Nope, not me." I crossed my arms over my chest. "I killed two of Evans's rustlers, both armed, in a straight-on shoot-out. How many guns did Morton and Baker have on them when you killed them?"

Brewer spat.

"How brave is it to ambush the sheriff and his deputies?"

"Shut up, both of you," interrupted George Coe.

I stepped away from Brewer, figuring I should warn Roberts of what he was riding into but knowing I'd get shot for my effort.

Roberts angled away from the trail and straight toward the barn, crossing the gully that ran into the sawmill itself and then aiming his donkey for Dr. Blazer's corner office.

"Let's take him," Brewer said, lifting his pistol from his holster.

Frank Coe grabbed Brewer's hand. "No, not yet. I know Roberts. Let me talk to him, see if I can get him to surrender."

I was disgusted with them trying to arrest Buckshot, especially when he hadn't even witnessed Tunstall's murder. I shrugged at George and pointed to the house. "I'm going upstairs to my room, George. I don't want to be a part of this killing."

George shook his head. "Nobody's gonna get hurt, Lomax. We're after justice, not blood."

"Some of you don't know the difference." I marched inside, past the diners, and up the stairs to my room, which looked down over the barn. When I got up there, I fell on the bed, not wanting any part of the unfolding events, but I couldn't help but overhear the conversation between Frank Coe and Roberts. They greeted each other warmly; then there was an awkward pause before Frank spoke again.

"We've got a warrant for your arrest."

"The hell you have," replied Roberts. "I didn't know you were the law."

"Brewer is, and I'm riding with him. Surrender to Brewer, and we'll get you back to town for a trial."

"Like you got Morton and Baker to town for trial?"

I got up from the bed and slipped to the window. I saw Roberts, a Winchester cradled in his arms, facing Frank. Roberts had apparently been planning to take lunch with Mrs. Blazer, because his two gun belts were hooked over the saddle horn on his donkey, which was hitched at the post by Dr. Blazer's office.

"There's Brewer and eleven more with him, Roberts. If you don't surrender, they'll just kill you."

Roberts grinned as he patted the Winchester. "Betsy here'll have a little to say about who gets killed."

"There ain't no sense in resisting and getting killed."

"Ain't no sense in giving in, neither. If I surrender, I die. If I don't give in, somebody else'll die with me."

Frank was perplexed that he couldn't get Roberts to see the wisdom in giving up, but the brave little cuss wouldn't surrender. Frank would've tried until night to change Roberts's mind, but Brewer apparently lost patience. He rounded the corner of the house with George Coe, John Middleton, Billy the Kid, and another Regulator I learned was named Charlie Bowdre, who had bad blood for Roberts. All had their pistols drawn.

"Roberts," yelled Bowdre, "drop the rifle."

"Not much, Betsy," Roberts shouted back. Frank Coe dove to the ground.

Roberts wheeled his rifle around so fast that he got off a shot at the same time as Bowdre. Their aim was good, Roberts taking a shot to the gut and Bowdre screaming as a bullet hit the cartridge belt hanging across his chest. Though staggered by the stomach wound, Roberts fired again, knocking George Coe's pistol and trigger finger from his hand. George screamed, but he charged at Roberts rather than turning tail and running.

Brewer, the Kid, and Middleton sent lead whistling for Roberts, but he must've unnerved them because not a one of their bullets hit him. His next bullet, though, struck Middleton in the chest, knocking him down and out of the battle.

George Coe stopped his charge beside his cousin and helped Frank up, and then both men ran for the corner of the barn and cover.

Roberts backed toward Dr. Blazer's vacant office, firing his Winchester until it was empty. Kicking the door open, he tumbled inside just as four bullets struck the wooden wall beside him.

By the blood on the ground I knew Roberts was feeling poorly, and by the panicked voices I knew the Regulators were scared.

Brewer was angry, screaming like a madman. "He's out of bullets. Take him!" he yelled.

The Kid, who considered himself as good a shot as ever walked the territory, charged for the door. Though Roberts had expended his ammunition, he must've found Dr. Blazer's hunting rifle on the wall and grabbed it just in time to give Billy the surprise of his life when he reached the door.

The Kid squeezed off a blind shot inside but was answered with a booming shot that seemed to echo like thunder across the valley.

"Shit!" Billy yelled, jumping away from the door just as another shot sliced through the air where his head had been. He rolled away from the office, then crawled on hands and knees to the back of the barn and out of sight.

The smoke-filled air carried Roberts's taunting laugh, which seemed to drive Brewer crazier. He shouted for

Blazer, threatening to burn the barn and house down if the doctor didn't go in and pull Roberts out. Blazer refused.

"He's gutshot, Dick," cried the Kid. "He'll die anyway."

"No, dammit," Brewer cursed. "I want him dead now. Keep shooting. I'll get him."

The other Regulators fired sporadically, and the next time I saw Brewer he was running in a crouch down the gully toward the sawmill. He must've been a hundred yards away when he dropped behind a pile of lumber and propped his rifle on the wood. He fired, and the bullet broke a window and rattled around the office, drawing Roberts's curses and apparently his attention. Brewer ducked behind the lumber pile and waited for the smoke to clear before he eased the rifle back atop the lumber, then lifted his head.

I saw his forehead but a second when a booming shot exploded from the corner office. I never saw a shot to match it in all my years. By the sickening thud I knew Brewer was dead.

So did Roberts. "How's that feel, you son of a bitch!" he yelled. "Who's next? Come on, you bastards."

Even with a bullet in his gut, Buckshot Roberts had drained the Regulators of their vinegar. Not a one had the courage to check on Brewer. They gathered their horses and borrowed Blazer's lumber wagon to start Bowdre, Middleton, and George Coe to Fort Stanton for medical help. I ran downstairs to see George. He was pale as a ghost and stared in disbelief at his mangled right hand. When he saw me, he shook his head and lifted his hand. "No fiddle playing for a while."

"Good luck," I told him, but the Regulators didn't linger around long enough for me to say more.

As they rode away from Blazer's Mill, careful to keep out of Roberts's sight, Billy apparently took over leadership of the Regulators.

I went to the corner of the house and called to Roberts. "They're gone."

"Who's speaking?" he called back. "This a trick?"

"H.H. Lomax. I've been lodging here the last two days."

"It's true, what he says." Dr. Blazer seconded me. "They're gone and we're not in this fight. We just want to help."

Roberts paused. "Come ahead, but come slow."

From opposite ends of the house Blazer and I converged on the corner of the barn, our knees turning mushy as we neared the door.

"It's us," I said. Both Blazer and I lifted our hands so he wouldn't mistake any gesture as a threat when we stepped inside.

Taking a deep breath, I moved to the door, gritting my teeth against the possibility of a gunshot. Roberts was sprawled on the mattress he had thrown by the door. His belly was leaking and soaking the mattress with blood. Even so, he offered us a sliver of a smile. "Was that Brewer by the woodpile?"

I nodded.

"I'll die a happy man, knowing I sent him to hell first."

Dr. Blazer examined the wound, but even a blind person would've known Roberts was a dead man. "There's nothing I can do."

We tried to make him comfortable, and a dozen men and women came to see him to get his account of the fight. He was lucid the rest of the afternoon and even joked about missing Brewer's funeral when we went off to bury the dead Regulator.

Roberts's shot had drilled Brewer right between the eyes and blown out the back of his head. The men at the lumber mill made a coffin for him, and we buried him that afternoon, digging another grave by his side for Roberts.

When we returned from the burial, Roberts asked where the bullet had hit and seemed pleased that it was square between the eyes. After that he didn't talk much more, just groaned and grimaced. As night fell he became delirious but lingered on until the next afternoon. When he died, we loaded him in his coffin and buried him beside Dick Brewer. I don't know that either of them would've liked being so close to the other, but we buried Roberts on the right side of Brewer. I figured that's where he belonged because he was in the right in this encounter.

After burying the brave Roberts, I left the mill, dropping Chisum's bid off at the Indian Agency and turning back for Lincoln and the convening of the grand jury.

Chapter Twenty-one

Lincoln was a powder keg waiting to explode when the grand jury finally convened. I was a bit nervous, too, fearing someone would remind the court that I had killed two rustlers in the shoot-out on Chisum's range. The cases that the jury was to hear included the murders of Tunstall, Morton and Baker, Sheriff Brady and Deputy Hindman, and Buckshot Roberts, as well as the embezzlement accusations brought against Alex McSween. I rested a little easier knowing that Dr. Blazer had been appointed grand jury foreman.

Judge Warren Bristol and federal district attorney William Rynerson were Murphy men to the bone and as honest as the typical lawyer—which wasn't honest at all. They took the truth and cut it up into so many pieces that it could never be put back together and anywhere resemble what it had been. As they began to go over the cases with the grand jury, Bristol and Rynerson told more lies than a roomful of incumbents. And judging by their statements, the Regulators rode with the devil and Murphy's men accompanied the angels.

I had my time before the grand jury, but they didn't question me long. They wanted to know what I knew of the Morton and Baker killings. I told them I did not see the shootings. Dr. Blazer then asked me

about what I had seen of the killing of Buckshot
Roberts.

I described the affair as best I could, identifying who
was there, though trying not to mention the Coes. Blazer
caught me and asked me point-blank if Frank and George
had been present. I admitted they had. After that, I was
thanked and dismissed.

I hung around the next couple days, awaiting the
grand jury's findings. I stayed with Sam Corbett in
Tunstall's store, spending a lot of time and as little
money as I could with him. After ten days the grand
jury emerged to announce its findings to a courthouse
jammed like a tin of sardines.

That pompous ass Bristol gaveled the room to order
and requested a report. Dr. Blazer stood up and looked
at the spectators. "In the death of John Henry Tunstall,
members of the grand jury find that the crime, for brutality and malice, is without parallel and without a shadow
of justification. Were they living, indictments would be
returned against Buck Morton, Frank Baker, and Tom
Hill for this despicable crime. As they are not, the grand
jury returns a single indictment against Jesse Evans as
the murderer of Mr. Tunstall."

The spectators cheered, drawing the judge's ad-
monishment.

When the babble died down, Blazer continued. "We
equally condemn the brutal murder of our late sheriff
and his deputy and therefore indict John Middleton, Fred
Waite, and William H. Bonney, also known as the Kid."

Several among the audience clapped and crowed,
though not nearly as loudly as with Jesse Evans's
indictment.

"As for the murder of Andrew Roberts, also known
as Buckshot Roberts, the jury indicts William H. Bonney,
John Middleton, George Coe, Frank Coe, and Charlie
Bowdre."

The spectators applauded again. They were tired
of the fighting, tired of living in fear, and wanted the

violence to end. Many of the spectators had avoided
siding with either faction and wanted them both to go
to prison—or to hell—where they belonged.

"In the matter of accusations of embezzlement
brought against Alexander A. McSween by Lawrence
G. Murphy, the grand jury has given substantial con-
sideration to both sides, but we are unable to find any
evidence that would justify such accusations. We fully
exonerate Alexander A. McSween of the charge and regret
that a spirit of persecution has been shown in this matter.

"Further, we believe that most of the troubles that
have attacked Lincoln County like a plague lie at the feet
of Lawrence G. Murphy. His dishonesty and his political
manipulations have so poisoned this county that it will
take years to recover."

The crowd cheered. Bristol slammed the gavel
against the bench, but spectators celebrated in defiance
of his effort to restore order.

"Further," shouted Blazer, "we find Murphy—"

"Silence," Bristol yelled at Blazer. "No more on this
matter, Mr. Foreman." He banged the gavel, then looked
at Rynerson, who sat with his head in his hands. "Court is
adjourned," Bristol cried, then stood up and walked down
the aisle for the door, Rynerson falling in behind him like
a puppy.

A couple spectators spat on them as they squeezed
outside to the protection of a squad of cavalry. Then the
spectators spewed out of the courthouse to celebrate the
indictments. The grand jury's findings were fair in all
the killings, though I hated to see the indictments against
the Coes for Roberts's death.

For once it seemed right had prevailed, and that
was a change of wind in Lincoln County. Not two hours
after the session ended, the decent folks of Lincoln
came together for a town hall meeting and celebrated
in the very room where the grand jury had made its
report. Standing outside by the window, I listened to

the proclamations of those who thought the county was over its troubles. I had my doubts—most of the indicted men were still running loose, save Jesse Evans, John Middleton, and George Coe, who were recuperating at Fort Stanton from their wounds. McSween was happier than a hog in slop. Though he felt vindicated, the son of a bitch was still a lawyer no matter what the grand jury had said.

I left two days after the celebration, but not before Lawrence G. Murphy himself pulled out of town, never to return. Up until Tunstall's death, he had dominated the western half of Lincoln County. After the killing, though, his empire began to crumble away, his business dying like men in Lincoln County. He failed to meet his contracts delivering beef to the Indian Agency because the Boys had been too busy trying to stay alive to take time to steal someone else's beef to meet Murphy's obligations.

But glad as everyone was to see Murphy ride off to Santa Fe, his departure meant the last chance for order in Lincoln County for a couple years. In his own way Murphy was as bad as they came because of the mayhem he created, but it was a controlled mayhem. With his departure, nothing kept the bad men in check. What decent people in Lincoln County had prayed for they finally got, but their lives only worsened and the violence became bloodier.

I made the two-day trip back to Chisum's without incident. As soon as I arrived, he asked for details on Murphy's retreat. "Finally outsmarted himself, didn't he?"

We learned the full extent of Murphy's problems ten days later when we got word his store had closed. Murphy had lost, but neither McSween nor Chisum had won. Roving gangs began to prowl Lincoln County, the Regulators looking for revenge, the new sheriff searching for indicted men, the cavalry trying to keep order without getting involved in civil affairs. One gang of men attacked San Patricio, raping several women and killing a couple men. I wondered how Rosalita had fared. Some roving ruffians fired several empty cabins along the Rio Hondo and Rio Ruidoso, burning to the ground the hard work of others.

The Kid and McSween, the main targets of the marauding bands, stayed on the run, the Kid being better at it than McSween, who occasionally dragged his wife along. Chisum's herds were targets, too, and he hired extra men to protect them.

A month after the grand jury indictments, the Kid and a handful of men rode up to Chisum's South Spring place. They were trail weary and dirty as a miner's fingernails. The Kid's eyes were glazed over with anger; I thought him a dangerous man. He saw me but ignored me, hollering for Chisum.

"John Chisum," Billy crowed, "we've got business."

It didn't seem to me they could possibly have too much to discuss, but Billy thought so. Sallie Chisum must've recognized the Kid's voice because she came rushing out to greet him, but she stopped immediately when she saw how haggard he looked.

While the Kid waited, impatiently drumming his fingers on his saddle horn, I queried him. "How's George Coe?"

Without looking at me, Billy said, "He got better, slipped out of the hospital before they realized it. He's riding free. Middleton recovered okay, though he's a little slow."

Since he didn't lower himself to look at me, I figured I owed him and Sallie a few insults. I took my hat off. "Kid, you still as friendly as you were with Mrs. McSween?"

Sallie gasped.

Billy eyed me slowly. There wasn't an ounce of fun in his gaze as he tried to stare me down. I stood my ground.

"It's not so, is it, Billy?"

He shook his head. "She's married and ugly. You're neither."

Sallie sighed like a schoolgirl.

I don't figure Billy ever touched Mrs. McSween, but I know his wick had been lit by other women aplenty.

"Where's your uncle, Sallie?"

"I'm here," called Chisum, ambling around the side of the house.

"Me and the boys here've got business with you, Chisum."

"What kind is that?"

"We came to collect our pay," the Kid answered. "Three dollars a day for two months."

Chisum scratched one of those big ears. "I don't remember hiring any of you, and I sure wouldn't have offered you three dollars a day. That's more than any of my hands make."

Billy pointed his finger at Chisum. "You're partners with McSween, and he said you'd cover our pay."

"Kid," Chisum replied, his voice tinged with anger, "whatever partnership I may have had with McSween's no concern of yours."

"We're fighting the House."

"There's no House anymore, Kid. It fell under its own corruption. All there is now is roving bands of outlaws, taking what they can get away with."

Billy wiped his lips with the back of his hand. "It'd be cheaper on you to pay us. You've a lot of land to protect, and you can't put a guard on every cow."

Chisum nodded. "I protect my own."

"No," Billy shot back, "your men protect your own."

"And I pay them for it, but I don't pay every saddle tramp that comes around threatening to steal my cows. I've had more cows stolen from me than you'll ever own, Kid."

Billy took his hat off and ran his fingers through his unruly hair. "You're about to have a lot more stolen. I made a good hand for Tunstall because he gave me a job."

Sallie stepped beside her uncle and grabbed his arm. "Please, Uncle John, give him work."

Chisum pulled his arm from hers. "He doesn't want a chance, he wants money."

"Please, Uncle John," she cooed.

Chisum spun around at Sallie, his sudden movement scaring her. "Young lady, go in the house. This is a matter between men. Whatever Billy's faults, he damn sure knows the value of money better than you do."

Sallie started crying, dabbing at her eyes with the sleeve of her blouse, but Chisum was steady as a rock. She turned and scurried into the house, embarrassed that she hadn't been able to change her uncle's mind in her favor.

Chisum turned to the Kid. "I figure you've been more right than wrong in these matters, Kid. I won't pay you because I don't owe you, but I won't run you off my property unless my men catch you stealing cows. That may not sound like much to you, but it's a chance for you to survive. I'm not saying I'm your friend, Kid, but I'm not your enemy, either, unless you turn on me. You ought to think about that."

Billy slapped his hat back on his head.

Chisum turned around and started for the house.

Before I could sound a warning, Billy slipped his gun out of his holster and cocked the hammer.

At the metallic click, Chisum froze. "Shoot me, Billy, and you'll be doing me a favor—you'll show Sallie what type of man you are."

I never saw Billy's hand quiver until that moment, but I think he was actually scared of an unarmed man he had the drop on.

"Is this the way Morton and Baker got it, Billy?"

"Shut up," Billy growled.

"No. You listen, Kid. I'm an old man. Had a decent life—and, for the most part, a good life. I've lived longer than you will. Just remember, every man you shoot takes a few years off your own life. That's why I never carried a gun, Kid, because I knew I'd live longer without one than with one."

"Damn you," Billy grated.

Chisum shook his head. "I'm going to walk back into the house. Shoot me before I get on the porch. If you can't shoot, then have your horse facing the other direction by the time I get there or I'll put the word out for my men to shoot you on sight." Chisum started walking.

Billy's hand quivered.

Chisum strode ahead.

Billy cursed, then released the hammer on his revolver and shoved the pistol back in the holster. "Come on, boys, let's get out of here. The smell is bothering me."

The Kid jerked the reins on his stallion and rode away from the ranch house. Chisum reached the porch, then turned around and watched him.

"I didn't know you could bluff the Kid," I started, "or stand up to Sallie."

Chisum sighed. "I didn't, either."

Never had I seen the cowman look so tired. He had finally stood up to Sallie and had just backed down a man whose reputation as a fearless killer was beginning to grow. "You know, Lomax, it's not hard to build an empire, if that's what my ranch is. What's hard is keeping it together. Maybe it's other people trying to chip away at what you've built to add to their own empires, or maybe it's just that I'm an old man and don't have the strength or the will to keep the place together. Sallie's life has been a lark because of the empire I built. When I die, no one'll look after her, pamper her the way I have. She'll find out how rough life can be. Maybe I should've been harder on her, but it wasn't in my nature."

I figured a bit of John Chisum died that day. Maybe it was his spirit; maybe it was the realization that comes to all old men when their time has passed. He stood there a long time, not saying a thing. I grew so uncomfortable that I finally cleared my throat and announced I had a few chores to do. Then I slipped away.

For the next two months, the Regulators, with Billy at the lead, roamed Lincoln County, looking for more of Tunstall's murderers and trying to avoid the sheriff's posse. The sheriff appointed by the county commissioners to replace Brady was an honest man who tried to apply the law equally to the McSween and Murphy factions, but the territorial governor replaced him with a Murphy adherent just as he had relieved Squire Wilson of his post as justice of the peace.

The casualties mounted. The Regulators killed another two men who had ridden with Tunstall's murderers. Later the Regulators and the sheriff's men arrived in Lincoln at the same time. In the shoot-out that followed, George Coe, despite his maimed right hand, wounded one man who later died, and several on both sides were injured, though not seriously. Captured in another shoot-out, Frank Coe was taken to jail but managed to escape.

John Chisum seemed to gradually grow wearier and wearier of the troubles and of ranching. I sensed he wanted out. His health was declining, though it wasn't obvious at the time. The last week in June, he left on business, and Sallie seemed unusually gloomy at his departure.

"He wants to sell the ranch," she told me.

I think she realized for the first time that her reign as the Princess of the Pecos was ending. The foreman tried to cheer her up, promising we'd have a big ranch celebration on the Fourth of July. There wasn't much to celebrate with John Chisum gone, but we did anyway.

The cooks started preparing a feast the day before, killing a couple beeves and cooking them over pits of embers. Just about dusk we were startled to see a gang of more than forty riders approaching the ranch house. Everyone grabbed carbines and pistols, uncertain who the riders were.

"It's Billy!" Sallie cried out. "Don't shoot."

Sure enough, it was the Kid and the Regulators as well as McSween and his wife. They were as weary a bunch as I'd ever seen. Their time on the run showed in their starved looks and wild eyes.

"Is Mr. Chisum about?" asked McSween.

"Nope," replied the foreman. "He's gone for a few days."

"Good," interrupted Billy, as Sallie walked to him.

"We wondered if we might sleep here a night or two," McSween said. "We're tired from no rest and little food on the trail."

His voice quivered, and I thought he was going to break down and cry right there in front of us all.

"The posse's been on our tail," Billy said. "They won't attack us here."

The foreman nodded. "We've plenty to eat. As long as you don't cause any trouble you're welcome to celebrate the Fourth."

"Thank you," said Mrs. McSween, her voice drawing a sour look from Sallie Chisum.

"Okay, men," called the Kid. "Mind your manners." He looked at the foreman. "We ain't stolen any of your cattle. Tell Uncle John that, will you?"

The foreman nodded. Billy dismounted and hugged Sallie for a moment.

"Things are going poorly for me, Billy."

Billy laughed. "You think things aren't bad for me? No bed sleep in weeks. No decent food. On the run all the time."

"No, not that," she said, her eyes welling with tears. "But Uncle John's gone, and may be selling the ranch. Where'll I turn?"

Her problems must've seemed small to the Kid. "At least folks ain't trying to kill you all the time."

"It's worse, not knowing what's gonna happen at the ranch. It's my home."

Billy took Sallie's arm and escorted her toward the tree-lined stream. "Everything'll work out fine," he reassured her. I was paying so much attention to the couple that I didn't see the Coes walk up beside me.

Frank slapped me on the back, and George offered me his maimed right hand, less the trigger finger he left at Blazer's Mill.

"I can still fiddle," George announced, taking my hand in his and shaking it warmly.

"George's fiddle playing wasn't hurt, but he can only count to nine now without taking his boots off," Frank joked.

"Or his pants," I said with a grin. "Good to see you boys."

Frank shook his head. "All this time I thought you were the dumb one, pulling out and not throwing in with the Englishman."

"He was narrow between the eyes, didn't think I could trust him."

George laughed. "Now we're on the run, and you're living the good life with a fine bed and a roof over your head."

We had a small supper after that; then most of us retired. I gave up my room in the ranch house to bunk with the Coes. Though a few men threw their bedrolls outside and slept beneath the stars, most claimed bunks in the bunkhouse. The Kid tomcatted around with Sallie much of the night and was the last in bed. Even so, he was one of the first ones up, going from bunk to bunk seeing who wanted to go with him to Roswell.

"What?" cried George. "Why do we have to go to Roswell?"

"To get Sallie some candy."

"Candy? Let her get her own candy," George replied. "This is the first night I've slept in a bed since I got out of the hospital."

"Sallie's sad, and I want to cheer her up."

"We're tired and want to sleep," Frank interjected.

"I've got to tell Ash Upson my news," Billy went on.

He went around, pestering a half-dozen fellows until they knew it was useless to argue. They stumbled out of bed, cursing Sallie for being moody and Billy for being a horse's ass about it.

"I'm not going unless Lomax goes," George insisted.

"Me neither," Frank chimed in.

"Lomax ain't invited," the Kid shot back.

"And why not?" George challenged.

"He's no Regulator, and he rides a damn mule."

"Well, hell," George replied. "He can borrow one of Chisum's horses since it sounds like he's second-in-command here."

George had stretched my responsibilities on Chisum's place, but I wasn't about to correct him.

"Just get up and get going," Billy finally said and strode out.

Within a half hour we were all riding toward Roswell, me on the yellow dun that had made me a hero. The store was doing a Fourth of July business when we arrived. Three women and two men were wandering about, picking out some canned foods for the Independence Day celebration.

The Coes, the Kid, and I were joined by Charlie Bowdre, Fred Waite, John Middleton, and several others I didn't recognize and didn't care to meet. The Kid bought a pound of horehound candy, a pound of peppermint sticks, and six cartons of ammunition. All the men had money to buy ammunition, and I was the only one who didn't pick up a new supply of cartridges.

The Kid spent some time talking to Ash Upson, who took notes and asked a lot of questions. It was midmorning and July hot by the time we left the store and started back for the ranch.

We had barely gotten out of town when a dozen horsemen dashed out of the trees along the Rio Hondo and charged toward us.

"Posse!" yelled Billy, pulling his pistol and firing first. The other Regulators did the same, except for George, who was still learning how to handle a pistol without a trigger finger. I didn't shoot. I was holding the reins on the damned yellow dun to make sure he didn't turn around and charge into the posse like he had the rustlers.

We had a running fight all the way back to the ranch, but no one was injured. The Regulators back at the ranch heard the gunfire and had their carbines ready to cover us on the ride in. With the outbuildings and corrals providing cover, those Regulators managed to put down a substantial fire that discouraged the posse from getting close enough to be a real threat.

That began the damnedest Fourth of July I ever had. The Regulators exchanged shots with the posse all day without effect. I'd never heard so many fireworks. The foreman issued orders prohibiting any ranch hand from taking shots at the posse.

When it was time to eat, the Regulators ate in shifts, half keeping the posse at bay while the other half ate. Everybody pulled a shift at the battle line except Billy. He stuck to Sallie like bark to a tree—even a blind man could've seen his sap rising.

Come dusk the gunfire tapered off, and we saw the posse slip back to Roswell to do battle another day.

After dark the Regulators gathered around McSween and his wife to discuss their options. They had been on the run now for weeks, and the strain was showing. They talked in hushed tones, keeping the ranch hands away, but George had slipped me in with the others to listen.

"I'm tired of running," McSween said. "I want to go back to Lincoln."

"It'll be a battle if we do," the Kid answered. "Some of us could get killed."

"We can get killed this way," McSween answered. "I'd rather die in my home than out here on the prairie."

Billy scratched his head, then nodded. "We're returning to Lincoln."

I couldn't believe that all these men, many of them decades older than the Kid, were taking his orders and following his decisions, but they were. As they began to move off, I got up to go, too, but froze in my boots when I heard McSween call my name.

Without answering, I turned and stared.

"I need to know where Mr. Chisum keeps pencil and paper."

I led him through the house to a desk Chisum didn't mind others using. The last I saw of McSween that night, he was writing his will.

Chapter Twenty-two

Folks in Lincoln came to call it "the Big Killing." There was no reason for me to go and plenty of reasons not to, like saving my hide, but I was drawn to Lincoln like a moth to a flame.

A few days after the Fourth of July, word reached the ranch that the Regulators, sixty or more strong, had reclaimed Lincoln from the Murphy gang. What few Murphy men still remained in Lincoln escaped to alert their allies, then returned in full force.

The McSween men forted up several buildings. In addition to Tunstall's store and McSween's house, they commanded the torreón, a house on the eastern edge of town, and a small Mexican cantina midway between. The Murphy forces claimed the west end of town, including the Murphy store and Wortley Hotel.

Both sides took to sniping at each other. It was pretty much a draw, though the Regulators controlled more of the town, reported a rider passing through on his way to Texas. The foreman, Sallie, and I listened to the rider's account, and I later told the foreman I needed to visit Lincoln.

"Can't let you do it," he said. "If people see you there they'll think Chisum's taking sides."

"You can't stop me," I answered.

The foreman nodded. "You're right, but I can fire you. Draw your wages and be gone by sundown. You ain't done that much for the ranch since you were butt-shot."

I had added a little meat to my bones, but I figured I'd earned it. "No gratitude for a man that killed two of the Boys, huh?"

The foreman shrugged. "At first I figured you were the brave one, but it was that loco yellow dun." He turned and walked into the ranch house. Before I could move to collect my things, which weren't many, Sallie Chisum threw her arms around me, making me think I might want to reconsider my decision to leave the ranch.

Then she ruined it all by opening her mouth. "Tell Billy I miss him and that I love him."

"If Mrs. McSween will let me," I replied.

Sallie let go of me faster than a sack of warm manure. "I never did like you," she spat, then spun around and strode away.

I had to admire her frankness like I had once admired her figure. I gathered my belongings, stuffed them in my saddlebags, then took my carbine, pistol, and holster. When I marched out into the parlor, the foreman was waiting there with my money, another seventy-five dollars' pay since April.

I took it. "Tell John Chisum I said he was a good man."

The foreman grunted as I left. I found Flash in the barn, and he seemed glad to see me. I saddled him, tied on my belongings, and climbed aboard, riding away without stopping in Roswell to see Upson.

In the July heat it took me two days to reach Lincoln. It was late afternoon when I neared the town, and I could see trouble—a thick plume of smoke arising from town—and hear it—gunfire around Tunstall's store. I slipped off the road and angled for the Rio Bonito, sticking to the trees to screen myself from possible snipers. As I advanced up the stream, I saw McSween's house spewing black smoke from the far end. The house was *U*-shaped, and somebody had apparently fired the roof at one end. The slow-moving fire would ultimately destroy the roof and all beneath it except the adobe.

As I advanced I saw, camped along the side of the road, a troop of cavalry going about its business as if nothing at all unusual was happening down the street. It didn't make sense to me, but so few things ever did. I learned later that the cavalry had come to Lincoln to protect the citizens, but it didn't look like they were protecting the folks in the McSween house.

From the Murphy men I could see hidden nearby—I counted at least thirty—I gathered that some of the Regulators were barricaded in McSween's place, McSween probably among them. If he was inside, I knew the Kid was too.

I learned later that Murphy's men had contrived to get the military drawn into the affair by sending a woman to Fort Stanton early in the five-day siege to plead for cavalry protection. The cavalry commander had acquiesced and brought his troops and a Gatling gun to town. He announced that any man who shot at the cavalry would be executed and that any building from which a shot was fired at the soldiers would be demolished.

Then, to make matters worse for the Regulators, the colonel had had the torreón cleared and troops stationed between it and the buildings on the east side of town, where other Regulators were holed up. He announced that any shot fired from those buildings would be considered hostile. In effect the colonel had isolated the McSween house from any allies and had allowed Murphy's men to surround it. I hoped Frank and George Coe weren't inside because I couldn't see any way to escape. Either the trapped Regulators would burn to death or they would be shot as easily as fish in a barrel.

I'd ridden into town expecting the Regulators to be in control and instead found the Murphy faction in command, with the help of the U.S. Army. It reminded

me of how things had been back in Arkansas during the
War Between the States. You never knew who was in
charge.

For a long time I watched the soldiers posted around
the camp, then saw a couple others standing in the torreón
watching the siege. I felt helpless and about as low as a
bootheel. That feeling bothered me for a long spell until I
realized that whoever was inside the burning house would
have to make a run for it. If the fire didn't force them out
earlier, they would probably wait until dark to make their
break, and if any did escape, they most certainly would
bolt for the Rio Bonito and the cover of trees. There they
would need horses to escape. I decided I would steal
horses for them. I rode Flash up the Rio Bonito to the
west end of town, dismounted in a thicket of trees, tied
him, then slipped across the road to the two-story adobe
building that had once been Murphy's store. Sure enough,
I found three dozen saddled horses tied at hitching posts
or running loose in the corral behind the store. I looked
around real careful, to make sure nobody was watching. It
seemed the fire down the street was like the circus come
to town, and everybody had left to watch the parade.

Certain everything was clear, I slipped to the
hitching posts and untethered a horse at a time, then
tied its reins to the saddle of the next mount until I had
a dozen horses in a string.

I was feeling confident as a Baptist with four aces
when I heard a screeching noise overhead and looked up
to see someone opening a second-floor window.

"What the hell are you doing with them horses?"
came a gruff voice. A bearded face and a carbine were
staring at me.

"Taking them," I replied.

"I can see that, dammit. Do you think I'm stupid?"

"The thought did enter my mind," I admitted, "since
you could plainly see what I was doing."

"You better give me a straight answer, partner, before
I shoot the hell out of you."

"If you don't shoot any straighter than you think, I'm not worried."

That riled him. "You son of a bitch." He lifted the carbine to his shoulder.

"The boss wondered where you were," I bluffed, "and why you weren't out shooting rats at McSween's like everybody else."

"What? That's a lie. Now, what are you doing with them horses?"

"Boss said to leave them by the Bonito in case some of the McSween rats escape. He wants to have the horses close enough that we can give chase. You understand?"

Lowering his carbine, he scratched his head.

"If you don't believe me, just go ask him. I hope he doesn't get too mad."

"That's okay," the fellow replied. "I just came back here to get some ammunition, then I'll be returning."

"Good," I replied. "Now get going."

He pulled his head back inside. My knees felt suddenly mushy at the close call; I was glad only the stupid ones had remained at the store. I untied and mounted the lead horse and circled my string by the corral. Hoping the dimwit upstairs wasn't watching, I bent over and lifted the latch, shoving the gate open so the other horses could slip away.

Figuring I had pressed my luck far enough, I rode up the road a quarter of a mile before crossing back toward the stream and returning to Flash. I jumped off the horse and mounted the mule, then worked my way back down the stream, which came within a hundred yards of the McSween house. The trees were thin in places and I was surprised no one saw me, but if they did they didn't raise a ruckus. I went about my business, loosing horses from the string and tying them in pairs to trees so any Regulator who made it alive out of McSween's house would have a chance at escaping on a horse. That done, I rode back downstream, then up the slope toward the army camp, figuring that was the best place to tie my mule and wait.

When I reached the camp, I heard a screaming voice coming from a white tent with the canvas rolled up. Mrs. McSween was giving the troop commander enough hell that he could've canned it for winter heat.

"My husband is going to die because of you," she yelled, "and all my belongings will perish with him and my house."

From what I could see, the colonel was a big, blustery type who enjoyed his rank and his authority. "My orders are not to interfere in civil matters. I will not do it. Now be on your way."

"No!" she shot back, enough venom in her voice to poison all the colonel's troops. "You meddled in civil matters by coming here and taking sides with Murphy's men."

"Damn you to hell, woman."

"Hell? You want to see hell, Colonel, then look down the street where you can see my house afire. That's hell."

The colonel strode out of the open tent and marched to two of his enlisted men. "Remove this woman. Throw her out in the street or on her burning house, if you must—just get her out of our camp." He turned to Mrs. McSween and tipped his hat. "These fine troopers will escort you. Good day!"

When the two soldiers approached her, she straightened her shoulders, stiffened her lips, and marched past the colonel. If a gaze could kill, they would have arrested her for murder.

As she passed, the colonel spat in her wake. It was obvious he wouldn't be calling on the widow McSween to go courting. Mrs. McSween stopped thirty paces from camp and stood in the middle of the road, staring at the soldiers. In a house nearby, I saw Dr. Ealy standing in the doorway with his wife, calling for Mrs. McSween to get out of the open and take cover.

I tied Flash as near as I could to the cavalry horses, then grabbed my carbine and marched past the camp, hoping that Mrs. McSween wouldn't recognize me.

I was doing okay until a cavalry officer yelled, "Halt!"

I pointed to myself.

The lieutenant nodded. "Where you going?"

"To help out," I replied.

"Whose side are you on?" he challenged.

"The law's side."

"So you're with the sheriff?"

"Yes, sir," I said.

He looked doubtfully at me and began to reach for the pistol in his scabbard until Mrs. McSween saw me.

"You, you," she cried out. "Get out of here. You never liked me or my husband anyway. You're going to kill him now? Why not kill me first? I won't survive without him." She held up her arms like she was about to be crucified. "Shoot me."

The soldier shook his head at me. "It'd save us some grief if you'd just shoot her, but if she don't like you that's all the recommendation I need. Go on. Good hunting."

I marched on, aiming for the torreón and glancing back over my shoulder in time to see Dr. Ealy run out of the adobe, grab Mrs. McSween's arm, and pull her inside. I guess I owed her thanks for helping me get past the guard, but it was hard to think about owing that woman anything other than a good punch in the mouth.

To the west the sun had dropped behind the mountains. The plume of smoke was rising high into the air and growing thicker. I didn't care to join the Murphy men around the burning house for fear I might be recognized, but I wanted to see what happened at the end.

I looked up at the torreón and saw a half-dozen soldiers atop it, watching the fire. That seemed like a good idea. I marched up and was challenged by a smart-mouthed trooper.

"Where the hell you think you're going?"

"Upstairs," I said, "where the lieutenant told me to go."

The trooper shook his head. "Lieutenant told me not to let anybody in except cavalry."

"Well, hell, son, I'd damn sure hate for you to get in trouble, but the lieutenant told me this is where I was to be, so I intend to be here. I'm a deputy."

"You don't look like a deputy."

"And you don't look like a soldier." I could tell he was still skeptical. I pointed to the cavalry horses. "Lieutenant told me to picket my mule with your mounts. You see my mule down there?"

He looked and nodded.

"The lieutenant's gonna have one of the troopers take care of my mule. Now, unless you want that chore added to your responsibilities, you better let me through."

The trooper mulled it over, then stepped aside.

I went into the stone tower and climbed the ladder to the top where the officers stood watching. They looked surprised to see me.

"Who are you?"

"The sheriff sent me to tell you gentlemen you best leave."

"We don't answer to the sheriff, we answer to the colonel."

I nodded. "You and I know the army's not to meddle in civil matters. I told the colonel the sheriff thinks it's only a matter of time before the outlaws have to break out. Sheriff wants me up here in case any get by so we can see where they run."

"That doesn't mean we need to leave," the captain argued.

"That's not how the colonel viewed it. You know the orders from Washington about not getting involved in civil matters. He doesn't think it wise for you to be seen up here with one of the sheriff's men when this plays itself out. Appearances, you know."

The captain scratched his behind in disgust. "The colonel's never been worried about appearances before."

The officers put their heads together and grumbled a bit.

"It's fine with me if you stay, but I wouldn't want to get you in trouble over it. Go down, talk to the colonel, and if he's changed his mind, come on back."

For a moment the captain hesitated, then shook his head. "Come on, men, let's go somewhere else for the fireworks." He led the others down the ladder, and soon I was alone atop the torreón. I propped my carbine against the rock wall and glanced toward the McSween place. The flames had turned down the east wing and were licking their way toward the back; they would be no more than an hour burning to the end of the house. Then the Regulators would be out of room and time.

After giving the officers a couple minutes to retreat, I clambered down the ladder to the door, pulled it shut, and barred it. Now no one would get in without my knowing it. I climbed back up the ladder and pulled it through the hole in the floor, then propped it against the circular wall. Grabbing my carbine, I climbed the ladder until I had a good view of the McSween place, or what was left of it.

As the sunlight died the fiery embers that were carried up in the draft with the smoke began to glow, making the plume look like the devil's Christmas tree. I hoped the Coes weren't trapped inside. As darkness enveloped the valley I could just make out Murphy's men creeping closer to the adobe building and taking up positions where they could fire into the back door, by then the only route of escape. The door opened out toward the Rio Bonito and faced a four-foot adobe rear fence, where Murphy's men were taking position by the dozens. There must've been fifty of them.

The Regulators had but a fool's chance to escape. Once they jumped out the door, they would have to turn to their right or run into the barrage from behind the adobe wall. Even if they made the right turn, they'd still have about thirty feet of open space to cross before they reached the knee-high picket fence. If they made it beyond the fence, then they might have a chance to hide in the gathering darkness.

From my position I couldn't see the back door, but I could see enough of the roof to know that time was running out. As the moment drew closer, the sporadic gunfire stopped, and everything was silent except for the roar of the flames and the popping of burning wood.

I aimed my carbine at the back of the house to give the appearance I was one of the Murphy supporters. The fire crept ahead until there was no more than ten feet between the leading edge and the back of the house. The Regulators had but seconds to escape or fry. My palms grew sweaty and the drift of smoke made my eyes water.

Then it happened.

The silence exploded with a barrage of gunfire from the back of the house. Out they ran like gophers from a waterlogged den. Billy darted out first, pistols in both hands firing in all directions at once, cursing as he ran, one of the few times I ever heard him say a bad word. I sighted my carbine on his chest and could have killed him had I pulled the trigger, but I'm sure that's what every one of Murphy's men thought that night as they took aim at him. Somehow Billy made it through the wall of lead and reached the picket fence, turning to shoot a Murphy man who jumped up from behind the adobe wall. Billy shot him in the head. All his target practice had saved Billy's life. Three of the four who followed Billy through that hailstorm of lead made it past the picket fence.

Though things were happening fast, I didn't recognize McSween among them. There was a pause, just long enough for the Murphy men to reload; then out charged six or seven more, McSween among them, but instead of running to the side, they ran toward the adobe wall and Murphy's men. The gunfire was intense, and one man fell. The others retreated to the house.

"I surrender!" McSween screamed, his voice at a high pitch of fear. "I surrender!"

Everything went quiet, and McSween stepped forward along with two other men, coming into the bright light of the flame. From somewhere somebody yelled something—I never knew what—and the night erupted in gunfire again. McSween took a half-dozen bullets, maybe more, and collapsed like a rag doll on the ground. The two other men fell on top of him.

With all Murphy's men firing at McSween, the others escaped in the darkness. Shortly I heard the sound of horses galloping away from the stream and knew the Kid and the others had found my mounts.

I have to admit I didn't care for McSween, but I didn't care to see him gunned down, either. One minute a man's alive and the next minute he's no different from a fence post. First John Tunstall, then Buck Morton, Frank Baker, Tom Hill, Sheriff Brady, Deputy Hindman, Dick Brewer, Buckshot Roberts, and now McSween. And besides them, there were two dozen more, like those around McSween's body that I didn't know. I felt sick to my stomach, wondering if my name would be added to the list before long.

For two or three minutes after the big killing, none of Murphy's men moved. They seemed to fear that some of McSween's allies lingered in the darkness to shoot them when they came out of hiding. Gradually one, then another, then a couple more stepped from behind the adobe wall or out of the shadows. They went first to their own man, the one Billy had plugged in the head, and found him dead as a man can be. A couple other men brought a blanket to wrap the body in and carried him off. Next, a crowd gathered around McSween, dragging from atop his body the two men who had fallen upon him. They laughed, then kicked his body and spat on it. Soon every man among them had paid similar respects to the late Alexander A. McSween. Then the murderers brought out bottles of whiskey, which explained the poor aim that allowed so many of the trapped Regulators to escape.

Before long they were shouting and singing, then dancing among the bodies, some fellow bringing out a fiddle to accompany the gruesome dance. The soldiers from the camp came in clumps to stare at the bodies and watch the merriment.

I just watched. They were mean, vicious men who worked for Murphy. McSween and Tunstall had believed New Mexico to be a civilized territory where they could dominate the economy within the law. They were no match for the lawless men dancing among the bodies.

For more than an hour the victorious warriors celebrated, until the flames of the house died like its owner. Then someone shouted, "Let's take over his store."

The crowd needed no further encouragement. They marched as a mob toward the store, quickly breaking in the door and ransacking it. I crawled back down the ladder and lowered it through the hole in the floor, then sat down and leaned against the circular wall, considering what type of danger I was in. It was hard to figure, and I became emboldened. Why just let Murphy's men take what they wanted from the Tunstall store? I'd built a strong fence for him with devil wire, and the Kid had gotten the credit and the pay. The Englishman owed me a few things.

I stood up, climbed down the ladder, unbarred the torreón door, and started for the store. I tugged my hat down my forehead and pushed my way inside. The men, crazed with liquor and greed, were taking armloads of goods. Me, I went to the ammunition cabinet, took six cartons of ammunition, and reached for the last remaining pistol, but another man beat me to it.

There was one other thing I wanted, and I wanted it bad—a bottle of liquor. All the bottles of bitters and medicines that we sometimes drank when we wanted to celebrate were gone, as was the good whiskey. But I knew where Sam Corbett usually hid a couple spare bottles of liquor behind the counter. I found them quickly, then marched out of the store as fast as I could so I wouldn't be recognized. I dropped one carton of ammunition, but rather than try to find it in the dark I went on, anxious to get out before anybody spotted me.

I made it to Flash, figuring I might be challenged by one of the soldiers, but not a one said a thing, them being so occupied with what was going on down the street. I heard the sobs of a couple women and recognized one of them as the newly widowed Mrs. McSween.

Flash fidgeted while I shoved the carbine in the saddle boot, then loaded the ammunition and one bottle of liquor in my saddlebags. I uncorked the other and took a healthy swig before untying Flash and riding to the outskirts of town. Just beyond the cemetery, which would have some new additions over the next couple days, I aimed Flash off the road and toward the Rio Bonito. Beneath a cottonwood tree that had muscled its way above some other trees, I dismounted, tied Flash, and began to do some serious drinking.

Liquor is a vile drink that generally got me in trouble. Fact was, had I not been drinking in Leadville, I might never have come to Lincoln County. Had I not been drinking in Leadville, I might have remembered whether or not I had killed that lawyer. This night I'd seen another lawyer die, and it didn't go down well with me.

The bottle was the only companion I had or wanted until I passed out. I awoke the next morning with a terrible headache. When I pushed myself up from the ground, I still had the empty bottle in my hand. I smashed it against the cottonwood trunk and staggered to Flash, untied him, and climbed on.

The sun had cleared the mountains to the east, so it was well past sunrise when I rode to the still-smoldering ruins of McSween's place. Four bodies were strewn upon the ground, chickens pecking at their eyes. I cursed and spat at them, then jumped from Flash and kicked at them until they scurried for cover. McSween's body was pretty well abused, but the others had been left alone and unmutilated except by the chickens. I examined each and breathed easier when I found that none was a Coe. I mounted up again and turned Flash to the west, riding by the House, intent upon leaving Lincoln County forever.

I might have succeeded had it not been for Rosalita.

Chapter Twenty-three

I followed the road from Lincoln and wound up in White Oaks, a small mining town about twenty-five miles northwest of Lincoln. All the talk was about the Big Killing and that Lincoln's day was over. The respectable folks of White Oaks were planning to petition for an election to change the Lincoln County seat to White Oaks. I had too much to drink in one saloon and started arguing against such an election.

"It'd bring more lawyers," I declared, "and then White Oaks'll go to hell quicker than a politician goes back on a promise."

Nobody except the bartender took me seriously, but he listened patiently after he saw my money roll. Since no other citizen bought my reasoning, I decided I wasn't spending any more money in a town of such closed-minded idiots.

All the drink got me to thinking about home and wondering why I hadn't returned to Arkansas for a dozen years. I still had about two hundred dollars in my pocket, and if I didn't drink it all up, that was enough money to get me back to Cane Hill to visit my momma, who was getting up in years.

With Flash to get me home, I headed northeast for Fort Sumner, a town that had survived the closing of the military post several years before. From Fort Sumner I planned to take the Texas Road and angle across the top of the Texas Panhandle, then hit Indian Territory and ride on into Arkansas.

When I finally rode into Fort Sumner, I had left Lincoln County for San Miguel County. Fort Sumner was a hundred miles from Las Vegas, another lawless town. The land south of Fort Sumner was cattle country, including the northern reach of Chisum's ranch. In other directions, though, there were more sheep. Civilization was approaching Fort Sumner, but nobody was in a rush to escort it in or to do something stupid like petition to make the town the county seat.

The town clung to the east bank of the Pecos River. To the west stood broken mountains and to the east the rolling prairie. The town had taken over the military post. The buildings surrounded a big square that had once been the central parade ground. All the army buildings had been claimed by civilians, the most important being Pete Maxwell, a wealthy man who lived in one of the double-story officer's houses. Maxwell had a well-furnished house with an orchard and garden fed by an irrigation ditch from the Pecos.

To the south of the square stood a long, narrow adobe building that had been partitioned into small dwellings used by poor folks or, in a couple cases, as cribs by the girls who worked the cowboy or outlaw trade. The quarter of the building nearest the river was occupied by the saloon of Beaver Smith, who ran the most popular drinking establishment in Fort Sumner. Bob Hargrove operated the other saloon, which stood on the opposite corner of the square near a store and a couple other smaller buildings. On the east side of the parade ground were the old barracks, which were being used as homes, stores, and such.

I rode into town, tied up Flash outside Beaver Smith's saloon, and walked inside. It was morning and there were already a dozen men drinking and two señoritas making the rounds and suggesting favors they'd be glad to perform, for a price, of course. I didn't pay too much attention to the ladies, just sidled up to the bar and ordered a shot of whiskey to clear the trail dust from my gullet.

The bartender was a skinny fellow who was arranging bottles on his backbar before he turned around and greeted me cordially. My jaw dropped at the sight of his right ear. It had been sliced along the side, and the top half drooped over, giving him the same ear marking as one of John Chisum's jinglebobs.

"What the hell you staring at?" he demanded.

"Just admiring your liquors. Better stock than I was figuring."

"You liar. You were staring at my ear, weren't you?"

He was ready to make an issue of my manners until I pulled out my roll of money. "I'm passing through, barkeep, and I can either drink here or find another saloon."

Smith smiled like I was his long-lost brother. "Nothing like a paying customer."

Before he got the words out of his mouth one of the señoritas was beside me, her arm in mine. As I looked around, I got the shock of my life. It was Rosalita! The last time I had seen her was at the dance in San Patricio.

Her eyes fixed on my money roll, she didn't even look at my face until I called her name.

"Rosalita, what are you doing here?"

She glanced at me with doe eyes and a white-toothed grin. "So much money," she purred. "Looking for a wife?" Her eyes and her grin narrowed when I didn't answer. "This is sheep country. Is that what you're looking for?"

Beaver Smith looked at me. "What kind of fool is he?"

Leaning across the bar, I grinned at Beaver Smith. "The kind that can keep from slicing his ear when he shaves."

Beaver cursed me until I shoved my money back in my pocket.

"Not as thirsty as I thought."

"No, no," cried Rosalita.

"Cut myself shaving." Smith laughed, mustering up all the sincerity of a snake-oil salesman. "That's a good one. Actually, a gang of Chisum's hands did that."

"Sí," said Rosalita. "They gave him a brand on his side, too."

"A long rail, just like they brand their cattle," Smith said.

"What for?" I inquired.

Smith shook his head. "A little misunderstanding over what I cut their liquor with. It wasn't cow juice like they said."

"Milk?" I asked.

"No," answered Rosalita, "piss."

"Damn," I replied. "I don't want a bottle of anything now."

Smith held up his hand. "Don't make a hasty decision, Mr.—"

"Lomax," I replied.

Smith scowled and leaned across the bar. "Any relation to Gadrich Lomax?"

"No," I said.

Smith growled, "He's the son of a bitch that told those cowboys I was cutting the liquor with cow juice. As I was saying, Rosalita, give Lomax a treat on the house."

"No more sheep comments," I demanded.

He lifted his arms like I was holding a gun on him. "None. You just let me know if you need help with anything."

I figured he wanted to help me spend my money, but I just grinned as Rosalita planted a kiss on my cheek and tugged me out the door and down the line of adobe buildings to her section near the other end. As she shoved open the door, I looked through the front window and caught a glimpse of rough furniture and a small potbellied stove. When I walked in behind her, she shoved the door to and barred it. The kitchen didn't look any better from the inside. Three chairs, a table, stool, half-full water barrel, woodbox, broom, and a few pots, pans, and dishes in wooden crates were all her earthly belongings.

She grabbed me by the hand and pulled me into the back room, where she conducted her business on a bed with stained sheets, a wool blanket, and a corn-shuck mattress. Over the head of the bed she had hung a crucifix. Like the front room, the bedroom had few luxuries other than the slop jar under the bed and the tintype of her on a small bedside table that also held a washbasin, comb, and mirror. Her clothes hung on a peg in the wall opposite the crucifix; her other belongings lay in a small trunk beneath the clothes. A wide window in the back wall let a breeze drift through.

Rosalita pulled the wool blanket off the unmade bed, then retreated to the kitchen. She returned with a cup of water, dipped her fingers in the liquid, then flicked droplets on the bed to cool it from the July heat. When she finished, she put the cup aside and helped me get comfortable. She added to my comfort the rest of the afternoon and into the night. I slept as soundly as a baby suckling on his momma's breast, and when I awoke about the middle of the next morning I was as rested as a grown man could be.

I reached over for Rosalita, figuring I could rekindle some of fire that she had produced before, but she was gone. I reached for my britches beside the bed, but they were gone. So was my shirt, my drawers, my socks. I cursed to myself and jumped out of bed. If my clothes were gone, so was my money. I was madder than a young bull at steering time. I found my hat on the floor, and just as I bent to pick it up, I heard a noise at the window.

Spinning around, I covered myself with the hat and saw Rosalita standing there.

"Buenos dias!" she said, grinning wickedly at my hat. "Do you still prefer sheep to women?"

"My clothes—what did you do with my clothes and my money?"

She looked hurt. "I thought little one might want to come out and play again?"

"My clothes? My money?"

She wiggled her finger for me to come to the window. I walked over, protecting myself with my hat. When I reached the window, she pointed to a clothesline out back. There hung my newly washed britches, shirt, socks, and drawers.

I grimaced. "My money?" I said, a little less surely.

Rosalita pointed to the small trunk. I marched over and lifted the lid. There in the corner, atop everything else, was my money. Meekly I closed the trunk and returned to her.

"Your pistol and carbine are under the bed, if you think I stole them. Beaver tended to your mule, and I did your laundry."

I leaned out the window to kiss her. She kissed me back with fiery passion, then broke free. *"Un momento."* She grabbed her skirts and ran around the end of the building. I could feel my sap rising. I dropped the hat and stood there waiting as she ran through the front door, not even taking time to slam it.

She needed me so, and I was ready to scratch her itch. When she came within reach I lifted my arms to hug her. She lifted her arm as I closed my eyes.

Then she hauled off and slapped the stuffing out of me. My cheek burned like she had hit it with a hot skillet. She started screaming and yelling, half in English, half in Spanish, talking so fast that I didn't know for sure what she was saying—that she might be an easy woman, but she wasn't a thief. She berated me so loudly I figured everybody in Fort Sumner knew of our little spat.

I tried to calm her by nodding at everything she said in Spanish, but she slapped me again. I shrugged and she slapped me. I shook my head and she slapped me. I was beginning to wish I had a rope so I could tie her up until she calmed down, but I'd never roped a tornado and wasn't sure I could tame this one. Like most big winds, though, this one blew itself out, and we both stood there looking at each other.

I shrugged. I didn't know what to say, but I figured she'd had enough of me. "When my clothes are dry, I'll pay you for laundering them and get out."

"You can stay."

"I'll be out by noon, so you can attend to business."

"I'm tired of that. You can stay longer."

"I'll leave after supper, then."

She shook her head. "You can stay longer. I'm tired of doing what I've been doing. Not going to do it anymore."

I was taken aback. She had been so passionate before, and now it seemed she was taking a vow of celibacy. "You're not going to do that anymore?" My frown must have given away my disappointment.

"With other men, no, but with you, yes."

I started to whoop and holler.

"You're here with more money than I've ever seen on a man. More than two hundred dollars—I counted it, but I didn't steal it."

She wanted my money, but she wanted it in an honest fashion, so I started boarding with her. Since I'd taken up a house with a woman, I figured I ought to get a job and support her, or my two hundred dollars wouldn't last any longer than an icicle in the July heat. After I got my clean clothes back, I walked over to Beaver Smith's and asked him for a job bartending.

"I've got a bartender already that works at night, Juan Largo. Besides, you've already stolen from me."

"What are you talking about?" I asked, figuring the fumes from his liquor had addled his mind in addition to wilting his right ear.

"You stole Rosalita. She's the best saloon girl I've ever had."

I didn't know quite how to take that comment, so I let it pass. "You need another bartender?"

"Juan Largo's fine," Smith replied. "Fact is, I could saw him in half and have two as big as you."

Well, I took that to be an outright lie, me being a right decent-size fellow, so I decided to return that night and check Juan Largo out for myself.

Rosalita made me a fine supper of beans and tortillas covered with a mash made from green peppers. It was tasty, and spicy enough to scorch your tongue and erase your mind. I waited until it was dark outside and Rosalita was lighting a candle in the bedroom. I went back to her trunk and took out my money, stuffing it in the pocket of my clean pants.

"I'm going to the saloon," I announced.

"No, stay."

Well, I was a man, and I wasn't about to let no woman I'd spent but one night with tell me what to do.

I put on my hat.

"You go, fine, but your money stays here. The gamblers cheat."

She pounced on me before I could get out of the bedroom and pressed her lips against mine, making a convincing case why I should do what she said. She pulled the money from my pocket and peeled off a single bill. "That will be enough."

I gave in, figuring I could still get my way by going to the saloon and having her when I got back. "Okay," I mumbled with her lips pressed against mine.

I took the money, telling her I'd be back in a bit. I marched out into the light of a phosphorous moon, but I could've found Beaver Smith's place in the dark by all the celebrating. I figured about the only thing noisier than drunks were politicians and revivalists, both no doubt more dangerous than a few sloshed men.

I strode into the noisy, smoke-filled saloon and did a double take. Beaver Smith was right. There behind the bar was the tallest man I'd ever seen. A surveyor could've started at his toes and spent two months mapping him out, he was so tall. He stood six foot five at the least and was skinny as a fence rail, so he appeared even taller. Though his face was in the clouds, I could tell he was a handsome fellow, with dark hair and mustache, thin lips, and an angular face.

I squeezed through the crowd of four dozen or more men and stepped up to the bar, placing my money on the wood. He howdied me and asked my pleasure. I told him whiskey as far as my money'd go.

"It goes farther with cheap whiskey," he said.

"Cheap is fine as long as there's no cow piss in it."

He shook his head. "Beaver'll never live that down. He cuts the stuff, but I've never seen him put anything bad as that in his bottles. They call me Juan Largo, which is Spanish for Long John, but my real name's Pat Garrett."

He had a soft, melodious voice that gave away his southern heritage.

"Lomax is my name. Henry Harrison Lomax, no relation to Gadrich Lomax."

Garrett grinned. "Lot of folks would like to get their hands around Gadrich's neck. I figure he's the one that started the story about the cow piss in Beaver's whiskey." He took my money and turned around to fetch a whiskey bottle.

He placed it and a jigger down in front of me just as two cowboys at a table began arguing a little louder than everybody else was shouting. Garrett cut loose with a shrill whistle, and the saloon went silent. He pointed his finger at the two wrangling cowhands. "Behave yourself before I throw you out of here."

Even in their drunken haze, the two cowboys knew to quiet down.

Garrett turned to me. "You're the one that Rosalita's taken a liking to, aren't you?"

I nodded, not knowing whether Garrett would be mad or just plain jealous about my success.

"Something about the Mexican women, I like. Like them so much, I married one."

"I ain't married yet," I admitted, "but figure since I've taken up with Rosalita I need to find some work around here. I've done a little bit of everything, including bartending."

Garrett looked at me rather hard.

I lifted my hands. "I'm not after your job."

"No, not that," Garrett said. "Beaver's got me working every night of the week. I was just thinking maybe I could have a few nights off every now and then. You could fill in, make a few bucks, a night or two each week. I've been wanting a little time to look into some ranching possibilities. There's no future in bartending unless you own the saloon."

Garrett was a likable fellow. We talked and got along well, partly because we had both hunted buffalo in Texas and knew a lot of the same men. He was a lot like me, trying to find his real calling and always looking for a way to make his fortune. Friendly though he was, he didn't give me any extra drinks when my money was used up.

I remembered I still had in my saddlebags a bottle of whiskey I had stolen from Tunstall's store during the looting. I asked Garrett if he knew where Smith had taken my mule and tack. He told me to check a corral and shed out back. I looked for a back door, found none, and wandered back out the front, leaving the smoke but not the noise as I circled the building. The earth glowed from the moonshine, and I was interested in glowing a little bit from the same thing. I found the shed easily, and sure enough, my saddle and saddlebags were hanging on a rail under the shed. I opened the saddlebags and felt damn proud when my hand touched the cool glass of the whiskey bottle.

Removing the bottle, I felt as excited as a fat man at an eating contest. I uncorked the bottle and took to sipping at it and enjoying it like a king. In thirty minutes I was feeling so good I began to sing and dance back toward Rosalita's. I must've been singing pretty good because a couple hounds began howling with me, and we must've made a good trio because people yelled their approval and threw money at us. The moon wasn't bright enough for me to find any of the coins, though I did get down on my hands and knees a couple times to look.

After an hour I'd finished the bottle and was feeling ready to visit my Rosalita. I should've thrown the bottle away, but I didn't. It'd brought me so much fun, I just couldn't bear to part with it even if it was empty. I ambled over toward Beaver Smith's saloon, singing as loud as I could, but the noise from the saloon drowned me out. I yelled for silence, and when nobody hushed I pulled my gun and shot it in the air, but everybody kept on doing whatever they were doing. I shoved my pistol toward the holster, making it on the third try.

I couldn't have been any happier when I finally reached Rosalita's front door. I lifted the latch and shoved, but it didn't budge. My Rosalita had barred the door. I knocked and called for her, but she didn't answer. There was only one possible explanation: She didn't have her clothes on and didn't want to come to the door naked. So I walked around the end of the building and started along the back wall until I came to her window. I could tell it was her window because I could see in the shaft of moonlight the trunk where she kept my money.

"It is me," I whispered, then hiccuped and apologized. "Sorry."

I shoved my hand with the bottle in the window, then tried to lift my leg inside, but somehow I got all twisted up and banged my head on the side of the window. I slipped back out. "Rosalita, come help me," I called, but she didn't answer. She must've been afraid to be seen naked in the moonlight. I stood there a minute studying the window, trying to figure out how to get inside. Finally I lifted my right leg over the windowsill and pulled myself in until I was astride it. Then I banged my head against the top. As I reached up I clunked myself with the empty whiskey bottle and fell inside the bedroom.

Just as I was shaking the mud from my mind and trying to make sense of all that had happened, I heard a scream that I could've sworn was a cougar. Then I heard the pad of footsteps on the floor and was struck by what I knew was a cougar's claws. I yelled and the cougar screamed, but this mountain lion was different. It knew Spanish.

Even as the cougar swatted at me, I realized Rosalita had come to my rescue and was cursing out the cougar as she tried to save me. I tried to stand, but the cougar swatted me down. When I looked up, I saw Rosalita standing in the shaft of moonlight, a broom in her hand, trying to knock the damn cougar away, but it was a sly, stubborn animal, clinging to the darkness in the room, never stepping into the moonlight where I could see it. I made a final, valiant effort to escape the cougar's fury and managed to rise to my knees. The last thing I remember was something whacking me upside the head, and then I saw stars.

When I woke up about dawn, I had a terrible headache and a knot on the side of my head the size of a horse apple. I got clumsily to my feet and staggered to the bed, trying to take off my gun belt, but it was missing, as was my pistol. I started stripping off my pants, got tangled in them, and tumbled into the bed, startling Rosalita. She sprang up from her pillow, screaming in Spanish and pummeling me with her fist. I knew she must be having nightmares from fighting off the cougar, and I tried to comfort her. But she kept pushing me away in fear, and I couldn't get my clothes untangled enough to thank her for saving me. Finally I gave up and went off to sleep, dreaming about how lucky I was to have a woman that would fight off a cougar. It was almost noon when I woke

up. I could smell a meal cooking, but my stomach was
churning and food was about the last thing I wanted in
it. My head was throbbing both inside and out. I called
for help.

"Rosalita, Rosalita." My voice crackled from the dry-
ness and the taste of sand in my mouth.

Carrying a broom, she strode into the room, her eyes
flashing, her teeth bared. Yelling in Spanish, she swung
the broom at me, catching me on the shoulder.

Now I was more confused than a nun in a brothel. I
didn't know what to say or do, so I yelled, "Stop, Rosalita,
stop!" I thought she'd turned rabid. I hit my waist for my
gun, but it was gone. She was hurting me now, and I
realized she must not understand English when she was
enraged. In desperation I yelled the only Spanish I knew.
Me gustan las ovejas mas que las mujeres!

She stopped beating me, then began to laugh, slightly
at first, then uncontrollably. She collapsed on the bed
beside me and patted me with her hands where only
moments before she had been slapping me with that damn
broom. All I could figure was, she was still distraught over
the cougar attack.

"You saved me last night. Thanks."

"What?"

"From the cougar."

She began to laugh again. "You thought a cougar
came at you?"

I nodded. What else could it have been?

She laughed harder. "It was me—the cougar was
in the bottle." She pointed to the floor and the empty
whiskey bottle.

Vaguely I remembered fetching it from my saddlebags. "A cougar didn't attack me?"

Rosalita pointed to the broom.

It began to make sense. "But why?"

"You come home liquored up and you won't have a
home no more with me."

"I was celebrating," I said.

"Celebrating what?"

"Getting work. Juan Largo said I can work a couple nights a week tending bar for him, bring in some money for us."

"A drunk like you tending bar? You should move out now, because you can't do it."

She got up and pointed to the door. "Go on, leave, now." She strode into the kitchen.

I jumped up from the bed, starting to chase her, but got tangled in my pants and fell to the floor. "I promise, I won't drink again. You can spend the rest of my money if I do."

She came back in and looked at me skeptically.

"Get it. Just don't spend it unless I come in drunk," I said, still struggling to get to my feet.

"Not even one drink," she said, folding her arms across her bosom.

"Even one drink and you can spend it all."

"You can stay," she declared.

As I struggled to get up, she fetched the money from the box and went into the next room to hide it.

Only problem with our deal was, I hadn't okayed the arrangement with Beaver Smith. That afternoon when I was sober and thinking straight, I went back to the saloon.

Smith saw me enter and motioned me over to the bar. "Juan Largo said you agreed to work for him a couple nights a week, that you'd been a bartender before."

"I've had experience," I lied.

"I'd let you do it, except a couple folks said you got drunk last night and shot up the square. Juan Largo said you'd had a few drinks but left without being drunk. I don't want a drinking man tending my bar."

"I was sober as a Baptist's wife," I protested. "I did fire my gun out on the square, but I saw a skunk, nothing else."

Smith shook his head, that slice of his right ear flapping like a bedsheet in the wind. "I guess I'll take you on, but if I find any money missing or too much liquor gone, I'll cut you free quicker than deadweight."

I couldn't argue with that and took up bartending. It was a fine occupation. The only thing hard about it was learning to spit in a fellow's drink when he wasn't looking or how much of a spittoon to dump into a keg of whiskey before it clouded the liquor. I never saw Beaver Smith cut liquor with piss from any animal, living or dead, but he had fewer reservations about anything else. Turpentine gave whiskey a little bite. Kerosene thickened it up a little. Water thinned it, and tobacco juice gave it color. After what I saw the first two weeks on the job, I knew I'd have no problem keeping my promise to Rosalita.

The next three months were a happy time for me. I heard news of Lincoln County—matters had only gotten worse, with thieving, raping, and killing. Word came that Chisum had sold the ranch but was going to keep running it for a while. The law was still looking for the Kid, who had lived up to his promise to steal Chisum's cattle if the cowman didn't pay him the wages he thought he was due. Only problem was, the Kid didn't stop at stealing Chisum's cows. He started stealing everyone else's and herding them to Texas, where he sold them, then stealing horses on his return trip and selling them in New Mexico Territory. Probably the saddest news of all was that Lawrence G. Murphy himself just up and died in Santa Fe without giving someone the chance to kill him.

With a job and a woman that shared her food and more with me, I pretty much thought I'd left those troubles behind, but that was before the fellow everybody was now calling Billy the Kid showed up in Fort Sumner.

Chapter Twenty-four

The trouble between me and Rosalita started at one of the dances that Fort Sumner held every few weeks. Despite my many dancing skills, I stepped on her feet a couple times, and she didn't like it.

"Did you learn to dance with sheep, too?" she growled, loud enough for a couple cowboys to hear.

Had she been my wife, I'd've punched her in the nose, but I was still sharing her food and her bed and didn't think that wise. Things might not have been so bad except those two cowboys took to making sheep noises. I kept my temper because they were saloon regulars, and I figured to get even by spitting in their drinks or mixing in some spittoon drippings.

When one of them cut in on me, Rosalita fell into his arms as easily as water drips out of a bucket with a hole. This cowboy, though, was clumsier on his feet than a three-hour-old calf. Rosalita smiled the first time he stepped on her feet, shook her head the second time, and slapped him the third time. Then she began to cuss him in Spanish. It sure made me feel proud knowing my dancing wasn't bad enough to get slapped.

"You must've learned to dance with an anvil," I commented. The cowboy took it personally and called me and my momma a few names that weren't fit for a dog.

I immediately suggested he didn't have the intelligence God gave a pile of horse apples. He drew back his fist and swung for my nose, but I dodged his punch and sent my fist plowing into his stomach.

The cowboy screamed and went for his gun, but it had been checked at the door, like mine, and he drew air. With our fists we tore into each other, landing enough solid punches to bloody our noses and bruise our faces and chests.

Several men jumped us, pinned our windmilling arms, and dragged us apart, cursing us for disrupting the dance. I struggled against them, but they were too strong and too mad. We were banished from the dance.

"He started it," I yelled as they dragged me to the door. "I haven't been drinking. He has." I struggled against them.

The cowboy was equally incensed. "That yahoo insulted me."

I glanced around the room, looking for Rosalita to come to my aid and or at least console me, but when I saw her, my jaw dropped. Standing beside her was the Kid, his arm in hers. She looked at him with doe eyes filled with desire. She seemed to have forgotten me.

"Rosalita," I called, "time to go."

She looked my way, her doe eyes turning narrow and hard. "Adios!" she mouthed as they tossed me out the door.

I demanded my gun and the cowboy demanded his, but they refused to give us our weapons until morning. If we couldn't settle it with guns, we wouldn't settle it at all. The cowboy shrugged and headed for Hargrove's saloon, leaving me standing there confused. When the music started, I slipped around the side of the old barracks building and peeked through a window. I saw Billy and Rosalita gliding around the dance floor. Had it not been for my bloody nose and my aching body, I would've done something about it.

Instead I stumbled across the parade ground to Rosalita's and let myself in. I undressed in the dark, swiped at my bloodied face with a wet rag, and crawled into bed, waiting for Rosalita to join me. It was after midnight when I fell asleep and well after dawn when I awoke. I turned over and reached for Rosalita, but she was as gone as an unchained dog. Angry, I jumped out of bed, grimacing at the pain in my nose and belly, then dressed and barged out the door, leaving it open as I strode across the parade ground for the dance hall. I burst inside and marched to the table by the door where two gun belts had been left from the night before. One was mine, so I grabbed it and strapped it around my waist, ready to settle the issue with Billy.

I charged back outside. As I studied the square and surrounding buildings, I realized something was different at Rosalita's. I had left the door open, but now it was shut. Rosalita and the Kid must have slipped in during my absence. I cursed her unfaithfulness. As I ran back across the square, I wished I had practiced my drawing and shooting as much as Billy had. I shoved open the door and barged through the kitchen and into her bedroom. She was on the bed asleep—or at least pretending to be asleep. I glanced around the room, then under the bed, but the Kid wasn't there.

"Where is he?"

Rosalita didn't move, still pretending to be asleep.

"Where is he?"

She stirred, turning to face me, and smiled. "Where have you been all night?"

"What?"

"Where have you been?"

"In bed," I said, shaking my head in disbelief.

"No, I've been in bed, waiting for you."

"No. You spent the night with the Kid, didn't you?"

She acted as innocent as a trainload of virgins.

"Where is he? I'm gonna show him you're mine."

"We just danced, then I came for you. That's all," she replied.

"And that's all it's ever gonna be." I slapped the gun at my side. "I intend to show him you're my woman."

"You're wrong."

I was going to argue with her, but she slid the cover from her neck to below her knees. All she wore was a smile. Billy didn't seem nearly as important then, and I forgot about him as Rosalita tended my wounds. By the time I started thinking of him again, I wasn't as mad as I had been.

"Maybe we should get married," I suggested.

"But why?"

"Be man and wife. Henry and Rosalita Lomax."

"Many think we're married."

"It's not the same as being married," I countered.

"I know. We marry, you'll slap me."

"You know I wouldn't hit you."

"Yes, you would, and you wouldn't let me dance with others."

"Dancing'd be okay," I answered. "We could move someplace away from him."

"Him?"

"The Kid," I replied.

At his mention, she smiled before she could catch herself.

"He's an outlaw, Rosalita."

"He's a good dancer."

"What else is he good at?" I challenged.

"Stories. He tells funny stories."

"You like him too much. He's nothing but trouble."

"I like trouble," she said, "like dancing with you at San Patricio. Many shamed me for it and drove me away."

"I'm sorry you had to leave San Patricio."

"Not me—I wanted to. Some of the women who hated me most were raped during the troubles. They deserved it."

"Will you marry me?"

"Not now. Maybe one day."

Her response wasn't an acceptance, but neither was it a refusal. I still had some hope in spite of the Kid.

Rosalita cuddled next to me, her hot flesh rekindling my desire. I figured I was about to get a second helping of her charms and would have had she not asked a question.

"What night do you work again?"

She doused my lust quicker than a Baptist preacher dunks new converts. "Why?" I asked, knowing all the time she was wanting to schedule her next visit with the Kid.

"I want to know how many more nights we'll have together."

"You're planning to see him again, aren't you?"

"No," she answered, then began to cry.

Nothing can make a man more helpless than a woman's tears, even when salty with lies like these. I hesitated to tell her, but decided to put her to the test once and for all. "Tomorrow," I said.

She turned off her tears. "We'll have the next night together."

"We still have right now," I said.

"No, we don't." She shot up from bed. "I have things to do."

She smiled, dressing quickly and escaping out the door.

I put on my pants and went in the kitchen, where I stuck my head out the window. I saw her talking to a slender, redheaded kid who didn't look much older than Billy. When she started to turn around, I pulled my head back inside and retreated to the bed, sitting down to pull on my boots.

Rosalita returned shortly, singing what sounded to me like a Mexican love song—though I admit, with my knowledge of Spanish it could just as easily have been a church hymn. She seemed happier than I had ever seen her, and it angered me enough to take a drink, but I didn't give in to the temptation for fear of losing my two hundred dollars.

Fuming over her betrayal, I put on my shirt, then strapped on my gun belt and marched past her as she began to build a fire for a meal.

"Do you want something to eat?" she asked.

"Later."

She said something in Spanish as I strode out the door.

I marched over to Pat Garrett's place and found him eating. He greeted me and introduced me to his Mexican wife. "Care to have a bite?"

Declining his invitation, I got straight to the point. "I know tomorrow night's my night to work, but could you spell me for a couple hours? Say, from ten to eleven or so?"

"Sure," Garrett replied, "if you'll return the favor some night when I may need it."

I nodded and turned around. "Thanks."

From Garrett's place I returned to Rosalita's. She pointed to a stack of tortillas on the table for my meal. They were as cold as her affection for me that night.

I was glad when the next afternoon arrived and I could report to Beaver Smith's. Business was slow that afternoon, and it stayed slow until after dark when men began to drift in alone or in groups of twos and threes. I was surprised to see the cowboy who had fought me at the dance step up to the bar. He looked at me but didn't remember me from the fight. I gladly took his order for whiskey and spit in his glass.

About an hour after dark, I heard the sound of several horses stopping outside. When the saloon door swung open, a half-dozen men swaggered in, Billy the Kid in the lead.

"Evening, Lomax," he said as he stepped up to the bar.

"The law still after you?" I asked.

He grimaced and nodded.

"Kind of makes it hard to settle down."

He laughed. "Makes things catch as catch can. How about whiskey for my boys?"

I recognized John Middleton and Fred Waite. Like the Kid, they had a hardened look about them. The other four I didn't know by name, though I recognized the one Billy introduced as Tom O'Folliard as the redheaded fellow Rosalita had spoken to the day before. Billy strode to a table, and the others followed.

I grabbed a bottle of cheap liquor and six jiggers, then sauntered over. Middleton and Waite were talking about getting out of New Mexico Territory and pleading with the Kid to join them.

Placing the bottle and shot glasses in front of Billy, I nodded my agreement. "You've had too many close calls."

Billy looked up at me. "I can take care of myself, Lomax, and I don't run out on my friends like you did."

"A dollar and a half," I said, holding my palm up in his face. "You'd've never escaped the Big Killing without me, Kid."

Billy shook his head and stared at me hard.

"A dollar and a half," I repeated. "It wasn't coincidence that a dozen horses were strung out like laundry by the Rio Bonito. It was me, Billy. I stole them and left them there in case you made it that far."

The Kid studied me silently as he fished a dollar and a half out of his pocket and dropped the coins into my palm.

"That squares my debt for you jerking me away from Jesse Evans's gang, Kid. Where are the Coes?"

He leaned back in his chair, rocking on the back two legs. "They got chicken and left."

"They got smart, Kid. You need to listen to Middleton and Waite. Leave while you still can, not carried out in a box."

Waite and Middleton nodded, but the others called me yellow.

"I'm staying," Billy announced, then pointed his finger at my nose. "Lomax, you're the one who better leave Fort Sumner."

"Why's that?"

"Because I might be interested in Rosalita." He gave me a cocky grin, but his cheek didn't poke out like it did when he was joking.

I retreated to the bar and the sawed-off shotgun that Smith stashed there for trouble. I kept an eye on Billy and his gang for the next hour. Then Billy ordered another bottle of whiskey, and not long after I delivered it to him, he stood up, stretched like he was tired, and moved out the door. The others sat at the table, talking low and studying every man who came into the saloon.

The Kid had left to find Rosalita, and I made up my mind I was going to kill him for that. It seemed forever before Juan Largo arrived and relieved me behind the bar. I untied my apron, tossed it to him, then started quickly for the door, straightening my gun belt. Before I could get away, however, Tom O'Folliard stood up and grabbed my arm.

"What's the hurry?" he asked. "How about sharing a drink with me and the rest of Billy's friends?"

I shook myself free, but not before two more of Billy's gang came over to help. They forced me to the table, O'Folliard pulling my pistol from the holster, and shoved me down in Billy's chair.

"Help me," I said to Middleton and Waite.

They shrugged. "We're not a part of this, Lomax," said Waite. "We're leaving the territory come morning."

Turning toward the bar, I called Pat Garrett. "Give me a hand."

"They're just being neighborly." He grinned.

"While the Kid pokes Rosalita," I shouted back.

O'Folliard leaned over the table and grabbed the bottle of whiskey and a dirty jigger. As he filled the glass over my head, I could feel whiskey dripping in my hair.

"Have a drink, Lomax," he taunted, but I closed my mouth and struggled to stand up. I didn't want to lose my two hundred dollars to Rosalita. While the other two pinned my arms, O'Folliard pinched my nostrils shut. When I opened my mouth for air, he tossed the drink inside. I spat whiskey, but O'Folliard jerked my head back and dumped a good cupful down my throat. I swallowed half and spewed half across the table, then gasped for breath while everybody in the saloon laughed at me.

"We just want to be your friends," O'Folliard said.

I cursed. "You're just trying to keep me from finding Billy with—"

O'Folliard jerked my head back again and poured down another dose of whiskey before I could finish my accusation. For a bit I wanted to kill them more than the Kid, but after about six doses of whiskey I began to see the humor in their "friendship," and before it was all over we were laughing and singing good songs.

Sometime after midnight I began to get groggy and thought I saw the Kid enter the saloon, but I couldn't be certain. The next thing I knew, I felt a hand shaking my shoulder gently. The room was dark and quiet as I opened my eyes. My thoughts were as muddy as a river on the rise, but I recognized Pat Garrett's voice. "Time to get you home," he said.

"Damn right," I answered, slapping at my holster for my gun in case I ran into the Kid. I couldn't find the pistol, though.

Garrett steered me through the saloon door and on toward Rosalita's. "You're home," he announced as he opened the door and pushed me inside.

"Come on in," I called to Garrett, waving at him.

He refused. "I need to get home to my wife. I was out later than I told her I would be."

"Hah," I said. "She's got you tamed pretty damn well. Rosalita ain't tamed me." Then I realized I was talking to a closed door. I staggered to the bedroom, pulling off my shirt and preparing to impose myself upon Rosalita. I heard her heavy breathing and reached the end of the bed without incident, though I swung a little wide and tripped over the trunk. Even as I fell to the floor I jerked off my boots, then shot up and ripped off my clothes and dropped into bed beside Rosalita, reaching for her naked body.

"Billito," she said. "Billito."

I didn't know much about Spanish, but I knew it wasn't my name she called out. I didn't mind, though, because she slid her warm body against me. Then I made a two-hundred-dollar mistake. I kissed her.

She came awake as my lips pressed against hers, and her eyes opened enough to see me in the pale moonlight. "It's you," she said, her disappointment as nakedly revealed as her body.

"Who'd you want, Billy?"

She spun over in the bed, remaining still for a moment, then just as suddenly whipped back around, grabbing my head and pulling it against her lips. I thought my passion might have overcome her, but she pushed herself away from me. "Drinking!" she cried. "You have been drinking again?"

"No, I haven't."

"I smell liquor on you."

"No. I mean yes. But I didn't drink. They forced it down me."

"The money is mine," she proclaimed.

I inched closer to her, but she shoved me away. "They made me drink it, Billy's men, holding me at the saloon and pouring liquor down my throat like medicine down a sick cow's mouth."

"No," she said. "Billito would not do that."

"You saw him, didn't you?"

She nodded. "You and I aren't married."

"I've been paying to support us."

"It's my place," she argued.

Here I'd plucked her out of the depths of whoredom, and she was sleeping with another man. I didn't know what to do or how to do it, and the longer I thought about it, the more confused I got. Sleep resolved my dilemma.

Sometime in the morning I heard Rosalita get up, dress, and leave. My head ached like it had been run over by a wagon, and my throat tasted like I had licked the trail all the way from Fort Sumner to Texas.

It was about noon before my head cleared up enough for me to make sense of much around me. I scooted up in the bed, sitting against the wall and trying to get my blurry eyes to focus.

Suddenly I was startled by a shrill whistle that seemed to bounce around in my brain. It had come from outside, and I looked in that direction, startled to see Billy the Kid standing there eyeing me.

"Morning, Lomax," he said.

I grunted. "How was Rosalita?"

"As good as I remembered," he said. "That's what I want to talk to you about."

"There's nothing to talk about, I'm not sharing."

Billy shook his head. "Get out of Fort Sumner."

"Why should I?"

"I'll be back, and when I am, I don't want to wait and see if you're working in a saloon before I visit Rosalita. I might have other plans for her."

"Nope," I answered. "You're not running me out."

The Kid nodded. "If you're not gone the next time I'm in town, Lomax, get ready to attend your own funeral."

He turned around and walked away.

I have to admit that a chill ran down my spine. I'd seen Billy with a gun. I'd seen him as fearless as God in boots, and I didn't know how to take him in a fair fight. But shooting him in the back seemed pretty fair, so I jumped out of bed, scrambled to the floor, and grabbed my gun belt, hoisting it up to my waist and slapping at my pistol. It was gone—I seemed to remember something about Billy's gang taking it at the saloon. I jumped for the window and stuck my head outside, looking for the Kid, but he had already disappeared.

Next I heard a half-dozen or so horses galloping out of town. I figured it was Billy and his men, riding off to rustle cattle or murder anybody who got in their way.

I wasn't going to let Billy the Kid scare me. He was ten years younger than me and not nearly as smart, the way I figured it. He was on the dodge all the time, while I had a paying job two nights a week. I figured I still had Rosalita to myself, except when he might come riding back into town.

By the time Rosalita returned, I had dressed. "Leave," she commanded.

"No."

She slapped me across the cheek and cursed me in so much Spanish that I'd've been a rich man had I got a dime for all the words my ears collected.

"Leave," she said again, pointing to the door.

I nodded, then started gathering my things. "You'll be sorry."

"Only the sheep will be sorry to see you've lost a woman."

"Now that you got my two hundred dollars, you think I'm broke," I bluffed. "There's plenty more I've got stashed places."

"Show me," she demanded.

"Nope," I replied. "I'll find a woman who trusts me."

Rosalita studied me.

"You can go back to taking men boarders every night."

She didn't know whether to believe me or not. I was as broke as the walls of Jericho, but she didn't want to give up the possibility of more money, easily earned.

I kept gathering my few belongings until she stepped to me and put her hand on my shoulder.

"You can stay. Just don't let the Kid know if he comes back. He'll kill you."

"Who do you like best?"

"You," she told me, but that was as big a story as my bluff about more money. She tried her best to give me those big doe eyes that were so inviting, but there was doubt in them.

For the next three weeks Rosalita and I lived like Billy had never returned to our lives. She was careful not to let me see where she had hidden my money, but I finally figured she kept it in the woodbox by the stove. With the cool crisp air of fall, we used wood for heat as well as cooking, and every time I put another log in the stove, she would watch the woodbox closely. She always insisted that I keep it full. One day, when she ran to relieve herself in the outhouse, I scrambled into the kitchen, dug through the woodbox, and found the money in a pouch at the bottom. I palmed it and refilled the woodbox, then jumped for the bedroom just as she returned. I managed to slip the pouch in my pocket before she realized anything.

Luckily that was a day I was scheduled to work. I left in midafternoon for Beaver Smith's bar. There was a crowd outside where a traveling photographer had set up his camera and was making tintypes for a dollar apiece. It was a curious operation, the camera being a large, cumbersome box atop a gawky tripod. The photographer had a big metal reflector taller than me that a volunteer helped him position for lighting.

I wasn't much interested in the goings-on, other than they were keeping business down and giving me a chance to count my money. I smiled when I counted out more than a hundred and eighty dollars.

I would've kept smiling, but a regular customer jumped inside, out of breath. I shoved the money in my pocket.

"Billy the Kid's across the square and heading this direction," he gasped. "And he says he's come to see Rosalita and to kill you, and not necessarily in that order."

Chapter Twenty-five

I thought it was a prank until I slipped to the lone window overlooking the square. My heart jumped to my throat and might have cleared my teeth had my mouth been open any wider. His right hand on his holstered Colt and his left carrying a carbine, Billy was less than a hundred feet away and walking straight for the saloon.

My hand began to quiver as I touched my revolver. It was shaking so that I'm not sure I could've hit him from two feet away if I'd ever pulled the gun. Billy appeared as steady as the earth beneath his boots. Then I remembered the shotgun behind the counter. A man didn't need a steady aim with it—I'd seen some of the bravest men on earth turn yellow under the gaze of a sawed-off scattergun's twin eyes.

I scrambled to the bar, where I grabbed the shotgun and cocked both hammers. The customers in the saloon retreated to the far corner as I stepped back to the window and waited. Billy advanced, his gaze harder than granite. His eyes were fixed so intently upon the saloon that I figured they could see through the adobe walls.

Standing by the edge of the window, I rested the shotgun's short barrel on the sill and waited for Billy to walk within sure range. Then I'd squeeze the trigger and cut him in half. I still liked Billy, but I liked myself better.

He drew closer.

I didn't know how he could not see me. Or the shotgun!

He lifted the Winchester and held it in both hands, ready for action, as he came within twenty feet of the building. I could almost feel his hot breath, he seemed so close and dangerous.

He was dressed about as poorly as I could remember, his work britches and boots worn and dirty. He wore a vest over a shirt and a loose-fitting sweater over them both. Around the same neck that a lot of lawmen wanted to fit in a noose, he wore two knotted bandannas. His pistol, butt turned outward, rode high on his right hip.

Coming within ten feet of the saloon, he squinted at the glare from the wide metal reflector that leaned against the wall by the door. My index finger touched the cold metal of the shotgun's twin triggers. I figured I'd call to him to throw down his guns, give him at least a hair of a chance. Just as I was about to shout his name, I heard another voice call.

"Kid, how about a tintype?"

It was one of those moments that change the course of a man's life. I was seconds away from killing Billy the Kid and becoming a well-known man throughout the West, maybe even returning to Arkansas as a somebody rather than the vagabond who'd left a dozen years earlier.

The Kid stopped to study the photographer and the bulky camera. "How much?"

"A dollar a pose."

Billy shook his head. "That's steep."

The photographer shrugged. "For you, Kid, two poses for a dollar. No less, no more."

Billy grinned, then adjusted his bandanna and straightened his lopsided hat. "My business can wait."

I didn't feel relieved, though, because all Billy had done was prolong my agony. I might still die.

Outside, the photographer maneuvered Billy into place, positioning him just right, twisting the butt of his revolver even farther away from his hip to accentuate it in the tintype. He had Billy stand with the butt end of the Winchester stock on the ground and the muzzle in his left hand.

"You've got to stay still," yelled the photographer as he slipped his head and shoulders beneath a black cloth and adjusted the bellows on the camera.

My mind raced. I had to use this momentary distraction to escape. But how? There was no back door or window. Only one way out of the saloon—and that route passed right by Billy.

Trying to get by Billy would be like trying to slip daylight past a rooster; only difference was, the Kid would shoot first and crow later.

Then the photographer said something that saved my life. "Somebody help me with the reflector."

This was my chance. I could hide behind the big reflector and hope Billy wouldn't notice.

"Somebody give me a hand," the photographer pleaded.

I left the cocked shotgun on the windowsill and slipped out the door, quickly sliding behind the reflector and grabbing each side with my hands.

"To your left, away from the door," called the photographer.

I obliged, figuring my life depended on it.

"That's good," he said. "Now lean the top forward just a bit."

I did what he said.

"Great. Now hold it there."

Hurry, I wanted him to hurry. I feared the Kid might peek behind the reflector, the bottom edge of which was resting on the ground just inches in front of my feet. I tightened my grip with my left hand and released my right. Carefully I slid my pistol from its holster.

"The reflector's moving," the photographer yelled. "Keep still."

Hell, I thought, *you try keeping still when you're not four feet from a man who's threatened to kill you.*

"Now, you be still, Kid. That's it."

All was silent for a moment. Then came a pop and flash as he lit magnesium powder.

I flinched and caught a breath of the pungent odor. The Kid cried out. "You blinded me."

"It's just temporary," the photographer answered back.

I moved the reflector to prop it against the saloon.

"One more," cried the photographer. "I promised the Kid two for a dollar. Keep the reflector still. It's shaking."

Damn right it was shaking I was shaking, even more so when I heard the Kid ask a question.

"Who's back there?"

I swallowed hard and thumbed back the hammer on the pistol, just waiting for Billy to poke his head around the edge.

"Stay where you are, Kid, or I'll never get done."

I grimaced, wondering if I wouldn't have been better off staying inside the saloon and just killing Billy when he walked in. I glanced back over my shoulder and saw the shotgun resting on the window's thick adobe sill. I thought about reaching for it, but I saw the cocked hammers and remembered the shotgun's hair triggers.

With another pop the magnesium flashed, throwing an instant veil of white light over the Kid, the reflector, and me.

"You done?" the Kid called.

"Am now," the photographer yelled.

Before I could make a move, the Kid circled around the reflector and paused there, just looking at me, his eyes squinting and blinking. He must've still been blinded by the flash because he just nodded and stepped through the saloon door.

In my nervous haste to put down the reflector and hide, I leaned it against the adobe wall and accidentally bumped the shotgun barrel. It swung around toward the inside of the saloon. I started to grab it but caught myself for fear I would discharge the shotgun in my gut. I froze as it slipped off the sill and fell inside.

The instant it hit the floor, the saloon boomed with two successive explosions.

Men cursed and screamed.

I shoved the reflector against the wall as a bullet thudded into the edge of the window, splattering me with bits of adobe.

As another shot whizzed over my head I realized I was no longer welcome around Beaver Smith's.

"What's happening?" yelled the photographer, grabbing his camera and lugging it toward safety.

I ran around the side, then along the back of the long adobe building, knowing Billy would be following me shortly. I figured I was about to die. As I looked over my shoulder I tripped over a pole on the ground and went flying. I hit the ground solidly, knocking the air from my chest and the gun from my hand. That fall saved me, because I had tripped over my escape route— a long pine pole that had been nailed with crosspieces to make a primitive ladder. I jumped up, picked up the ladder, shoved it against the top of the adobe, then darted for my revolver, grabbing it and thrusting it in my holster. I scrambled up the ladder onto the flat mud roof, hoping not to crash through the ceiling into one of the compartments below. It was a perfect hiding spot, the roof itself being a couple feet lower than the top of the adobe wall. Nobody could see me unless they climbed up. Quickly I pulled the ladder up after me and waited.

In a moment I heard men pouring out of the saloon. "Lomax did it," cried one of them.

"Where'd he go?" the Kid yelled.

"Out back," cried another.

I sure had a lot of friends. Maybe they hadn't been pleased with the cut drinks I'd served them. Or maybe they were upset over the shotgun's discharge. Anyway, they were mad. I held my breath as I listened to men charging around the building.

"Check the shed," the Kid yelled.

I heard footsteps running in that direction. "Nothing here but a mule."

The Kid cursed. "I'll find him if it takes all day."

He did spend the rest of the day searching for me. I heard scattered bits of conversation about me just disappearing in thin air. Fortunately the air was cool and the sun subdued so I didn't grow unbearably thirsty, but what had been advantages during the day turned to disadvantages after dusk. The fall air turned cold, and I shivered the night away, my teeth chattering so loudly that any minute I expected folks to figure out where I was hiding.

Dawn came cool and brisk, and I was still shivering like a leaf in a breeze when I heard horse hooves and cattle bellowing. I glanced over the top of the wall and saw some fifty cattle being herded by Tom O'Folliard, Charlie Bowdre, and a few others I didn't recognize. By the jinglebob of the cattle's ears, I knew who they belonged to.

The rustlers drove the cattle right by Rosalita's door, whooping and hollering to the Kid about what kind of night's sleep he'd gotten. From what I'd heard during the night, he'd gotten plenty, though not necessarily sleep.

All the rustlers laughed when Billy apparently stepped to the door. "You'll get a mite cold if that's all you're wearing to Tascosa," O'Folliard teased.

"You boys ride on. I'll catch up with you. And one thing, boys, if you see Henry Lomax, you let me know. He and I've got a score to settle. The fool tried to assassinate me yesterday with a shotgun blast. Only problem was, his nerves weren't any better than his aim."

O'Folliard laughed. "Want us to take care of him for you?"

"Nope," the Kid answered emphatically. "*I* want to kill him. Now you boys go on, and I'll catch up with you."

"Today?" Bowdre joked.

Billy laughed. "As soon as I finish my business."

The rustlers rode on as Billy shut the door. It wasn't long before I heard Rosalita and him rutting again. I tried to ignore the fact that Rosalita liked Billy better than me, but that was about as likely as Billy believing the shotgun blast had been an accident. Rosalita was forever mine, except when Billy the Kid was around. Then she was temporarily Billy's. I decided right then I was going to face my problem the only sensible way I could. I would leave New Mexico.

When I heard Billy tell her good-bye, I lifted my head above the top of the adobe wall and watched him stroll across the square toward Bob Hargrove's saloon, where he'd left his horse overnight. I saw him mount up and gallop to the northeast to catch up with his gang. Even after he rode out of sight I waited for another hour, just to be certain, then lowered the makeshift ladder over the wall. As I climbed down I realized for the first time that I was still wearing my bartender's apron. I untied it and flung it aside, then marched to the shed and quickly saddled Flash. I led him to the back of Rosalita's and climbed in her window, startling her.

She jerked the covers up in false modesty. "Where have you been?"

I pointed under the bed. "Hiding there."

"That is a lie."

I gathered what few things I had in her dwelling.

"Get out. Go find you another sheep." She cursed me in Spanish.

I cursed her in English.

She cursed me in Spanish and English.

I couldn't top that, so I bundled up my things, grabbed my hat, and crawled out the window. "What are you going to do when my money runs out?" I yelled as I cinched things down on Flash.

"Find me another as foolish as you." She laughed smugly.

"Then you better start looking."

Rosalita flung the covers back and dashed into the kitchen. I heard her throwing kindling and wood. She loosed a terrible shriek and dashed back to the window as I turned Flash around. Spewing insults like a tornado spews debris, cussing at a hundred miles an hour, she shook her fist at me, her naked bosoms jiggling with each emphatic point. I enjoyed watching her lecture.

I angled Flash toward the shed, where I found Beaver Smith eyeing Rosalita as she showered me with profanities in two languages.

"I'm leaving," I told him. "With the Kid out to get me, I figure I'd best move on."

Smith nodded, his ear flapping. "Where'd you hide? The roof?"

My eyes went wide and I licked my lips. "How'd you know?"

"The ladder wasn't behind the saloon like it usually is."

"Why didn't you tell?"

"Why should I? You never stole from me and never told customers how we cut the whiskey. Even if you were spitting in the drinks of some customers, as long as they didn't know it, it saved me money."

I grinned. "Thanks, Beaver."

He shrugged. "I suppose you want your pay? I figure I owe you ten or eleven dollars."

I decided a man who wouldn't divulge my hiding place could be trusted with a few dollars of mine.

"Mail it to me in a couple months, Beaver."

He nodded. "But where?"

I figured I could tell him and he would keep the word to himself. Last thing I wanted was for Billy the Kid to be chasing me all over the Southwest, trying to kill me because I had come near killing him. "Tombstone, over in Arizona Territory. There's word they're finding silver."

"I'll give you two months, then send it to Tombstone."

I tipped my hat to the saloon owner and nudged Flash ahead. I didn't know if I would ever make it back to New Mexico Territory, but I knew for sure I wouldn't be back in Lincoln County until Billy the Kid was dead or in jail. Billy should have left months ago, but he began to think he was invincible. Not me—I knew I was mortal, and maybe more so around the Kid.

Pointing Flash westward, I guided him along the road to White Oaks. It was late October or early November of 1878, and the weather was cool. I met several hard-looking men on the road, some outlaws, no doubt, and some lawmen or cattle detectives looking for the Kid and his gang. They didn't bother me, apparently figuring that a man who rode a mule couldn't know much or have enough money on him to be worth stealing.

I spent one night in White Oaks, buying a little ammunition and some supplies for the trip to Tombstone, then started out the following day, taking the trail south along the Rio Grande River toward Mesilla, a sleepy little town with a Catholic church on the north end of the small square and low-slung adobe buildings on the opposite side that served as the district courthouse.

Outside of town I crossed the Rio Grande on a ferry and kept moving west toward Arizona. The land was speckled with sagebrush and not much else; the isolated mountains were as barren as if they had been born the day before.

I don't know when I left New Mexico Territory for Arizona Territory, there not being much difference between them, besides the fact that New Mexico still had Lincoln County and Arizona didn't. I cut south toward Douglas, then up to Bisbee before hitting Tombstone.

Not two months after I arrived I checked the post office and found a letter from Beaver Smith. Inside, as promised, were eleven dollars and a note that Rosalita had taken my departure harder than he would've expected.

I spent the next two years in Tombstone, using the hundred and seventy dollars remaining from Chisum's pay to open a saloon and invest in mining properties. I might have been rich had I not got caught in the middle of a feud between two hardcases, but that's another story.

All I know is, I was sitting pretty well and gradually picking up bits and pieces of information about the activities in Lincoln County. Perhaps the most startling was that Pat Garrett had given up his job as a bartender to run for sheriff. He was promising to end the violence and bring Billy the Kid to justice. That seemed like a pretty bold promise because so many other men had tried and failed, but if anyone could do it, Garrett could. He wouldn't run from a showdown like I had, I was certain.

Toward the end of 1880, the *Tombstone Epitaph* reported that several of Billy's gang had been captured or killed, including Charlie Bowdre and Tom O'Folliard. The way the story sounded, the new sheriff was chasing the outlaws without pause.

Then came a story that Pat Garrett had given New Mexico Territory a Christmas present with the capture of Billy the Kid. I felt sorry for the Kid, figuring his exceptional luck had finally run out. Even though he was out to kill me, I hated the idea that he had wound up captured. It would've been best for him to die at the wrong end of a gun rather than the business end of a rope.

The news was interesting, but I didn't think that much about it. I had lived in and survived Lincoln County, just as I had survived Leadville and the unfortunate demise of a lawyer. I had no intention of going back—until I received a second letter.

As I took the envelope from the postmaster, I recognized Beaver Smith's handwriting even though it had been two years since his previous letter. I ripped the end off and found two messages inside, one in English and the other in Spanish. The one in Smith's handwriting I was able to read with some work:

I don't know that this missive will find you, but Rosalita wanted to send you a message. I am sending it with this letter. I don't know what it says, though she has really taken to missing you since the Kid was captured. Aren't women odd?

Next I studied Rosalita's handwriting, which was pretty and delicate, unlike her temper. But that was all I could make out of it other than misspellings of my name. I asked the postmaster if he knew anyone who could read Spanish. He said he didn't know anyone and didn't care. I was impressed by his honesty, but that did nothing for my curiosity, so I left the post office and wandered back to my saloon, asking one of the Mexican helpers if he could read Spanish. He nodded and I gave him the letter.

He skimmed it real quick, then gave me a grin. "She wants you back."

"What?"

"Your señorita wants you back."

I couldn't believe it. "Read the letter."

The boy took a deep breath and began to read:

When I refused to marry you before, I was wrong. Please return to me and we shall become husband and wife as soon as the time is right. Please forgive me for our past differences, but I was wrong. Love, Rosalita.

It still galled me that she had thrown me out for Billy to begin with and that she would crawl back to me only after the Kid was in jail. I mulled over her offer for several days. I had to admit, though, she was a fine woman at pleasuring a man. My sap kept rising at the thought of being with her again. Finally I decided to see just how much Rosalita really meant to me.

I left my saloon in the hands of the three men who worked the bar and mounted Flash for a return journey to New Mexico. It took me a little over ten days to reach Fort Sumner. I stopped at Beaver Smith's, and he greeted me with a warm handshake.

"Billy hasn't escaped jail, has he?" I asked.

Smith laughed. "You're too jumpy. I bet Rosalita'll take a little starch out of your worries."

I shook my head. "I don't know why I came. She doesn't care for me. It's Billy."

"Billy's days are over now that Pat Garrett's sheriff. Juan Largo won't let Billy escape."

"I opened my own saloon in Tombstone," I told Smith.

"You still spitting in customers' drinks?"

"No, that's my bartenders' job."

Smith laughed. "So you're finally making decent money. Money enough to support a wife."

"That's a possibility," I admitted.

He nodded. "I think she's in her room."

I slipped from the bar to her door, rapping lightly upon it.

When she opened the door, she froze in surprise, then charged me and threw her arms around me, smothering me with kisses. I figured that was a little too warm a welcome, especially when she pulled me inside, shut the door, and led me straight to her bed. She made up to me the rest of the afternoon and night until I was too tired to bat my eyes. I got as deep a rest that night as I can ever remember and woke up the next morning to the smell of breakfast cooking.

I dressed and marched to the kitchen.

"I'm glad you came. I didn't know if my letter would bring you."

"It was your charms that brought me."

She smiled. "Your charm is growing." She placed a breakfast of eggs and tortillas before me.

"When do you want to get married?"

"After the trial."

"What trial?"

"Billito's trial," she replied.

I grimaced. "I didn't come to help you forget Billy. Either marry me or live with Billy's memory."

"No, I want to marry in the spring, make a new start on life."

"Sounds damn foolish to me."

"Maybe so, but love makes you foolish."

I shrugged.

"Once I see Billy in jail, then I'll marry you."

Chapter Twenty-six

Now, I admit it was a foolish decision staying in Fort Sumner when I had my saloon business in Tombstone, but Rosalita couldn't cut herself free from New Mexico just yet. My brain told me I should up and leave her, but I could barely get out the door each day without coming back to her at night. Of course, I knew if Billy ever escaped, her love for me would turn colder than a grizzly's butt in winter. But Billy wasn't escaping. We heard they kept him under guard day and night even when he was locked in his Mesilla cell.

Rosalita kept pestering me to take her to visit him, but I told her I'd be damned if I was going to Mesilla in winter weather. She reminded me we would marry only after I took her to see Billy one last time. Word drifted to us of events in Mesilla. In January and February the damned lawyers started muddying the waters. Billy's lawyer kept buying the Kid time and delaying my wedding. March rolled around. By then I knew I needed to get back to Tombstone and check on business there and in Benson, where I was considering opening another saloon. I offered to take Rosalita with me and start over in Arizona, but she put me off, saying she didn't feel like a long ride. I didn't feel like one either, but I was having to make one because of her stubbornness.

I left the first of March and passed through Mesilla a few days later. I was tempted to stop and visit the Kid, but rode on anyway. Everything turned out okay in Tombstone. I left Flash there to rest him for the return trip to Fort Sumner and rode the stage to Benson. I survived an unfortunate robbery on the trip, which is another story, and afterwards decided not to open up a saloon in Benson because it would require constant trips from Tombstone, and I didn't know that I trusted my wife-to-be around so many single men.

Feeling a little more confident that my bartenders hadn't been swindling me out of money, I gathered part of my profits and started back to Fort Sumner, figuring a thick roll of money would convince Rosalita she should go ahead and marry me.

I arrived in Mesilla just as the Kid's trial was commencing for the murder of Sheriff Brady. He was guilty as sin, and I was just glad that the law didn't realize I had witnessed the murder. The Kid's lawyer had already gotten an indictment for the murder of Buckshot Roberts thrown out on a damn technicality. Seems the federal indictment against the Kid and others assumed the murder had taken place on the Mescalero reservation, which was federal property. Instead, it had taken place on Dr. Blazer's private property. It seemed idiotic to me that they would debate that. After all, Roberts was still dead.

I feared some other odd legal interpretation might keep the Kid from being executed for killing Sheriff Brady. I never saw such a brutal murder as Brady's, nor as many lawmen as were attending the Kid's second trial. A pair stood outside the door, inside the door, at each window, and at each side of the bench. I made it inside only after I was relieved of my holster and checked for other weapons.

The courtroom was maybe fourteen feet wide and likely twice that long. It was packed and hot from so many bodies pressed so tightly together. I wound up in the front row and only then because another lawman stood up from one of the spectators' benches as the lawyers entered the room, followed by the Kid and three more guards. The lawman whose seat I took stood facing all the spectators squeezed on the dozen or so backless benches.

The Kid turned around to look at the crowd. He had a grin bigger than a washtub, and it got bigger when he saw me. "Where's your shotgun, Lomax?"

The three deputies at his side glared at me, as if I was in a plot to free Billy.

"It was an accident, Billy."

The Kid shrugged. "Don't guess it matters, right now," he said. "I saw the tintype. There were fingers at the edge of the reflector. Were those yours?"

I nodded.

Laughing, the Kid lifted a manacled hand at me. "So you were behind the reflector. I was blinded by the flash. You should've killed me then, because when I get out, I'll be gunning for you."

The Kid had more confidence than a sodbuster after a spring rain, I had to admit, and he spoke as if there was no doubt about it.

"The time for leaving was two years ago, Billy. You should've left then. It's too late."

Billy just laughed again. "They'll convict me."

"They should," I said. "You killed Brady, and that changed everything, Kid. The county was on your side until then. You shouldn't have planted those fence posts upside down."

The Kid's smile disappeared and his eyes narrowed. "They'll convict me, but they'll never hang me."

Our conversation was interrupted by the arrival of Judge Bristol, the same judge who had presided over the grand jury that had indicted the Kid for the murder two years earlier. We all had to stand for the horse's ass, then settled back on our hard benches while he got to sit in a padded chair. He started pontificating over all this legal folderol, and I quickly grew bored.

When it came time for the lunch recess, I'd had enough. "See you, Kid," I said.

Billy grinned. "Look at my feet."

I did. They were bare except for the leg irons around his ankles. He lifted his manacled hands and shook his head. "I'll get out of these and out of jail. Tell Rosalita when I do I'll come by to see her."

Now I laughed. "She'll see you because I've promised to let her visit you once in jail. After that she's promised to marry me."

"She likes me better, Lomax. Ask her where she keeps the tintype I gave her of me."

"Hell, Kid, I thought she kept it so she'd have a picture of my fingers."

Billy grinned, his cheek poking out where he wriggled his tongue. "We'll see, Lomax. We'll see."

I went out with the herd and bought some tortillas from a Mexican vendor who was set up on the plaza for the court business. I mounted Flash and rode out of Mesilla. Rather than ride the road, I angled toward the new railroad track that had finally split New Mexico in half from north to south. It pretty much followed the Rio Grande, and I skirted them both as I headed north, joining up with the road ten miles outside of Mesilla. In the little over two years that I had been away from Lincoln County, New Mexico Territory had changed. The telegraph followed the railroad and made it possible for news to travel faster than men.

By the time I reached Fort Sumner, I learned the Kid had been convicted of Brady's murder and sentenced to hang on May thirteenth in Lincoln. I found Rosalita in mourning because she had learned the same thing. She was so distraught that I had a hard time convincing her to let me in her bed.

"No, no," she said, dashing for the broom and picking it up like she was going to sweep me away.

"We're gonna be married," I protested.

"No," she sobbed, "not until I see Billito again."

"I'll take you when he gets back to Lincoln," I offered. "That's where they'll hang him."

She sobbed even louder, swatting at me with the broom.

I grabbed the broom from her and tossed it aside, then took her in my arms. She hugged me and nuzzled against my chest, but I had the feeling she was thinking of Billy instead.

Two days later I lived up to my promise. I borrowed a wagon and a team from the prosperous Pete Maxwell. We put bedding in the back, and Rosalita carried her small trunk of clothes, evidently intent on dressing well for Billy.

It took us a couple days to reach Lincoln. We arrived late in the afternoon, and Rosalita wanted to go straight to the jail to see Billy. I didn't know how she would take seeing Billy in that hole in the ground, but I was in for a big shock. The jail had been abandoned. A Mexican kid explained to Rosalita that the jail was now in the courthouse. That didn't make sense to me, because the building just down the street that had always served as the courthouse was locked up. I mentioned this to Rosalita, and she questioned the Mexican kid. When she gave me the answer, I was as shocked as I could be. Murphy's store had been bought by the county and was now the Lincoln County courthouse. It seemed odd that a building that had been responsible for so many crimes by Murphy and his cohorts was now the building where justice would be dispensed. Of course when I realized that judges and lawyers would be populating the building, it didn't seem odd at all. There'd be just as many crimes seeping out of that building as there had been before.

I hoped I might see Sheriff Pat Garrett, but instead ran into a deputy at the door. His name was Bob Olinger, and he was an ugly, cocky sort of fellow who probably wasn't smart enough to dump water out of a bucket with the instructions written on the bottom.

"What do you want?" He stared at me with muddy eyes that matched the tobacco staining his teeth.

"Wanted to see Billy Bonney."

He grinned, giving me a better view of his ugly teeth. He had a square, chubby face and was strutting about like he ran things.

"Can't see him."

Rosalita began to sob.

Olinger grinned and took to chewing his tobacco harder. "One of the Kid's señoritas?" he asked.

"My wife-to-be," I replied. "Where's the sheriff?"

"Why, Pat's gone to White Oaks," Olinger replied, "and won't be back until day after tomorrow. He's buying lumber for a gallows. We'll be having a hanging May thirteenth, you know. Until Pat gets back, I'm in charge." He hooked his thumbs in his gun belt.

I pointed to Rosalita. "Let her see him ten, fifteen minutes."

"Nope," Olinger said. "Pat Garrett left specific instructions. No one is to see him or any of the prisoners except between ten and eleven each morning. The Kid's a dangerous one, you know, and Garrett left his best deputy in charge of things."

"Then let me speak to him."

The deputy shot me a stare. "I'm him."

With his attitude I figured Olinger would've made a damn good lawyer had he been playing with a full deck. He wasn't. Maybe he'd make a better target. I was beginning to wish the Kid would escape and thrash Olinger on his way out.

"Now," Olinger said, "I'm ordering you to move on and go about your business. There won't be any chance of you seeing the Kid tonight."

Rosalita, charming wife-to-be that she was, cursed Olinger, then said she was ready to leave. She pointed to a place out behind the courthouse where we might spend the night, but Olinger seemed to want to torment me.

"Nobody's allowed to camp on courthouse property."

I steered the team around and drove the wagon back down the street, figuring to stay near Tunstall's store. We passed the site of the McSween home, its ruins long since picked over by scavengers looking to salvage anything that might be useful. I doubted they found much.

We spent the night together beneath a cottonwood tree. Rosalita had a restless sleep, and I didn't do much better. We woke up early, with three hours to kill before we could visit Billy. Rosalita convinced me we should move the wagon down by the Rio Bonito where she could bathe and I could watch. At the stream she was overly modest, trying to hide her charms from me as if I had never seen her naked. When she was done, she dried off and dressed, putting on a green skirt and a new blouse. She combed her hair, rouged her cheeks, and colored her lips until she looked better than I ever remembered. It bothered me that she was doing this for another man, but this was a man who would be hanging from a gallows in another three weeks.

When she was ready, I helped her in the wagon and took her to the Wortley Hotel for a bite of breakfast. I was hungry, but I was also a bit jealous. I hoped she might spill food down her dress and soil it before seeing Billy, but she barely nibbled at the food, and I wound up eating it myself.

Though we still had a half hour before the courthouse opened for visitors, Rosalita insisted we go there and stand at the door. It galled me that she wanted to spend every possible minute with the Kid, but I felt a little better knowing it would only be sixty minutes.

A line had already formed of people planning to visit the other prisoners. As best I could tell, Rosalita and I were the only two there to see the Kid. When the door finally swung open about a quarter to ten, I saw another deputy instead of Bob Olinger. He introduced himself as Jim Bell and said all entering the jail would have to check their gun belts and be searched as well. I didn't cotton to leaving my gun in the same building with Olinger, so I slipped from the line to the wagon and unbuckled my gun belt, rolled it up, and placed it under the wagon

seat. I was pleased that Rosalita watched me, especially
when she smiled. Maybe she was getting over the Kid
and ready to accept me as her husband.

She hugged me when I got back in line with the other visitors, mostly Mexican women and children. Deputy
Bell announced that after he had searched each of us, he
would escort us all upstairs as a group. I'd never met
Bell before, but he was a decent sort, respectful of the
women as he looked them over, never touching a one
in his search for weapons. He frisked me and the two
other men in line, then locked the outside door behind
him when he was certain no other visitors were coming.
He apologized as he led us up the stairs. "Shame we have
to keep the courthouse locked up, but until we hang the
Kid we've got to be careful."

At the head of the stairs he turned around, facing
the rest of us. "Who's to see the Kid?"

"I am," said Rosalita.

"Me, too," I added.

Hearing no other responses, Bell nodded. "All the
rest of you go this way," he said, pointing to his left,
"and you'll find your folks and friends." He let the other
visitors pass, then looked at me and Rosalita. "You two
come with me."

At the top of the stairs I glanced left and saw a
single deputy standing guard at a room with about six
men inside.

"We keep the others separate from the Kid," Bell
explained as he led me and Rosalita into a wide room in
the northeast corner of the building. There sat Billy the
Kid, playing solitaire with a dog-eared deck of cards on
a board in his lap. His bare, manacled feet were chained
to metal rings in the floor, and the chains on his wrists
jingled as he played cards. Billy looked up, smiled at
Rosalita, and nodded at me.

Sitting in a chair opposite him was Deputy Bob
Olinger, chewing tobacco and patting a shotgun in his
lap. "Come to see the condemned man." He laughed.

"Billito," Rosalita cried and rushed toward him.

Olinger, though, shot up from his seat and grabbed her hand, jerking her to a stop before she could reach Billy.

Rosalita cried out at his tight grip on her wrist. Billy flung his lap board and cards to the floor and lunged as far as his chains would let him.

Olinger shoved Rosalita aside and swung the shotgun around for Billy's gut. "Just try something, Kid. I'd enjoy killing you, you son of a bitch."

The Kid growled, "You'll never kill me, Bob. You're too fat and stupid."

Olinger's face turned red with anger, but Bell stepped in. "Take your seat, Kid," he said, then turned to Olinger. "Don't taunt him."

Olinger scoffed, "He's trash." He looked at Rosalita. "You can approach him, but don't get close enough for him to touch you."

Rosalita stepped forward, tears rolling down her cheeks. Billy told her to cheer up, that he would get out of this mess.

Bell eased by the window, where he could see between them to make sure there was no opportunity for Rosalita to slip the Kid a weapon.

After a few moments they began to talk in Spanish. Olinger looked to Bell, who shrugged.

"What did she say?" Olinger demanded.

Billy looked at Olinger. "She said you're the biggest horse's ass she's ever been around, and she's been around some big ones." He laughed.

Olinger patted the barrel of his shotgun. "Just try to escape, Kid. All I'm looking for is an excuse to kill you, save the county the expense of hanging you."

The Kid laughed again. "You'll die before me."

Bell took a step toward Olinger. "Leave him alone, Bob. You've been baiting him too much. Kid, you best talk with the young woman because you're running out of time before eleven o'clock."

Rosalita began to cry, but Billy told her to be strong. Their conversation flowed back and forth between English and Spanish; none of the rest of us in the room understood it all.

I took a seat by the door and waited impatiently for Rosalita to finish her last visit with the Kid. From my chair I could see the sheriff's office across the hall and the arsenal that Garrett kept in it. The hour passed slower than a circuit rider's sermon, but it finally drew to a close as Rosalita and Billy spoke their intimate feelings in hushed Spanish.

"Time to go," Olinger announced, patting his shotgun.

The Kid turned to Bell. "Let me give her a hug and a kiss."

"No!" shouted Olinger. "She might slip him a weapon."

Bell nodded. "Okay, Kid, but we'll have to search you."

The Kid laughed. "Wish you'd let Rosalita search me."

I didn't think that was very funny, but Olinger did. He glanced over his shoulder and smirked at me.

Rosalita stepped to the Kid and kissed him on the cheek. He held her as best he could with his chained arms.

"That's enough," Olinger cried out. "Get away, girl."

Rosalita stepped backward, then turned to face me, her eyes overflowing with tears.

Bell lifted his pistol from his holster, then placed it on the windowsill before advancing to the Kid and searching him. Of course there was no weapon on him, because there was no way Rosalita could've slipped him anything but a kiss. Satisfied that Billy was still unarmed, Bell backed away and retrieved his own gun. As he slipped it into the holster, Bell motioned for us to leave.

"Rosalita," Billy called as we stepped to the door, "don't marry Lomax because I'll be getting out of jail soon."

Rosalita just grimaced.

I turned to the Kid. "You shouldn't have set those fence posts upside down, and you should've left Lincoln two years ago."

Bell herded me and Rosalita to the head of the stairs where the other visitors were waiting, then marched us all down the stairs. I was the last in line, save for Bell, and at the foot of the stairs I ran into an unexpected acquaintance: Gottfried Gauss, the cook on Tunstall's ranch. Blind though he was, he must've recognized me by my voice.

"Vell, iffen it's Lomax. Vanten some coffee? I cook for the county now."

"I'm still alive because I quit drinking your coffee, Gauss."

The old German swatted me on the shoulder and laughed, thinking it was a joke.

Bell pointed the visitors out the door, and I told Gauss so long. Outside, Bell grinned at me. "That old man makes the worst coffee I ever drank."

"Shame of it is," I said, "he thinks it's good."

Rosalita, still in a sorry state over Billy, marched alone to the wagon and climbed in, taking her seat and bending down a couple times like she was reaching for something on the floorboard. Bell and I visited a few moments, him worrying that the Kid might try something and give Olinger the opportunity to kill him.

Bell shook his head. "Billy's a likable fellow, not a bully like Olinger. Shame, isn't it, that the Kid let it get out of hand."

I nodded and shook Bell's hand. "Good luck, Deputy." At the time I shook his hand, I didn't know that Bell had less than two hours to live!

Anxious to head back to Fort Sumner and get married, I bounded off the porch step and out to the wagon, drawing myself quickly aboard. Rosalita seemed nervous, and I attributed it to seeing Billy for the last time. As I untied the reins and started the wagon forward, she told me she needed to heed nature's call.

"There's outhouses in back. My belly is hurting," she said.

That explained her bending over in the seat a couple times. She was trying to relieve the pain. I swung the team out into the dusty street, then turned it behind the courthouse toward the two privies. Carefully she climbed down from the wagon and strode to the one men generally used.

"You want the other one," I said. "The seat won't be wet."

Rosalita ignored me, going in and shutting the door behind her. I attributed it to her nerves again. While she was occupied, I retrieved my holster. It seemed awfully light, and I saw the reason why when I put it in my lap. The revolver was missing! Some son of a bitch had stolen it while I was in the courthouse. I cursed and placed the empty gunbelt on the wagon bench just as Rosalita emerged from the outhouse.

She was smiling, so she evidently felt better, but the smile withered when I held the empty holster up.

"Some bastard stole my gun," I announced.

She hesitated, then smiled. "You can get another one." She pulled herself aboard the wagon, and I turned the team back for Fort Sumner. I still had my carbine so we weren't unarmed, but I felt naked without the pistol.

We took it slow and easy on the way back to Fort Sumner, Rosalita seeming edgy the entire way. We made it back three days after we pulled out of Lincoln. We'd no more than arrived in town than I had the biggest shock of my life when Beaver Smith came out to greet us.

"Guess you heard the news," he said, scratching his gouch ear.

"What news?"

"About the Kid. He's escaped."

Rosalita squealed with glee.

"Killed two deputies, a Bell and an Olinger."

I bit my lip. Olinger might have deserved to die, but not Bell.

"Word is, Pat Garrett's out to kill him this time, not risk another escape."

Rosalita's excitement dimmed.

"How'd it happen?" I asked.

"From what I hear, nobody's certain, other than Bell took the Kid to the privy while Olinger was eating lunch at the hotel. From somewhere, the Kid got a gun, killed Bell, and then ambushed Olinger when he ran back to the courthouse to check on the gunshot."

I turned to Rosalita, knowing full well where the Kid got the gun, my gun. She and the Kid had discussed the plan in Spanish on our visit, and then she had stolen my gun.

She cocked her head and gave me a proud smirk.

"It's time for us to get married," I announced.

The smirk died on her face. "I want to marry in the summer."

"The summer? You said the spring last time."

"I changed my mind."

"Now that Billy's out?" I challenged.

"Now that I've changed my mind," she said, jumping from the wagon and striding for her door.

Beaver Smith shrugged. "She'll never marry you, not until Billy's dead—and he's got more lives than a cat."

I scratched my head. "I'm not letting him run me off again, though I've got business in Tombstone to attend."

Smith shook his head. "You'll be making a lot of trips, then."

I stayed in Fort Sumner the next two weeks, buying me a new handgun and plenty of ammunition just in case Billy and I crossed paths. In late May I spent two weeks traveling to Tombstone, where another feud was

growing, and checking on my saloon before returning to
Fort Sumner.

The talk of Lincoln County was about how Pat
Garrett, stock association detectives, and bounty hunters
were scouring Lincoln County for Billy the Kid. Word
was that Billy's crimes had made him famous back east,
and he was now the subject of dime novels. It was the
damnedest thing how folks would glorify a criminal, albeit
a likable one. I came to figure he was stupid, though, if
he was still haunting Lincoln County when so many men
were out to get him.

In the three weeks I was in Fort Sumner, Pat Garrett
might have slipped in and out of town four or five times,
trying to get the jump on the Kid. Come late June, the
Kid was still roaming unfettered. I had more business in
Tombstone, so I left once again. Every time I left, folks
in Fort Sumner said I was chickening out, afraid the Kid
would kill me for this or that. I even heard a few took
bets on whether or not I'd return each time.

It was after the Fourth of July before I was able to
return to Fort Sumner. After each Tombstone visit, I kept
hoping Rosalita would leave with me for good the next
time. But she stayed, and the Kid was still on the loose.

That changed, though, before my next trip to Tombstone.

Chapter Twenty-seven

Rosalita was cold to me the first three days after my return. I didn't know whether it was because the Kid had just been there or he was overdue. I had bought a new pistol, and I was ready to settle things with him. Too, Rosalita had begun to weary of Billy's unpredictable schedule.

My fourth night back in Fort Sumner, Rosalita and I carried a bench from her kitchen outside and sat in the long shadows of early evening. It had been another hot July day, and we were sticky with perspiration. We didn't say much, just sat there holding hands and wishing we had as much money as Pete Maxwell, whom we could see sitting on the long covered porch of his huge house, just beyond an orchard of apple and peach trees. Maxwell retired early to his bedroom, which opened out onto the porch. Shortly, his room glowed yellow from the lamplight.

The night was typical of Fort Sumner in the summer, hot and lazy. Everything seemed to move slower, the men going afoot or on horseback to the saloons, the dogs roaming the square, and the hogs scavenging for something to eat. We noticed three riders traverse the square just after dark, one sitting tall in the saddle. I thought it might be Sheriff Garrett but discounted that because the men rode on across the square and out past Maxwell's house.

Rosalita leaned her head against my shoulder and began to nuzzle against me. I was feeling pretty confident, not just about the night ahead but about our future together. I'd shown Rosalita my money roll of close to five hundred dollars and convinced her I'd be able to support her and provide her things she wanted. But at that moment money was the last thing she wanted.

I teased her a bit. Every time she made a motion for us to retire inside, I kept my seat like I wasn't nearly as interested as she was. That made her more anxious. When I finally stood up, she almost shoved me inside, closing but not barring the door. A slight breeze slipped through the open kitchen window and out the bedroom window. Rosalita was rabid as she unbuckled my gun belt and placed it on the kitchen table, then pushed me toward the bedroom. She shoved me onto the bed and straddled my legs, jerking off one boot, then the other. I had never seen her like this, and I was enjoying it. She fairly ripped off my shirt and tossed it at the end of the bed. Then she unbuttoned my pants and pulled them free and tossed them toward the window and the shaft of moonlight that angled in.

There I was in my socks and my drawers. I rolled over onto my side of the bed, and she ran to my side, standing there and beginning to undress. Her dark skin shone in the moonlight as she ripped her clothes off. I could feel my sap rising as she uncovered her breasts, then pulled off her skirt and drawers. I was as ready as a preacher peering at a collection plate.

Rosalita giggled.

Just as I reached for her, she fell suddenly silent.

Then I, too, heard it—a soft rapping on the door.

Rosalita froze. Her face showed fear for an instant, then pleasure.

"Rosalita," came a whisper.

I recognized the voice. It was the Kid.

"Billito," Rosalita answered.

I shot up from the bed, grabbing instinctively at my side for my revolver. I touched nothing but the flesh of my leg.

I heard the front door open, then close.

Forgetting me, Rosalita dashed naked into the kitchen. "Billito, Billito," she cried, "I have missed you."

"I've missed you," answered Billy, "but I see you're ready for me."

I heard him wrestling off his boots and dropping them to the floor.

"Take off your gun, Billito, hurry."

Bless her heart, Rosalita was stalling him for me. I slipped quietly out of bed.

I heard his gun belt drop on the table.

I scooped my pants up from the floor and was trying to shove my foot in the pants leg when I tripped and stumbled into the table by the bed, knocking the tin washbasin to the floor.

"*Quién es?* Who's that?" Billy cried out, then answered the question. "Lomax, isn't it? Out of my way," he yelled.

Dragging my pants, I clambered out the window as Billy came charging inside.

"Damn you!" he yelled.

As I struggled to get my pants on, I heard Billy rush back to the kitchen. "My gun, my gun, Rosalita."

"No, no," she cried. "Don't use a gun."

Bless her, I thought. She did love me after all. Then she spoke again, raising a doubt in my mind.

"A gun will make too much noise," she called. "Use my butcher knife!"

I was still struggling to get my pants on when I saw Billy crawling out the window after me. I jerked my pants up, but my hands were shaking so that I couldn't button them. I started running, but my feet were bare. Pain shot through them as I stepped on stones and thorns, dashing toward the Pecos and the trees, Billy chasing after me. At least he was barefoot, too, or I'd've been dead, sliced to pieces by the Kid.

Reaching the riverbank, I turned north and ran toward Pete Maxwell's place, desperately seeking a place to hide. I ran and ran, glancing over my shoulder for Billy, catching sight of him occasionally. At least Rosalita had talked him out of his gun, or I would have been dead.

My heart was pounding, and my breath sounded like the huff of a steam locomotive. My feet were killing me. My mind was reeling. How could I escape him? How could I survive against a man who had dodged hundreds of bullets in a dash from a burning house? How could I escape from a man who had broken out of the Lincoln County courthouse, killing two deputies? How could I escape from a man who gunned down the sheriff of Lincoln County without a bit of remorse? I didn't know. I ran on instinct—or panic.

I tripped over a log, then shoved myself up and scrambled to my feet. In the soft moonlight I was able to dart through the trees and brush, but the moon's glow made it easier for the Kid to keep an eye on me. I leaped over an irrigation ditch that was carrying water to Pete Maxwell's orchard and hit the ground hard, twisting my ankle. It exploded with pain, and I knew the race was lost now. I limped and staggered forward, knowing the Kid was gaining on me. It was over. I would be stabbed to death. The Kid would win out after all and live up to his promise not only to escape jail but also to kill me.

My only chance now was to make it back to the square and raise a cry for help. If I was going to die, I wanted people to know who had killed me, so maybe he would hang for my murder as well as Brady's. I staggered away from the stream and started toward Maxwell's house, keeping as close to the trees as I could. My change of direction worked for a moment because the Kid ran on down the river, allowing me to stretch the distance between us, but just when I thought I had it made, I landed hard on my lame left ankle and cut loose a scream. For a moment I saw Billy change directions; then I stumbled behind some trees and lost sight of him. I was nearing Maxwell's house, running beside the irrigation ditch.

When I reached the back edge of Maxwell's orchard, I came to a little footbridge over the ditch. My ankle was burning with pain, and I could run no more. I slid into the irrigation ditch under the bridge and hid as much of me as I could beneath the water, hoping the Kid would pass me by.

I waited and waited for what seemed like forever, but it could only have been seconds before he came up. I heard his heaving breath and nothing more. He seemed to stop over me, and gasp for breath; then he crouched and crept closer to the house, clinging to the edge of the irrigation ditch as he advanced deeper into the orchard.

Holding my breath so I could hear, I lifted my head enough to look into the orchard. I thought I heard the voices of two men among the trees. Suddenly I made out Billy freezing in the orchard and saw two men not twenty feet from him.

"Quién es? Quién es?"

"Huh?" said one of the men.

Billy darted out of the orchard toward Maxwell's porch, then into Maxwell's bedroom.

"Quién es? Quién es?" he yelled.

After a moment of silence, he was answered by first one and then another gunshot.

Instantly two men dove out of the bedroom onto the porch and rolled away from the door. The two men in the orchard drew their guns and crouched behind trees.

"What is it?" shouted one of the men in the trees.

"I think I just killed the Kid," came the voice of a man hunkered down on the porch. It was Pat Garrett. I crawled out of the irrigation ditch, shaking myself like a wet dog and limping forward.

"Is he dead?" yelled the orchard voice.

"Not sure," Garrett replied. "You wanta check it out?"

"Hell no, Pat," called the voice. "You're the one that winged him, not me."

There was a nervous silence for a moment. I limped toward the house. "He was just carrying a knife," I called. "He didn't have a gun."

"Who's saying that?" Garrett asked. "Is that Henry Lomax?"

"Yeah, Pat."

"You sure no gun?"

"Yep," I answered, "or I'd be a dead man."

"Maxwell," called Garrett, "there any guns in that room?"

"No, sir," responded Maxwell.

"Then everybody keep quiet," Pat yelled, "so I can see if I can hear anything." He crept closer to the door, then stopped and listened.

Finally Pat dug some matches from his vest, struck one, and held it in front of the door. "Can anybody see anything?"

"Not for sure," yelled one of the men in the orchard as both slipped closer to the door.

After the first match burned down to his fingers, Garrett shook it out and lit another. He stood up slowly and walked into the room, a match in one hand, his gun in the other. In a moment the room was aglow with yellow light from a lamp. The two men from the orchard trotted up to the door, then Pete Maxwell. I was the fifth man to see the Kid's body.

Garrett rolled him over and pointed at the crimson spot on his left breast. "Hit him in the heart," he said.

I limped over to the body, shaking my head. "You should've left Lincoln County when I told you, Kid."

By now the gunshots had attracted a crowd outside Maxwell's bedroom as word passed through Fort Sumner that the Kid was dead. I heard one terrible scream and incessant sobbing and recognized Rosalita's voice. She clawed her way through the crowd at the door and fell upon his body, kissing his dead face, screaming Spanish profanities at whoever had killed Billy.

Garrett dragged her away.

My ankle ached, so I limped over to Maxwell's bed and fell upon it.

Rosalita's hard gaze landed on me. She pointed her finger. "You killed him. It was you, bastard."

I figured she was a mite upset but that she would get over it. I was shocked myself at the way things had turned out. I could just shake my head as she was hauled outside. Still, she wailed and screamed like a wounded panther.

As word passed through town, feelings ran high against Pat Garrett, his two deputies, and me for being involved in the killing, because the Kid was popular with most folks in Fort Sumner in spite of any problems he had had in Lincoln County. The four of us stayed the night in Maxwell's bedroom, the Kid on the floor where he had fallen. With the money roll that had somehow managed to stay in my pants pocket, I bought some of Maxwell's clothes to wear until I could get back into Rosalita's place for my own. The crowd was surly and some shouts went up to lynch Garrett, but mostly those were the whiskey-addled ravings of men without the courage to do anything other than incite others to do their dirty work.

We didn't get much sleep that night, though Billy didn't seem to have any problem, and we were glad when morning came. The local justice of the peace called a coroner's jury together, and they quickly listened to Garrett's side of things, then examined the body. They ruled that the death was justifiable, then turned the body over to Rosalita and several other women who were quite fond of the Kid. They toted him to a carpenter's shop where a coffin was made and his body placed within it.

By late afternoon I was riding Flash behind the funeral procession that went to the old military cemetery. There Billy the Kid was laid to rest.

I figured Billy's death meant I'd soon be married to Rosalita, but I was wrong, as I'd been about most things that involved women. I steered clear of her for two days, then approached her at her place, still limping on my bad ankle.

She met me at the front door, her arms folded across her chest.

"I figure we can get married now."

Rosalita just stared at me, shaking her head. "You killed him."

"He should've left years ago," I replied.

"He stayed because of me."

"But he's gone now and we can get married."

"No, never. I will always love Billito." She sobbed.

"We can go to Tombstone, start a new life, the two of us."

"I never want to see you again. I could never see you without remembering him."

I could only shake my head. I had waited six months for her to make a decision, and the decision she finally made meant I would wait forever. I stepped toward her.

"No," she said.

I pushed her aside. "I'm getting my things." I marched into the bedroom. As I gathered my new pistol, my boots, shirt, hat, carbine, and the few other belongings I'd managed to acquire in Fort Sumner, I glanced at her bed and saw the tintype of Billy on my pillow. That told me for certain she would never get over Billy enough to marry me.

When I had collected everything, I strode past her, trying to disguise my limp as much as possible. I said nothing to her, and she said nothing to me. I saddled Flash and loaded him up, riding out of town in midafternoon. I never returned to Fort Sumner and never saw Rosalita again, though I heard she had a child not eight months later. It was a girl and certainly my child or Billy's, though I knew whom she would claim as the father.

The death of Billy the Kid made Pat Garrett a celebrity. He was a good, honest lawman, the type always in short supply. Garrett even wrote a book called *The Authentic Life of Billy the Kid*. Though he wrote the last couple chapters, most were written by Ash Upson, who finally had a book that sold well, even if his name wasn't on the cover.

I rode from Fort Sumner toward Lincoln and two days later spent the night with Sam Corbett. The way we added it up, twenty men had died on the street of Lincoln over the previous five years. When I rode away from Lincoln for Tombstone the next day, I vowed never to return. I had enough bad memories from that street to last me a lifetime. Though I still had money in my pocket, I was in a sorry mood when I came to the ferry over the Rio Grande. It didn't help matters when this oily huckster got out of his buggy and slithered over to me. He was one of those types who wanted to talk whether you wanted to or not.

"You look like a smart feller," he said, "the kind that knows a good investment opportunity when he hears about it."

"I ain't interested," I said.

"Sure you are, when you hear the details."

I shook my head and dismounted so I could walk around the small ferry and stay away from him, but he followed me like a puppy follows a boy.

"Please, mister, just a moment of your time," he said.

I shrugged. We were nearing the opposite bank, and I wouldn't have to listen to him long. "Go ahead."

He grinned. "Allow me to introduce myself. I'm Gadrich Lomax."

"Who?" I wanted to confirm what I had just heard.

"Gadrich Lomax."

Before he could say another word, I drew back my fist and punched him in the nose, hit him so hard that he flew back into the rope railing and tumbled into the Rio Grande.

He came up spitting blood and water. "What was that for?"

"For giving me a bad name," I shot back.

As soon as the ferry hit the opposite bank, I mounted Flash and rode for Tombstone, feeling a bit better about life.

ABOUT THE AUTHOR

A native West Texan, PRESTON LEWIS is the author of a dozen western novels as well as numerous nonfiction articles on western history. In 1993 Lewis won a Spur Award from the Western Writers of America for his story, *Bluster's Last Stand*. An active member of the WWA, he currently serves as vice-president. The author resides with his family in Lubbock, Texas.

Spur Award-winner Preston Lewis continues H. H. Lomax's outrageous eyewitness accounts of the most infamous men on the western frontier in. . . .

THE REDEMPTION OF JESSE JAMES

When young Henry Harrison Lomax runs away from his Arkansas home to visit his two brothers soldiering with the Confederacy, he triggers a chain of events that lands him in the saddle with the youthful Jesse James. Along the way Lomax discovers a hidden cache of Confederate gold, but finds he can't spend it, not with soldiers from both armies on his tail and his nemesis, Pooty Burke, sticking to him like burk on a troo.

By chance, Lomax finds himself fighting Yakees with the rebel guerilla band led by Frank and Jesse James. By choice, in the dark days after the war, he rides again with the James brothers. Caught up in their dangerous world, Lomax—despite his many misgivings—helps them commit the first civilian bank robbery in American history.

When the remorseful Lomax comes face to face with Jesse's mother—and her frying pan—he decides it's time to find a new job and saddle pals. But escaping from the James gang is harder than spending Confederate gold, and Lomax finally must resort to a ruse to make the break and go straight—and pray he never runs into Jesse James again.

Turn the page for a preview of *The Redemption of Jesse James*, on sale in August 1995 wherever Bantam books are sold.

Chapter One

I never much cared for Jesse James. He was about as likable as a rabid mongrel, but sorry though he may have been, he was downright lovable compared to his momma. Now there was a cur of a woman. She was rough as a cob and twice as ugly, which is a bad thing to say about a man's momma, even if it's true.

I never took to her and she never took to me, though she did take out after me a couple times, once with a frying pan and once with a shotgun. Some said Jesse James finally ran me out of the Ozarks, but that just wasn't true. My conscience and his mother are what sent me packing west.

The truth of the matter is I might never have met any of the James family had it not been for Abraham Lincoln. Old Abe—not some cannonball over Fort Sumter and not slavery—brought on the War Between the States, and the war brought out the meanness of folks in the Ozarks.

Until then the Ozarks was as near to heaven as a young boy could find, short of getting into some girl's sack drawers. We lived on 128 acres of land bordering Jordan Creek about a mile south of Cane Hill, Arkansas. Things weren't so bad the year the war started, since most of the fighting took place up in Missouri. That spring we planted corn, Irish potatoes, wheat, and vegetables on the twenty-four acres of land Pa and his sons, myself included, had cleared of trees and stumps over the years.

The way I figured it, if Pa and Momma had brought me into the world, they should've made my life easier rather than putting me to doing chores. Almost from the day I was born, I was ready to run away from home. Pa was in the goldfields of California, trying to get rich, when I was birthed on January 9, 1850. Momma named me Henry Harrison Lomax because all my brothers had been named after presidents, like my father, George Washington Lomax. She told folks my initials but not my name, insisting that Pa would be the first one she would tell, me being his offspring. Around Cane Hill folks took to calling me Hurry Home Lomax since no one knew my real name. Even after Pa returned in 1851, some folks still called me Hurry Home.

Momma said I was born with the worst case of wanderlust she had ever seen. If I hadn't had the urge to move before my pa returned from California, I sure did after he got back. When he told his adventures and spoke of places with romantic names like the Sierra Nevadas, the Pacific Ocean, and the Golden Gate my feet'd start to moving and my mind'd go to wandering. I knew that one day I'd get to see those things for myself.

Through the end of 1861, we figured the war would bypass our out-of-the-way place, even though my two oldest brothers had already enlisted by then. For all of 1861 it seemed both the Union and the Confederacy had forgotten about our corner of Arkansas. We got in our crops that fall and felt about as smug as a hog in a corn crib.

That all changed in 1862. War has a way of spreading like a bloodstain, and it began to drip over the border into Arkansas. If the damn Missourians had seceded from the Union like they should have, we might've never had to worry about hiding our valuables and hoarding our food, but they didn't have the guts God gave a worm, so they stuck with the Union.

In February of 1862 we first heard of trouble in

Arkansas—a little fight at Potts Hill, then a tiff over at Sugar Creek, and finally a skirmish in Bentonville. When March came around there was a run-in at Berryville and finally a hell of a fight at Elkhorn Tavern in neighboring Benton County. Elkhorn Tavern claimed a thousand or more Confederate casualties and probably half again as many Yankee dead and wounded. Fact was, Confederate soldiers blindfolded could outshoot Yankees in daylight and in dark, but there were just so damn many of them blue bellies that we couldn't make ammunition fast enough to wipe them out. It was like attacking a plague of locusts with a flyswatter— you knew you had to be killing plenty, but there were thousands more crawling at your feet. Since the Yankees couldn't outshoot us, they damn sure tried to outloot us. They'd swipe an acorn from a crippled squirrel, and there were times us home folk couldn't take a leak without a Yankee trying to steal it.

At the start of the war my two oldest brothers, Thomas Jefferson and John Adams, enlisted, wound up in the 3rd Arkansas Infantry, and were sent east to fight. We all went to Fayetteville to see them off. Momma insisted on getting a tintype made of the family, which became her treasure because it was the only one we ever had of us all together. Only Tom returned from the war. We lost John Adams Lomax to the North, just never heard from him again after Gettysburg. Tom lost an eye, but came home after the war. Me and my brothers, of course, were mightily disappointed that we couldn't go east with Tom and John to assist with the spanking. I mostly wanted to see some new territory, even if it was east rather than west, and if I had to fight Yankees to do it, that was okay with me. I think Jim, Andy, and Van were interested in whipping Yankees, but they were of courting age and figured it was a good way to impress the ladies.

Now, not everybody in northwest Arkansas rallied round the Confederacy. Some just up and joined the Yankee army. A good number more, likely of inferior intelligence and breeding, felt sorry for the Yankees, them being so far from home and their mommas, but not sorry enough to join them and not men enough to stand up to the rest of us. These fellows took to the hills, hiding out and avoiding us saner secesh.

Gordon Burke was one of those. His place bordered ours across Jordan Creek. He was so dumb he didn't know ground beans from coffee—and he was the smart one of his brood. His wife, SincereAnne, was plainer than a log cabin and wouldn't have had a man look at her, much less marry her, if it weren't for her eyes. They were crossed.

Gordon and SincereAnne Burke had three girls—RuthAnne, LouAnne, and DeeAnne—before they got it right and had a boy. They named him Joe Don, though for the life of me I can't understand why it wasn't JoeAnne. Most folks around Cane Hill, though, came to call him Pooty Burke because he had this talent all us other boys admired. He could stink up a hollow quicker than a polecat.

I always figured the aroma of his pipe music was what turned his mother's eyes ajar. And I suspect the noise was what made a coward of his father—it sounded too much like artillery.

After the battle of Elkhorn Tavern, the Confederate government sent General T. C. Hindman to Arkansas to raise the soldiers necessary to drive the Yankees back up to Missouri where they belonged. The appointment of General Hindman taught me there was one thing more powerful than Momma, and that was the damned government. Hindman declared martial law and began to enforce the conscription act against every able-bodied man in the region. It wasn't enough that two of my brothers had volunteered to fight Yankees; the damned government decided it would volunteer the rest of them. Just a few months before, us four homebound Lomax boys had been willing to sign up for the glorious adventure, and then the damned government came along and didn't give us a choice. Not only that, they were taking our horses, mules, food, and fodder for the cause. We were fortunate to keep two old mules. What the rebel army didn't take, the damn Yankees tried to loot. It got where your friends were no better than your enemies.

James, Andy, and Van marched off to war as part of the 34th Arkansas Infantry. Pa was exempted from service, since his crippled leg made him unfit for what infantry do the most—march. The army deemed me too young for soldiering. Pooty's pa was considered able-bodied—there being no requirement for an able mind—and was ordered to join the Confederate Army just like my brothers. That's when Gordon Burke decided he couldn't fight to preserve slavery, no matter that he would've been fighting to protect his home and family. So, like a lot of other Union sympathizers, he left his family and took to the hills.

That summer General Hindman issued an order permitting small groups of Southern men to operate behind enemy lines as irregular troops, whom we came to call bushwhackers. So not only did we have legitimate Confederate and Union troops wandering the hills trying to kill each other, we had secesh and Union irregulars ambushing each other and plaguing every household in Arkansas. Anytime you met folks, you had to be careful what you said because you never knew for sure whose side they were on. If you insulted the president, it had better be the right one—Abe Lincoln or Jeff Davis—or it was treason on the spot and you could get shot, hung, or knifed.

I never knew for certain if Gordon Burke was a bushwhacker or just a coward. I just know the day the Confederates came back to collect the so-called volunteers, he had retreated into the hills. So we found ourselves neighboring a known—but cowardly—Union sympathizer. Though I think Pa leaned toward the Union, he had five sons fighting for the Confederacy, so we were considered secesh.

For a while our lives didn't change much, though having only two broken-down mules instead of the other six strong ones the rebel army took did cut into our farming. Everything remained the same otherwise. I still thought Pooty was dumb, and I knew for a fact his sisters were so ugly flies wouldn't land on them.

Pooty couldn't take a joke—like the time I found a momma cat and her kittens beneath a rock pile. I convinced him it'd be fun to catch them and kill them. I told him if he'd poke them out with a stick, I'd catch them so he wouldn't get scratched. He thought that was a good idea. He found a dead limb and got down on his hands and knees, then hesitated and studied me real hard.

"This ain't a bobcat den, is it?"

"Nope."

"Promise?"

"Cross my heart and hope to die."

He nodded confidently and shoved the limb in.

"It's a polecat den," I said.

Pooty jumped back, but it was too late. Momma skunk sprayed him in the face. I'd never seen anyone turn green before, but Pooty did and took to puking. He ran away screaming and jumped in Jordan Creek, but skunk vapors don't wash off that easily.

He ran to SincereAnne, and I could've sworn the odor straightened her eyes for a minute. She got some vinegar and tried to wash the stink off, but for all her scrubbing, it cut the aroma only slightly. If vinegar failed on clothes, the only other solution was to bury them. I suggested they do that with Pooty, but no one saw the humor in it, especially not SincereAnne.

For all our differences, the War Between the States finally brought me and Pooty together, much to our disgust. Come late summer, after most of the able-bodied men had been conscripted and the rest had taken to the hills, cavalry from both armies roamed the countryside looking for each other. In addition to that, the bushwhackers on both sides became predators, at first tormenting those households unsympathetic to their cause and then, as the war wore on, tormenting everybody that was weaker than them. After several farms around Cane Hill had been hit by one side or the other, Pa sat down at the supper table one night and announced that SincereAnne and her kids were coming to live with us.

I about spit out the cornbread and cane syrup I was eating. "Why? They ain't orphans," I said, looking to Momma for support.

"Times are mean," Pa answered, "especially for a woman and kids alone."

My sister Melissa, who was three years older than me, crossed her arms and shook her head, giving Pa a stare that would've melted wax. "No beaus'll come calling me if those ugly Burke girls move in." I admired Lissa's way with words.

Momma, though, wasn't as appreciative. "That's not a nice thing to say about those girls."

I couldn't help but come to Lissa's aid. "You always told us to tell the truth, Momma."

"They can't help it," she started, "if they're ug—homely."

"Sure they can," I shot back. "They can wear sacks over their heads."

"Henry Harrison Lomax," Pa said, his voice rising like a bad wind, "the decision has been made for their safety and ours."

"Ours?" I couldn't believe what Pa had said.

"Between the soldiers and the bushwhackers, things aren't safe for anybody, so folks are pairing off, Union families with secesh families."

Nothing else was said at the supper table. We'd all seen Pa when he'd made his mind up. Once he did, he was harder to budge than a fat lady on an anvil.

I went to bed that night lower than a mole's belly and prayed that all the skunk perfume had faded from Pooty's face. The idea of losing the war didn't seem nearly as upsetting as the idea of Pooty moving in with us. It wasn't fair, what with his sisters being so damn ugly. At least with Lissa and Harriet, who were damn pretty, he was going to have some decent scenery to look at. Me, I was just going to have to pray I never saw his sisters in the altogether, or it might turn me into a gelding.

For all my brothers, the war had already begun. For me,

it began the next day when Pooty Burke came to stay with us. Had he stayed where he belonged, I would never have had the pleasure of meeting Jesse James or kissing Amanda Fudge.

Chapter Two

Come midmorning that awful next day, Pa hitched up our two broken-down mules to the farm wagon and ordered me to go with him to the Burke place. Though our homes weren't two hundred yards from each other, we had to go upstream half a mile to the nearest wagon crossing, then back down to the Burke house. I wasn't too pleased to learn that we would be carrying some of their furniture and belongings back to our place. As far as I was concerned, Pooty could tote them across Jordan Creek himself.

SincereAnne Burke was standing on the porch, arms crossed, foot tapping on the wooden planks, as we approached. The Burke hounds took to yapping and howling at us. When Pa halted the mule team beside the porch, SincereAnne greeted him. "It's about time you showed up."

Pa released a deep breath, then rattled the reins. The confused mules hesitated, then jerked the wagon forward when he shook the leathers again. "Good day, Mrs. Burke," he said as he circled the wagon around and started back for the crossing. My smile must've been wider than a crescent moon. Pa wasn't going to take any more sass from the Burkes than he was from his own family.

SincereAnne looked like she had been slapped with a piece of raw liver, her eyes moving in opposite directions. She ran after the wagon crying, "George, George, please."

I waved good-bye and stuck my tongue out when I saw Pooty run out onto the porch. I almost bit my tongue off when Pa drew the wagon to a halt.

Before SincereAnn could say anything, Pa pointed his finger at her wrinkled face. "I ain't your husband and I won't be spoken down to like I'm married to you. I'm trying to be neighborly and watch out for you and your girls until all the meanness is through. And don't call me George again. It's Mr. Lomax to you and your offspring."

Pa aimed the wagon back to the Burke cabin and stopped beside the porch. "Come on, Henry," he said, "let's load up their belongings and get home."

SincereAnne was just as courteous as a Sunday School teacher. "Whatever you want us to do to help, Mr. Lomax," she offered, "you just let us know. Girls."

I about gagged when the three Burke sisters appeared on the porch, dressed in their best gingham dresses and matching bonnets. They were uglier than woods in a field, but had the good sense to wear their bonnets so you only saw them from the front.

"Point us to what you want loaded," Pa said, leading me into the cabin, "and have Pooty give us a hand."

"You mean Joe Don?"

I giggled as I passed Pooty, but he stuck out his foot and tripped me.

It took us a half hour to load two beds, a couple rocking chairs, three trunks, and all the food in the house. Then we cleared out the smokehouse and took from the barn what tools Pa thought we would need.

Finally, Pooty brought out the shotgun, the only weapon Gordon Burke had left his family before fleeing like the coward he was.

"I'll take that," Pa said, grabbing it from him, breaking it open, and checking the load. It was empty. "Where's the shells?"

"Aren't none," Pooty replied.

"Hard to hunt or defend yourself without shells."

"He can always club them to death," I suggested.

Pa put the gun in the wagon and told the girls to climb aboard. I averted my eyes so I wouldn't have to see their faces. Pa looked at me.

"I figure on walking back," I announced, not caring to be seen with a wagonload of ugly.

Pa's eyes narrowed, but before he could order me otherwise, we were distracted by a commotion barreling out of the woods. A black stallion was charging our way.

"Wait!" called the rider in a soft feminine voice.

Everyone tensed for a moment until Pooty announced, "It's just Amanda." He rolled his eyes.

I'd never seen a girl ride a horse like that, but here she came, heels flailing against the stallion's flanks. She charged to the very corner of the cabin, then reined the horse up hard, jumping off as it stopped. She landed on the ground as gracefully as a panther, and I was struck when I saw she had been riding bareback. I was even more impressed when I studied her. She had hair the color of fresh straw and eyes as green as spring in the Ozarks, and she was just beginning to fill out her dress, which meant she was about my age or a little older. Amanda was everything the Burke sisters were not, and I was smitten.

"I came to say good-bye," she announced.

"We're just moving across the creek," Pooty said, rolling his eyes again.

"I wasn't talking to you," she replied, then looked up at the three Burke girls. They climbed out of the wagon, and each gave Amanda a teary hug. For the first time in my life I was jealous of RuthAnne, LouAnne, and DeeAnne Burke.

"We're not that far away, just across the creek," RuthAnne reminded her.

"I'm not supposed to cross the creek, but Father won't know, I guess, as long as I don't tarry."

"It's not far," I put in. "I can show you."

Amanda released RuthAnne and looked my way. "Who are you?"

"I'm Henry Lomax, and this is my father. The Burkes are coming to live on our place."

"Amanda Fudge is my name," she said.

Pa shook his head and climbed into the wagon. "Time we were going, girls," he said.

I had heard of the Fudges, but they pretty much kept to themselves, Amanda being their only child and them sheltering her as much as they could.

"You're welcome to ride with us, Amanda, down to the river crossing and then back to our place."

"I'd like to, but I can't be gone too long or Father will know I went farther than I should."

"Pa," I volunteered, "I can ride double, and we can cross the creek here. I'll show her our place so she'll know where to come for a visit."

Giving me a slight smile, Pa nodded. I was happy as a duck in water until Pooty spoke up.

"I'll ride with them."

"The horse won't carry three," I protested.

Amanda gave me the cutest smile ever sent my direction. "Sure it will."

Though I had just met her, I thought I saw mischief in the twinkle of her eyes and the curve of her lips.

"Then everybody get moving," Pa said as he rattled the reins and turned the wagon toward the crossing.

Amanda vaulted up on the horse's back in the blink of an eye and pointed at me. "You next." She edged the stallion toward me and I jumped up, swinging my leg over the animal's back, then slid behind her and slipped my arms around her waist.

"You ready, JoeAnne?" I asked Pooty. To my delight, Amanda giggled.

As Pooty growled and made a leap for the horse, Amanda flicked the reins, and the stallion stepped away. Pooty splattered against the horse's side and fell to the ground.

Amanda whispered over her shoulder, "When we get in the creek, push him off when I say now.'"

I laughed. Pooty thought I was laughing at him and took to griping and wailing.

"I'm sorry," Amanda purred. "The stallion's frisky."

Pooty bounced up from the ground, took a running start, then stopped to make sure the stallion wasn't going to flinch again. The animal stood like a rock. Pooty jumped again and clambered aboard.

"I won't ride fast, boys," Amanda said.

Pooty settled his crease on the stallion's back, then whistled to his hounds.

"You boys ready?" Amanda asked.

"I am," I said.

"No tricks," Pooty said.

Amanda turned the horse toward the creek and started at a walk, with Pooty's hounds trailing us. When we reached the stream, she let the stallion blow and water for a moment. Pooty was whistling as we entered the creek's lazy waters. Halfway across, Amanda yelled, "Now!"

I jerked my elbows forward, then backward, ramming them into Pooty's gut. He stopped whistling and gasped for air. Amanda shook the stallion's reins, and the animal bolted forward.

I grabbed her waist. Pooty screamed, flailing to grab hold of my waist or shirt. As the stallion charged across the creek, Pooty tumbled off. I glanced around in time to see him splash into the creek.

The stallion emerged from the stream, then hit the bank and quickly climbed the steep slope to the plain where our cabin and fields awaited.

Amanda and I were whooping and hollering at the trick we had played on Pooty Burke. When we reached the house, I jumped down and took the reins, tying the stallion to a porch post. She slid off, both of us still laughing.

"That was fun," she said, then leaned over and kissed me on the cheek. It *was* fun, but not near as much fun as the touch of her lips.

Momma and Lissa came out on the porch. They stared at us for a moment, and I knew they were about to ask a whole lot of questions, but Pooty never gave them a chance. He came barreling up the creek embankment, straight for me.

I doubled my fists and stood there in my best prizefighter pose, trying to impress Amanda even more.

Pooty had the look of a wild animal in his eyes. He screamed wildly and charged headlong into me. I swung for him, but he dove for my waist, driving me to the ground and knocking my breath away for a moment. We rolled around in the dirt, swinging and clawing for each other, mostly missing. Pooty was enraged and I was embarrassed that he had knocked me down in front of Amanda.

"Stop it," Momma yelled. "Stop it!"

When we didn't, she waded into the battle, jerking me by the arm and flinging me toward the porch and screaming at Pooty to stop his fighting. Pooty and I were heaving for breath, madder than wet cats. Momma was yelling, Harriet and Lissa were screaming at us, and Amanda was giggling like she enjoyed every minute of it.

Momma pointed us each to a different end of the porch, then turned to Amanda. "What happened, young lady?"

Amanda smiled like an angel. "I gave them a ride from the Burke place. Pooty fell in the river and—"

"They pushed me," Pooty cried.

"—he blamed Henry and me for knocking him off."

Now, I knew it was a lie, but it didn't seem so bad coming from lips as sweet as hers.

Momma knew she couldn't settle it so she shook her head. "When your pa gets home, we'll get this straightened out."

Amanda smiled. "I need to get home or my father'll be angry."

Momma nodded. "See that you do."

Amanda tossed me a grin, then untied the stallion and bounded on. I caught a flash of pale leg and decided it was worth it, no matter what punishment I received.

About twenty minutes later, Pa drove up with the wagonload of ugly. Momma was waiting on the porch, her arms crossed, her foot tapping. SincereAnne saw Pooty and jumped out of the wagon, running to see what had happened. Pooty explained his side of things, which was nearer the truth than my side, but Amanda had plowed a good furrow for me to spread a little manure in, and I embellished her account.

Pa shook his head. "I don't know who's telling the truth and who isn't."

"I do," SincereAnne interrupted. "Joe Don doesn't tell lies."

Pa shrugged. "Maybe so, maybe not. This reminds me of a couple ox I had one time. They were obstinate and wouldn't take to a plow or each other. Both of them were all piss and vinegar. You know what I did?"

"Shot the one named Pooty?" I volunteered.

Pa glared at me. "No, I yoked them together for a month. They turned out to be the best-mannered pair of oxes I ever worked."

"You ain't yoking me," Pooty said.

"No, sir, I'm not, but you two boys'll do all your chores together, you'll sit together at meals, you'll clean up together, and you'll make your bed together until you learn to behave like civilized people instead of Indians."

My only consolation was that I hadn't been fighting one of Pooty's ugly sisters. I'd've preferred being lynched to having the same punishment with any of them.

We went about three weeks that way, each of us wary of the other and disgusted with our mutual punishment. The worst by far was having to sleep in the same damn bed. I swore I could still smell the skunk on him.

And then one night about three weeks later, our punishment didn't seem so harsh and our personal vendetta didn't seem near as important as we had thought.

That was when the night riders first visited our place.

From out of the American West comes an entirely
different kind of legend....

BLUEFEATHER FELLINI

Max Evans

"The most gloriously strange novel of the West
that ever fell into my hands... A strange, utterly
compelling masterpiece."
Dalo L. Walker, *Rocky Mountain News*

From award-winning writer Max Evans comes this bold
and visionary new work, blending the mythic Old West
with the stark realism of the twentieth century, creating
a unique and dynamic voice in American fiction—
filled with magic, passion, and drama.

"A true and grand epic...*Bluefeather Fellini* is the
American novel for our time—for all time."
—Robert J. Conley, author of *The Way of the Priests*

AN ARMY SCOUT AND A COMANCHE WARRIOR...
BOUND BY A HATRED THAT WOULD NEVER DIE...

ENEMIES

Geo. W. Proctor

They had sworn to kill each other—an Army scout
haunted by the brutal slaughter of his wife and child,
and a fierce Comanche warrior who'd suffered his
own tragic losses. And it's only a matter of time
before these two enemies meet, alone, on the battle-
field—warrior to warrior—in a bloody showdown
that can end only one way....

"An authentic, richly detailed novel set in a
neglected period of the American West—the
twilight of the frontier. Fascinating reading!"
—Chad Oliver, award-winning author of
The Cannibal Owl